The Reclamation

About the Author

Roger Howell frittered away his best days mapping geology and poking around old mining districts of the central Rockies. Long hours were given to slow, serial daydreams while walking ridges or watching drillrigs smoke and whine. In spite of those qualifications he eventually was promoted to management, where quiet times are rare and daydreaming less appreciated. So, he quit. Now he is walking ridges again and jotting down some of those serial musings.

Roger grew up in Idaho mostly, in Montana some, and in Oregon a little. He attended Boise State University, U.C. Santa Barbara, Gonzaga University, and Clemson University, receiving degrees from three of the four. He's worked as a professional geologist, hydrologist, and environmental engineer in all corners of the western U.S., Alaska, northern Canada, most of South and Central America, Philippines, and Russia.

He is married to a geologist, a painter, and an ever-patient woman, and they have two beautiful daughters and a street dog. *The Reclamation* is hardly his first fiction, but it is the first novel he's gotten around to publishing.

ROGER HOWELL

THE RECLAMATION

Copyright © 2019 Roger Howell
All rights reserved.
ISBN 9781081518219

This story would not be possible without the inspiration of the smart, independent women in my life—who are just about all of the women in my life. My mother left me the gift of dissatisfaction; sisters Helen, Barbara, and Julie shared the interesting times; wife Susan lets me know that contentment is okay too; and my girls Clara and Eleanor give meaning to all this reflection. Strong women, all. I am very lucky in that way.

Author's Note

Stibnite Idaho may be the most remote town of any size in the lower forty-eight. It lies fifteen miles up an awful dirt road from Yellowpine. Yellowpine is another sixty miles of dirt from McCall, which finally is somewhere. Cinnabar is five miles more remote than Stibnite, but it no longer counts as a town.

The mineral deposits of Cinnabar and Stibnite were discovered in the 1800's. For nearly a century the district lolled in obscurity, with just a few shallow scratchings to support the unhurried hill people who lived there. The Second World War lifted the towns from their slumber, sometimes with a boot.

The district was put under the charge of the U.S. War Production Board. The Army was desperate for mercury, tungsten, and antimony, and those strategic metals gave Cinnabar and Stibnite first pick of the best miners and equipment in the country. Still, I'm told, to have walked the streets or drink in the taverns then you might never have understood that these towns were at war. Nothing but the faintest notion of the crusade ever penetrated so deeply into Idaho, over the dusty miles of pine forest, through the layers of granite stacked up around the district.

My own father did, in fact, sign on with the mine recruiters, and he brought with him to Cinnabar my mother, JoAnne, and my sister, Helen. If my mother's heart sank at the sight of wall tents lining half the muddy main street of Stibnite, she may fairly have wept when she topped the ridge and looked down upon the rough-wood and tarpaper shacks of dark Cinnabar. Or she might have been relieved, finally, to be home with her child and the man she loved. When she and I returned to Cinnabar years ago, we did not speak of those things.

It is important to note that *The Reclamation* is not meant to be a chronicle of any sort. I have interwoven memories of Cinnabar and other mining camps I've lived and worked in, and I've not been careful with geography, nor with history, nor with the layout of roads and businesses. If I've included family anecdotes—my mother trapping martens in the winter woods and working a sluice for gold—these accounts end well short of biography. JoAnne and Jolene were both barely educated women who yearned to be more, and who pushed themselves to read and explore. You use what you know to flesh-out what you would invent. For the record I was not born in Cinnabar, nor did any of my family die there. And for the record, all of the characters and events in this story are fictional.

—*Roger Howell, Golden, Colorado*

THE RECLAMATION

1

The war ended, and mining ended, and the town ended in short order. I was a child then and one of the last to leave. I'd been told we would go, that we had to. But I didn't understand what going meant back then, not even when the electricity stopped, and the streets went dark, and our house grew silent and cold.

I rose early on the spoken day and tiptoed down a hallway full of crates and trunks, all bound with straps and marked with my father's name but no address. My grandmother was up early, too. She'd started a fire in the kitchen range, and she bent over a rolling pin in the yellow light of the fire, making biscuits for our trip.

"How will our stuff find us in Nevada?" I asked.

She rolled the dough over the board. "How will the Lord find us where we're going?" she answered. The fire crackled and smoked behind her. I must have started to cry. "Harlan, Hush!" She slapped the breadboard; a wisp of flour curled into the firelight. "Your father's gone ahead to find work," she said. Then almost kindly: "This'll all catch up to us sooner'n we need it."

We had hotcakes to eat, and we ate them quietly, sitting on a trunk with a wooden box for a table. *Take all the butter and syrup you want*, I remember. The wall above where we sat showed a clean square where a painting had hung. The painting was gone and the wallpaper, where not faded and sooted, was filled with bright flowers. I'd never noticed the flowers before.

The picture had been of desert bluffs and blue skies, the land of Ali Baba's thieves. Grandma saw where I was staring, and allowed, "It was your mother's favorite."

I nodded, though it made my chest ache to hear the words spoke aloud. Grandma said, "Your Uncle Harly painted it, else we wouldn't have bothered to take it."

We left the dishes unwashed in the sink and the fire burning in the stove. The road glistened with slush and red mud as we marched with suitcases past doors swinging open, past gaping houses and gardens gone to seed. Tarpaper hung loose from the house on the corner, torn by September winds. No one had nailed it back with chicken wire, so it draped like black flags over bare, yellowed timber. Orange flowers clung to the edges of another yard, and pumpkins and squash lay in the garden. That house wasn't empty yet, and I strained to see if someone might be watching from inside, marking our passage. My grandmother pulled me by the hand, brooking no delay, no chance to look back.

Ahead of us, fleeting shafts of sunlight knifed through mist and dark pines. The door of the grocery was locked, and strangers were nailing boards over the windows. We lugged our suitcases through the town of Cinnabar, past the Merc, which had been closed more than a year, and past the garage where all the windows were painted white. The government office was closed; the sign above the door still showed an eagle perched on an artillery shell. *War Production Board*, it announced. Through shattered windows, moldering posters of hard-working men and women hung on graffiti-marked walls.

At the mine portal our road dipped beneath timber loading chutes, and we took care passing under them. Workers were closing up the mine entrance at the main level, swinging big wooden doors and using bolts to set heavy iron cross bars. Grandma finally set down her suitcase, and we rested our arms and watched as the mine was shut in.

THE RECLAMATION

The road over to Stibnite had washed out, Grandma told me, and no one had repaired it. Her words were thin and meted out between heavy breaths, and it was odd she would confer with me like that. We hiked a long way up the road, where the slopes oozed blood red all around us. Crimson waters ran in the road, and we jumped the rivulets and swung and dragged our suitcases through the gore.

The car didn't come for a long while. We sat on our suitcases and I watched the town below for signs of life. Through the treetops, a lone two-track dirt road took out from the heart of town and headed away from us, northward. The road ended before it was out of sight, and I wondered if roads often start and end where you can see them. The road turned into a trail as it bent around a rocky point, but even the trail faded to a trace before it re-appeared in the next valley. I followed it with my eyes as far as I could, to where it vanished into grey, rocky canyons that joined one to another to become a deep darkness.

"Who named it the River of No Return?" I asked.

Grandma didn't turn but sat on her suitcase with her arms around her middle. "It's nothing to be minding now," she scolded.

"But what explorer went down the Salmon River and learned about the canyon and everything, and then returned after all to give it that name?"

She'd been watching uphill for the car, but now drew her eyes back to the town and the canyons beyond. "It ain't who went that named it," she explained, "but who waited behind."

*

It was ferruginous clays, of course—the blood-red water flowing down the road so long ago—just iron-rich mud. And my father did find work, for a while. We moved on again and he found more work and lost that too. I always expected I would return to Cinnabar. I didn't think it would take sixty years.

The road out of Stibnite, Idaho and back over to my place of birth climbs northward around switchbacks still muddy and rough in places. Our headlights wind through dog-hair pine and aspens standing tall and ghostly in the half light of early dawn. We jolt and bounce over rocky outcrops, and splash through snowmelt coursing down the double tracks of the road. Crescents of snow block the way where we finally top the ridge, but I bust through with my lead truck, sending slush and ice crystals flying into an opaline sunrise.

High on the ridgetop the air is cool and our breath fogs in front of us. Birds chatter and curse us from the edges of the clearing, but we take time for a coffee from our thermoses and to get our bearings in the light of the new day. A couple of the guys, the roustabouts, light up smokes. I take one when it's offered. Our trucks carry equipment and some initial provisions, and the heavy tools of road work—essentials for a camp we'll set up in the old town site of Cinnabar. From there I can conduct my mine evaluation without the long drives over from Stibnite each day. The rest of the project crew have chosen to stay in Stibnite, with its hotel, café, and bar—the bar being the deciding factor, I think.

We have to chain up our tires before heading down through the north-side turns. When finished, Mike Lovitt takes the lead. Mike's a good hand, a solid geologist with field experience, and he's mounted a blade to his front bumper to plow ahead. A third truck carries the three roustabouts who bummed me a smoke and who will help with the camp setup. I don't know their names, though Mike does. Snow lies in long patches on the north side, filling roadcuts under steep banks and in dark, shaded ravines. I hang back to give Lovitt plenty of room to make his passes, and he works steadily, angling the snow off the roadbed. His blade plows up wet forest soil, kinnikinic, and juniper, and I roll my window down in spite of the chill to take in the bouquet.

Winter-fall trees block the road as we descend and complicate the plowing; we have to chop and saw our way all down the switchbacks. Lovitt expects me to stand back for the logging and brushing, to let the working men tackle it. But I'm not so old yet I can't run a chainsaw. Two-stroke engine exhaust wafts around me, chips of damp wood gather in my hair, and these and sweet pine sap complete the medley of springtime aromas.

We work our way down out of the snowdrifts by noon and the day grows warm, and still there are trees and brush to clear from our way. The lower road passes through clay-altered rocks of the mineralized trend, and the road base here is saturated with snowmelt from above. Clay cakes our tire chains—that blood-red clay—so the chains don't grip, and we half slide down the road. These lower reaches will dry in the days to come, and brown dust will rise in clouds from under my wheels and follow me as I come and go.

The afternoon is well along by the time we roll into Cinnabar and I step at last from the truck. The town itself is just a few broken rows of sagging shacks standing in tangles of wild rose and raspberry. Most of it has burned or fallen down, I guess. Still, it is small, even accounting for the factual collapse.

Maybe seven hundred people lived here in the war years, but there is little left of all the place once was. I scrabble in weeds and rubble and peer through glassless windows and broken doorways while the others stop for a late lunch. I can't find the pile of tin and timbers I'm looking for. It doesn't matter.

Mike asks if I've decided, and I tell him I'll take the main level of a nearby shack in what once was a home with kitchen and parlor and two bedrooms up a steep, now-fallen flight of stairs. The roof there seems to be intact and the floors solid and generally level, and the packrats haven't soiled the place beyond use. A cot, camp stove, and a table of sorts will furnish my rustic apartment.

The roustabouts help to sweep the place, nail up plastic, and wire a generator in the wood shed for a space heater and a computer. A lantern will let me read at night, and that about covers my needs. My food and beer I'll keep in a big ice chest, which Mike and I pack with snow. Steaks I'll grill on an old mill grate over a fire pit out front.

Mike, I could tell, questions my perspicacity in this matter, and the others will have a laugh at my expense in the bar tonight. But they said their goodbyes and made their way back up through the slick red mud and the snowbanks. Their noise and exhaust fumes have gone.

North from town a storm is brewing: heavy, dark clouds tower over the Salmon River gorge. The clouds glow on their undersides, back-lit by the yellow down-canyon sun. On the porch of my new place, though, the late afternoon grows sweet with sage and willow, and with old pine boards baked by the heat of the day. Fir and aspen have grown up on the surrounding hills, and low hawthorn and alder brush now cover the deep scars of mining. The brush shelters a lot of birds; jays and wrens I think, returning with the season. But for their commotion, the valley sits still and quiet.

The storm turns my way and will be on me before dark, so I toss the beer bottle into a rusted barrel and pack and drag the rest of my gear from the porch into the shack. A small trunk of papers and memorabilia, the last thing I threw onto the truck, is now the last piece to be carried in. The trunk is full of family stuff, the leftovers of dreams and days long past. I should not have brought it—there are no new treasures or troubles to be found inside. Still, I have come full circle to Cinnabar and the trunk and its contents have as well, so I'll no doubt sort through the Pruitt saga one more time before the summer is done.

Dinner sizzles on the Coleman stove as a light rain spatters outside; the sky and the room have grown dark. In the focused glow of the lantern a faded wallpaper stirs to life: an exotic pastiche of orchids and pineapples and palms. A miner's wife once ordered ten rolls of this pattern delivered to the heart of the wilderness. She'd have been young, poor, and unsophisticated. She'd hoped the tropics would lift her spirits. Maybe it did; hope is a funny thing.

A cool wind drives the rain, and the wind flutters the corrugated tin all through the neighborhood.

The trunk I brought with me holds the hopes and memories of another miner's wife. Inside the trunk are packets of black-and-white photos, paste jewelry, pins, combs—things a young woman would keep. And she was... young, that is. And she was a riddle, even back then. Reserved with her friends, I'm told, this young miner's wife was not well known even to her own family. The trunk holds a pelt of a small animal, a handful of books and letters; the stuff of her dreams, I suppose, though it doesn't amount to much, boxed up like this.

But a photo on top of the pile is worn with handling. The young woman smiles through the creases in the glossy finish, and her smile makes my chest ache again, as when I was a kid. It is Jolene, the young miner's wife, my mother. She wears a simple house dress and leans back against the edge of the kitchen table, her arms crossed. A painting of desert bluffs and clear skies hangs on the wall behind her; dark tresses tumble past her shoulders. Her head is cocked to the side and down, but her eyes glancing up through twists of hair hold the camera rapt. Her own smile is bemused: *Where did you come from?* she wonders. Her eyes fill the old kitchen with light; they reveal no pain, show nothing of the despair that would swing like a wrecking ball through so many lives. My God, she was young, and lovely, and at peace in the photo. I would leave her that way if I had any kind of heart.

Where did you go? I wonder again. *Did you really lose your mind, or just your direction?*

'In the end,' folks used to say, 'she lost hope.' They meant to be polite. I lay the photo on the packing crate table and find a bottle to open with my dinner.

Six decades of sun and wind have worked the nails loose from the panels of corrugated tin, and the tin makes an awful tearing, shrieking noise when the breeze picks up. My shack rocks in the breeze and it shakes in a heavy wind, and rain splashes its way through nail holes and seams in the roof. Sleeping is not easy.

2

Dew shimmered in the lilacs as I stepped from the shack. The morning air was cool and tangy with sage. I threw the empty bottle into the barrel and ate my breakfast to the pinging of tin roof panels warming and bending in the sun.

A geological contact zone zigs and zags up the north slope of Lookout Ridge, and I've traced its course all morning to a rocky knob where pine boughs catch the late-morning breeze and scatter sunlight over grüs and boulders. A red-tailed hawk kept me company as I climbed, hunting the slopes, hoping for a chipmunk or a rabbit scared up by my boots. She soars away now over treetops just out of my reach.

The climb was steep, and the air is thin, and in the shade it chills the sweat on my back. But the whining and rumbling of the drillrigs don't reach me here. I find a flat rock and swing my pack down. It's an early lunch stop—too early, really—but I'll wish I had this breeze, and the shade, when I push down into the canyons. Lunch is peanuts and raisins and warm plastic water. In forty years of field work I haven't come up with something more agreeable. The hawk sideslips on the wind until barely a fleck remains of her far up the valley.

The geological mapping will take a big part of the field season, and I have no one to help me. I used to; a junior geologist started out with me this morning, but he is gone now. Baitman, I think was his name; Dave Baitman. Andy hired him to assist me, although I asked him not to.

THE RECLAMATION

"Just let him carry your pack, Harlan," Andy argued. "He has a master's degree and I hear he's pretty sharp."

Today was the kid's third day on the job and his first working with me. He drove over from Stibnite and met me at sunup down by the old Midas shaft, where we started our mapping in good exposures of the geology. I told him to take off his sunglasses.

"Why?" he asked.

I didn't get cross. I said, "Because with sunglasses you can't tell when you pass from an alunitic alteration assemblage into kaolinitic; the color change is too subtle in the forest soils."

"With a hand-held spectrometer you can shoot the soils and get the mineralogy. That's how we did it at Berkeley."

"We're not mapping with a spectrometer," I reminded him. "We're mapping with our eyes."

"There is no color change," he told me. "It's white and white."

I took a breath and waited, as Andy has asked me to do. I waited almost half a minute, then explained, "It's eggshell and snow goose. Take off your sunglasses or I'll fire your ass."

He took them off but kept grousing about it, so I fired him. The drive back to Missoula is six hours by way of Lolo Pass, and he can wear his shades the whole way.

The hawk has flown on, out of sight. Across the valley from my rocky knob towering headframes stand like pickets, keeping wary guard over dark, crumbling shafts. Fingers of waste rock reach out from the shafts, gripping fast to the hillsides. Where rilled by years of runoff the waste dumps are vividly, toxically layered with white and orange and arsenic-green rubble. Rusted rails, oil drums, and other debris litter the tops of the dumps. All of these signs of once having been—the scars, the piles of rock, the rusted tin and timbers—align on a broad geological trend that sweeps through the valley. It's easy to see if you notice things like that.

I write up my notes and touch up my map between handfuls of lunch. The trend below becomes a pencil line cutting across topography, a contact between blue and pink, between sedimentary rock and granite.

As I work, the sun passes behind a cloud and re-emerges, and the changing light gets the birds chattering in the pine branches above me. Cinnabar opens again in the hollow far below, her tin roof panels baking in the afternoon sun and glinting as the wind lifts them.

The geological contact leads down from the rocky knob and over a spur to the northwest, to the wet, willow-choked valley of Cinnabar Creek. I fold my map, grab my pencils, and follow. The contact disappears under the rushes and alders but re-appears again on the far hillside. I mark its trace in pencil on my map and pursue. It weaves back and forth up the hillside and across the next ridge and down into another canyon, and so follow my boots and my pencil line. Where the rocks dive beneath forest litter my line dashes, then dots, then ends.

This hollow is not named on my map, but I believe they called it Alec's Canyon. Grass and low-bush huckleberries cover the ground so that the contact can't be mapped through. I'll pick up its traces another day. A clearing opens in the forest below the trail where the trail bends toward the sound of water, and the clearing is cool and splashed with sunlight. Blue jays caw and scold as I step forward into the glade. The chorus is familiar, but the memory is old, and I'm not sure if I really remember the place or only remember having remembered it long ago. Nearly hidden by brush and bramble, a small cabin stands in a shaft of spring sunlight. But for the jays all is quiet; a breeze stirs the crowns of the trees, but the air by the ground is still.

It's easy enough to pick through the bramble, and the door of the cabin swings in with a little shouldering. A stove, a table, and a cot stand in dust and shadow just as I remember remembering them. A roof timber has broken and fallen at one corner and bent the iron bed frame, but otherwise the roof is solid and the room dry. An old quilt still covers the cot; tattered and soiled, torn apart by rats and squirrels for nesting material. Tools hang from pegs on a wall. A shelf holds two pottery cups and two plates, a pot and a kettle, a tin of tea. Crumbled remnants of old magazines lie on the shelf, too, destroyed by the insects and the vermin, they're mostly now piles of pulp and kaolin.

A few dusty books sit on the table, and I pick one up and blow it clean. It is Walt Whitman's *Leaves of Grass*, sixth printing. The pages are stiff and brittle, and brown stains—fingerprints—mark some of the passages. Small and delicate, they could be a child's prints, but they were left by a woman. They are of dried blood. I lay the book back in its clean rectangle.

†

My father led us into the deep woods, and I remember still how my legs ached to keep up. The air was warm and sweet, and the trees towered in the sky, cloaked in late summer green. Dad kept walking, farther than I'd ever gone before, and he carried a heavy pack—so heavy I didn't think even a horse could carry it. But he'd swung the pack up with one hand and ducked his shoulder into it, then put his arm through the other strap and hunched it up on his back and tightened the hip strap.

"Keep up," he yelled back, "I don't want a mountain lion eating my lunch."

I carried a pack with our lunch in it. I'd put a book in my pack, too, when he wasn't looking, and he must have seen the book when he checked that the lunch was all there. I expected a knuckling for it, but he screwed up his lips and didn't say anything.

I hurried over boulders and roots in the trail, ducked tree branches, and made sure I didn't fall behind. The book wasn't heavy, at least at first. I pushed myself to keep pace. I hadn't been out of the hollow since Grandpa died; I'd never gone anywhere with my dad before.

I didn't see the cabin at first; it was still in shadows when we stepped into the clearing. Birds called from every tree; the place seemed haunted. I thought Dad thought so too, because he entered the clearing slowly, haltingly. He worked inside the cabin, cleaning and fixing things up. I stayed outside, out of the way but close, and didn't make a lot of noise.

Sunshine filtered down through the treetops in shafts of yellow light; seeds and bugs floated in and out of the shafts, catching fire and glowing. Willows sweetened the air around a marshy seep, where the water gathered into a pool, and I played with dry leaves, floating them like boats across the water. When the breeze picked up the birds hushed, the tall aspens rustled, and my flotilla sailed in battle line over the pool.

Dad straightened the magazines and blew the books clean and stacked them neatly on the table. I wondered what books they were but kept quiet and out of sight. He washed cups and plates and swept the floor. My father hammered and sawed a good part of the day, and split a stack of firewood. He brought logs back from the forest for the roof; he worked up on the roof a good while. He hammered on the door until it closed properly and re-hung a shutter for the window. The bedding was taken from the bed and shaken out, then put back on the bed. He spent a long time making the bed neat and smooth.

My father spoke to me as we left. He had hardly spoken all day, but we turned back and gazed long on the cabin in the fading light. He said, "This is all I can do, Harly, but this is the end of it, I think. We have to move on."

"To Nevada?" I asked.

He dropped his eyes and laughed softly but didn't look happy. He said, "Yes, to Nevada."

He said some more, after a bit, but I don't remember the words, just that he put his hand on my head and said something to me that was important to him. We walked the long trail back home in silence, and he picked me up and carried me high on his shoulders when my legs got tired. I forgot the son of a bitch ever did that.

3

Another storm blew through last night, and the remains of Cinnabar hammered and shrieked as I sorted through photos and memories. Sheets of tin scraped and slapped against timber rafters and banged against the sides of my shack. The roar and spatter of the downpour, when it came, nearly drowned out the crash of metal, and the room swirled with a fine mist. The plastic we'd nailed around window frames snapped and fluttered in the wind but kept me mostly dry as I worked in the light of the lantern.

The squall continued late into the night but brought no more dreams. I tossed another empty into the barrel as the sun rose and made myself a breakfast. A third drillrig arrived during the night, and the bulldozer has been sent to prepare an access for it.

Andy Carson is arriving from Spokane today, and I told him to meet me at the New Main adit. We're going to re-open the portal today, and I thought watching some excavation work is something a corporate vice president would appreciate.

I came across the portal about a week ago, nearly hidden by thick willows and alder brush. The foliage is fed by waters that for many years have seeped from the adit, soaking the rocks of the broad waste dump and coating pebbles and leaves and narrow-gauge rails with a thick, red-orange colloidal ooze. Behind the tangle of willows, a pile of fallen rock and soil blocks the tunnel entrance. But when I scrambled to the top last week I could see through the gap between the debris and the rock crown above, and when I shined my light in, it looked partly flooded but open a good way back. We thought it worthwhile to clear out the portal to see if it's possible to re-open the whole thing for underground mapping and sampling.

I'm having a crew slash out the brush and the tangle ahead of the backhoe work, and they are going at it with machetes and chainsaws in the midday heat. Pickup trucks, rusted barrels, and piles of brush and bramble crowd the flat waste-rock dump outside the adit. Andy parked down below the dump on the flat mill tailings that fill the bottom of the upper valley. Andy is a big man, and he drives a big Chevy pickup—the Luxury-Edition, with lots of chrome and a leather interior. He chose to walk up from the bottoms rather than get his truck scratched or muddied.

Andy squares himself down on the tailgate of my pickup and another man sits with him, but I can't remember the other's name. He is about ninety years old. I'm afraid I looked annoyed when the old bastard showed up. But he and Andy brought sandwiches and sodas to share, so I put away my bag of peanuts and raisins and made his acquaintance. In the smoke and the tinny buzz of chainsaws we enjoy roast beef on sourdough and gaze out over the town and the valley. The old bastard waves his arms and gives us an account of the history of the mining district. As of all mining districts, it is a cyclical story of hope and ignorance.

The mines of Cinnabar and Stibnite were worked for nearly a hundred years by a few shallow shafts hidden behind twisting, dusty miles of granite and pine. War brought city people to the ridges and hollows, along with quotas and deadlines. The military needed the district's antimony, tungsten, and mercury. Gold and silver mines across the west were shut down for the war effort, but Stibnite and Cinnabar worked and grew.

There was a little gold in the veins, too. There always is with mercury deposits. It is the gold that brings us back today.

Earl waves at the various road cuts and trenches—that's the old bastard's name: Earl Something. He identifies the weathered, broken headframes on the far hill, the multi-hued waste rock dumps, the loading chutes, and machine shops. He points out the larger piles of tin in the town site that mark places of business: Baughman's Grocery, the long sixty-man boarding house, the Mercantile. The Merc he gets wrong, though, and I point out the mistake.

"That would be the hardware, there," I say. "The Merc was half a block east on the other side of the street."

"By God, you're right." He turns and considers me. "What did you say your name was?"

I ignore him, and he doesn't say anything more about it. The backhoe kicks over, and the unmuffled roar and a heavy black smoke put an end to our conversation. We give the roustabouts another minute to clear out their equipment, then show a thumbs up to the backhoe operator. He starts mucking out the rock and mud with the long back arm of the hoe, swinging the bucket around and dumping the muck on the far edge of the clearing. Earl has been watching me since I spoke up about the damned Merc.

When the hoe breaches the debris dam, crimson mine waters gush out and course over the top of the waste dump. We have to jump aside to avoid the deluge. The slurry cascades down the side of the dump, washing deep rills into the rock and gravel fill. We stand and watch the iron-mercury solutions pour out unabated for about an hour until I notice, finally, it is channeling through cattails and reeds at the base of the dump, then flowing overland to the dry tailings where Andy is parked. It partly flows over and partly soaks into the tailings, leaving Andy's truck in the middle of bright red anastomosing channels.

Cinnabar Creek flows below the tailings pile, of course. "We should check it out," I suggest.

The three of us: Andy, Earl and I—Earl won't stay behind—hop in my truck and head down for a look. The roustabouts follow us partway, with tow chains to pull out Andy's truck. We follow the red slurry down the length of the dry mill pond to a wet-stack timber dam, which holds back about thirty feet of sandy mill fines. The solutions pool and filter into the tailings above the dam, and bright-red seeps ooze from between the retaining logs below.

"Have you found an environmental manager yet?" I ask Andy.

He jerks his eyes Earl's way, and says loudly, "Sure have. She'll be here next week. A real pro."

Earl isn't listening. He's walked to the edge of the tailings dam and is looking down over a broad area of burnt timbers and tin, broken glass, and tangled pipes; down where Mill Branch joins the main stem of Cinnabar Creek.

"It's the old Cattail Lounge, by God." He laughs and wags his head. "The Cattail was something in its day, boy; practically the town hall here in Cinnabar. It was the miners' tavern, you know; a good place to drink, dance, and fight. So I'm told, anyway." He puts his hands on his hips and gazes quietly for a minute. "The engineers and merchants all hung out somewhere else."

I look down. He says, "The Owl Club, I'm pretty sure. Across the street from the Merc." When I raise my eyes, he's looking at me again. "However, this here was the Cattail," he says.

Andy speaks up: "Harlan lived here, too. He was born here during the war."

I suck in my breath and shake my head. For Christ's sake, it's not for him to say and nobody else's business. "I was seven years old when I left. I don't remember anything."

But the old bastard is staring hard at me now. "Doctor Pruitt, you say?" He straightens himself and shuffles over my way.

"I didn't know anybody in town," I tell him again. "I don't remember a Goddamned thing, really."

"Harlan Pruitt," Andy offers.

A smell of oldness surrounds Earl as he leans in. His skin is pink and translucent in the sunshine, and his eyes gape through thick glasses. "I'll be damned," he laughs, "if you don't favor your mother."

I step away and clear my throat. "So, you knew my mother back then?" I retreat toward the truck.

"Everyone knew Jolene and Ray," the old bastard says. His magnified gaze pans over the town site. "Everyone knew the Pruitts."

THE RECLAMATION

Andy's truck wasn't damaged in the mudflow, but the roustabouts did a number on the leather and the carpet when they waded over and towed it out. Mike Lovitt and the laborers, in the meantime, shored up the tunnel entrance with heavy timbers so we can enter and exit without fear of rocks rolling down on us from the unstable highwall. He put up a couple square sets, braced them, and covered them with plywood.

The mine waters were still spilling out as we left the portal. But another downpour is due overnight, and hopefully that will help dilute the mess before it makes it down Cinnabar Creek to Meadow Creek and flows past the Forest Service office in Stibnite. Andy left. He's driving Earl back to Stibnite, then heading out to Spokane to talk with some environmental consultants. The day was pretty much shot for me too, so I headed early back to the shack.

My father signed on with the mine recruiters in Boise shortly after Pearl Harbor. As spring came on, he traveled north to McCall, and from there eastward through the narrow canyons to Yellow Pine and on in to Stibnite. He found a house and sent for his wife and their child: my sister Myrna.

A photo shows four young people standing at a table and a fifth behind them, a little in the shadows. All five smile into the camera, and I can't help but smile back. My father and the other man at the table, it would be my Uncle Harly, wear western-cut plaid shirts with pearl snaps. It is the Cattail Lounge, I'm quite sure. The mirror behind the bar caught the camera's flash, but nothing of the photographer. Two men in uniform stand at the bar. They're not military, but neither are they quite police uniforms. The two are half turned, watching the crowd.

Jolene is there, of course; she wears a mid-length buckskin jacket with fancy beadwork on the front and long fringe down both arms. I know the jacket; it hung dry and yellowing in a musty attic with a few other moth-balled clothes: dresses and blouses, a heavy cloth coat, women's shoes cracking and curling in boxes. Did I want to take these, too? "Naw, hell," I told them. "What would I want with any of that?"

My mother and father are in Cinnabar, so the photo can be no earlier than 1942—three years before my birth. It is no later than 1942, either, because they are all smiling, and my father hasn't put on the swollen, sullen look of a drinker. He's tall and young; lean still, though you can see the power already wound tightly in his arms. Jolene seems happy, so September has not yet happened. She nestles her head in the crook of Ray's shoulder and her whole face smiles. Her dark, diamond eyes crinkle for the camera, almost laughing at it. The photographer focused on those eyes; everything else fades to background.

The other lady was probably with my uncle. She's awfully fashionable for Cinnabar, in a print dress and a button-front sweater, bobbed blond hair, and bright lipstick; quite pretty for the day, though not in Jolene's league. The man in the shadows is different— different from everybody in the room. A pullover hangs around his neck, tied by the sleeves. He raises his glass to toast the camera.

Of course, the blond girl has to be Dorothy Giem. I knew Dotty years later when her hair was quite gray. They were friends, she and Jolene; they'd grown up together outside of Boise. I fill my cup and lean the glossy photo nearer the lantern.

†

The camera's flash made them blink. Jolene thanked Ray's friend and took her camera back. She wound the film and snapped the lens down and stuck it into her purse. Harly went back to his conversation, and Ray to his beer. Dotty slid the sweater from her shoulders and hung it over the back of the chair. "Dance with me, Harly," she pouted.

Harly put his arm around Dot and squeezed her. "You bet, babe," he said, we'll catch the next one, I promise." He let Dotty slip from his grasp and returned to the man in the shadows. Harly's big handsome face lit up as he spoke, and his arms rolled left and right to frame his question, like a hawk soaring on an updraft. His friend used his hands, too, to explain his reply and it seemed they were talking about flying. Harly was learning to fly back then.

Dotty crossed her arms and stared across the room. Jolene gave Ray a look, and Ray stood from the table and said, "C'mon Dot, let's put on some tunes and show these jokers how it's done."

He took Dotty's arm, sauntered over to the jukebox, and dropped in a nickel. He pulled Dotty close and said, "Pick something good; something to make this old barn bounce." Dotty picked a Glen Miller, probably, and maybe an Arty Shaw, and the men at the bar shifted over to give them room as the music began. It was a swing tune, and Ray knew what he was doing, so the bartender switched the light on over the dance floor and people turned to watch.

Harly came back and sat at the table, but Ray and Dot had already gone to dance. "How are you getting along in Sin City?" he asked over Miller's trombone.

"Cinnabar?" Jolene answered, smiling. "You don't make a convincing Baptist, Harly. And the only sins around here are too much drinking and too much ogling of other people's clotheslines." They got on well, she and Harly—so the folks said—they talked easily together.

"Yeah," Harly threw back his head and grinned, "I was being sarcastic. This town is something else, isn't it? It may not be the end of the world, but you can see the end from here." He smiled a solid, square-jawed smile, and brushed a lock of black hair off his forehead.

Jolene smirked, and turned to watch her husband and Dotty dance. The jukebox in the corner reflected pink in the lacquered pine paneling, and the lights over the dance floor sparkled off the liquor bottles. The music was scratchy, but it was deep and loud, and it filled the room. So when she said, "Hon, you can't get deeper in the sticks than Cinnabar," she said it almost fondly. Jolene dropped her head and considered a moment, a smile caught between her cherry lips. "But we have it good here, Har," she said quietly.

"We've got it safe, if that's good."

"It is. Safe is good. We were on our way to California, you know."

"You'll still go, won't you?"

"Oh, Harly, someday we will; we haven't forgotten. This isn't where we meant to be, and it isn't where we'll end up. But I'd rather have Ray with us in shot of the end of the world," —she smiled, acknowledging his joke— "than getting shot at on a Japanese beach somewhere."

She looked up and nodded to Ray, who started back to the table. Dotty laughed, though, and pulled Ray back as another song began.

"Harly, don't start talking to him about going to war," Jolene said quietly. "He has a good job and he doesn't have to go. Neither do you, you're exempted. Ray saw to it."

"What the hell do you mean Ray saw to it?"

"No, I didn't say it right. He saw your name on the list is all I meant."

Harly considered her and shook his head, but smiled, and let it drop.

She said, "You're helping just as much to win the war right here, anyway."

"Well, aren't you just a War Board poster?" He leaned around in his chair, and they both sat quietly for a few stanzas of *Chattanooga Choo-Choo*.

"I'm not going to talk him into going, Jo. I couldn't talk him into it or out of it, and you know that. Ray does what Ray does."

The song ended, and another began, and Jolene said, "Well, don't talk to him about war at all, then. Don't give him ideas." She laid her hand on his arm, "Take me dancing, Harly. I like this song."

They stood, and Jolene shed her jacket, and they stepped onto the dance floor where Ray and Dotty were already swinging to the tight, three-part harmony *"...the next day the cap' went out and drafted a band..."*

Shooting a grin at Ray, Harly took Jolene's left hand in his right as she leaned and swooned toward her husband, then Harly pulled her quickly to him, brought her hand up over her head as he stepped forward and rolled her into his left arm to *"...now the company jumps when he plays reveille..."* In one beat Jolene reached with her right hand across her middle, and Harly took it in his left and twirled her out in a two-handed spin once, twice, three times around to *"...boogie woogie bugle boy of Company B."* He let go of her left hand and shot her out to the very limit of his grasp, snapped her back in, switching hands at the midpoint to *"...eight to the bar...*, spinning her and darting her out to the limit again.

Ray laughed at his brother and his wife, and gave Dotty a spin. Shooting Dot out and pulling her back, he let go of both her hands as she turned helplessly, spun around once himself, and reached out with his left to catch her flailing right hand. He pulled her in and wound her into his right arm and spun her out again. Dotty let out a scream as the Sisters sang *"...Toot-toot diddelyada, diddelyada, toot-toot..."* Harly gave Ray a hip check as both couples circled in and out, and Jolene laughed so hard tears streaked her face. Harly spun her and flung her across the floor, catching her a dozen times an inch from falling, before pulling her back and spinning her into another fall. The lights and the music swirled like a carousel and people's faces whirled past her, smiling and shouting; the plank floor bounced like the top of a drum. Before the song ended both girls were screaming and laughing and barely touching their feet to the floor. Even the two men standing at the bar, the federal marshals, laughed and gave the couples a hand.

Harly grabbed Jolene's jacket and Dotty's sweater and they all ran out to cool off. Ray and Dotty lit smokes on the broad, plank porch that wound around the Cattail. A dog barked in town, probably at a raccoon.

"What'd your flying buddy have to say?" Ray asked when they'd all caught their breath. "What's going on outside? What's up with the war?"

Jolene waved at the mosquitoes and caught Harly's eye. Harly said, "Nothing. Nothing's happening. It's all a big snafu from one front to the other. Everyone sitting around waiting for boots or bullets or something else."

"You want to go though, don't ya?" Ray asked.

The moon was at its peak and had just cleared the pines on top of Lookout Ridge. Harly grinned with eyes closed and shook his head but not to the question. He hooked a boot between the balusters and leaned back over the railing of the porch letting the blue moonlight wash over him. The deck began to tremble as other dancers got up and moved to the music inside. Crickets screeched around them.

Ray slapped at Harly and grinned. "Get your feet on the ground, boy."

Harly dodged the slap. "There's nothing for me here," he said finally. "I have to get out before I die in this empty hole."

Dotty's jaw dropped at his words, like she'd been hit, and Jolene said, "Oh Harly, you don't mean that!"

"Oh hell, Dot, I didn't mean anything toward present company." He jumped up from the railing and reached for Dotty. "I just need to do something more with my life, see a little more of the world than I've seen. I didn't mean nothing personal."

Dotty pulled away. "No, you never do," she said. She stepped on her cigarette and walked into the pink light of the tavern. Jolene rolled her eyes and stomped after her, and was angry the rest of the evening that Harly could be such an ass.

Ray waited until they were inside, then laughed aloud. He flicked his cigarette into the willows and slapped at his younger brother, hitting him this time. He said, "For all your reading, you're one ignorant fucker, you know that?"

"It's a hell hole, Ray, you can see it." Harly stood and slicked back his hair. "We're mining too fast; no one's watching out. The government's in everybody's business."

"It'll sort out."

"Men'll die if it doesn't."

They all talked Dotty out of going home. Harly put in more nickels, and Jolene chose a couple more songs, and this time Harly took Dotty and they danced slow to Artie Shaw. Jolene leaned her body in against Ray, and he folded her gently into his arms and sang along, *"...Thanks for everything, for taking the skies of gray, and making them blue..."*

THE RECLAMATION

Dotty was still upset and said, "No thank you," when Harly offered to walk her home, so Ray and Jolene walked her up the hill to her rooming house. The moon was already behind the high ridge; it didn't shine in the hollow but for an hour or so, and the dirt street was dark and hard to walk.

Harly stayed behind for a couple more. The place emptied and there was only the clinking of glasses being washed. The tongue-and-groove walls and ceilings of the Cattail were sanded and finished with a glossy lacquer. The bar and back bar were one-of-a-kind: they were faced with a tight corduroy of lodgepole pine saplings, each no bigger around than a rib bone. Knotty-pine tables and chairs scraped heavily across the plank floor.

The bartender wouldn't serve Harly after a while, so he stumbled out and found his way home by starlight through streets loud with crickets and dogs.

*

I last saw Dorothy Giem in the early eighties. Even after a couple of husbands and as many divorces she smiled to speak of Harly. The Cattail Lounge was the miners' tavern, as the old bastard said, and it stood at the lower end of town where the springs and seepage from mill tailings kept the ground marshy and the air cool and full of bugs. I was in it a few times as a kid. I came in the back way with my grandmother to fetch my father out late at night. The place burned down before I left town; it burned the whole night. There must have been a thousand thin, stunted saplings covering the long back bar, and fifty gallons of lacquer covering all that pine. God, it burned.

4

With a week gone by in my new old place I'm getting used to the faded wallpaper and the banging roof. I'm working my way into the old trunk, too. The trunk and its contents, the knickknacks and photos, came to me years ago from a distant cousin. I'd have thrown it out if my wife hadn't put her foot down. She's sentimental in that way. But she's my ex-wife now, and she's turning our attic—her attic—into a painting studio, so the trunk has come back to me again. When I heard I was returning to Cinnabar it seemed fitting to bring it along.

I found a poem among the papers in the trunk. It isn't dated or signed, and there is no title. I found it pressed between pages of a notebook. The hand is rushed, with long, crooked loops:

> *Crow, your coming's a curious sign*
> *Should you not attend the bereaved?*
> *Do you come by chance, to steal my bread,*
> *or is something dearer you'd thieve?*
> *But answer this, and you shall dine*
> *if your soul's not black as your crest:*
> *Tonight shall my beauty lay her head*
> *on stone or bough or breast?*

THE RECLAMATION

It goes on for several verses, and I made myself read to the end. I like poetry, but this one cuts sharp as a knife. Someone else wasn't pleased with it, either: it was wadded up, before being straightened again and folded.

Mike Lovitt found me considering the poem down by the old West End Mine. He came barreling up the road, kicking dust into the sunrise. "We have a problem," he said climbing from his truck. "Honorario's drill rig is down. Looks bad." I folded the poem and slipped it into my map case.

The drillrig was smoking and roaring as I drove up. Shouts announced my stepping from the truck and preceded me to the deck—shouts in Spanish to the *pendejos* hustling about to carry that sack or get that wrench. Honorario, the head driller, was too busy even to acknowledge my arrival. His winches whined, and cables clanked against the mast. The big diesel engine raced, and all was as it should have been. Except the machine yanked and twisted at the drill rods, and the rods weren't moving.

The rods—the steel pipes we use to drill the exploration hole—are stuck in the ground. Honorario nods at last. A helper dawdles nearby, adjusting and re-stacking boxes of core; two others hurry around carrying sacks of drilling additive on their shoulders, trying to look essential while the boss, the senior project manager, glares. Anyone can see they're useless. The rig roars and clanks.

Honorario and his cross shift have tried freeing the rods with all of the safe, standard techniques. Nothing has worked; the rods remain fixed in the ground like the enchanted sword in the stone. Honorario is no Arthur, and the idea makes me shake my head. He sees me laugh and is discouraged all the more. Drilling mud sprays through the leaky swivel in sunny arcs.

I leave my drilling foreman to his levers and knobs and his helpers to their charades and find a pallet of drilling-fluid additive in the shade of a pine. Shoving and scooting a few sacks around, I make a seat from where I can monitor the goings-on. Two of the helpers hammer loudly on a down-hole tool. I've sat on sacks of bentonite for forty years and nothing has changed.

The dust from my arrival still hangs in the air, and my bandana wipes gritty sweat from my brow and neck. I ignore the hammering and write up a few notes, and the sun flickers down the valley over mine shafts and dumps and scattered remnants of houses and sheds.

Honorario cuts the rig's engine, and the drill site goes suddenly, oddly quiet. He walks over, his hard hat in his hand. "We're stuck in a mine opening," he complains before he has stopped walking. "You didn't tell me I might drill into a stope with this hole."

Stopes are the excavations left behind where ore has been removed, and they're nasty ground to be drilling through. Sometimes stopes are back-filled with waste rock, sometimes they're filled with timbers, sometimes with iron rails and machinery. Usually they're empty.

"It's not a stope," I tell him. "The map shows no old mine workings where you're drilling."

"It sure drills like a back-filled stope."

"It's not a Goddamned stope. This mine was under the control of the War Production Board. The Bureau of Mines stamped the map of underground workings—it can't be wrong. You got your bit stuck in a simple fracture zone."

Honorario purses his lips and looks down. "All's I know... she's stuck." He turns slowly, examining the trees and hillside, the valley and far ridges, hoping I'll make the decision for him. "What do you think?" He completes his turn and looks back my way. "We use the hydraulic jacks we might pull the steel apart—lose the hole."

"Honorario, there are no right decisions in life. There is your decision and there is no decision. No decision is usually worse."

He gives up on me. "We use the jacks, then. We got no choice."

I nod, and Honorario stuffs his hard hat on his head and stomps back to the rig, yelling and gesturing to his crew to get this and do that and not stand around like a bunch of *pendejos*.

I leave him to it and return to my map and notes. A plume of smoke wafts over the drillpad, and the diesel engine races again. Honorario's voice lifts above the roar, shouting to his helpers.

Within an hour the jacks have worked the drill pipe free. The crew start "tripping" the rods, pulling them with the winch and cable, unthreading the joints with three-foot-long pipe wrenches, and standing them against the mast in twenty-foot lengths. The trip takes another hour.

The last length comes out and the workers lay the pipe on the deck, and with their long wrenches begin to disassemble the core barrel. Excited cries in Spanish tell me they've found something.

"Your fracture zone is made of wood!" Honorario shouts while still thirty feet away. He can barely stifle a grin. He hands me fragments of old mine timbers: wet and rotted, smeared with clay and grease. I can smell the anoxic blackness from where they came. "We dug it out of the drill bit."

"Well, it's a Goddamned stope!" I toss the slimy fragments to the ground.

He doesn't reply but arches his brows and pans away.

"What the hell is going on?" I ask, "Someone was mining the wrong part of the mountain."

Honorario shrugs and keeps his gaze on the far hills.

I breathe in and hold it. Birds twitter in a thicket of scrub oak a stone's throw away, and I wonder if birds sing the whole time or if they wait for the clamor of drilling to subside. "Well shit," I tell him, "if this one's unmapped there might be more unmapped workings. Put on a new bit, and I guess keep your torque down and your fluid pressure up."

He nods, and strides back to his crew, grinning no doubt as he jumps onto the deck. The diesel engine roars again as I rise. I steady myself against the pallet of sacks and watch the birds take flight.

From the porch of my borrowed abode I watch a column of dust rise far up on the east end of Lookout Ridge. Trees sway and topple at the source of the dust, where a bulldozer pushes out an access road. A drillrig waits behind the bulldozer, mast-down, for the road and drill pad to be completed. Another drillrig stands at the west end of the ridge, already mast-up and drilling. It raises a thin pall of smoke against the late afternoon sky, and if the wind is right tonight I'll fall asleep to the thrum of its engine.

I found the old Stibnite cemetery after leaving Honorario this morning. I'd gone into town for supplies and stopped at our office for a bit and was overtaken by questions and problems from the junior staff. I pried myself away for a walk in the afternoon and took the side streets, dodging into alleys and trails until I found myself among a few landmarks and barely remembered ruins. I wasn't looking for the cemetery but came upon it at the end of a wooded track.

Abandoned cemeteries clutter my memories—probably because played-out mines and their ghost towns clutter my days. Invariably, wooden crosses stand crooked, and hand-chiseled headstones crumble under years of weathering until just a few letters and numbers can be made out: *this name, of that family, who lived her share of time; a loving wife, a precious child.* The Stibnite cemetery is no different, except perhaps in the attenuated period given to living and dying in this place: 1942 to 1945, inclusive, with few exceptions.

The grounds were overgrown when I entered, and weeds and soggy leaves showed through creases of last winter's snow. Wooden fences still surround long-forgotten plots, although the plots have been invaded by aspen suckers and small fir trees taking advantage of the growing space and the rich soil.

My own family plot, when I stumbled upon it, was not as overrun as I would have thought. There were three granite tablets over three grave sites—just as I remembered them—with only one grave, my grandfather's, ever invested with family bones:

Here Lies Axel Montgomery Pruitt, 1885-1951.

Next to that: *In Memory of Harlan David Pruitt*—who died, as anyone in Idaho could tell you, in the calamity of '45.

THE RECLAMATION

And then, *In Memory of Myrna Lynn Pruitt, Beloved Child*—who wandered away while her mother was distracted with one selfishness or another, and was lost to the wilderness, not six years old, before the leaves had quite turned in the autumn of '42.

Three granite tablets. There would never be a fourth.

*

Two of the three drillrigs broke down over the next couple of days. One got going again on its own, but the other wasted a good part of yesterday and last night sitting idle. It was Bernie's rig that was down. Bernie is my other drilling foremen. Honorario runs a big Longyear-44 out of Phoenix. Bernie supervises two rigs, two LF-70s out of New Brunswick, and it was his number-two that was broken down. I understand Bernie's English even less than Honorario's.

I was discussing the drilling progress with Bernie, and we were yelling quite a bit when Andy showed up in his big, white, Castle Mining pickup truck. Andy was supposed to be back in Spokane. He returned sooner than I expected, and I must have looked surprised.

"You'd know when I'm coming if you stayed in Stibnite instead of your rusted rat-shit ghost town," Andy says. "There's a cafe there and a hotel…"

"There's internet and cell coverage in Stibnite," I answer.

"That's my point, Harlan."

"That's my point, too."

A young woman rode up with Andy in his air-conditioned cab, and she thought my point funny. She laughs as she climbs out the passenger door.

"Hi, I'm Madison Davy." She wears field boots and a field vest, and a geologist's loupe around her neck. "Maddie. There's a rig on the west end of the ridge that's down, too, if you weren't aware," she says.

I don't know what to say to that. I generally don't like anyone telling me my Goddamned drillrigs are broken down. "Thanks." I force a smile. "It had been reported to me."

Andy takes a moment to slip on his field boots. He drove all the way up the canyon in loafers. He says, "I saw Tracey and what's his name, Lovitt, at the core shack. Where's Baitman today, out mapping still?"

"Who?"

"Baitman, Dave Baitman. Tall kid, long hair?"

"Oh yeah. I fired his ass a week ago."

Andy leans his back-end against the truck with a stockinged foot hanging in the air and one boot in his hands. "You didn't, Harlan. You did not!" He slips the second boot on, gets that foot to the ground in time to stem his fall, and says as he straightens up, "Does the name Baitman not ring a bell? His uncle put up a quarter of the money for this project."

Andy wears steel-toed cowboy boots, and his trouser cuff is half tucked in and half out of the top of his boot. He says, "A quarter of our budget! Why in God's name did you fire Carl Baitman's nephew?"

"There was nothing more I could teach him."

"A week ago, and you didn't tell me? I was here on Wednesday, and you didn't say anything?"

"I didn't think you were going to micro-manage the personnel."

"Baitman's fucking nephew!" He holds his head with both hands. As he pirouettes he catches that Bernie is upset, too. He turns away from where the girl and I are standing and steps over to talk with him, hands still raised; he could be surrendering to Bernie. Bernie shouts '*tabernac!*' a lot. I don't know what tabernac means.

I and the girl, Madison Davy, listen from near Andy's pickup. "Andy hired me to head up the environmental program," she offers.

"What?" I'm certain I misunderstood. "Who are you working for?"

"Andy."

"No, I mean, this is going to be a complicated project. What company...?"

But she shrugs and gives me an open-eyed smile. She looks like she's nineteen years old: an eager, sincere college type; shoulder-length dark hair and tourmaline-blue eyes. Quite pretty, really. She wears designer jeans, which are impractical for field work—I mean Christ, there's no room even for a pocketknife—and heavy leather hiker's boots. I'm guessing Middlebury or Williams, somewhere in New England.

I say, "Really? You ever worked on a project like this before?"

She mentions a few small studies over a few summers. "I've since finished my PhD," she says. "Dartmouth."

"Dartmouth." I nod. "You ever been a discipline-lead on a major Feasibility Study?"

"I am now. Andy warned me about you."

I ignore her. Andy slides his palms down his face as he walks back to us, and I ask him what Bernie's problem is. He shakes his head and says, "You might cut him a little slack for a shift or two, Harlan. If you can manage that."

I ignore that too. We drop the tailgate of Andy's pickup and lay out some project maps. I ask Andy to give the geological summary to Miss Davy because I'm still a little taken back that he hired her to head up the environmental program. I climb into the bed of the truck, sit on the sidewall, and follow the presentation upside down. I can keep an eye on Bernie this way, too. The two of them stand facing the open tailgate and the maps.

The young woman absorbs the geological discussion pretty well, I suppose, and brings the talk around to environmental challenges for the project. I take over, though it annoys Andy, and emphasize the potential for contamination of streams and groundwater.

"Acid mine drainage?" she asks.

"Yeah, acid drainage is pretty much a sure thing here."

Andy shifts his hands from his pockets to his hips and exhales a couple of times, but I describe for Davy about a dozen rock types that will require testing. She stands silent, gaping, as we roll up the maps, a little like a fawn in the headlights. I knew she would.

When the sun tips below the treetops the air high up on the ridge cools quickly. Andy and I pick our way around the idle drillrig and around a series of mud pits to the edge of the drill pad. We scramble up the slash pile, onto the trunk of one of a dozen large pines bulldozed to clear the pad. The air is mostly still, but strong winds aloft blow tall clouds over our canyon, and the clouds billow and glow and light the ground around us in an eerie salmon-rose color. I nod to Andy at the red light of the setting sun burning below on the old tin roofs and timbers of Cinnabar.

"It's a rusted shithole," he says.

"Your young Miss Davy is inexperienced, Andy. She's smart, but not smart enough to appreciate what's about to hit her. You need a real environmental study done here, one that can withstand a lot of scrutiny."

"She'll be fine. Why in God's name did you get her all excited about mine-water issues?"

"She's your environmental manager. What should we talk about, endangered owls?"

"There aren't any, are there?"

"No."

"Then yeah, owls. We don't want to screw with water issues."

"Don't be stupid," I explain. "We're sitting in a cherry stem of the River of No Return Wilderness. We are not going to sneak this project through." I reach down and hammer at a boulder scraped up along with the trees. "Acid drainage from these rocks is a practical certainty. There's no getting around it, so we'll report it straight up. When the shit hits the fan—and it will—we can cuss and wave our arms and eventually offer mitigation."

"Mine-water mitigation, Harlan?" he yells. "Are you serious? You're tossing fifty million dollars on the table!" He Goddamns me a couple times as the sun drops below the last line of ridges and the whole valley glows ferric red.

"Look, Andy, you'll never mine here unless you commit to mitigation. We keep the Sierra Club, and your Miss Davy by the way, interested in water. Let 'em beat us up over acid mine waters, and they're going to overlook some other small things."

He turns to face me, hands on hips. "What other small things?" he asks.

"Beats me. Things we don't know about yet and don't want to know; things that can't be mitigated."

Andy understands what I'm saying, and he nods, though he won't cool down for a while. Mining is a flaky business. It always has been.

5

Jolene grew up somewhere in the Idaho farm country. There was a river, fields, and treed country lanes, but I don't know how I know that. I don't know, either, if it was a happy home or a poor one. She had a sister, whom I met once, and I have a few cousins whose names I may once have known. But that's it. It's as if my mother barely existed before her path crossed my father's.

The black-and-white photos lined up across my table show two young people in work clothes and flowered prints, smiling as though youth is all you need. My mother and father met at the state fair in Boise. Jolene was still in high school. They eloped, or 'ran off,' as my grandmother would have it. Ray worked dam construction on the Columbia for a while, and the pictures show him in a steel hard hat with lunch box in hand. Jolene kept a rough-lumber house—barefoot, as they say, and pregnant. Little Myrna came along, and she learned to walk in an apple orchard.

Ray tried commercial fishing on the Washington coast, but Jolene, 'the shrew' in my grandmother's telling, never stopped complaining about the rain in LaPush. The war came, and the job in Cinnabar, and they moved here. Myrna turned five with no brothers or sisters.

The Cinnabar photos are mostly of the out of doors. The first packet shows a warm, graceful summer in the high country. Five-year-old Myrna is in many of the shots. But the series ends in early autumn with the aspens and cottonwoods just starting to change. Then there are a few loose photographs, not part of a set. One shows my father holding a heavy maul. Bare to the waist and hard as marble, he's stacked a couple cords of wood behind the house. His face is chiseled lean—leaner than I remember it—with a straight black hairline and wide, dark eyes.

Another photo shows Ray and Harly standing in front of two elk and three deer dressed and hanging from a high cross beam. The leaves are gone from the trees and the ground is dusted white. Both men wear plaid and denim and hold Winchesters. Jolene is dressed much the same and sits on a stump hugging her knees to her. Her cheek rests on her knee; her eyes are empty and set well beyond the photographer; her brows are arched, and her lips parted and turned down.

Autumn is beautiful in the high country, as I recall the season. Light frost steals in as the days shorten, and rims of ice grow overnight around boulders and twigs in the streams. The air at dawn can be biting cold, but afternoon sunlight shines through yellow aspen and cottonwood so brightly it hurts your eyes. But Autumns are awful in their brevity. I never knew my sister, of course, and I never knew the full story of her loss. No one else knew either, I guess, because every retelling was a little different. All the stories included a family picnic, and all ended with a whole town searching the hills and canyons as hope faded with the fall colors.

The rest I know from the people who lived on our street, who may have seen or heard small parts of it but were fine, somehow, retelling it in whole.

†

The men regrouped and tried again as the aspen turned gold and the underbrush scarlet. They re-thought their strategies and searched new trails. As the days shortened, the searchers grew tired and their numbers thinned. When the trails slickened with fallen leaves and the frosts set in hard each morning the men pulled back one by one, and at last stayed home. Neighbor ladies who'd brought casseroles and pies now bore knowing looks, whispered remarks, and sorrowful nods. *'God called her to him,'* a few explained. Others asked, *'Who was watching that child, anyway?'*

September ended, October followed slowly, and nights and days began to come one at a time again. Ray still had to make a living, and Jolene was left with her house to keep.

Jolene stood in the kitchen window as the sky changed and gusts of wind twisted down the street catching up the dresses of her neighbors, blowing laundry off the lines, and lifting dust, ash, paper, and weeds in soaring, swirling devils. The dishwater went cold. She left the sink and the dishes and ran out the mudroom door and into her narrow yard.

The sky above was deep blue, and there were no storm clouds to be seen; none of the towering, billowing forms poets describe, just a diffuse, gray-white mass descending upon the town. Toward the northeast where the canyons tumble away, one distant ridge and then another faded into the awful whiteness. She closed her eyes to the onslaught, but still she heard the clatter and rush of the coming front. She pressed her hands to her ears and stood shivering in the wind, but every breath brought her the smells of the frozen tundra from where the storm blew.

Wind in frantic gusts bent trees low and scattered thin eddies of corn snow and leaves. Jolene ran back into the house, and ignoring the kitchen, threw herself up the stairs to her closet. She dug out whatever winter clothes she could find: wool army pants, boots, and a heavy sweater. Back down in the mudroom she donned her wool mackinaw, hat, and gloves.

The icy wind bit through the weave of her clothing and chilled her bones, but she hurried away from the warmth of her home, following the road out of town until it turned into a trail. She followed the trail a mile or more to where it, too, disappeared to a trace under barely-trod leaves. The wind picked up, and the sky above her was washed of blue at last. Snow began to fall in earnest, and it stuck to the chilled ground and clung to tree branches.

Jolene turned and turned, seeing the world change before her eyes. Colors were stripped from the hills and life sucked from the foliage; the scenery faded away to white and gray even as her trail disappeared under the accumulating snow. She called out, over and over, but her voice lost itself in the gale. The ground whitened, and snow gathered on her shoulders and in her hair. Still she pushed on until nearly blinded by the blowing flakes, chasing feint movements along the darkened tree line, and slogging through deep meadows after sylphs and shadows.

Exhausted, she gave up and sheltered beneath a draping fir as the day and the season died. In the empty grayness before dusk she huddled and whispered prayers to the storm.

A deer passed by close enough to touch, and then another. Jolene rose, and all around was cold and dark and blowing. Her hair was matted with snow against her wet face, and she struggled to keep her feet in the wind. Already drifts had built up and she stumbled in them. Her body was numb, and her mind numbed as well, and she couldn't find her trail: the wind had blown it away.

Ray and Harly were readying packs, filling thermoses, and lacing winter boots, preparing to go out into the blizzard. Tears wet the eyes of both men, while a couple of others, coworkers called in haste, helped them with the equipment and pored over a set of maps.

The door blew open and wind and snow swirled into the room. Jolene stumbled into the kitchen, matted in snow, scraped and raw. She fell to her knees, catching herself on the edge of the table. Ray dropped to a chair, head in his arms, and wept openly as Harly and the others helped Jolene to a seat and helped her out of her stiff, frozen mackinaw.

Harly offered her a cup of hot soup from the thermos. "It came on stronger and faster than I thought it would," she said when she had sat awhile and could talk. "I got turned around and had to drop down to the valley floor to get my bearings." Her hands shook as she sipped a little of the soup. "The going was tough down in the bottom. The willows and deadfall were a tough go in the dark."

"Jolene, what in God's name...why were you even out in this blizzard?"

"I wanted to watch the end of the world." She looked from one to the other, expressionless. "Harly once told me you can see it from Cinnabar, but you can't properly."

The two coworkers looked around, embarrassed, and said they'd best be getting back to their families. Harly saw them out with thanks.

"This isn't a Goddamned joke," Ray cried after the others, but Harly, had gone. "We had no idea where to even start looking for you."

"Don't ever come looking for me!" She jumped up and wheeled around. "Neither one of you knows this country like I do. Neither one of you can find your ass with both hands. I'd just get home and have to go back out and look for you."

Ray stood, knocking his chair over, and raised his hand. But he pulled it back down before Harly could take a step. "You didn't leave a note or anything," he yelled, shaking. "Hattie said you might have headed up the north road, but she wasn't sure. Would it be too much to leave a Goddamned note?"

"Now I have to leave notes? Should I draw a map, too?" She paced around the kitchen with tears in her eyes. "I just wanted to see... I wasn't looking for anything. Leave me alone!"

Ray ran his fingers though his hair, and spoke quietly, "I never stop you from doing anything you need to do." He righted his chair and sat and dropped his head into his hands. "Is it too much to leave a Goddamned note so I know where to find just one body I can bury?"

Jolene wheeled, choked back a cry, and dropped to the floor next to the fire. She buried her face in her knees and pressed her fists to her temples. Harly waited a moment, then knelt and hugged her, and with a word to Ray, excused himself and stepped out into the storm.

THE RECLAMATION

Ray wiped his eyes with the balls of his hands. "It's not your fault, Jo," he said. "It wasn't your fault."

She didn't look up but stayed on the floor hugging her knees and rocking as the wind tore between the houses. The fire in the range died, and the kitchen went cold, and still Ray couldn't raise her.

*

There is nothing in my family trunk to counsel me as to what came next. Some trials of the soul no pictures record, nor are souvenirs gathered in remembrance. Family explanations were kept from me as well, whether out of kindness or guilt.

But with October dead and gone, and November bringing ever shorter days, and with December's early snows closing the roads and trails, Christmas fell suddenly upon them with carols and lights and indiscriminate good cheer. I don't know exactly when my mother failed, I only know she spent the last days of 1942 in the Stibnite hospital. 'Her accident' is how the polite folks described it, but of course it was no accident. *Your mom was crazy*, is the clearest explanation I ever heard, and that from the artless tongues of children. That and, *Jolene Pruitt why'd you do it—made a cake and cut right through it.*

6

A poem about a damned crow kept me up a good part of the night. I slept in fits and starts, and woke to the smell of lilacs and sage, rat shit and rust. But I'm getting used to it, and to the chatter of birds in the pre-dawn mist. There was no time for breakfast, so I drank a Coke and ate part of last night's dinner sitting cold in the pan. I cleaned my head and teeth, gathered up my underground gear, and tossed the empty into the barrel.

Matt Cairn is supposed to be here from Butte this morning. Andy asked him up to assess the condition of the New Main workings. From the porch there is movement in the deep shadows up at the portal, and knowing Matt, it's probably him and Andy already looking things over. I have to hurry up the road. The truck's tires are cold and stiff, and the ruts jar my kidneys.

Matt already has his diggers on as I swing my truck in and park beside Andy's truck. Matt is a contract miner. He's a good four inches shorter than I, but hard, and broad at the shoulders. He'd be sun-browned in another profession, but his face is pale, even rosy from living and working under the ground. Matt brought a thermos of coffee with him. I accept a cup, and we stand and talk a bit. Hard-in against the ridge the sun hasn't topped the trees yet, and the air is cool and crisp; birds make a hell of a racket in the darkened foliage. Andy doesn't rush us because he isn't going in with us and he understands what we're facing.

The coffee goes cold, and I toss it and get into my diggers: yellow slicker bibs and jacket and knee-high, steel-shank rubber boots. I sling a broad utility belt around my waist and buckle it tight. Matt hands me a lamp for my hard hat, with a battery pack to wear on the belt, and a heavy self-rescue canister.

"We don't know what kind of air we'll find," he says. "We'll need to carry the oxygen-generating rescues."

The damned oxygen-generating apparatus weighs a full ten pounds on the belt, but I buckle on the gear as Andy sits on his tailgate watching. Andy is our safety plan. I don't know what he'll do if we get into trouble underground, except tell the authorities where to find our bodies. No one else is around, and the nearest mine-rescue team is in Kellogg, about six hours away.

There's nothing left but to head on in. I unlock the screen gate across the portal. Cairn holds his OVM—his organic-vapor meter—inside the opening for a minute and the reading is okay, so he walks in twenty feet and checks the air there. Birds still call from the trees above, and I listen for a second, then follow Cairn in. I step into a foot of water pooled against the sluff, and we splash through tentatively, getting our bearings. The most dangerous area is right at the entrance where surface weathering weakens the rocks, so we wade in another twenty feet before checking our gear again.

We swing our packs up over our shoulders and turn our backs to the light. Darkness pushes back on us immediately as we wade forward, but our eyes adjust, and light refracting through the gate behind us reflects off the surface of the pool, illuminating the tunnel for almost a hundred feet ahead. The second-hand daylight makes a dim light, but it's light, and more than will be found beyond the first turn.

Around the bend we wade into utter darkness but for the narrow beams of our cap lamps, which slice meekly out at the emptiness. Our heads swing side to side almost involuntarily as we move forward, waving the lamp beams before us like talismans. Circles of white light dart across wet, clay-spattered walls, sweeping after the darkness, leaping onto wooden beams, and dying for a heartbeat in each deep cross cut. Our eyes fix on the brightness at the ends of the beams while our feet move in darkness, picking a way over the wet, uneven floor.

At three hundred feet into the mine, the floor rises and flows with water but is no longer under water, and it is strewn with rocks fallen from the back above us and from the ribs on either side. Narrow-gauge iron rails run down the middle, covered in many places by the fallen debris. The cap lamp beams reflect eerily off shallow pools and glimmer on the surfaces of the tunnel ahead. The air is warm and stagnant, unsatisfying to breathe. It reeks of moist clay and rotting timbers, of long-emulsified grease and oil, acrid sulfates and iron oxides—there is no smell like it anywhere the sun ever shines. At about five hundred feet in, Cairn checks his OVM again before proceeding, and I do the same. The meters will warn us if methane or carbon monoxide levels rise, so we can evacuate. If we step into a pocket of hydrogen sulfide, the meters will tell us what we're about to die from.

"Do you trust your OVM?" Cairn asks me.

"Oxygen holding at nineteen-point-seven, elevated CO_2."

"Trust there's no methane in here?"

It's not geological methane that we would encounter, but methane brewed up by the acid solutions eating at old timbers. But hell, if you don't trust your meter you shouldn't be in here at all. "Yeah," I say. "Why?"

He half laughs and strikes a match on his jacket zipper. We don't die. He lights a cigarette and hands me one, too, and the smoke in our cap lamp beams drifts ever so slowly in the direction of the portal. There is a slight breeze in here, not enough to feel, but enough to flush out gases as they build up over the years. One of the shafts on the hill must be connected somewhere to these workings.

Cairn nods at the left rib with his beam. He wants me to see that the tunnel here is mostly in good shape. He'll have to do some rock bolting in places to hold up the back where it has loosened, and new timbers will be needed where fracture zones weaken the rocks.

I nod. We toss our smokes away and move on. Our boots scrape and splash on the floor and our breathing is loud to my ears. There

THE RECLAMATION

are no other sounds but those and the echoes they stir, and a faint dripping of water ahead.

At eight hundred feet in from the portal the country rock passes from hard granite into fractured sedimentary rocks, and the condition of the tunnel worsens. Thick aprons of rubble collect at the bases of the ribs here. The aprons coalesce in the worst zones, and the rubble forms dams that hold back pools of mine water. Cairn and I march like zombies in the deeper water: hunched over, shuffling and dragging our feet to keep from splashing or falling into unseen holes, swinging our arms stiffly for balance.

Cairn nods up at the back, and again I swing my beam over. It will require bolting through here. Men talk little underground. You might think miners would talk a lot, for the companionship. But voices in a tunnel echo flatly and give no warmth or enjoyment; the hollowness of your voice only reinforces the inhuman dread of the place. There is never a lot of talking.

The main adit connects a dark maze of crosscuts and drifts that tangle their way through the mountain. We'd be lost without a map, which I keep in a case, as dry as possible. The map seems to be fairly accurate except, of course, a lot of the mapped workings are no longer accessible: rock falls and cave-ins have closed them.

Our lights probe into the drifts—those tunnels that follow the veins—and into the overhead stopes from where the ore was removed. The conditions in the ore zones are pretty scary; we don't go in far and we don't stay long. My Uncle Harly died somewhere back there, and according to the stories, he still lies under the rocks. I grew up hearing at night the crack of timbers over head, men's cries in the darkness, and the echo of footsteps in desperate retreat.

Cairn and I shuffle on, our boots scraping, our bright talismans swinging side to side, cutting a way through the gloom. The air becomes hotter as the tunnel drives deeper, even accepting the work is hard and we are anxious. At about half a mile in the air gets wetter, too, and our light beams grow and slightly brighten in the mist. Groundwater oozes from fractures in the wallrock and rains down from the back. It pools nearly to the tops of our high mine boots.

Where water impounds behind piles of sluff now, we skirt the deeper parts, keeping against the unstable ribs, taking care not to rub too hard against the old wood pillars that still hold up the rock above us.

Cairn says, "The drifts and stopes are in bad shape. Most I've looked into are caved badly." His first words in I don't know how long: the turning of time means little without a solar reference.

I nod. "The veins they followed contain a lot of clay. It weakens the rock." The loudness of my voice unsettles me.

At three-quarters of a mile in from the portal the lamps throw white, fuzzy cones of light in heavy, steamy air, and the glow shimmers off the wet rust-stained walls. Orange iron-oxide stalactites hang from roof bolts and from timbers. It is hard work: the sluff on the floor and the pooled water are deep here, and we stoop under roof timbers barely over our heads. There is no place to stand upright, no place to kneel to take the pressure off our backs. The weight of my gear cuts into my beltline and I stop often to brace myself, hands on knees, to catch my breath. The unrelenting darkness weighs just as heavily.

Cairn reminds me to check my OVM again, and to keep it in front of me. I try the snap buckle that holds my self-rescue in place, opening and re-closing it. I hate this shit.

At about forty-eight hundred feet in along the main adit, the back rises abruptly above us and we stand upright at the edge of a tall passage where long wooden beams in intricate trestles and trusses make up a strong supporting framework. Behind the beams and pillars, solid shiplap holds back crushed, broken rock. "Holy Christ," Cairn whispers, "this is some bad ground here!" The floor is heaved, and the rails bow up and twist. Cairn is fascinated by the timbering, by the structure supporting the weak rock.

Orange and green solutions ooze from between the planks. "What the hell kind of mineralization is this?" I ask. "High-grade ore and bad ground always seem to go together, don't they?"

"Listen!" he tells me, then shuts up, and we hold our breath and the old timbers groan around us, barely heard but straining still under the weight of the overburden, bending and creaking and defying the earth after all these years.

The darkness closes in and smothers us. I close my eyes to it, and the whining of the timbers grows and pounds in my ears.

"Have you seen what you need to see?" I whisper to Cairn.

"I saw that much half an hour ago," he whispers back. "Let's get the hell out of here."

I don't answer but turn and start slogging out. I need to stand upright and feel wind on my face. Mostly I need sunshine, or moonglow if that's what it's come to. I'd settle for the gloom of twilight.

7

We walked out into sunlight so bright it hurt our eyes and found Andy asleep in the cab of his truck. I said goodbye to Matt Cairn and left it to Andy to complete the contract details. They drove back to Stibnite together, and I'll see Matt again in a couple of weeks. I was done for the day.

I've never liked abandoned mines, odd as that may sound. The darkness of this one, though, won't leave me. So, I dragged the family trunk out onto the porch where I could sort through the photos in the waning daylight. The thing is, there was no blackness in that mountain until there was a void to fill, and no void until the miners dug it out. My own people created the darkness that haunts me.

My grandfather came to Cinnabar years before the war, it appears. Tall and tanned in the photos, he moved from Kansas and the wide-open prairie. I don't know what caused him to abandon those broad horizons, to leave the sunflowers and windmills and to bend himself down to labor beneath the earth. I don't know where or when my grandmother Ethel joined him.

But they are not my concern today. I've found nothing more from that fatal autumn of '42 and have just one photo from the winter. It is of Jolene on snowshoes in a bright but low-angle sun. She wears heavy woolen jodhpurs with canvas gaiters over her boots, a knit sweater under an open wool mackinaw, and a backpack slung over her shoulders. Fancy leather mittens show beadwork on the gauntlets, and she wears a furry billed hat with ear flaps. Her brow, though, is furrowed and her jaw set, and anyone would think she was setting out on a fateful expedition. I expect that my Uncle Harly took the picture, and his shadow falls across the foreground.

Ray had set up a trapline in the hills west of town. He coaxed Jolene to come along at first, maybe to get her out of the house or maybe to keep an eye on her while he was out. In any case, the pelt I found in the trunk is of a small, creamy-brown animal the size of a large house cat. It is probably a pine marten. Ray would have had no patience for trapping, but Jolene took to it single-mindedly, or so the folks remembered. It's hard to believe my old man would have let her go alone into the wilderness in her state.

†

She re-laced her boots, sticky with beeswax, and set them on the folded newspaper by the stove to stay warm through the night. Ray sat at the table and smoked his cigarette as she readied her gear. He waited to talk to her, she knew, but she kept busy and avoided his looks. She'd fried chicken for supper because it was his favorite, and she worried he would tell her he didn't want her going anymore. Last time he wasn't happy about her traipsing alone into the woods.

Ray wasn't fooled by her fried chicken, and Jolene wasn't surprised when he said, "Will you stop, please, and talk to me about this?"

"Ray, I've got so much…" she began, then hushed and stood still, her dark eyes cast down, her lip caught between her teeth.

"Jo, I'll buy you a damned fur if you want one so bad. You know I can afford it now."

She opened her mouth to speak but caught her breath. "I know you can," she said. "And I know you would, too. But can you buy me some sunshine, Ray?" She brushed the hair off her forehead and tried to smile for him. "I didn't see the sun at all today. It doesn't top the ridge but four hours this time of year, and the hollow was fogged over for all that time."

"Hell, I ain't seen the sun in over a month." He stubbed his cigarette into the tray.

"I know, and I don't know how you can do it. I'd go right out of my mind, I know I would." She moved from the kitchen to the mudroom and hung a bag of greasy bait to stay cool overnight, shutting her eyes tightly when her back was turned. From a hidden corner she brought out her backpack, already half packed, and in the kitchen finished loading it with wire and twine, pliers, a sheathed fillet knife, and some kippered meat and fruit for lunch. She made a show of packing the safety kit Ray had put together for her.

Ray said, "It's like you aren't even with me half the time when you're right here in the room. You got no warmth for me anymore."

"We made love last night," she murmured.

"That isn't the point, Jo."

"It sure seemed like the point last night." She pouted, then grinned a little.

Ray caught her around the waist as she tried to hurry by and swung her down onto his lap. She shrieked, and laughed, and let him kiss her on the mouth. He tasted like cigarettes but smelled like he'd showered at the mine and used hair tonic, so she kissed him again.

"I worry, baby. You spend so much time in the woods—there's...well there's nothing there, Jo."

"Please, let's not talk about it!" She twisted to get up, but he held her tight until she settled down. She laid her cheek on his shoulder and closed her eyes. "I just need some sun, that's all. It's so dark and dead in this valley."

"I know, baby. It's just, I don't think I could live if anything happened to you."

"You'd be better off without me, as nasty as I've been."

Ray brushed the long, dark hair from her face. "It isn't you. It's...I know this isn't a square deal." He rocked her gently, and she leaned into his shoulder until the kitchen became still and quiet. "Have you tried going out in the town?" he asked.

"Some."

"No one's being mean to you, are they?"

She shook her head, "It's the kindness I can't stand."

He exhaled slowly. "Would you not go on this hike if I told you no?" he asked. "If I said stay home, would you do it?"

"I don't know. Maybe. For as long as I could."

He sighed and kissed the top of her head. "You'll carry matches and the army sack? Don't be going anywhere without that down bag."

Jolene shifted around and faced her husband squarely, astraddle his lap. She wrapped her arms around his head and hugged him a long, hard time. "I'll take matches, baby. And I'll come home to you."

Snow fell through the night, cold and dry, and the next morning clean new drifts lay thick over the dirty snow that had fallen back in November. Ray was up before she was, and he was thoughtful and made a fire in the kitchen range, so it was warm when she came down. Jolene boiled a pot of coffee and cooked sausages and hotcakes. They ate at the kitchen table under a bare light bulb swinging slowly on its cord as the wind whistled outside.

"It's awful cold, Jo. You can change your mind; tomorrow will be warmer," he said.

But Jolene wouldn't listen to sense. "It's cold because it's clear," she said.

"Well, then, stay on your blaze line. Tell me you'll do that honey, please?"

"I won't go twenty feet off my line, and if the weather turns bad I'll turn straight for home, and I'll drink water and keep my matches dry, and nobody has seen a bear in these hills in fifteen years."

"Doesn't mean one hasn't moved in."

"Ray, if I see a bear I'll lead him right back to town, so you can shoot him. I'm so sick of elk meat I can't see straight."

She smiled for him, and he smiled back. She rolled up her sack of bait, stuffed it into the pack, and tied it all closed, then stuffed a magazine under the top flap. "Harly loaned me a pair of aviator glasses for the sun," she said.

"Well, I hope you'll need them." He exhaled, squeezed her shoulder, then turned and poured another coffee. Jolene packed Ray a lunch of cold chicken. For herself she rolled some sausages in hotcakes, wrapped them in wax paper, and stuffed them into the inner pocket of her coat.

The pack was heavy but manageable as she and Ray stepped together into clear, windy starlight. The air sparkled in the light of the kitchen window and froze the hairs in her nose, and the new snow crunched and squeaked under their boots. The cold bit her through her clothing, and Jolene said they'd better get moving or they'd freeze. With a hug and a nod, then, Ray started toward the lights of the mine, and she headed toward the cobalt darkness in the west, carrying her snowshoes in her mittened hand. She stopped once and called "I love you," but in the wind Ray kept walking, and she didn't want to yell louder and wake the neighbors.

The drifts came up to her knees, but too unevenly in the town and willow country for Jolene to use her snowshoes, so she slogged at first. The snow deepened and evened in the trees as she climbed up valley, and within a few minutes she was able to put on the snowshoes. They floated her above much of the tangle and ground debris in the woods, and the going was easier. She left the ghostly white aspen of the lower valley and gained the fir and pine as the sky in the east turned light purple.

The ground lay steeper as she neared the pitch that would take her to the broad, flat top of the ridge. Her climb began in earnest in the pink light of pre-dawn with fresh snow clinging to the pine boughs and her breath freezing in clouds in front of her. The snow became drier and lighter and did not support her weight; even with the snowshoes she found herself slogging nearly knee deep in the powder as she topped the ridge. The trees thinned, too, and no longer protected her from the biting winds. But the winter sun clawed over the eastern horizon as she stopped to catch her breath on the crest, and through pine boughs she watched the gilding of the ridges as far as she could see.

She did not drop down into the next canyon, back into the shadows right away, but found a tree well at the crest where the wind had exposed the rocks. There she took off her snowshoes and sat awhile in the rising sun. She pulled the water jug from her pack and drank. The hotcakes and sausages kept next to her body were still warm, and they tasted sweet and salty, and smoky like a wood stove. The sun took its time rising, and the shadows retreated; morning wind whispered in the pine needles above, and the swaying boughs dropped a fresh dusting of snow that sparkled as it drifted down. No other sounds reached her, and no smells but her breakfast; even her pine tree was too cold to give off a scent. The sun in her eyes made her squint and smile too much, and her teeth froze. She laughed in spite of herself as she warmed them with her tongue.

She let the sun climb a few more degrees in the sky, then strapped her boots back into her snow shoes, got her bearings from the surrounding hills, and started side-hilling down the far side. She got onto the good game trail she sought and worked her way to the north, up canyon. A blazed tree marked the trap line where it started out from the trail, and she tied a red bandana to a branch, left the trail, and started up the line.

To her left, in through the trees about a hundred yards or so from the game trail, a small cabin stood in a glade. A spring flowed nearby in summertime, and the ground there in winter was bare of snow, dark, and misty. The cabin once belonged to an old prospector named Alec who, folks said, disappeared into the wilderness some twenty years back. Small drifts of snow blocked the doorway, but she cleared them with a snowshoe and shouldered her way in.

A little snow dusted the floor and the room was frozen but in fair shape, as she'd left it last time. She started a fire in the small iron stove, and when she saw that the smoke was drawing even and white, she stuffed in more wood, prodded the embers, and made the fire crackle until the blaze seared her face. She made herself a cup of tea, and when the room warmed a bit, took off her coat and boots and stretched out on the cot. Propping her head on her rolled-up coat, she read from a stack of magazines she'd left for herself.

Silver Screen was full of the goings on of Hollywood; she had read it cover to cover three times. Clark Gable, surprised by the photographer, stood next to Myrna Loy, and everyone knew they were in love. Jolene lay back with the creased and dog-eared magazine. The elegant couple stood in shiny silk and black tie at a table by a pool, with palm trees towering behind them. There was probably a band playing just off to the side; Louis Prima, she bet, and they would dance all night, although they hadn't moved from the table in two years.

Red Book offered dress patterns for all the latest fashions, but they were depressing, with nothing but the plainest fabrics to be found in the shops these days. The new fashions were three years old, and who was there to dress for, anyway?

She tossed the magazines aside and rolled and stretched her arms under her head. The morning light teased her through the small window, glowing through the thin smoke and creeping from the shelf to the edge of the table, to the teapot, and gleaming at last on the spoon. She closed her eyes for a bit and tried not to let thoughts gather, but she found that tears had wet her cheeks.

She rose and stretched, and put on her warmed boots, then stuffed the stove with firewood and banked it down so it would burn slowly all day. She donned her coat and mittens and headed back out into the winter day.

It was still mid-morning and the sun shined brightly through the trees. She started up her line in a light breeze with a fine sparkling of snow falling from the branches. Within minutes she came to her first snare, marked by a blazed tree ten feet from the trap. The snare was set about four feet above the snow in a tangle of fallen trees. It was not sprung. She pulled a hunk of pork from the oil cloth sack and re-baited and re-set the snare.

She moved on through tangled brush and dog-hair pine. There were twelve traps to check, about a quarter of a mile apart. At the third trap she found her first prize. The wire snare had caught the marten around the neck, just at is was meant to do. The animal had leaned in to grab the bait and tripped a bowed stick, and that had sent a bent sapling snapping up, closing the snare and pulling the animal up to hang about six feet above the ground. Jolene reached up, pulled the marten down to her, and bent the sapling to her in order to loosen the wire noose. The animal was frozen hard as a board.

She re-baited and re-set the trap, then tied the marten up in a tree with a length of twine. She would pick it up on her way back down.

A second marten hung from trap six, and she began to feel the excitement of a successful line. But at trap number seven she found not a marten, but the lower leg and paw of the animal hanging in the snare. Jolene took off her snowshoes to climb up onto the logs where the trap was set, and she stood staring at the paw for the longest time. It had been caught by the leg instead of by the neck, and it hadn't died quickly. A badger might have taken the body, but Jolene didn't really believe that. The marten had chewed off its own leg to escape.

She re-set the trap and started to climb down off the logs, but her cheeks felt cold and she touched them and found that tears had come again to her eyes. The distraction caused her to slip and fall into waist-deep snow. She floundered, unable to clear the water off her face because her mittens were caked with snow, and she cried until her face nearly froze. When she finally was able to climb back onto her snowshoes she forced herself up the line, rushing to regain the warmth of the climb.

A third animal hung at trap ten, and there was nothing at trap eleven. She re-baited and re-set each trap as she came to it. It was past noon and Jolene pushed herself now. The water jug was nearly frozen, and she shook it to get a couple swallows of slush as she climbed. The sun was undependable, darting in and out of fast-moving clouds, confusing and angering her.

The end of the line lay in steep terrain near the head of the canyon where deep snow covered all but the tops of the smaller pines. Hunger and fatigue slowed her climb until each step became an exertion. But the sun came out brightly after all, and the snow crystals all around her sparkled in brilliant colors. The last trap was also empty. It was too high, really, for pine marten, but the view was wonderful. The wind blew soaring horsetails of snow over the surrounding ridges, and it swirled up fierce snow dragons far below her that twisted and snaked across frozen glades. Jolene sat to catch her breath and watch the spectacle below but floundered again in light powder deeper than she was tall. She rolled over and flattened herself, and floated awhile on the soft, cold surface. The ground winds blew stinging ice crystals, but her body was empty and aching and it felt heavenly to lie still. The sun burned her eyes, and she narrowed them to slits so tight it pulled her mouth again into a smile.

8

Honorario finished his drill hole but we had to case through the errant stope in order to drill beyond it. He ended up leaving an expensive length of drill pipe in the ground. We bulldozed a new drill pad for him about two hundred feet to the southeast, and he's drilling again on a parallel line.

Or he was. He broke into another unmapped stope. These Goddamned mine workings aren't right. They don't follow the official map.

"The damned thing isn't on my map!"

"Ask Earl," Maddie suggests. "He worked in the engineering office in the forties. He might remember." She steps over my way, to where the Salmon River Canyon opens suddenly to view. She catches her breath and teeters at the vast emptiness of it.

Maddie Davy has settled into Stibnite and for the last week has stayed nearly invisible. I guess there was a lot of paperwork over that mine-water spill. We've run into each other a few times, and she's not unpleasant for an environmental manager, except of course with regards to the spill. She really got angry over that. All in all, though, she's as you might expect from Dartmouth. I asked in the first week to discuss my expectations for her work, but she pulled out the *'environmental-is-an-independent-review'* argument. "Good point," I told her. "You stay independent. Let's talk about my expectations for the use of the project trucks, drillrigs, field technicians, generators, probes and meters…" That pissed her off, boy.

"Who the hell is Earl?" I ask.

"You'd know if you stayed in Stibnite with everyone else." She pulls, haltingly, from the canyon view. "Only fourteen locals live there, and he's the only one old enough to have worked when the mine was going."

I inhale deeply and brace my hands on my hips, but she adds, "He runs the hotel."

"Oh, yeah. I met the old bastard a couple weeks ago."

Maddie is at Honorario's rig watching them try to set casing through this new stope. She stopped by to load up the boxes of core drilled before the mishap, to take them into town to the logging shack. The drillrigs remove a continuous sample of rock, or 'core' as they advance. We log the core to understand the geology, and we send splits of the core to the assay lab for analysis.

Maddie doesn't have to transport the core; we pay roustabouts to do that. "Anyway, I'll help you," I say as we walk. "Why don't we throw the boxes into my truck and we can drive in and see Earl together."

Maddie agrees because she wants to ask him a few questions too, but says she'll drive. She has to come back afterward in any case, to line out the night shift. "I'm fine with the driving," she says. "You can relax and enjoy the scenery."

"I'll drive," I say. "I've been driving back-country roads longer than you've been alive."

"That's partly my point." She smiles prettily as she speaks, but continues to load her pickup, not mine. "Come on, maybe you'll enjoy having a chauffeur."

"I don't need to be chauffeured," I tell her, "or patronized. I'll drive to town." I pick up two boxes of core at once, which I shouldn't do, and carry them to my truck.

"Your driver's side fender is crumpled." She calls after me, "That's new."

"It's creased," I call back, struggling to drop the tailgate while balancing the boxes on my knee. "And that has nothing to do with anything. Bernie's idiot helper parked in a blind curve. If you're suggesting that I..."

"Your right headlight is smashed out," she says, walking over to my truck.

"The wind blew a Goddamned tree across the road. Look, I don't need some Dartmouth..."

She says, "Your rear end is bent so bad you can hardly open the tailgate."

"I backed into a fucking rock! You've never backed into a fucking rock?"

Maddie jerks up the two boxes I just stacked in my bed and with a sideways glance carries them back and stacks them in the bed of her truck. She loads the last box from the rack, slams her tailgate shut, and tosses her day pack in behind the driver's seat. "You coming?" she asks as she climbs in. "Or are you gonna walk?" She isn't smiling.

One of the helpers hurries over to open the door for me. "No!" I shout, waving him away. "No abra mi Goddamned puerto!" I climb in on the passenger side and close the door firmly. I haven't checked Maddie out in back-country driving, which should be done before a pickup is turned over to anyone. This is a good opportunity, I explain, to gauge how she handles the roads.

"Fine."

She works the clutch and the stick shift okay and generally avoids the worst chuckholes and rocks as I point them out to her. She drives fast around the tree-lined, sandy curves, and through the thick brush; faster than I think prudent, so I suggest she slow down a bit. She exhales audibly, but then smiles, and slows.

"Are you in four?" I ask. "I always keep it in two-wheel drive until I get into trouble, then I use four to get out of trouble."

She exhales again. "I keep it in four-wheel drive whenever I'm on dirt," she explains. "That way I don't have to use the truck's momentum to get over steep or bumpy stretches." Tilting her head my way she says, "I can drive through bad spots more slowly." She turns her attention back to the road but adds, "It reduces wear on the tires and the clutch, and it saves gas."

"It used to be we had to stop and get out to shift into four-wheel drive," I explain. "You had to lock the hubs manually."

She raises her eyebrows but keeps her eyes on the road and doesn't answer.

Ridge Road between Cinnabar and Stibnite crests Lookout Ridge in a broad, rocky clearing where an ancient fire took out the trees. Low sage, bunch grasses, and wildflowers cover the ground there now. The openness is always a pleasant surprise after driving a long way through thick woods. "There won't be much of a sunset tonight," I say.

"*Penstemon*," she says.

"What?" I ask. She was looking at the flowers.

"*Penstemon strictus*. What did you say?"

"Not a cloud in the sky. You can see practically to Lowman. We won't get a sunset."

"It'll frost tonight," she says, looking the other way. She drives through the clearing slowly and down-shifts before plunging into the draws and ravines of the south side.

"What did you mean back then; what did Andy tell you about me?" I ask.

She lets a moment pass and says, "That you're the best exploration geologist..."

"Yeah, skip that shit. What did he actually tell you about me?"

She clears her throat and says, "That I should be patient because you can be irascible at times."

"Andy doesn't know words like irascible, and I'd like to think you can answer a question without bullshitting."

She swings her head my way and gives me another pretty smile. "You're right," she says, and turning back to the road, "Andy told me I'd need a thick skin because you've gotten to be a mean, abusive asshole in your old age."

That sounds more like Andy to me, but I don't answer right away. We've entered a boggy stretch where groundwater seeps out and flows across the road bed. It's muddy and bouldery, and you have to pick your way through carefully, which Maddie is not doing. I point out the better route at several junctures, but she follows her own course, even when I raise my voice. We get through the bog, her jaw clenched, and her eyes narrowed. Climbing up the far grade she accelerates but shifts too soon, lugging and nearly killing the engine. I don't say a thing.

The road bends around into a copse of tall aspens where the sun, now at its zenith, shimmers and flickers through the leaves, sprinkling light all around us. "I'm not that old," I finally reply to Andy's words.

She nods. "You've still got a ways to go, then," she says. We ride the last mile in silence.

Earl owns the hotel in Stibnite where Maddie and our junior geologists are living, but he doesn't live there. He also owns the TNT Café, and the bar next to it with the liquor store in back. Earl owns the laundromat down the street, which sells detergent and fabric softener from the same window that delivers the U.S. mail. He was not at any of his places of business. Maddie learned where he lived from the postal clerk/laundress and drove us up to a big house on a knoll where sunlight and flowers brighten the lawn behind a low wrought-iron fence.

I remember the house. It is of red brick, tall and ornate in the Victorian style and boasts a broad, curved portico and gingerbread trim and dormers. The woodwork is brightly painted, and the grounds are well kept. We found Earl in the garden around back. He apologized as he let us inside but insisted on washing up before joining us in the parlor.

The rooms are high ceilinged, and the walls freshly painted; the carpets show a little age, but otherwise the house is well maintained. Maddie studies framed photographs above a maple sideboard. They are of the same vintage as the photos I've been going through in my shack; almost all black and white, and of people, horses, and airplanes. There is no mineral collection, at least not in the parlor, and no rusty mining memorabilia clutter the place.

Earl joins us at last, carrying a tray with iced tea and lemon cookies. He has changed from his gardening coveralls into a yellow cardigan sweater and a pair of tan corduroys. Earl is a small man, but he might have been medium-tall, even well built, when he was younger. He stands respectably erect anyway, for eighty-six or seven, and his stride is steady, if not quick.

Tea is hardly my drink, but I accept a glass, and ask Earl if he possesses or could direct me to any mine maps or documents—anything saved from the mill fire of '63. "A lot of the underground workings are turning out differently than shown on the engineers' maps," I explain.

Maddie, though, breaks in and asks about his gardening and the problems of keeping Goddamned roses alive in this climate. Earl shares that it all depends on how and when you prune them back and cover them as winter comes on. Many times he has found himself in minus-twenty weather shoveling snow over the burlap-wrapped bushes for extra insulation.

That's fine, and I wait patiently, too, through the hardier irises, lilacs, and peonies. Maddie is especially taken with the peonies. I ask again about the mill fire. Maddie asks Earl how he came to live so well and so long in such a remote and unlikely place.

That's fine, too. It is interesting Earl has lived so long, but I would like to get some information before his luck runs out. The two of them, though, seem unconcerned the afternoon wears on. It turns out Earl stayed out of the draft as the sole support of his mother and has run the TNT cafe since he was eighteen. There were times, Earl recalls, when he might as well have joined the army, violent as the streets got right here in Stibnite.

"Crime, here?" Maddie asks.

"Not like city crime. No, poor people don't take from poor people. I meant the workers striking for fair conditions, and the government's suppression of them."

THE RECLAMATION

I find his words a bit out of place, but when I look up there is no irony in his face. He says, "The miners could never keep up with the War Board's quotas, and the pay and safety conditions, I guess, were pretty skimpy. Even the women marched at times, over nothing in the shops to cook or to sew with." Earl pauses, and gazes beyond the walls for a moment. "Nothing a heavy boot couldn't take care of. Usually it was put down by the federal marshals. Direct and forthright, too, damn them. Occasionally they called in the National Guard."

"Wouldn't be the first labor unrest in a mining camp," I say. "Pretty common, really."

"How many you heard of where a strike was considered an act of treason?" Earl doesn't want to argue, though. He turns to me open eyed, and I un-purse my lips and un-furl my brow. He says, "The maps were not destroyed in the fire of '63. Most of the maps and engineering records were never kept at the mill in Cinnabar. They stayed in the engineering office here in Stibnite."

"Great, where can we find that office?"

"It burned down in '75."

Maddie can't check her laughter.

"But," the old bastard continues, now grinning, "a lot of the mine maps had been taken out and copied by then; by Amax, I think." Earl pours Maddie another glass of tea and tops off his own. I wave off a freshener. "In any case," he goes on, "they got most of what maps there were, and they passed them on to Anaconda Corporation when those crooks took over, and Anaconda would have passed 'em to Inspiration Mining, and so on. They all thought they could make a go of this district. Maybe someone will someday. Maybe you folks. Anyhow, I think you have what maps there are."

I unroll and show him the mine-level map I'm working with and ask if he is familiar with it. He puts on his glasses, runs his finger over the traces of the workings, and mentions a few names of veins. But no, he can't recall much detail. He ran his mom's cafe, for the most part, and worked a little as a clerk in the engineer's office.

There had been trouble over the maps at one time, he believes, but he can't recall the specifics.

"I was afraid not." I roll up the map and stand to go.

"You do look like your mother," Earl says, "but you remind me an awful lot of Ray Pruitt."

"The old man wasn't much for small talk?" I ask, as I roll a rubber band around the map. I glance with raised brows to Maddie, a signal she should say her good-byes. But Maddie's eyes narrow and sweep from Earl to me and back; her lips part in a curious smile.

"He wasn't much for small anything," Earl says. "But I don't mean that ungenerously. Ray—your father—got things done, all right. I don't know that everyone agreed with his methods, but he was a doer." Earl takes off his glasses, rubs his pink eyes, and leans forward in the wing-back divan. I take a step toward the door, but Maddie crosses her leg over her knee and throws her arm over the back of the chair.

"That's why Ray was a favorite of the boss's," Earl says. "He was tight with Oscar Hammond." Earl reaches slowly for his tea, sips, and slowly sets the glass back on the table. "This was Oscar's house, of course."

"I figured."

Earl lifts his knee with laced fingers and leans back. "Ray didn't get along too well with the boss's son, Farrell, although Jolene and Farrell were friends. Myself, I noticed Jolene, early on—early that first winter. Later, she and Harly and Farrell would meet for coffee at the TNT. But I noticed her clear back in the dark of winter. Hard to miss her." He pauses for a moment and glances up at me, but I move my eyes to the window just in time. He says, "She would come over the hill to shop; she came alone and kept to herself. I didn't understand till I got to know her, but I think she came over here from Cinnabar just to find some peace."

I never thought about it, but hell yes, she must have. It had to have been difficult living under the gaze of such an insular community, what with the whispers and insinuations.

Earl sees me lean on the wing chair and pauses for a second. He clears his throat and sits up. "Then there was Harly," he says with an odd cheerfulness. "Harly was a swell guy; everyone loved Harly. Your uncle was king of the Cattail, but he had no time for that. He was out to win the war and make a fortune. Of course, you know how that ended."

"Yeah, I know."

"I don't," Maddie says.

"Harly and Jolene, and—who was it, Farrell? —were all friends, though?" I ask.

"Farrell Hammond. He leant them books, and I guess Harly and Jolene amused him. He owned the only library in town." A cloud passes over the house and the room darkens. Earl notices. He smiles, though, and nods to the room across the hallway. "It's still the only library in town. You're welcome to borrow any time you'd like."

The rolled map drums on the back of the wing chair, but that doesn't get Maddie moving either. I ask, "This map was signed off by 'F.H.' Would that have been Farrell Hammond?"

"No. Farrell was chief geologist, but he was no miner. Scared of the underground. F.H. was an engineer; Fred somebody. Fred Hogue—a hog of a man." Earl's eyes crinkle into a laugh. "That's Farrell there in the photo, standing in front of the plane. Farrell's on the left and your Uncle Harly's on the right."

I glance again at the photo and recognize Harly at once. I recognize the other guy, too. He stood in the shadows at the Cattail the evening of the dancing.

Maddie stands and takes up the framed photograph. "They were awfully good looking, weren't they?" she says.

Earl shrugs. "They were different as two men could be." He lets go of his knee and tosses his glasses onto the coffee table. Looking away through the lace curtains, he says, "Of course, they'd both be dead not two years after that photo."

"Who was Jolene?" Maddie asks.

"Ray's wife," I answer.

We drive back over the ridge through deep shadows and brightly back-lit trees. It's beautiful but dangerous too, and I've reminded Maddie several times it is just after shift change and to keep an eye out for drillers on their way back in to Stibnite. Drillers are idiots after a long shift; idiots until they get about five beers in them, and then idiots again at six and more.

"Harlan, you're from here, from this place? You didn't think that was worth mentioning?"

"Everyone's from somewhere," I tell her. "Where are you from?"

"New Haven. But we're not trying to mine New Haven."

"Then you'd better not tell Andy about New Haven. This is a blind curve."

"Does Andy know this is your hometown?"

"Of course, that's how he got me signed on to this train wreck."

"It wasn't the stock options?"

"I didn't have anywhere else to go."

Maddie looks at me as if I said something weird, and I have to explain, "I was lined up to lead a feasibility study at Silver Ridge outside of Winnemucca, but the funding was held up."

"Do you have a family?"

"Do you mind?"

"But this is a home-coming for you, right? A return of the native, a closure?" she asks.

"No, I wouldn't say any of those three things. Do you ever just drive and listen to your own thoughts? Why do people your age never listen to their thoughts? Does the internet take that away?"

"And you're ready to open-pit your home town?"

"There's nothing left of that Goddamned town; it all died half a century ago. Really, can we just watch for drillers and drive?"

9

One of the books from the trunk is stamped *"From the Library of F.A. Hammond."* Well, I'll be damned. It is Hardy, a Classics Edition of *Return of the Native*. A number of other books are stamped in the same way. The dust jacket of this one holds a photo, undated. It shows a gathering of men on the main street of Stibnite. They mill about in front of an office; the Bradley Mining Company, I think, although the sign is obscured by smoke rising from a pile of trash and tires. Uniformed men make a rifle line a block away.

At mid-morning the shifts at the mines and mills would have changed two hours earlier, and by now working men should have been at their day shifts or readying for bed. The men in the crowd pull winter coats closer around and stamp heavily in their boots. They stand in groups—few stand alone—and they lean their heads together to speak. Some glance outward at the marshals.

A few people scuffle along the walk: housewives caught doing their morning shopping, now hurrying away from trouble. A flag on its pole snaps in the breeze, but for this instant there is no sound, and no color but black and white.

†

An unexpected opening of sunlight burned steam up from the street, and the morning breeze sent the vapors snaking low over the frozen, rutted mud. The breeze had tangled Jolene's hair and caught up her skirt and, though icy cold, had made her laugh a little as she'd tripped and side-stepped to the grocery. She stood now, bags in hand, and studied the sun as it darted between clouds. She breathed in deep, and reached down to take a hand, but there was no hand to hold.

Jolene closed, then opened her eyes, and stood a while longer as sunlight and shadows rotated and white strips and patches of frost on the wooden walkway shrank and died. A few might have noticed her standing there, but she showed no concern. The cold and dark of that first winter had been fully as bad as folks had warned, but she was nearly through it. There was no reason for Harly to worry or for Ray to fuss over her; she was through it. She remembered the laugh she'd had with the morning wind, and touched her hand to her mouth, then raised her head and stepped into the street.

If an order was shouted, a whistle blown, or a warning shot fired, she didn't hear it. But as she studied another sliver of greasy sun Jolene found herself in the midst of running, shouting men. She was bumped hard and knocked sideways; her feet slipped on the icy mud and she fell to one knee. Her grocery bag was kicked from her by another runner and she watched a couple of oranges roll away. She'd hardly dared to buy the oranges, and now the sight of them made her ashamed. She reached to retrieve the oranges but was bumped again and landed on her hands and both knees.

The crowd stopped, then, and turned. A man tried to help her up, but at a shouted order the crowd surged back the way it had come, leaving Jolene in the mud and the smoke of the trash fire. Her groceries were scattered, and the oranges ruined. She managed to gain her feet, and in the middle of the street stood transfixed by the sounds of the melee; of shattering glass, fire bells, chants, and police whistles. Smoke rose black and thick, and swirled in the sun between fast-moving clouds, making the scene in front of her flicker like a stop-motion film.

A pistol banged, then rifles cracked in unison, and the crowd turned and fled in her direction again. She turned and ran but was caught up and swept along with the mob, nearly losing her footing until strong arms grabbed her around the waist and spun her, pulled and hauled her across the flow of the rushing mob. A tall young man swung her up onto the boardwalk. They pressed into a recessed doorway, their faces nearly touching, and there the crowd of men slammed into them and sheared past them.

The man smiled an apology, reached behind her for the doorknob, and together they fell back into a café.

The place was empty but for a young waiter holding a broom, eyeing them closely. The youth, perhaps seventeen years old, was medium tall, and thin, with a mop of dark hair. He glanced through the window up and down the boardwalk, and without a word swung his head and nodded toward the backroom. Jolene followed her rescuer into the pantry where another, broad-shouldered man sat, head in hands. It was Harly, and Jolene gasped at the blooded napkin he held to his head.

"Harly, what happened? You're hurt."

"Jolene? Where in hell did you find her?" Harly asked the man from the street.

The café waiter looked in just then and said, "You can't stay. They're poking into shops."

"Right, then," the first man said, and he helped Harly to his feet and started out the back way.

"You wait here a spell," Harly said to Jolene, "then head back to home. You didn't see me, okay? I'll be fine."

With a nod to the young waiter, the two men stole into the alley. Jolene watched for a second, then stepped out too, and followed behind—pressing against the buildings when Harly and the other did and dodging behind cover. She followed them through a tangle of tents and shanties where eyes watched from shadowed doorways, through gardens, and into the woods where Jolene caught up to the men. The three climbed a low hill thick with underbrush to a big house atop the hill. Uniformed marshals guarded the front of the house, but they managed to dodge behind garden sheds and clothes lines and slip in through the kitchen door. They washed quickly, then walked unseen down a hallway and into a warm, leather-bound room with a small fireplace, a desk, and full shelves of books on two walls. No one spoke.

Jolene stood by the fire and flounced her dress to dry the spots of mud where her knees had met the street.

"Should we find Harly a doctor?" she asked at last, her voice shaking. She left the fire and leaned against a bookshelf with her hands clasped behind her. She wanted to cry and felt that ordinarily she would.

Harly said, "I'm fine, really. Hand me a handkerchief, Farrell—you remember Farrell, don't you Jo?"

"I, um…" she tried to clear her head. "How do you do? Where are we, is this your home?"

"My father's house, although the library is my particular domain. We met one time, I believe—at the tavern in Cinnabar, last September. I'm afraid you stepped into the street at the wrong time."

"In September?"

"No, today."

"I don't remember. I don't remember you." Jolene looked from Farrell back to Harly, her brows still creased.

Farrell said "We can't get Harly help right now. It's serious business, I'm afraid. He could be in a lot of trouble if he's found to have been in town."

"He could have a concussion." Jolene still shook, and now her chest ached, and she was surprised to have to hold back tears. The effort made her sound angry.

"I'm fine, Jo."

Still leaning on the wall of books, she folded her arms across her chest and asked, "Well, what is Harly in trouble for—and why are you helping him. Or are you helping him?"

Harly said, "Jo, if anyone asks, we've been here all morning talking about books."

"What do you mean?"

They heard voices in the hallway, and boots muffled by carpet. Farrell traced his finger across a row of books and tossed two onto the desk. Harly guided Jolene to a chair and sat on the arm next to her. He flipped through one of the books as Jolene watched, confused, and laid it open on the desk for her. Harly whispered, "We're just a book club. We like books." He nodded to the open passage and winced as he put the cap back over his wounded head.

Two gray-uniformed marshals stepped into the library with a big, well-dressed man. It was Oscar Hammond—Jolene recognized him from the company Christmas affair. There was a moment of silence, then Oscar said to Farrell, "These men are concerned over your locations for today." His German accent was heavier than she remembered it.

Farrell said, "We've been here all morning. Tuesdays, you know."

Oscar turned his head but kept his gaze on his son. "So I know. There was a riot in town, did you know that? They want to give the world over to the communists." He glanced Jolene's way, but right through her. "And all you care about is your philosophies."

The head federal—the captain, Jolene assumed—looked her and Harly over more carefully. Jolene realized Harly did not look like a philosopher, even with the cap, and her own hair and clothing must be a mess. She looked down again, into the open book. The captain asked Harly, "You're from Cinnabar, aren't you? Why aren't you at work?"

"Night shift."

"Then why aren't you sleeping?"

Harly tilted his head and held the lawman's eyes but said nothing. The marshal asked, "And just what have you been doing all morning?"

"Reading, as Farrell said. Discussing. We like the same books."

"Reading what, exactly?"

There was a heavy silence. Jolene looked up from the book and cleared her throat. She said to Farrell, "I don't understand why a man can't, um… step twice into the same river?"

Farrell smiled and nodded. "Heraclitus meant there can be no 'same' because the universe is ever in flux; everything changes, nothing remains the same."

Oscar Hammond sighed heavily, and the captain screwed up his lips and shook his head at the three of them. "Get home," the officer said to Harly and Jolene, "Get back over the hill. If you're on the streets past sundown, you could be shot."

Oscar pulled the door closed, and the men's steps faded down the hallway. There was a long moment with just the popping and hissing of the stove until Jolene asked, "But does the river change, or the man?"

*

That could well have been the start of it. I know, more than anything else I was told about my mother, that she became captivated, even obsessed with books. She drove over to Stibnite to borrow them, and to visit and talk about them—constantly, according to my grandmother who remembered it disapprovingly. But yes, it could have started as simply as that.

It is possible too, I suppose, that my old man asked my uncle to help out a bit with Jolene. It couldn't have been easy for him, either. *Come by and visit once in a while, Harly. Bring some of those books you and your college friend read.* And Jolene would have read a book or two, just to get some peace. Then Harly suggested, and Ray wouldn't let it drop, that she should get into Stibnite now and then—*Get out of this hollow, honey. Maybe go in with Harly to that book club of his. Have a cup of coffee.* The coaxing rose to nagging, and they both were such damned nuisances that she would have let Harly drag her along.

Harly was in deep with the labor movement—that much the folks still spoke of around the house. And young Mr. Hammond could have been, too, or so I gather from Earl. Having Jolene there and a stack of books on the table would afford them a plausible cover for their meetings. But what did Jolene get from it? Would she have yearned for conversation and company? I think in her state she would have dreaded both. But that's just me thinking.

THE RECLAMATION

†

"What a swell hand warmer," Farrell said. "Is it mink?"

"Um, no." Jolene stepped back, but smiled. "It's marten."

"Pine marten?" Farrell reached to feel the muff. "*Martes humboldtensis*; is it of local pelts? I read they were indigenous to these hills."

She pulled her hands back reflexively, although the muff would have covered her wrists. She worked hard to get the words out, "I, uh… I trapped the martens, just this winter. It took three animals to make it." Her voice shrank almost to a whisper. "I tanned the pelts and cut and sewed it together." She felt the room closing in, but let Farrell take her coat and Harly help her with her chair. "No," she answered Harly's amusement, "I don't think there are enough martens between here and McCall for a full-size coat." She tugged at the sleeves of her blouse, clung to a smile, and told Farrell, "Really, it's just an excuse to get out of that sooty hollow and up into some clean snow and sunshine."

They ordered breakfast right away, although Jolene could have done without. Harly was famished, and he insisted on treating her. Talk started politely about springtime, fast approaching, and the new businesses rumored to be coming to town. They waited for their breakfast and spoke a few words about Farrell's new book, *The Grapes of Wrath*, although Jolene wasn't sure she'd read the name John L. Lewis in the book. Breakfast came, and Jolene thumbed through a travel atlas between bites, letting Harly and Farrell whisper about the UMW and about new rules and their legal basis; about engineers and security agents unknown to her.

She let her gaze wander over the room, seeing no one paying the least attention to her. Folks walked by on the boardwalk, a pane of glass away, and did not even glance in her direction. She swallowed, smiled softly, and turned back to the men at her table. Farrell cut his ham with the knife in his right hand, she noticed, and ate from the down-turned fork in his left. Harly ate as she ate, setting the knife down and transferring the fork to the right hand at each bite.

"We've been rude. We've been ignoring you," Farrell said to Jolene after…she didn't know how long, her coffee was cold.

"No please, I know it's awfully important, what you have to talk about."

"And what is that," Harly asked, grinning.

Jolene said, "I guess… the fair distribution of wealth; the exploitation of working men like you by those who own the means of production—like Farrell, I suppose."

Farrell sat back and struggled for words. "Like… my father. I assure you my own means…You've been paying attention."

"These photos, they're of New York, aren't they?" She tugged at her sleeves and spun the book around. "That's where you're from, right?"

Farrell apologized again for leaving her out. He said, "I've just returned from there, I…"

"No one is exploiting me," Harly said.

Jolene asked Farrell to describe the city streets, then. "And the country between the big cities, what is it like? How does one city end and the next begin?"

Farrell raised his brows to Harly. But Harly said, "Oh please, do go on." He drummed his fingers on the edge of the table while Farrell described the city lights, the crowded subways, union halls, and the colorful anti-war marches.

Farrell's mouth formed nicely around his words, Jolene decided, but his eyes were too flighty, unsure of his reception. He was handsomer than she'd thought at first; he could be the damned Arrow Shirt man. He didn't act handsome, though. His head ducked when he made a strong point, and he smiled apologetically when he used big words.

Of course, he'd been to Boston, too, and it was the same there, with busy sidewalks, unnecessary shortages, and drunken blackout parties. Harly fidgeted, but a smile grew on Jolene's face as she watched traffic pass beyond the window. She'd had Farrell all wrong.

THE RECLAMATION

"You really care nothing about being here, or any of this do you?" she said.

Farrell stopped mid-sentence, and again sat straight in his chair. Harly waved to the young waiter, who dashed over with the coffee pot. "I wouldn't say I care nothing," Farrell answered. "It's more I do care, a great deal, *about* nothing."

Harly sighed theatrically and clunked his cup down. "It's nothing to you, then? I suspected as much." He winked for Jolene. "These are real lives, not idle theories, college boy. I'm a real person; we have real needs."

Farrell spread his fingers on the table, "I appreciate that, Har. Of course it's everything in a temporal sense. I only refer to the vanity of all things; the transience of human endeav… Where are you going?"

"It's still an odd way to put it." Harly had risen from the table and now walked to the door. "Look I have to take off."

Farrell watched him disappear down the boardwalk. He shrugged but seemed unsure what to do with his hands once Harly had gone. Jolene's own smile wore thin, and she gave it up and let her eyes drift to her plate. She cut her cold ham holding the knife in her right hand and brought the meat to her lips with the down-turned fork in her left. It would take practice.

"Are you enjoying Cinnabar—the rustic life?" Farrell asked, but then he turned red, shifted in his chair, and said, "Of course rusticity might be more charming as an adventure rather than a living." He cleared his throat. "Not that… Well, anyway, it's a pretty spring so far, isn't it?"

They finished their coffee without speaking more. When they were ready to leave, Farrell retrieved Jolene's coat and held it for her. "Is that a Yale ring?" she asked.

He stepped back with the coat in hand. "It's, umm… Sort of, I guess. It's Sigma Gamma Epsilon, a geological fraternity."

She put her arm through a sleeve and turned as he eased the coat over her shoulders.

"Do you like to read?" He asked. He busied himself restacking the books he'd brought.

"I don't really know. I used to read to…" She looked away. Every book she could recall was filled with pictures of bunnies or princesses. She leaned on the coat rack to steady herself as the room spun. "Sometimes I get hold of a magazine," she said softly.

"I'd be happy to loan you whatever you'd like."

She looked up and met his eyes for a moment, until he turned away. "I don't know what I'd like," she said.

"I'll help you. You were embarrassed to say you'd trapped your fur. Why? I think it's marvelous."

Jolene had to back away a step. Farrell seemed too close suddenly. Maybe people stood close in New York, but it was too close, and the café had gotten stale and smoky. "It's not a talent suited to a lady, though, is it?" she managed. She fastened the coat and looked toward the door. She needed to get out into the air and… just get out, dammit, and breathe.

He noticed her glance, and side-stepped with his arms behind his back. "That depends on the lady," he said. He smiled broadly, but there was another long pause as Jolene watched a cloud shadow race up the street. He said, "You came with Harly today, but you don't like being here, do you?"

The question brought her back. "Harly is getting himself into trouble."

"Besides that."

"I don't like being anywhere," she snapped. But she drew in a breath, pushed her hair back, and managed a thin smile. "When the weather isn't too bad I get myself out for hikes in the hills."

"Ah, Eustacia Vye." Farrell nodded, clasping his elbows. To her sideways glare he waved and explained, "Oh, she's a wonderful character in an old novel. I'll bring it next time, I promise. But for now," he pulled a book from the stack, "have you ever read Thoreau?"

"Is Thoreau a book or an author?"

THE RECLAMATION

He handed her a worn copy of Walden. "Henry David Thoreau," he said. "I hope you'll read this. I believe he may have written it for you."

10

The drilling program has been going forward in fits and starts, and we're way behind schedule for late June. It's the damned unmapped stopes on the north side of the ridge that are slowing us down. The south side of the ridge is drilling like butter, and all the underground workings are where they're supposed to be according to the maps. But the north side is a troublesome mystery. Those unmapped workings, though, are becoming a little more predictable. They may define a single, broad vein system trending obliquely off the main mineralized trend. Someone was mining there, but no one was keeping records.

We're letting oil and hydraulic fluid drip all over our drill sites, Maddie informs me, and we could be fined for that; even shut down until it's corrected.

"I haven't been shut down in thirty years."

"Harlan, some of the mud pits, not all of them, but some are not constructed to specifications."

"What specifications? Every mud pit is different. We build pits to hillside conditions."

"If a mud pit fails," she is compelled to remind me, "we'll have drilling fluids and additives cascading down the slopes, eroding the soil, getting into the streams..."

"Cinnabar Creek has been toxic for years."

"That isn't the damned point! We're governed by non-degradation language..."

"I've dug a thousand mud pits over the years."

THE RECLAMATION

"And how many have failed?"

"None! Anything else?"

Her breathing is deliberate and audible even over the roar of Bernie's engine. Bernie's rig is making good footage across the swale, and it whines like a diesel racecar. She lets the mud pits go. "The drill roads are being bulldozed more deeply than they have to be," she says. "I know the cuts expose the rocks for mapping, but it's also on the edge of illegal."

Maddie has been seeing one of the rangers at the Forest Service office in Stibnite. Tracey at the core shack let it slip. She's young, I know, and we're stuck in the middle of nowhere for months, I know, and it's none of my Goddamned business whom she sees. But she's part of a team here, and her team and the Forest Service team are playing toward different goalposts. At the very least there are questions of fiduciary responsibility…

And mud pits fail sometimes! Aquifers produce more water than you expect, heavy rain at the wrong time, any number of things. "What difference do the roadcuts matter, Maddie? We're going to open-pit this whole Goddamned ridge."

"No, we're going to complete a feasibility study. How many studies get final approval? Even at this stage the chances are twenty to one we'll be reclaiming these roads. I'm just saying we could take greater care now, so the reclamation will be easier down the line."

I can't even express an answer. You just don't participate in a venture with that kind of failure-first attitude. It's unprofessional. It's…

"Harlan, cool off, you're getting way too angry about this," she says.

"Why? Are you afraid someone my age might have a stroke?"

"Your age? Hell, you're giving me a stroke."

I laugh at that, although I don't want to. More quietly, she says, "Harlan, I'm not trying to tell you how to do your job, I'm just trying to do mine."

We both sit and rest, she on her tailgate and I on a blue plastic cooler. The late morning sun shining directly in her face does not flatter her. I mean, she's still quite pretty for as young as she is, but her eyes are sunken, just slightly, and there's a darkening underneath; again, just a little. Her face is more drawn and her brow more furrowed than when we met not a month ago. Over-work and direct sunlight can do that to a young woman.

Maddie needs to see Earl, though we were there just a week ago. She has questions about groundwater—about spring and well flows. "Do you want to go?"

"No, I don't need to bother him."

"He serves a good cheeseburger at the TNT. Pickle, chips, beer. What are you having for lunch?"

"Peanuts and raisins."

"Oh. I guess if you're watching your cholesterol..."

"My cholesterol is fine. I suppose I do have a few things I could ask the old bastard. You'll drive?"

Earl waits in one of the two large windows that front the cafe, watching for us. He's watching for Maddie, in truth, but doesn't seem to mind when I walk in with her. Earl's wearing a blue cardigan sweater buttoned over a pressed shirt, and cuffed slacks. No one else in town is wearing clean, pressed clothing. No one else for eighty-six miles.

Maddie shakes his hand, and I don't know, maybe she's just trying to start some small talk, but she says, "Look, I brought Harly's nephew."

An old man will lean back in his chair, chin up, staring off through the wall, and he'll catch a breath before he takes off on a long remembrance. "Yes, they came here a lot," Earl begins. "They liked to talk about books, and about flying..."

"Did mining affect wells in the town?" I ask. "What about springs? Did anyone ever mention a change in spring flow rates after blasting, or maybe water-level changes when one or another heading was opened up?"

"I don't know, I'm not a hydrologist."

THE RECLAMATION

Maddie looks at me like I must be from Mars. "Earl, did the people leave town all at once," she asks nicely, "or was there a gradual fall-off of population?"

"It emptied quick." He laughs. "Darned few people died of old age here."

"But why did the mines of Stibnite shut down right after the war and the Cinnabar stay open another six years?" she asks.

"Oh, well, Stibnite couldn't afford to keep her pumps running. Most of the pay zones by then were well below valley level. The groundwater inflows shut 'em down. The Cinnabar veins were higher in the hill and still gravity-drained through the adits."

"I thought you weren't a hydrologist," I say.

"Well, that's just common sense."

"Maybe you noticed, Earl," Maddie asks, glancing at me like that again, "when the discharge from the New Main adit at the Cinnabar began to flow reddish orange?"

"Well, you know," he says, nodding and cleaning his glasses, "let me think about that." He likes her, and he works on an answer for her. They talk quietly about mine waters.

Five tables crowd the floor of Earl's TNT cafe. The table tops are of coral-colored Formica. The chairs have robin's-egg-blue, padded vinyl seats and backs. Earl must have had the vinyl replaced fairly recently. A counter with half a dozen attached stools takes up the inner half of the café, and the cash register sits at the close end of the counter. The waitress hangs our order on a big wheel for the cook to read as he works the grill behind the counter.

From where we sit in the window, Main Street extends out of sight to the north, although storefronts accompany the road for only about two and a half blocks. All along that length the street is edged on the east side with a wood-plank sidewalk, splintery and broken. A deep, broad valley opens up to the south, and the airfield still occupies the upper end of it. A frantic orange wind sock can be seen flapping and pointing this unlikely way and that. Beyond the airfield rocky, forested hills rise up steeply and march southward forever.

Roger Howell

†

From the window of the TNT Jolene watched cloud shadows race across the hills, lighting up and darkening the scenery. By April the snow in the valley no longer laid clean and even; some distant ridges already were burned bare, and even in the shadowed gulches deep tree wells pocked a tattered blanket of white. And so the cold, damp breeze had brought to her the aromas of early spring as she'd moved along the boardwalk; of last fall's grasses lying wet and decaying under the retreating snow, of pine-wood smoke, and of sweet, tangy willows pushing up into the sunlight. It had made her smile. Now she felt as if she might suffocate in the heat of the wood stove, even here in the window, and she wished she'd let Farrell take her jacket when they met at the door.

She glanced back from the window and twisted her lips at Farrell's answer to Harly: "... We're shadows on the wall of a cave."

She thought, *I'm tired of caves,* and wondered if it was a literary reference, finally, or if they were talking again of the doings in the mine. She didn't ask. The morning was so much more interesting outside than in that she followed the conversation in bits and pieces. The several times she'd tried to interject, the men had talked right past her; a lot like last week and the weeks before. *I might as well be a shadow on a cave,* she thought, and the idea made her laugh aloud.

"I don't think he meant it to be funny," Harly said.

"I'm sorry, who meant what?" Jolene asked. She stood to remove her coat then hung it on the rack by the door.

"Your favorite philosopher."

"I'm sorry, I was watching outside." She straightened her collar and cuffs and took her seat.

"No man can step twice into the same river," Harly repeated.

A beam of light broke through the clouds and caught her fully in the face. She dropped her head, and from under sunlit curls asked, "A real man in a real river, or a shadow man in a shadow river—or one of each?"

Harly slunk down in his chair. "You answer her, college boy," he laughed.

Farrell had watched from one to the other, and the exchange made him smile. "Jolene, is it your role to point out the asses among us?" he asked.

The door opened, and a wonderful coolness blew over her shoulders. The bacon and wood-stove atmosphere was swirled away by the dewy aromas of springtime. She breathed deeply without turning from the window. "I'm sorry. It's been forever since we've had nice weather, and I'm not sure what Plato and Hercules have to do with springtime in Idaho."

"*Heraclitus.* I suppose the short answer is..."

A man and woman rose to go, scraping their chairs across the floor, causing Jolene to lose the thread of Farrell's answer.

Harly called, "Earl, I'll have another beer, Buddy." He saw Jolene glance over and smirk, and he shrugged. "Yeah, night shift this month. The bigger wonder is I can stomach eggs and hotcakes for supper."

Earl made change for the couple at the counter, then hurried over with another can of beer. Harly gave the young man a punch on the shoulder as a tired waitress began to clear the dishes from the vacant table. The couple retrieved their hats and coats from the coatrack, and again the bacon smoke swirled around the room.

A newspaper cluttered the table, and Jolene folded it and said, "Harly, tell me about the *Wealth of Nations*, then. Although that seems a big bite when we can't do much about the wealth of my pantry."

"Adam Smith, um... economic scale... it's all tied up together." Harly looked to Farrell and added with a bob of his head, "I sort of cherry picked through his *Inquiry*. You were right; it is a little dense."

"I'd love to hear all about the drama," Jolene said. She narrowed her eyes and smiled suddenly as a passing car shot another beam of sunlight her way.

"Well, it's.... it is primarily about the division of labor...

81

Jolene listened with her chin in her hand, her lip curling now and then almost to a grin. "What did Mr. Adams…"

"Mr. Smith."

"Mr. Smith goes to Washington?" She asked, biting her lip.

"… and dehumanization of the worker. The important thing is, the work creates the person, the person isn't born to the work, Jo. We aren't bound by nature to our tasks."

"We are in the winter when the passes close." She wrinkled her nose and hid a grin behind curled fingers.

Farrell looked up and said, "Philosophiae quotidien. David Hume would approve."

Harly set his beer down abruptly and explained, "Smith's treatise was written several hundred years ago, and primarily as a warning about the excesses…"

"Well," Jolene broke in, "I'm returning Farrell's *Gone with the Wind*. It didn't deal with excess wealth… or maybe it did. Anyway, I did have fun reading it."

Farrell seemed less nervous today, and he'd grinned through Jolene's teasing, but she saw him look heavenward at her words. He leaned back and threw an arm over the back of his chair, then asked with a smirk, "What did you think of Scarlett as a female hero in a book of such marshal theme? Scarlett seemed to care more for her own fun than for the South. Are women really so uninterested in the so-called cause?"

Jolene felt herself flush, and the grease smoke smelled suddenly nauseating. Harly said, "Farrell, she's just…" He set his beer down, sighed, and looked away.

Jolene sat still and looked ahead as the room seemed to quiet. Farrell started to speak again, then stopped, and looked off to the side, through the window and down the empty, muddy street. His cheeks reddened, and he winced, but just then Jolene started to answer. "It might seem like Scarlett didn't care, Farrell. But…"

"Jolene, I'm sorry, I shouldn't have…"

"No, listen, dammit!" She shut her eyes for a moment, then cleared her throat and said more gently, "Excuse me. What I mean is,

Scarlett couldn't be uninterested in the cause because, well, she *was* the cause. I mean, Mitchell created Scarlett and put into her everything she loved and hated about the South. She was silly and selfish like you say, but heroic, too." Jolene stopped and with eyes narrowed, raised her cup to her lips, then set it down quietly as she'd seen Farrell do to gain a moment. She cleared her throat. "Scarlett lost... Well, she lost everything, didn't she? But she never lost her spirit. And mostly" —she waited until she was sure her voice wouldn't break, — "mostly she found a way to survive and move on." Jolene looked down and smiled. "And that, I think, is what Mitchell hopes for the South."

Harly glanced Farrell's way. Farrell shifted his leg from his knee, and squaring himself, put his hands flat on the table. After a moment he said, "You read this book."

"Of course I read it."

The last breakfast customers left, and Earl sat on the counter listening to the friends in the window. "Did *Gone with the Wind* really happen?" he asked across the empty floor.

"Certainly," Jolene called back.

"Well, not exactly," Harly said. He pushed his chair onto its back legs, and taking up his beer, said, "It's not the real world, Jo. It's just a novel."

"Fiddle-dee-dee!" Jolene grinned, and it was a real grin, finally, broad and radiant. She said, "Margaret Mitchel grew up around people who lived through the whole war. Your Adams..."

"Smith."

"Smith wrote his so-called *Wealth of Nations* in a mansion full of servants. That's not the real world, Har." She stopped, bit her lip again, and fought for another bright smile. "Everything about that novel is true except maybe some facts."

Harly tried to argue scientific objectivity. "Help me out here, college boy," he joked.

But Farrell would not jump in on his side. He sat still, eyes open and lips parted, watching Jolene even as Harly's eyes turned his way and narrowed. "No, I'm not going to help you," Farrell said. "You're going to lose this one, I think."

*

Earl does serve a good cheeseburger, and Maddie and I had iced tea. I don't drink during working hours, not even beer.

Most people left Stibnite shortly after the war as the markets for bullets and airplane engines crashed, and the prices of antimony and tungsten followed them down. What was left of value in the ore, a little bit of gold, by itself could not offset the cost of dewatering. The shops and markets closed one by one, stranding the people still working and living in Cinnabar. The garage and filling station shut down, then the jail, and finally the school.

Cinnabar held on for another five years, fighting the remoteness and the falling mercury prices until just a skeleton crew remained. Only a couple dozen folks were left in both towns by the time I left in the early fifties. Earl kept his mother's cafe open through all the steady decline, and but for a few trips to Boise and Spokane, lived here his whole life.

I swear to God Maddie would stay all day long if I didn't make a point of rising and stepping toward the door. Rain began to fall heavily as we ate our lunch, but rain doesn't stop the drillrigs from turning.

Maddie kisses Earl on his cheek and says, "Thanks, sweetheart."

"Well, that's just patronizing," I tell her as we climb into the truck.

"What now, Harlan?"

"There's nothing more demeaning than an old man being called 'dear' or 'sweetheart' by a young woman."

"How would you know?"

I ignore that. Low, gray clouds hang in wisps and tatters, darkening and menacing our drive back. The rain has made the road a slippery mess, and one ought to pay attention to the hazards. But I'll just go ahead and die in a fiery crash; I'm weary of the argument.

THE RECLAMATION

At the crest we both need to make phone calls, and Maddie in her red raincoat talks for quite a while at the edge of the clearing.

The project plan for weeks has been to get Matt Cairn out here to open up the old workings, so we can map and sample underground. Andy needed me to stand around in the rain and call so he could tell me that Cairn and his crew left Butte on Monday and should be here tonight or tomorrow. There's absolutely nothing that information does for me. I'm not going to lay mints on their pillows, and I'm sure as hell not going to stand out at the pass, flagging down their trucks.

"Jesus Christ, Harlan, I thought you'd like to know, is all. Is it raining there or something?"

"I'll see them tomorrow or the next day when they get in," I shout over the rain and wind. "They'll be self-sufficient, right?"

"Oh, God yes. Matt knows you well enough he won't ask for a screwdriver. It's raining there, isn't it?"

The rigs are all cutting good rock when we check on them. The crews have hung blue plastic tarps from the masts and staked up the corners to make open-sided tents of sorts, where they can work out of the downpour. Oddly, the rain seems to lift the morale of the men. Even Bernie, standing under his spattering, fluttering tarp, nods and answers my questions without the usual invective. I don't have a damned tarp though, and the afternoon seems to me a good one to catch up on some paper work.

Mike Lovitt found me at camp reading old geological reports, and he looked pretty shook up. "We have another problem," he said stepping through the door. "The New Main tunnel. The Goddamned entrance collapsed."

"Was anyone hurt?"

"No, it must have happened last night or this morning. Maybe all the rain caused a slide." He looked a little shaken. "I was heading underground this afternoon to take some readings and water samples."

"It hasn't been up a month." I put aside the reports and grabbed my rain gear. "You can't put up a square-set to last a Goddamned month?"

And sure as hell, the portal is messed up. The entrance is now partly blocked with a pile of mud, rocks, timbers, and plywood all mixed together. Heavy supporting timbers sprawl out from under the debris at awkward angles. Maybe Mike's right, maybe this damned rain caused a small rock slide to take out the timber frame.

I inch as close to the fresh highwall as I dare and shine my flashlight beyond the caved debris into the maw of the mountain. The halogen beam barely glints off rocks and timbers for a few hundred feet before dying in utter darkness. Mike yells on the radio to bring up a crew and a backhoe. I say, "Tell them to bring a locking gate and frame, too."

A fall of timbers and rock is always a tangled mess, but it should retain some engineering sense. This one isn't right. The timbers could not have been kicked out like they are by a glancing force from above. This could not have been brought down by a mudslide; it had to have been pulled down. And sure enough, there are scrapes near the bottom ends of the support timbers consistent with a tow chain.

I don't say anything to Mike when I step back to the pickup but listen as he finishes his call with the construction foreman. "They'll have a backhoe up here in an hour," he says.

A little mine water still seeps over the edge of the dump, but no discoloration has shown up in the waters of Cinnabar or Meadow Creeks, as far as I know. No fish have floated belly-up past the Forest Service office, and nobody has said anything about the mine water spill around town. At least I don't think so. "Tell them to lock the son of a bitch tight," I say. "Cairn's crew are on their way. We'll shut it up till they get here."

11

The vial holds maybe a quarter ounce of gold dust. The yellow flakes swirl in the water when I shake it and settle quickly under a layer of black sand. It was in among her things. Jolene was known to work an old sluice box up in Alec's Canyon where a little color could still be won when the water was running. She might have found the sluice box on one of her long hikes. How she came across it is not important, except my father would not have been happy if he'd known what she was doing. Alec's Canyon was still within the Cinnabar Mining Company's land position, and you didn't take gold from any part of the Company's claims. As I think about it, it might have been Grandpa Axel who told Jolene of the sluice box. The old man hated the Cinnabar Mining Company and their Goddamned land grabbing. It might have been him out of spite; his own son turning into such a shameful company man.

†

Jolene pushed through scratchy green boughs and vaulted the trunk of a fir tree, a wind-fall from the winter storms left blocking the path. Remnants of snow lay on the ground, dirtied by plant litter and mill ash. Yesterday's bright sun had softened the snow to slush but the slush had hardened again in the cloudless night, so now she crunched through the thin aprons still lining the shoulder of the trail. She left Cinnabar in her wake. Unpainted frame houses in broken rows disappeared, and tar-paper shops and tangled power lines fell behind a turn of the trail, and the smoke stacks and the tall bunkhouse were finally lost to sight behind a screen of purple willows and morning mist. At last, the rolling and scraping of the mill and the banging of the ball drums fell silent, and the crisp, light calls of birds rose up and filled the stillness.

Most years, the Idaho high country is impassable in March and April. The snow by then is no longer deep enough or continuous enough for skiing or snow-shoeing but hasn't yet melted away to where a person can walk the trails. For more than two months then, Jolene would have sat house-bound, mopping boot tracks from the wood floors, cooking eggs and biscuits and coffee, and listening to Ethel go on.

She searched the meager shelves of meager shops for something to buy with Ray's paycheck; going out when foot traffic was lightest, dodging the stares and whispers of the townspeople. She cooked potatoes and canned beans, and elk steaks, and elk roasts, and elk stews; she hung wash on the line and took frozen shirts and underwear off the line. And she watched for the sun wherever she could find it.

Ray worked late most days, and then stepped out to the Cattail most evenings after dinner. He made shift supervisor, and there were equipment breakages, safety issues, and labor conflicts to deal with, and these were usually dealt with more easily over a drink. So Ray sometimes would come home half drunk, and then Jolene would cook him another late meal. There were times she'd have to stay out of his way or come as soon as he called her, and she wouldn't talk to him of Myrna then, because he could get angry. He put his hands on her, and she accepted it and sometimes enjoyed it, if he wasn't mean.

Once a week or so if the weather and road conditions allowed Jolene would get out to the coffee shop in Stibnite to trade in her books for new ones. At the TNT she talked of poems and places and ideas far from the mud and the meddling and the sameness of days in Cinnabar.

Now on that first morning freed from the bonds of spring breakup Jolene struck out from town in heavy boots and denims, a bright woolen mackinaw, and a pack over her shoulders. She climbed out of the mist and got into the aspens, still bare and ghostly, as the sun rose through a gap in the eastern ridge. The thick white aspen trunks and the lacey branches glowed in a crisp, pink light. Unseen birds called out a dawn greeting. She stopped to catch her breath and to listen a moment to the sound of the birds. "Whose woods these are, I think I know," Jolene called back. "And they are not the Company's, no!"

Drifts of snow still clogged the gullies and the deeper creases of the hills, though they would not survive another week of mid- May sun. The snow became troublesome in the thicker pine forest, but not impassable—not today. She warmed quickly with the climb and unbuttoned her mackinaw to the cooling breeze. She drank in the spring air, heavy with the rich, sweet sap of winter-felled boughs thawing in the sunshine.

The trail drew her up and over the ridge, the same trail to the clearing in Alec's Canyon. The cabin was as she had left it in February, but she spent no time in its dark confines today. She stuffed a couple of her magazines into her pack, took a long-handled shovel and an old steel pail from the porch, and headed down to find the sluice box.

The woods were thick and green in the draw, and the snow was deep. She crossed over boulders in the stream and broke through tangled alder to a clearing atop a knoll and stood finally under the clear blue sky. The sluice box was there, right where she had come up into the clearing. The old, weathered sluice rested in a rocky draw, where waters spilled around both sides of a knoll and joined to form a stream.

Jolene set down her pack, took off her mackinaw, and laid it on the bare ground. She lay down upon it, using her pack for a pillow. After months of inactivity her legs were tired from the climb, so she rested a while in the dappled shade of a pine and read from a Redbook magazine. The magazine was printed before the war, and the recipes inside all began and ended with ingredients she hadn't seen in a year. The household tips were silly—fix cracked plates by boiling them in milk. *Really, and where do I find the milk?* she wondered. *I'd trade all my plates for a gallon of milk.* She tossed the magazine aside.

Syringa filled the creek bottoms around her. The white flowers sweetened the air, and they surely smelled just like orange blossoms. Jolene had never smelled orange blossoms, but so she'd been told, and she tried to imagine California covered in tangy-sweet orange blossoms from beach to beach. She lay back and closed her eyes until tears trickled onto her cheeks. The magazines were useless; next time she would bring one of Farrell's books.

The sluice box was weathered to grey, its sides and riffles battered, the nails rusted. But it was solid and useable. Meltwater splashed down the creek a few paces away, and Jolene used the shovel to scrape out a channel for some of the runoff to flow into the top of the box. She left the water to wash down the sluice, picked up the shovel and bucket, and walked up into the raw hillside cuts where old-man Alec had worked the oxidized soils. The bleached rocks laid bare by the diggings were rich with the smells of kaolin and of sulfate solutions bleeding from oxidized pyrites. Jolene would not have known that, naturally, but her head filled with the earthy smells, and with the sweet syringa and tart alder brush.

She scraped the red soil, a crusty gossan, into the bucket and lugged it down to the sluice. She dumped the bucket in at the top, letting rushing water carry the soil and clots down the twenty-foot wooden box. The load clattered and shushed as it descended, as the clots broke apart over the wooden riffles; the gravel and cobbles rolled and thumped and bounced through.

She filled another bucket and dragged it over the bleached ground and dumped it down. The work was hot, so she took off her shirt and hung it on a tree branch. There wasn't a soul on the mountain today but her. But now she was doing her wet, muddy work in her brassiere, and a brassiere in wartime was worth more than the gold she was digging up. The brassiere, too, had to come off, and she worked her sluice box half naked in the warmth of the spring day, in the dappled light of the clearing.

THE RECLAMATION

She dug out and carried over another bucket of soil, rocked the sluice back and forth, and banged the sides with her shovel handle as the gravels descended. She dreamed as she worked—of a gold necklace to wear with that pine marten stole, or of a new dress she didn't have to sew from a pattern. She may have dreamed, by then, of buying a bus ticket—but she was careful where she let her thoughts go. Perhaps she enjoyed the sunshine on her back and the solitude and the rich earthy smells, and thought only of those.

A plane flew toward her, low and straight as she dragged more red gossan across the clearing. The plane had swept over the shoulder of the hill and now buzzed right at her. "Goddamn it!" She dropped the bucket and dove into the thick, tangled underbrush. It might even have been Farrell's plane! She sat herself down in the scratchy tangle, mortified, hugging her knees to her, feeling the gloom rise up again, fighting to hold it back. "For Christ's sake, leave me alone!" she cried.

She forced her way back into the clearing, only to hear the buzz of the engine again. The plane re-appeared in a tight turn over the ridge, and she had to duck under the foliage a second time. The plane was Farrell's for sure, and the fool wagged his wings this time as he flew over. Jolene laid under the brush and cried until she laughed.

Now what symbolism will our shy Professor Hammond insist on, she wondered, *catching me naked in the woods?* She shouted to the sky, "The wilderness, the dark forest as a trial—or as lost innocence?" She scoffed. "Or, my God, base immorality? Am I rocking the sluice box as I'd rock my lover's bed?"

She waited and listened, then struggled over with another heavy load of red soil; unable any longer to fight away the laughter. She barely could grip the bucket handle. *No*, she decided, *poor Farrell would surely look to Longfellow; dreary old Longfellow.*

"Longfellow," she shouted to the trees, "and his forest primeval; the murmuring pines, bearded with moss and in garments green." She stood upright and stretched her back. "Yes, that's what it would be. He would call me Evangeline... but he has no idea."

She worked the buckets of soil until the mid-day was spent, cleaning the riffles from time to time, washing the residues into her pan and swashing grains down to black sand and yellow flakes. She worked steadily in sunlight and shifting shadows and re-thought her clothing as the afternoon cooled. Cobbles and pebbles rolled and rattled down the sluice box. The rocks bounced and thumped on the bottom of the wooden channel and the sand hissed over the riffles. Jolene's voice lifted sweet and clear above the rush of the mountain stream and over the clatter of the sluice: not dreary Longfellow, but Donne and Marlowe, and St. Vincent Millay. The words pulsed and pounded, and tumbled through her like rolling stones, and she didn't care that she wept with every verse.

Jolene was late getting back to town, and found Ray not to be home. She'd forgotten Ethel's damned birthday! She sponged off quickly, threw on what was handiest, and ran across town to the folks' house. The parlor lights shone brightly, and dinner had already begun.

"We're happy you could join us, Jo," Ray said, setting down his knife and fork.

She saw he was angry, and a little tight. "Happy birthday, Ethel," she said. "I'm so sorry, I lost track of the sun."

Ethel barely looked up from her plate. "Running around in the sticks all day. It's a wonder you can find your way home any better than poor..."

"Mom!" Harly interrupted.

Jolene hurried around the table, laid her hand on Ray's shoulder, then sat in the empty chair at Axel's right. Axel patted her hand. Harly sat across from her.

"You're sunburned," Ray said.

"Yes, so it feels. Well, this is just a lovely dinner."

"So it feels?"

"It feels like it. It feels like I got burned a little."

They ate in silence for a minute. Harly, at last, set down his fork and told the table he had flown in with Farrell that day. Jolene looked up from buttering a roll, and Harly was beaming. "You know," he said, "Farrell let me take the controls today. We flew in from the northwest this time, and right over Alec's Canyon I swear to God, but we saw the strangest sight."

Jolene looked away and worked to control a flash of anger.

"Well, what was it you saw, then?" Ethel asked. Jolene began to flush, and she wondered if everyone would notice.

Harly said, "You know, we were so lost at one point... as we rounded a mountain, right there in a hillside clearing, well I swear we caught a glimpse of the fair and fabled Lorelai."

"Alec's Canyon?" Axel asked. He glanced to his right.

"Now, it could have been a mountain nymph; possibly a siren of old. But I believe it was Lorelai, and had our engine not been whining so, her seductive song might have called us to our doom."

"You're full of shit, as usual," Ray said.

"We had to circle around once to make sure our eyes weren't playing tricks. But there she was again, beckoning and tempting us out of the sky." Harly laughed a big, robust laugh. Axel grinned guardedly, although the others weren't so sure. Jolene kept her eyes down and avoided Harly's looks for the rest of dinner.

Harly jumped up and cleared dishes from the table as Jolene hurried to finish her sweet potato. He carried in a cake—Jolene's cake—and set it down in front of Ethel, candles afire.

Ethel had a small piece but didn't care for it so much, though Harly and Axel did. "Hattie's started a sewing bee with some of the ladies from the church," Ethel said, without looking at Jolene. "You need to get yourself in it. Get out and do something useful..."

"Ethel, thank you for your concern, but the ladies of the church don't need my help and I get enough of theirs on Sundays."

"...do something useful," Ethel went on. "Your wandering and moping don't change a thing, and Ray fixing his own meals half the time..."

"Mom..."

Jolene stared ahead and tried to remember the sound of the sluice box and the breeze through the pines. She picked at her cake. "What shall I sew then, Ethel? A winter scarf, a school dress?"

"If you're waiting for the world to feel sorry for you, well, nobody does and nobody will, and you brought it all on yourself, if you listen to anyone."

"Mom, enough!"

Axel said, "Listen now, all of you! *The judgments of the Lord are true and righteous altogether.*"

Jolene didn't look up, but murmured, "*He hath judged the great harlot who corrupted the earth with her fornication...*"

"I was quoting the Psalm, child, not Revelations."

Harly had risen to clear the table, and now he caught Jolene's eye as he reached for her cake plate. He smiled an apology and said, "By the way, Farrell sends his love."

"What the hell does that mean?" Ray asked. "Does anyone remember this is my Goddamned wife?" Ray had had a couple drinks, and his speech was thick-tongued.

Jolene exhaled slowly, "It's just a polite greeting, Ray."

"You don't need to worry about your wife around Farrell Hammond," Ethel spoke again. "He's queer as a three-dollar bill."

"Mom, he's not queer," Harly said, and laughed. "God, he's just a college type, is all. And where else am I going to find free flying lessons?"

Ray said, "I'd just like to know when I'm going to get my wife back."

"I'm right here, Ray. You wanted me to get out and get involved in things. You made me get out."

"In neighborhood things; I don't know, maybe a sewing bee. I'm always explaining why my wife is with the boss's limp-wristed kid."

She leaned her head back and pushed her fingers through her hair. "Explaining doesn't seem like such a heavy cross to bear."

"Are you going to back-talk like that?"

"Farrell is nice to me and he's intelligent, and at least if he was queer you'd know he wasn't grabbing at my ass."

"Who's grabbing your ass?" Ray asked.

"Oh, Jesus."

Axel raised his hand. "Don't take the Lord's name, dear."

"He's a gentleman," Jolene said. "And who else is there to talk to around here? Night-shift miners?" She turned her chin from Ethel. "The miners' simple wives?"

Ethel pursed her lips and jerked her head away. Ray slapped his hand on the table, making Jolene jump. He bit his words, but then said, "Well, don't get too tight with him, cause someone's gonna kill the faggot before it's over." Ray sounded all the angrier for his words being slurred.

Harly had stepped out to the kitchen with some dirty plates, and now he leaned in the doorway, filling up most of it. "Oh, Christ Almighty." he said.

"What's that supposed to mean?"

"It's two words, Ray, how much could it mean?" Harly held a wet cloth to wipe the table, but Ray had risen, and stood in his way.

Ray said, "I guess it could mean Christ Almighty, I wished I'd thought of that first. Or it could mean, Christ Almighty, keep your voice down so they don't know it was us that did it." He pushed his chin toward Harly, "Or it could mean Christ Almighty, don't talk about us queers like that. Which is it Harly?"

"Or maybe it just means," Harly said, tossing the dishcloth onto the table and squaring up, "Christ Almighty do you have to sound like an ignorant hillbilly every time you open your mouth?"

"Knock it off, you darned fools!" Axel yelled over the table. "You try my patience, all of you." He spoke to both boys but glared at Ray, and Ray looked back at the old man and nodded.

Jolene sat with her head down and her hands shielding her eyes, trembling slightly. She heard Ethel next to her say, "Anyway, you don't need to be visiting with that queer no more."

Jolene stood with her fingertips on the table and her head bent forward. "Ethel, I'll see who the hell I want," she said softly.

Ray wheeled on her. "You watch your tone, girl!"

"Farrell's just a friend, and he's at least seen the world." She moved, wearily, toward the doorway. "He's not just an ignorant hillbilly."

She didn't mean to use those same words—or maybe she did. Ray brought his hand up and out in a single quick motion, and the back of it caught her behind the ear as she passed and spun her around like a rag doll. She crumpled at the foot of the table and didn't move for a moment.

Harly stepped over and knelt by her, taking her hand. Ray leaned his head against the doorframe, clenching and opening his fists. "Happy birthday, Mama," he said.

12

"Naw, I doubt he ever hit her."

"What makes you say not?"

"I mean, I didn't know him that well, but from what I saw, Ray was wrapped around Jolene's finger."

"Yeah well, things happen behind doors," I answer. But really, I don't know if it happened that way or not.

Earl finds another beer in the cooler, and I hand him the opener. "And sometimes things don't happen," he says. "She never let on at the cafe that he was mean to her or she was scared. Your mother was nobody's victim."

In the valley to the northwest an afternoon breeze is trying to kick up. Today's been warm until now, no clouds at all. But as I watch, a light breeze shakes the aspens and waves the tops of the taller fir trees. Earl says, "Look, I know you're trying to make sense of things, but it's not that easy. Real people are complicated."

"He was a mean son of a bitch. There's nothing complicated about that."

"You knew him afterwards. Ray Pruitt was never someone to mess with, but he wouldn't have hurt Jolene. She was his treasure. I don't think you appreciate how beautiful your mother was. Or how strong."

"Not strong enough."

"That's not for me to say."

Earl is in Cinnabar today. Maddie drove him over to watch the goings on at the New Main portal. She set him up with her blue cooler and a camp chair in the shade of a poplar, and that's where I found him about mid-morning. Matt Cairn arrived from Butte yesterday afternoon and his crew and convoy of equipment trickled in through the early evening. Apparently, they all got to talking at the bar last night, and Maddie ignored health and safety protocol and liability considerations and encouraged Earl to come over and watch.

Cairn's men have been transporting equipment and supplies all morning over the narrow, twisting Ridge Road between Cinnabar and Stibnite, and tomorrow they will begin the work of opening up and shoring the old underground workings.

The morning started calm and bright for me. I sat on my porch enjoying the crisp June morning and had just poured a second cup of coffee when the first flatbeds came into sight. They worked their way down the ridge and through the switchbacks, kicking up dust that glowed here and there in the light of the low-angle sun. I threw my gear together and drove up to the portal.

Matt Cairn was already there, and we had another coffee from my thermos. I said no thanks to a cigarette, and we had a laugh about Andy Carson and his budget and schedule. Cairn explained there wasn't a lot of flat ground at the portal where he could stage his equipment, so I led him and a couple flatbed trucks through the streets of old Cinnabar to the mill site, where there's plenty of room for an equipment laydown.

When I returned from the mill Earl was sitting under the poplar at the edge of the waste-rock dump, pretty much in everyone's way. He at least was dressed properly in a pair of blue dungarees, a plastic hardhat, and work boots. I carried the cooler, which I noticed was full of beer and ice, and we moved onto a stack of bundled, creosote-treated mine timbers. There we got a good view of the action without being part of it. Beer is never allowed at a mining property work site. I don't know what the hell Maddie was thinking.

Creosote fumes rise in the heat of the late morning sun and burn our eyes and throats. "Why did Ray allow her to spend so much time with Farrell Hammond?" I ask, setting the bottle of beer back behind my leg.

Earl waits for a loud flatbed truck to drive past before starting his explanation. The truck carries a load of steel plates and rods—rock bolts for holding up the tunnel roof. Another flatbed behind it is loaded with rolls of heavy wire mesh. Cairn waves both on to the mill laydown.

Earl has to wait a bit longer as another truck rumbles by. "You know it's funny that question still gets asked," he says, finally. "Folks back then asked the same thing. I heard it. I'm sure Ray got an earful of it. I don't know, maybe he liked the idea his wife was socializing with a Hammond. More likely—and let's be generous—he understood Jolene needed... something to focus on."

"And," Earl says with a smile, "maybe he liked that she was a little above the gossiping and the bickering and the simpleness of the other miners' wives. Because she sure was. Now, that didn't win Jolene many women friends in town, I can tell you. But I don't think she cared a hoot about that. She had one good friend, a cute blonde girl."

"Dotty."

"That's it, by God! Dotty." He slaps his leg. "Dotty was cute. No rocket scientist, but a real cute gal. She came by a couple of times, but that's all."

"Harly liked her, right?"

"Sure, everyone liked Dotty. But she left long before any troubles began."

Cairn waves two large flatbeds onto the dump, and we both stand to see what's on them. It turns out they're self-contained shower units and a changing room. Cairn sees our beer and turns away, shaking his head.

"And you know," Earl goes on, "it wasn't like it was scandalous. I mean the three of them met for coffee in the light of day. Some folks whispered, but fools are gonna do that. Farrell and Jolene were good friends, and Harly, too, at least at first. They talked mostly about books, travel, and politics; the war, and what it meant. Farrell was a pacifist. Harly agreed with him philosophically, but not in a practical sense. Harly was eager to get into the war."

"How did Farrell get on in town?"

"How do you mean?" Earl answers. "Because he was educated? Because his hands were clean? Or do you think maybe he was a little effeminate?"

"I don't know how he was, I was just asking. In the pictures he doesn't look like he was cut for a mining camp."

Earl sets down his beer and leans his elbows on his knees, his fingertips pressed together. He looks a while down the valley for an answer. "Nobody with any kind of sensibility is made for a town like this one was," he says. "Farrell's dad's mine was exempt from the draft, and that's about the whole story of why he was here. He hated it, I think. He never said so, at least not to me. But he had to hate the Goddamned redneck attitudes, those illiterate hillbillies. You didn't say anything back then. You didn't stand against the mines or their goons'd be on you, and you didn't dare seem contrary or different or a lot of ignorant, intolerant thugs would be on you. You think your old man was a mean son of a bitch, but let me tell you, he was enlightened compared to most of the fucking bovines who lived here."

Earl is embarrassed by his language. His gaze wanders to his boots for a minute, and I sit and listen to the wind picking up in the valley. He finds his beer, empties it, and says quietly, "Ignorance breeds fear and fear breeds hate. That's how Harly explained it once."

Cairn's men have the portable showers set up and a pipeline run in from a spring by early afternoon. Laden trucks ease down the ridge, and empty trucks work their way back up. I wonder where and how they pass each other. A pair of long, low-boy trailers have somehow made it over; they carry a track-mounted roof bolter and a rubber-tired mucker/hauler for the heavy underground work.

"I don't understand," Earl says. "Why are you opening up the underground? Is that the target you're developing?"

"Oh, hell no. There's no money anymore in ticky-tack underground mining. We want to outline enough bulk ore that we can dig up this whole ridge with an open-pit mine, stack the low-grade material on a three-hundred-acre pad, and leach out the gold with cyanide solutions."

I watch for a reaction but see none. He says, "That's what I thought. Then how come the tunneling equipment?"

"We need this opened up to get in to map and sample."

"I wonder if some things aren't better left closed," he says.

A tanker truck finally brings diesel to fill the tanks that were off-loaded in the morning. Other than trucking and unloading, there isn't much to see. Maddie shows up in late afternoon and asks if us boys had a good day. We throw Earl's stuff into her pickup. He takes one more look around then climbs into the cab.

Maddie takes me aside for a minute. "Do you have a permit to mine?" she asks. She's still sore about the mine-water spill.

"Who's mining? This is exploration. It's covered under our general disturbance permit."

"Harlan, you're digging below the water table and discharging to Waters of the U.S. We need an NPDES permit."

"Not for an existing excavation."

"It wasn't existing—or not actually, until you re-opened it."

"It's a pretty gray area though, right?" I suggest to her that in view of the grayness, she might not want to share all the details, yet, with her friends in green.

"Harlan." Maddie keeps her voice low. "I'm not going to lie."

"Of course not. Just don't telegraph things is all I'm suggesting. Nobody is going to break the law or cause… long-term damage here."

She shakes her head and looks around at all the equipment brought in today, and at the red mine waters still trickling from the portal. Her lips screw up as she kicks the toe of her boot into the crusty orange residue topping the dump.

"Look," I tell her, "everyone needs you to do your best work and always stick to the facts. Remember, the world's better off with you at your job than with someone less conscientious."

"Yeah, well, it doesn't seem like I'm helping anything at all, here."

"You got me to build better roads and mud pits. That's something already."

I toss her blue cooler in back, and the empties rattle and clink. She nods and even smiles a little as she walks around the back of her truck.

She's young and doesn't understand yet the remarkable lies you can tell just sticking to the facts. She and Earl head on back to town. I call it a day, too, and return to my tarpaper palace.

*

In the photo I stand on wooden steps, with my father sitting behind me on the next step up, stiffly holding my shoulders. It's the only picture I've ever seen of the two of us. I remember the steps and the house; it is not among the houses still standing. A middle-aged woman peers accusingly from the half-open door behind us. My father and I are dressed well, but we don't smile. The woman, my grandmother, also wears Sunday clothes; she seems awfully young as I hold the photo in the lantern's light. My grandfather died when I was six and was buried in the Stibnite cemetery. We must have dressed up for that affair.

The sun was already up. I'd slept late, and my chores weren't done, so I hurried to dress and not be noticed. Dad must have heard me; he lifted the blanket separating the kitchen from my back-porch bedroom and stood disapprovingly in the doorway. I didn't remember that I had done anything else wrong, besides getting up late. His face was red and his glare watery and unsteady. He seemed drunk, though I doubted he could be so early on a week day.

"I'll fill the wood box straight away," I said, and moved to step into the kitchen before his anger rose. He blocked my way, so I figured I was going to get a slapping after all. I raised my eyes and asked him, "Did I do something else?"

He said, "Your grandfather is dead."

I thought he was accusing me of killing my grandfather; that's what it sounded like. So I lifted my chin and blurted back, "Huh uh!"

THE RECLAMATION

He rapped his knuckles hard against my head for my disrespect and then knocked me to the floor for I didn't know why. Grandpa had died, and now I understood the many hushed voices in the kitchen until late last night.

The clothes fit tightly; they were borrowed, and my father was annoyed to have to sit with me for a photograph. He flipped his cigarette into the garden and called out, "Mom!" then held me straight with both hands to make sure the picture would only have to be taken once.

My grandmother fed me and clothed me, kept me clean and quiet for the most part, and saw to my school and religion. My father bothered with none of that, nor with much else, really. When he was home and sober, which was seldom, I was in the way, or careless, or slow, or always had my nose in a Goddamned book. I was nothing but trouble when he was sober. When he was drunk, I stayed clear of him.

13

Matt Cairn got his guys working the next day, timbering up the entry and cleaning out and bracing the main adit. They didn't need me telling them where or how, and that gave me some extra time to hang around camp writing up notes and getting the geological map into shape. The afternoon, though, found me stiff from sitting hunched over the map table, so I got out for a walk around the old town. I'd been meaning to poke around some of the ruins but hadn't felt the spirit lift me until then.

A few of the places strike a familiar note, if just barely. The cardinal directions have not changed from my childhood, but the scale of the place is all wrong. The piles of rubble are too few and too small for the houses and the times that I recall. Rows of untrimmed lilac bushes border the abandoned yards of a few whom I knew, and stubborn clumps of rhubarb and horseradish cling to garden plots.

But I don't know what happened to the people who lived between the rows of lilacs, although I imagine everyone is dead by now. It is odd that the least among them would have survived to come home again. My friends, few as they were, I once thought lucky—luckier than I. But of course, they all had their own ghosts to conciliate. The bullies whom I suffered had to have gone through life dumb and scared, and mean for it—and hated, the poor bastards. And all the others: the ignorant, timid, and spiteful souls. Small towns can be small.

The weather was fine, so I walked, and found myself eventually at Applegate's Mercantile—or what was left of it. It's embarrassing, but I need new mantles for the Coleman lantern and damned if I didn't walk to the old Merc half in mind of getting some there.

The boardwalk is still intact in front of the Merc—it is the last stretch of it left in town. The front facade of the Merc is in one piece, too, albeit laying almost flat with wild rose tangles growing up through glassless windows. Traces remain of the forest green paint, and of the white door out of which smells of liniment and lamp oil would drift on a warm day; and new denim and leather. I found an old bench in the weeds on the street side of the boardwalk; one of the benches where old men would sit—and lonely kids sometimes—just to wait for a bit of traffic if any should come. The bench isn't rotted as badly as you'd expect, and it wobbles just a little as I watch out under an afternoon sun.

†

The sun burned Jolene's eyes but warmed her shoulders through a thin cotton shift whose floral print had faded from many washings. She hadn't bothered to iron the dress when she pulled it from the bottom of the closet. She sat alone at the table on the porch, sipping a cup of Farrell's tea.

She'd laid in bed until well after Ray's boots stopped clomping on the kitchen floor but sat up when the sun came through the window and wouldn't leave her alone. Ray had taken the curtains down two weeks earlier when he'd found her upstairs in the afternoon lying on the bed with the curtains closed tightly and the room dark. He'd set the kitchen table and chairs out on the porch then, too, and he sat with her sometimes when the evenings were fair.

The tea tasted like somewhere—nowhere in particular, just somewhere; anywhere far from granite ridges and dust and pine trees. Jolene considered scooting her chair around to where it was more shaded, so she wouldn't have to squint into the sun. She decided instead just to duck her eyes under her cupped hand as her elbow rested on the table. Hunched like that, she could see past Ellen's house and up the side street as far as Baughman's Grocery.

No one moved on the wooden walks, although it was mid-morning. Her neighbor Ellen could be seen and heard hanging wash in her back yard, but otherwise there was little life in the town. A car drove up the street raising dust, and stopped at Applegate's Mercantile. It was a shiny blue Buick, and she was surprised to see a woman get out of it. It was Greta Hogue, the chief engineer's wife; Jolene recognized the platinum hair.

It was Tuesday, Jolene's day at the TNT, and she wished she could cross over the ridge today. She wanted to return her book, *Tess of the D'Urbervilles*, and to ask Farrell about Tess. Why did Tess let them treat her like that? Why in hell didn't she shuck it all and leave—take care of herself? But the bruise on Jolene's jaw was still visible, even under makeup, and she was certain she shouldn't show herself in that condition.

Ellen yelled at unseen trouble makers and hung her load of dresses, dungarees, and diapers—one child's outfit after another until Jolene was so angry she could shout herself. But her attention was drawn back to the Merc, where Greta walked out with an armload of packages. Barney Applegate held the car door for her. Greta wore a new summer dress—store bought, Jolene could tell from two blocks away—and high heels. Jolene sat up. *Heels, in this town!* She breathed in deeply and sipped her cold tea. *But what of it?*

A baby started to cry through the upstairs window of the neighbor's house on the north side. Jolene tossed her tea into the garden and jumped up, sending her chair clattering across the porch.

The Merc was empty when she got there; a pleasant surprise at midday. She took a deep breath and entered with a smile.

"Good morning, Jolene. Isn't Greta Hogue something, though? How can I help you this fine summer day?"

"I need a new dress, Barney, I'm here for a pattern and some material. What about Greta?"

"Well, I mean..." he leaned in, "A new car in a wartime economy? And she almost single handedly keeps that Montgomery Ward truck hauling up the canyon."

"Well she's entitled to some diversion, I suppose, living with that hog… with that Fred Hogue, after all."

Barney turned away and nearly choked on a laugh. "But how can I help you today, Jolene?"

"Something nice; a worsted wool I think. Summer is fine and good, but winter's nipping our heels, and I won't have a decent thing to wear out of the house."

"Jolene," Barney hesitated. "We have no wool, not a stitch."

"But winter is coming."

"It's a good ways off."

"I don't know how I've let things go, but my whole closet has just gotten threadbare."

"Wool's all gone to army uniforms, every yard of it. We have the gingham you see there, and I've been saving a bolt of good sturdy cotton twill."

"Barney, gingham is too damned—excuse me—light for a winter dress, and cold weather's just around the corner!"

Barney Applegate was a small man with thin tufts of gray hair clinging to the sides of his head and thick steel-rimmed glasses. When I was a kid he would sit all day on the bench out front, after his stroke, while Berta Applegate ran the store.

He opened his hands to the ceiling and let them drop. "Not a thing I can do," he said.

Without looking up she sighed and said, "Show me the twill, then."

"It's just the one bolt." Barney reached under the counter, brought out the yard-wide roll of fabric, and held it up for her to see.

Jolene's eyes arched, and her smile went to a grimace. "What the hell... what kind of color is that?" she asked.

"Well it's a green… taupe, I believe."

She stepped closer. "It's khaki! I'm not going out in a Goddamned army dress. For heaven's sake!"

"I'm afraid it's just the gingham then. I think we might get one more allotment before fall, but you better not count on it."

Jolene rubbed her palms into her temples, but there was nothing either of them could do about it, so she looked over the ginghams for a decent print. She held up a red white and blue design. "What do you think, Barney?"

"I think the 4th of July will be here long before winter shows itself."

She closed her eyes and shook her head slightly, but said, "Three yards, then."

Barney laid the cloth out and took up his shears while Jolene looked around. "There are no pins on the shelf, Barney, are they back of the counter now?" she called over.

"I haven't got a pin in the place, Jolene."

"Well, where else am I going to find pins? Pins aren't like nails you can pull out of a damned fence. How in hell are we supposed to sew without pins?" She caught her breath and leaned with her hand against the frame of the window. A warm wind slipped between the loose panes and the weathered, poorly puttied mullions. Frost would build there before long. Now the separate panes of glass broke up the town and the hills beyond into eight loosely connected scenes, each dustier and sootier and emptier than the one next to it. She wished to God she'd stayed on her porch.

Down the street through one of the panes a bus pulled up in front of the boarding hall. "Good heavens! There's a Northland bus in town. When did they start service over to here?"

"It's something isn't it? Once a week through the summer months, now."

Jolene smiled. "Where do you suppose they go?" Several men stepped off wearing clean work clothes. They swung duffel bags over their shoulders and headed into the boarding hall. No one got on the bus, although Jolene watched for a while.

She gave up waiting for departing passengers, losing her smile as well, and went on with her shopping. "Barney, where are the spools of thread?"

THE RECLAMATION

Applegate stepped from behind the counter and answered carefully, with hands clasped at his chest. "There are packets of cotton thread right there on the shelf, in lots of colors."

"I need spools of thread to work with the Singer."

"Well, they aren't winding it on spools for now; they send it in packets."

"Well, that's just stupid; they have a machine right there to wind the spools. Why in heaven's name can't they wind the thread on the spool?"

"Jolene, it takes a few minutes to wind the thread on an empty spool. If you bring me a spool, I'll do it for you."

"I don't have any old spools. Nobody told me I'd have to save the empty Goddamned thread spools!"

"It's okay, Jolene."

"No, it's not okay!" Tears started, and her voice rose. "This is just bull crap. They tell us it's all about the war effort. They tell us our sewing is helping win the war and then they can't even give us a spool of thread. Is a damned plane going to crash somewhere if they wind the thread at the factory? It wouldn't take the fools anything at all to wind the Goddamned thread onto a Goddamned spool!"

Barney reached uncertainly, touching her on the shoulder. "I have some extra spools in back, Jolene. Tell me what threads and I'll wind them for you."

She caught her breath and wiped her eyes. "No, dammit, I'm okay." She stepped back to the window and leaned for a moment, wiping her nose with a Kleenex. The Northland bus had gone. "Thank you so much," she said. I'll wind the thread… if you can loan me a couple of old spools."

14

Rain or shine doesn't matter much underground. That's the whole thing about underground. Maddie and I entered the New Main adit after an hour of Matt Cairn's safety orientation. After Matt worked her over, in fact, I was pleased Maddie still had the gumption to enter at all. We found some diggers that fit her and strapped on a lamp pack and a rescue canister—the heavier unit again because we planned to go back into some dead headings. We found her some steel-shank rubber boots that weren't too big, and we brassed her in.

"What does that mean?" she asked.

"This brass tag on your belt matches the brass tag here on the board. It's so Security knows who's in and who's out. If there's a fire underground, the brass will identify your charred remains."

"Sweet."

The main adit, as far as Cairn's crew have opened it, is in okay shape, and we've collected groundwater samples from the fractures in the ribs and from roof-bolt holes along much of its length. Maddie cross-references the mine locations against the geological map to make sure we're getting a good coverage.

A few of the connecting drifts between stopes have been opened and shored up as well, and the mineralized fractures and veins there provide good groundwater samples. Cairn wanted us to hold off our sampling for another week or two, until he had the place in better shape. But Maddie needs to get the samples to the lab. The tests can take months and will already push our deadlines.

THE RECLAMATION

Maddie keeps her OVM in front of her with every step in the dead headings and drifts, where the air might still be stagnant. Each sample takes about twenty minutes to fill the bottles, record pH and conductivity, and write up the notes. I let Maddie do all the writing because the mundane task of sticking your nose in a field book can be calming.

"We don't need samples from there," she calls over to me. "That whole vein set is pretty well represented now."

"I'm just looking."

"What are you curious about?" she asks.

In fact, the accessible drifts aren't that interesting to me. It's the closed ones, the cave-ins, that make me wonder.

On our way back out with another load of water samples, we pass near to the bad ground at forty-eight hundred, then have to wait for the big mucker to pass. The roar and vibrations of the machinery, the diesel exhaust, the bright lights and back-up horns frighten Maddie, I can tell. To me it is so much friendlier and safer here than in the stillness of a dead heading, but to Maddie it is confusing and scary, and I see the edge of panic rise in her. I pull her to the outward side, away from the activity, where we can watch the work in relative safety.

Cairn's foreman, Jake or James, a young guy, comes out of the bad ground covered in white clay and streaked with bright red drippings, including in his hair and beard. The main adit is unstable everywhere they've shored it through the zone, and the caving doesn't stop for a hundred feet. "Looks like the whole Goddamned thing wants to come down," he says. He lights a cigarette; Maddie and I both wave off the offer. With his thumbs in his utility harness, he turns and says, "The boys are betting this is the ground where the miner is buried."

"Who's buried?" Maddie asks.

Jake smiles like he was hoping Maddie would ask. But before he can answer, the loader rumbles up with a bundle of timbers in its scoop, and he has to guide it up and unload it in the work zone.

When he's gone, I explain, "One of these drifts came down and killed a man years ago. They never got his body out."

"Goddamn it, Harlan," Maddie says, backing up a step. "You didn't think that was worth telling me?"

"You're not afraid of ghosts, are you?"

"That's not funny. I just think it would be courteous of you to let me in on what everyone else seems to know. We're down here with a dead man?"

"I wouldn't worry when you're with me; he's bound to be a friendly spirit to his own kin and namesake."

Maddie's not amused. "What happened?"

"I don't know if it was in here. But in one of these caved drifts Harly died."

"Your uncle?"

"Yeah. They never recovered his body."

"What happened?" she asks again.

"Well, you'd think there would be a lot of versions of it, but there's only one. My father was the only person with Harly when the roof came down on him."

She hunches her shoulders and looks up.

†

It was the start of night shift, but most of the mine was standing down for equipment repairs. Ray had arranged to meet Harly and Farrell Hammond in a drift where they'd had a lot of trouble with the ground. They discussed where and how it had to be shored, and a possible new, safer heading. It couldn't wait for the day shift; things were too unstable.

Some machine or another was broken down and being hauled to the surface, and only a maintenance crew was underground, making repairs in the south-side crosscuts. Safety lights were on at two-hundred-foot intervals, but otherwise the lights strung up in the timbers along the way had been shut off. In wartime, even privileged mines have a hard time finding lightbulbs. The mine was quiet but for water dripping from roof bolts, and valves and fittings hissing from the compressed air still being piped in all along the length of the adit and drift. Somewhere in a distant heading someone was hammering on a heavy iron grill, and they heard and felt the dull metallic plinks through the rock. Otherwise, though, it was their own voices and the scraping of their boots on the wet floor, and the groan of new timbers already straining over their heads.

As they talked things over, Ray and Harly felt a slight shift of the ground under their feet. It's not unusual in a new cut for the ground to adjust slightly, and an experienced miner can feel it sometimes. Hammond seemed unaware. The timbers groaned and popped. To Ray it sounded no different than before, but to Harly it did. Without a word he took hold of Farrell and Ray and yanked them toward the entry. They hadn't stumbled more than a few yards, though, when one of the beams cracked like a rifle shot above them. Ray's natural reaction was to duck away, and he fell to the floor and rolled against the rib, but he rolled to the in-by side of the broken beam. Farrell ducked away as Ray had, but Harly landed on the out-by side. The other roof supports began to tremble around him.

"Ray?" Harly yelled through the spattering mud and breaking wood. "Are you okay?"

"We're okay, but we can't get past the fall."

"Hold on. I'll get some timbers."

Harly ran out a few yards and found a new timber leaning against the rib. He threw it over his shoulder and headed back in. He shoved the timber up against the broken beam, just enough to get some leverage on it, and setting his back against the timber he shoved with his foot against the rib and wedged up the broken beam enough that Ray saw light through the sluffed rock and broken timbers. He pushed Farrell through then struggled out himself.

Harly backed off from his timber a little, but other beams began to groan, so he pushed it back up and steadied it with his shoulder, bracing with his legs. "Get out," he yelled to Ray. "Get help and bring timbers. I can hold it."

Farrell already had run out in a panic, and now Ray headed out at a run too, but he didn't get to the main adit before everything came down in a blast of mud and timber, lifting him and blowing him against the opposite wall, breaking his arm and a half dozen ribs.

"They were never able to get the drift open again," I explain. "It caved as quickly as they could muck it and brace it, and they finally gave up."

"When did that happen?" Maddie asks.

"I'm not really sure. Before I was born, because I was named after him."

"And it happened here?"

"I don't know that, either. This is the general area where Honorario and Bernie are losing all their drill steel. Cairn's men are betting it's haunted."

We load the sample bottles into three coolers and tape the coolers closed. They'll be brought out in the bucket of the loader later today, because I'm not about to carry them nearly a mile to the portal. Maddie and I walk the whole way, though, and she's flushed and excited when we finally march out into afternoon sunshine.

"That was great!" she shouts, frightening birds from the trees.

"So, you're going to be a miner, now?"

"Oh, hell no. Once is enough, but that was great!"

*

Cairn's crew got a good part of the main adit cleaned out and shored up over the next ten days, and the surface drilling progressed in that time with no major mishaps. The Fourth of July snuck up on us without my taking notice. Maddie told me something about a bonfire, but she didn't say it with conviction, and I was busy anyway. Not many of the junior hands missed the party, though, judging from their productivity in the days following.

Unfortunately, the drillers and the underground crew took the day off too, and while the mountain was abandoned someone found his way up over the ridge and helped himself to some mischief. The water line to Bernie's rig number-two was cut, and the pump down by the creek was smashed up. If that had been all, it would have been annoying but not out of keeping with some people's general dislike of mining. But someone, probably the same someone, also tampered with the diesel fuel for the underground equipment. Within minutes of fueling, the big engines sustained some pretty serious damage.

Matt Cairn's crew was delayed an extra two days as they cracked open the diesel engines, cleaned out the cylinders, and replaced rings. Cairn was vocal in his disappointment with the human condition. He couldn't figure out who would do something like that—besides a tree-hugging, son-of-a-bitchin' prick. I told him I would round up the usual suspects. He didn't laugh, but I don't think he actually has me on his list.

Maddie couldn't remember who hadn't been around during the picnic—besides me. "Was Mike there the whole day?" I asked.

"Lovitt? You're not serious?"

"Just asking, is all."

"No, he left early. He has a girlfriend."

"You're kidding! Well, how about what's-his-name, your friend?"

"If you really need to know, Dan has an alibi—for the whole night. And go to hell for asking."

"I didn't ask."

There are padlocks on everything now, of course, and Cairn insisted on putting a locking gate across the main road over Lookout Ridge. It won't help at all. Whoever did it came up a back road.

"How do you know that?" Maddie asked.

"I was mapping up on Deer Point," I explained. "I'd have seen someone come over Ridge Road."

"Who knows the back roads well enough?"

"Well, our crew all do, and the Forest Service personnel all do, and I imagine all of the locals do." I put the gate key on my key ring. "Let's keep this discussion to ourselves for a bit."

"God, yes!" She shook her whole body and drove away.

15

It's a rare color photo. Jolene wears a house dress plainly cut—with short sleeves, significantly, —and a button front, a simple collar, and a sash of the same material to tie it at her slender waist. It's a cotton weave printed with red, white, and blue designs. Ray wears wide, pleated slacks and a T-shirt. He belts his slacks up high, nearly at the bottom of his ribs, as most of the men do, and he wears starred and striped suspenders over impossibly broad shoulders.

†

She breathed in, held it, and unfolded her end of the table cloth as Ellen unfolded the other end. Jolene shared a smile with Ellen, who wondered that Jolene's tablecloth was not made of silk. Ellen was setting up a lunch for her large family at the next table and was eager to give a hand to Jolene, who hadn't been out much socially ever since… well, since the heartbreak.

"It's oilcloth, Ellen, just like yours."

"Well, I didn't mean nothing, Jolene. It's just that if Jack was doing as well as your Ray, I think I wouldn't have the same modesty that you show."

"Ray works in the mine, just like Jack."

In the photos Ellen is half a foot shorter than Jolene. She was my neighbor for all my childhood in Cinnabar. Ruddy-skinned and red-haired, she was short of temper as well as stature, and it was best not to cross her. But she fixed me a sandwich, or tied up a wound, or found me a warm jacket more times than I can count—when no one else was there.

"I guess if your husband is a foreman…"

"Supervisor, now," another woman corrected her. It was Hattie.

"…you get your vegetables at the market. Canned soup and things. But Jolene, the potato salad looks wonderful, so many boiled eggs. And the chicken is… Well, you have a lot on your mind, of course, and with it being just the two of you and all." She straightened herself and deflected a look from Hattie. "What I mean is, who cares about a garden anyway. You can get your vegetables in the market if you want to. There in the Stibnite market, I guess, is where you like to shop."

Hattie straightened the edge of the tablecloth and set a Mason jar of water and wildflowers on Jolene's table. "A garden isn't everything, Ellen," she said. Hattie was a little taller than Ellen, but stouter, with a Sunday-school look. 'Aunt' Hattie to me until her consumptive death, she and Grandma Ethel conspired to purge the devil from my misfortunate soul. "Jolene has her interests outside the home, haven't you sweetheart?" She couldn't help but snatch glances at Jolene's bare arms.

Jolene turned with her hands to her breast, cursing herself silently for wearing the damned dress today. "Well, yes, when the weather permits," she answered Hattie. "When the weather, um…" the sun burned her eyes and the smell of pickles and greasy chicken suddenly clung in her craw. "I like to get out of the hollow…" She sidestepped to the end of the table and looked out. The airfield was filling up, there seemed to be a thousand people jostling about, grabbing and gabbing at one another, shouting and staring. She turned again and nearly bumped Ellen, who stood with a gift of pickled beets. "Oh, thank you," Jolene managed. She couldn't bring herself to unfold her arms to reach for the jar. "If you'll just set them there on the table," she whispered.

"Interests outside the home winter and summer," Hattie went on. "And of course, so many trips over to Stibnite. Why is it we can't have our own doctor in Cinnabar? That would make it so much easier."

Jolene stayed at the far end of the table and busied herself sorting the silverware. "I'm not in Stibnite but once a week or so, and it's just to trade in books, is all."

"Of course, the rest of us have our work cut out." Ellen said. She talked through the noise of half a dozen sun-browned children who were keeping her own table in a state of commotion.

Ethel joined them and stood at the table as if waiting for Jolene to finish. Ellen ignored the shrieks of her brood, and nodded to Jolene's mother-in-law, with whom she did not get along. Ellen said to Jolene, "But that sure is a fine, new dress you're wearing. Don't you think so, Ethel? I haven't worn a store-bought dress since Butte."

"I sewed it at home," Jolene answered softly.

"No!"

"It's just some cotton calico I saw at the Merc." Jolene walked around Ethel to lay out the flatware, not looking up at the other women. The sun warmed her shoulders, but it was not yet at its zenith. It wasn't noon, and folks wouldn't politely pack for home until nine or ten o'clock that night. She hugged her arms to her and pressed her eyes shut for a moment, then walked away with one hand in her hair.

Farrell stood with a small group of mining engineers who could think of nothing to talk with him about other than his friendship with Harly Pruitt. The engineers' wives sat at a table nearby, but he'd left their conversation as well. The women's talk had focused on shopping and shortages, and who could procure things for them. So Farrell smiled to see Jolene ambling about, and waved to her to join his group. He introduced her around and the whole party chatted for a few minutes.

Inspiration finally struck the engineers, and they called Farrell over to discuss the upcoming ballgame, leaving Jolene in the middle of a private conversation between two of the wives: Greta Hogue,

THE RECLAMATION

with her platinum hair, and Tammy Reed. The two wives leaned in, resting their elbows on a table set with canned ham, store-sliced bread, salads, and a whole pineapple.

"I met Fred at Oregon," Greta was saying. Greta was quite pretty and wore red lipstick and a red hair ribbon. She wore bright red shorts, too, and a white shirt tied by its tails in front.

"Where in Oregon?" Jolene asked.

Greta cocked her head and smiled. "*At* Oregon; the University of. Fred was studying engineering and I was studying French."

"You can study French? French language or French history... or French culture?" Jolene sat at the picnic table with her arms down between her knees.

"Yes, all of those."

"That sounds wonderful. What kind of degree do you get studying French?"

"Well, I didn't stay in school after we got married, for heaven's sake."

"Oh. Of course not."

Tammy had attended Smith. She dressed in a blue pleated skirt and a red and white sailor's blouse. "I have an associate degree in English literature," she replied to no question. "Ollie was studying at Amherst—engineering of course. Amherst hosted a lot of dances for us Smithies." She shifted her eyes conspiratorially. "I didn't have to drop out, because... well..." She leaned Jolene's way. "But you're an outdoors girl, aren't you Jolene? You understand the woods are lovely, dark, and deep..."

"But I have promises to keep." Jolene said, then winced at her own words. "I just like to get out of the house when I can, out of the bottom, and up into some sunshine. Don't you like getting out into the fresh air?" she asked the two women.

Tammy said, "I couldn't be nearly the woodsman you are. I don't think I even own a pair of boots." She swooped her head Greta's way, nearly sweeping the table with her dark brown hair.

"And I don't think my skin could take the sun as effortlessly as yours does," Greta added. "Why, I'd just burn red as a lobster."

"You make me sound like Annie Oakley." Jolene saw Farrell turn from his conversation with Ollie and Fred and smile her way. "I like to read," she suggested.

"What kinds of things do you like to read?" Tammy asked. She brushed back her hair, sending prismed light shooting from her ring finger.

Jolene's eyes scanned the crowd for a gap she might dash through. But she smiled instead. "Novels mostly, and poetry." She sat up and crossed her ankles as Greta was doing. She breathed in and released it, smiled brightly, and leaned forward with her hands in her lap. "I'll read whatever I can find, really. But with a house and garden, as you surely know, and dinner to get on the table, there's not a lot of time, so the hiking isn't as much as you might think."

"Why, no!" Greta said, "With all that on your plate, and... everything else. Well, you really are the stuff heroes are made of."

Jolene's cheeks warmed. "I don't know what you mean," she said.

Tammy pursed her lips and looked away. Greta caught her breath, smiled kindly, and explained, "It's a silly literary allusion is all."

"I'm not familiar with it." Jolene's hands trembled, and she struggled to control an impulse either to jump and run, or to strike at Greta.

"Well, Jolene..." Tammy began.

Jolene glanced from Greta to Tammy, and then up, to where a jay called from the top of the cottonwood above her; the sun shined from near its zenith, now. Crowd noise caught her attention, but only for a moment. She cut Tammy off in mid-sentence. "Thomas Hardy wrote about the 'raw stuff of gods', and maybe that's what you mean; Eustacia Vye, and all that." She didn't turn but continued to look up into the branches. "But Shakespeare wrote about 'the stuff dreams are made on' and that's probably where Dashiell Hammett got 'the stuff dreams are made *of*' in the Maltese Falcon. But in truth I don't remember that in the book, just in the movie, and of course Humphrey Bogart was referring to gold where Prospero was talking about the illusion of life, so it would hardly be the same thing."

THE RECLAMATION

She caught her breath, pressed her eyes closed for a moment, then turned at last. "No, gold would not be the same thing. In any case, 'the stuff *heroes* are made of,' I don't know where that comes from." She stopped and exhaled hard, afraid that one more word would cause her voice to break. She managed, "...To double dangle prepositions, I suppose."

Tammy and Greta both raised their eyebrows and turned up the corners of their mouths. "Shakespeare and Dashiell Hammet in one breath," Greta exclaimed. They turned slightly from her.

Jolene struggled to say no more. Blood pounded in her ears and she felt her chest vibrate with the effort to be silent. When she glanced over the heads of the engineers' wives she saw Farrell looking back her way. He leaned with one hand on a tree, the other in his pocket, and ducking his head down and back to catch her conversation, smiled broadly at her, almost laughing. Jolene felt herself go red as Greta's shorts. She jumped up, and nodding curtly to Tammy and Greta, explained she had to get back to her own table or ruin the Goddamned dinner. She hurried away, jaws clenched, raking her hair with her fingers.

Farrell caught her up after a few yards. "That was fun," he said.

"I'm glad you were entertained. I made an ass of myself."

"You didn't."

"I can't believe... why in hell did you let me read Shakespeare?"

Farrell laughed, then turned in the direction of his picnic group with hands on his hips. "You committed an unforgiveable faux pas, Jo. You spoke above the reach of people who believe they should be superior but vaguely understand they are not. Are you going to the ballgame?"

"I..." She wasn't expecting the question and paused. "I should 'cause Ray's playing. But I don't want to. Are you?"

"Yes. I'm playing," He swung his fists in a batter's arc. "Don't look so surprised. I had to learn something at Yale."

"Something more than to be a smug, condescending stinkweed?"

He laughed again. "Stinkweeds we all may be. But no one can condescend to you."

"They've both been to college."

"It was obviously wasted on them." He moved sideways and squared himself in front of her. His face softened and lost its jollity but not its pleasantness. "You should go to college, Jo."

She shook her head, lips parted, trying to gauge whether he was being mean or fatuous. "Pigs don't fly, Farrell."

"No, but doves do." He reached to touch her shoulder.

Jolene stepped back, her jaw caught between words, and her eyes fixed on Farrell's suddenly unfamiliar face. She shook her head again and walked past him into the milling crowd.

She was breathless getting back to her own family lunch. Axel Pruitt sat at the center of the picnic table with Ethel on his right and Dotty Geim on his left. Ray sat facing his father, and Harly sat at one end with Dotty across from him. That left Jolene to face Ethel.

Axel surely had been a powerful man, but when I knew him he'd wasted away to a tall, erect frame with big, bony hands of surprising strength. His face was lean and stern, with sunken eyes under black bushes of eyebrow. He folded his hands on the table and led his family in prayer with a rasping, cavernous voice. Axel prayed for the country in its time of war, for the miners in their time of inequity, and at length for his family in their time of wandering.

"Amen," Ethel said. "It's awfully fine you could join us for lunch today, Dorothy. Isn't it fine, Harly?"

Harly raised his eyes to his mother's question, but his mouth was already full of potato salad. He struggled to chew and swallow.

Dotty said, "Thank you, Mrs. Pruitt. It was kind of you to extend me to, uh... ask me."

Harly was swallowing and trying to wash the potato salad down with beer, so Dotty spoke to the table at large. "Well, anyway, imagine us getting together like this. I hardly see you all anymore, since I moved back over the hill." She smiled and smoothed down a crisp yellow-print dress. She wore stockings and heels, too; an awful lot for a summer picnic, and her hair and face were done nicely. "I'm so pleased to run into you, especially, Harly," she said, and pushed a blond curl from her forehead.

"Well hell, Dot, if I'd known you'd be looking so good in your summer outfit I would have showed up at dawn." He winked, and Dotty blushed. He said, "Earl got me a new Spokesman Review yesterday. Shall we see what's happening in the world?"

Dotty leaned toward Harly, and Ray turned and winked at Jolene. Harly shuffled and folded the five or six broad sheets of the Spokane daily and offered them to Dotty. "Oh, I'll get ink all over me," she complained. "Tell me what's going on, Har."

"Well, there's a darned war going on, Dottie."

"Harlan Pruitt," Ethel said, "do you think anyone is so thick they don't know about the war?"

Harly shifted on the bench and folded the page, "General Patton captured a whole German army in Tunisia." He held the paper, and Dotty studied the photograph and the imbedded map on the front page. She smiled and glanced sidelong to Jolene.

"North Africa," Jolene explained.

"Africa? Now why are we fighting in Africa for heaven's sake? Don't we have enough Negros?" Dottie asked.

"I hear the Bradley Company's brought in four niggers to work in the Stibnite mine," Ethel said. "It won't be long before they bring 'em to Cinnabar. It's that Eleanor Roosevelt's doing."

Harly said, "They're negros, mom, and they get just as hungry as anyone else." Jolene breathed in hard as the sky seemed to darken and the table to spin for a moment under her. "Patton is marching through hell," Harly went on, "while we crawl through perdition."

She laid both hands flat on the table to steady herself. What in hell had Tammy meant by, "*...and everything else.*" No more or less, she knew, than Ellen meant by, "*It being just the two of you, and all...*" No more than any of them ever meant.

Ethel spoke to her from across the table. "Well, are you going to have something to eat? You're skin and bones."

"Yes, thank you." Her breathing still had not caught up to her.

She reached for a slice of bread but paused when Axel asked Harly, "You fixing to ask your friend Farrell over?"

"There's a three-dollar bill for you," Ethel muttered. To Jolene she said, "You were rude to Ellen and Hattie both."

A crow darted across her vision then circled above them. "You don't belong here," Jolene blurted. She closed her eyes tight, held her breath, and wondered if there was a table anywhere…some halfway point with neither a Tammy nor an Ethel; somewhere she could breathe.

Ethel was still talking: "You let the oil get too hot for chicken. You can see it burnt. But Ellen's pickled beets are a blessing and Hattie's corn pie…"

The crow was looking for something to steal, it occurred to Jolene. She followed its flight for a moment but then had to close her eyes to it.

"You can see as much," Ethel said again. "But I guess it's complicated."

Jolene put the butter knife down. "It isn't complicated Ethel. It's simple as the day is long." The damned crow lit on the grass between her table and Ellen's.

Ethel said something more, but Jolene missed it for the sudden pounding in her ears. Behind her, Ray was telling Harly, "Maybe if you could sweet-talk your crew into a day's work, meet a quota once, we'd all see a little redistribution of wealth."

The crow hopped about, pecking at popcorn and bits of crust. *What do you want with us*, Jolene thought. *Just our bread, or is it something dearer you'd steal?*

Harly said, "It'd be a sight easier if we could keep 'em alive long enough to do a day's work."

"Men are dying in the mines?" Dottie asked.

"No one's dying!" Jolene answered, more loudly than she meant to. Her hands shook; the crows black feathers gleamed iridescent in the noonday sun, and her heart skipped when it looked right through her.

Harly turned, surprised at Jolene's tone. He said, "No one's doing too much living either."

"No." She closed her eyes and breathed deeply.

Ethel passed the basket of sliced bread to Harly and asked, "What are you going to do if they put niggers on your crew? Why can't your labor union stop that?"

"Christ Almighty, leave it alone!" Jolene shouted. The crow hopped twice and took flight. Jolene jumped up from the table. "Give it a rest, please," she said more quietly, untangling herself from the picnic table bench. But when she raised her head and tried to walk away she was blocked in every direction by neighbors, strangers, and children all staring open-mouthed, leaning their heads together and whispering. Ray and Axel both rose, and Harly too. The men looked from one to another, then slowly sat again.

Jolene unclenched her fists and turned after a moment, walked around the table, and kissed Axel on the top of his head. She patted Dotty's shoulder and nodded to Ethel, who didn't look up. "Are you okay, Jo?" Ray asked quietly as she completed her circle. He swung to the end of the bench and stood. "Don't take it personal, honey."

"Oh, I'm fine," she whispered. She put her hands behind his neck and tip-toed to kiss him on the forehead. "I hate these damned picnics is all."

"You love these picnics."

"Do I? Maybe I do." She leaned her forehead on his chest. "But I just have a headache, dammit, and I'm gonna walk it off."

She started away but turned, wiped her eyes, and smiled again. "And you need to wear a hat, you cave troll. All this bright stuff we call sunshine, and it'll burn you red as a lobster." She found two cloth hats in the picnic box, a white one and a red one. She breathed deeply, marshaled a smile, and held both aloft. "Which one?" she called over to Ellen and Hattie.

The two ladies were surprised by the question and stumbled for an answer. "It doesn't matter at all," Ellen finally decided. Hattie raised a hand to her throat. "I'm sure you'll look lovely in either."

Jolene kept the red hat and stuffed the white one on Ray's head. She strolled from the table, then, from her people, with hands clasped behind her, weaving between tables piled with pickles and corn and sandwiches, through families assembled for a day of oneness. Shouts of friendship flew between tables. Jolene kept a smile on her face but met none of the eyes that turned to stare. She nodded as she walked, to no one in particular. A string band practiced on a stage still being hammered together, and tow-haired children darted by her and dodged her in their games. Flushed wives passed plates and grabbed tediously at the children, their wrung-out eyes following Jolene as she came and went, lest she sway too near to their pallid, beery husbands. Miners and millworkers and shopkeepers side-stepped her, or backed away, or turned to let her pass.

She wandered from the would-be strangers to the quiet bank of Meadow Creek and stepped into the shadows of stout cottonwoods and bitter-sweet willows. The trail meandered through tatters of mid-day sun, through tall grass and brush and a litter of leaves and fallen branches, following a cool path down by the water. She did once love Fourth-of-July picnics; she was sure of it.

Something rustled in the brush across the stream, and Jolene pulled branches aside but didn't see what it was. It fled from her into the fir and spruce beyond the low stream terrace. She hurried in that direction, to the water's edge, and sat to remove her shoes and socks. The brook was icy cold, and she waded with her shoes in one hand and her skirt up in the other. The stones were smooth and slippery, and water splashed over her knees at mid-stream.

On the far side she followed on over a carpet of spruce duff to the foot of a steep rise of granite. Climbing through a scratchy tangle, she came up onto a sunny rock that looked out over treetops past Meadow creek, to the airfield and to the town beyond the airfield. She sat on the rock, drew her knees up and breathed freely at last, letting the sun and clouds roll over her.

A wind came up, and she raised her eyes to watch the picnic below. Greta's red shorts made it easy to find her and Tammy sitting at lunch with their engineer husbands. Jolene wiped at her cheeks and wondered if they would ever slice that damned pineapple, or let it sit all day to admire. Her own table was disappointingly non-unique among the many others, and no different from Ellen's or Hattie's table, but for the sun-browned children swarming there. Hattie and Ellen—one child coming after another, as if it was the easiest thing in the world to do.

Brightly colored townspeople teemed over the field. She listened, but the wind in the trees and the splashing stream drowned out their sounds. The small figures wandered and joined into groups, broke apart, and swirled into other groups as she watched. *Dry lives like dry leaves*, she thought. She rested her cheek on her knee again. *Blowing and rolling, whirling and bouncing.* She wiped her nose and laughed. "Heedless, hapless, hopeless chance." She closed her eyes and barely breathed. "*Scattering, mustering, massing and blustering ... life's impossible—no, irresistible... dance?*"

Jolene opened her eyes again to the field and the colorful jetsam. She pushed her hair back from her face, and laughed, and wiped more tears from her eyes. The sun warmed her shoulders, and she noticed it had moved in the sky, so she rose and started down from the rock, back to the stream and to her people. She crossed over the water and sat on a smooth white cottonwood trunk to put on her shoes. But when she stood again she did not take the well-trodden path but changed course a second time. Nothing mattered—and whether she returned just now or not, it would still be nothing.

Meadow Creek bent back across the far end of the airfield, and there a few planes were parked out of the way of the party. A military plane, painted ugly green, was tethered at the ready. It was probably there to pick up a load of mercury from the Cinnabar mill. Farrell's plane, tied next to the military plane, was white with a yellow band down the length of the fuselage. It had broad wings sitting up high, directly over the cockpit. A Fairchild something, Jolene remembered, but she wasn't sure what that meant.

She listened to the shouts from far down the airstrip. The ballgame had started. She should go watch; she should try, at least. But a fight would start soon enough, and the masks would all be pulled away. Someone would slide into second and break someone else's leg, and they would all get into it—scared and hateful. Harly would get into it, and Ray most assuredly. Farrell would stand on the pitcher's mound, hands clasped over his head observing, narrow-eyed.

The metal skin of Farrell's plane gleamed in the afternoon light, and she reached high and ran her hand along the smooth leading edge of the wing as she walked under it. The metal felt cool to her hand. She glanced over her shoulder toward the picnic, then stepped quickly onto the strut and peeked inside the cockpit. Two small seats fit tightly up front, and she wondered how Farrell flew the plane sitting next to Harly with his broad shoulders. The interior was smaller and plainer than she expected, but the complicated instruments on the front panel impressed her and she jumped down satisfied. The propeller was of lacquered wood, smooth and graceful. She ran her hand along the double curve from the thick rounded stock to the sharp-edged tip.

Farrell saw Jolene climb onto the plane's strut at the far end of the field and watched a moment from the edge of the ballgame. Harly had given his at-bat to another miner, and at the edge of the parking lot he shared a laugh with a couple of the engineers, and a swallow of whiskey from a brown paper bag. He noticed Jolene, too, before ducking into the car for a few minutes.

16

The underground is a lot more welcoming now than when Maddie and I entered the first time. Cairn's crew re-timbered the portal then mucked, shored, and rock-bolted their way into a lot of the crosscuts and drifts. It's now more of an operating mine: lights have been strung up and fresh air blows in. The ribs and floor vibrate with rumbling, grinding machinery, and thunderous booms roll down the tunnels like cannon shots. Men shout and warning bells clang, and all join together to hold the darkness and silence at bay.

Reassuring as all that may sound, though, at nearly a mile in from the portal the conditions at forty-eight hundred west are as awful as when Cairn and I first looked on it. The timbering work has gotten dicey. Groundwater gushes from fractures in the ribs, back, and floor and runs in thick red slurries around our feet. The back sags and has fallen in numerous places while Cairn's crew tried to get bolts and netting in place. The crew's morale has fallen, too, and progress here has slowed.

Cairn and I stand in a strong wind carrying hints of summer forest, neoprene, and grease. We stand directly below the end of the ventilation tubing as far as they have hung it, and the end of the tubing snaps and flutters over our heads like storm-warning flags. It is loud and distracting, but the air is cool.

The fluttering of the vent tubing, the rock bolting, and the mucking are loud, and we're in everyone's way, I guess. Cairn guides me to one side or another, so I don't get killed as I examine the wallrocks and take compass attitudes on some of the fractures. More likely he doesn't care an awful lot if I get killed, but I'm slowing his crew as they try to get things done.

We move out a few steps where we can talk more easily, but still there is little to say; we mostly point at fractures in the rock with a word or two, or nod with our cap lamps at bad ground that needs more shoring. Cairn lights a cigarette, and the smoke draws briskly toward the portal.

A diagonal cross-cut should join the main adit at this point, according to the alignment of the damned stopes the drillers have been hitting. But there is no cross-cut, and it's no wonder: a set of sheared fractures cuts through carrying white clays and ground-up quartz vein material. It is weak rock—too weak to support a tunnel with a solid back. Extensive box timbering was used in the old days to shore up the main adit where it passes through the weak zone, and Cairn is having his crew replace some rotted timbers, but he's leaving the structure in place. "It's a hell of a job they did here," he judges. "Never seen anything like it. But they engineered a framework to hold up, and by God it's held so far."

Before I can reply, Cairn puts his arm on my shoulder and pulls me in close against the rib. A deep bellowing noise approaches, and bright lights round the corner, blinding us. The mucker, a low-slung, center-pivot loader, backs by us with a full scoop, and its rumbling vibrates through our boots and on up through our bones. Heavy diesel fumes spew at us, and suffocating heat blows from its fan as the machine passes a foot away. The loader moves by, and we follow in its lights and noise another hundred feet or so, to where it turns around in a muck bay before heading out.

Although I didn't see the cross-cut I expected at forty-eight hundred feet, the muck bay at forty-seven hundred extends in the right general direction. A ten-foot pile of sluff and debris fills the end of the bay, but a space between the sluff and the back gives me a vantage into a tunnel beyond. I have to detach my cap lamp to see into the narrow gap, but in the hand-held beam it's obvious this once was a lot more than a muck bay. It was a major drift, and it has collapsed, violently, along a good length.

Cairn calls me down from the sluff pile—it's not safe up there. I hook my light back onto the front of my hard hat, and we stand in our crossed beams and discuss the collapsed drift.

"I know," he says. "You can see here in the debris that pipes and wires and some pretty big timbers were thrown out when it came down."

"How long ago?" I wonder.

"We found the bay pushed out and a lot of old gear stacked here, so it must have been used as a storage bay for quite a while. It probably caved several years, at least, before the mine shut down."

"Well, I'll be damned."

"How far's it go in?" he asks.

"I have no idea; there's nothing on our maps."

*

"What's that?" Maddie came up on me from downhill, and I didn't hear her because Bernie's drillrig is finally turning and making a lot of noise. She found me going through one of Jolene's books.

"It's a book. Why don't you let someone know you're coming?" She's dressed as though she's been running. "Have you been running?" I ask because it seems like a person should get plenty of exercise in our day-to-day work.

She ignores the tone of my voice. "I can see it's a book. Are you reading poetry?" She leans over to see the title. "Percy Shelley, as God is my witness! Who's going to believe this?" She snatches the open book right out of my hand. But Maddie and I have been getting along, so I don't show my annoyance. "What's that you're holding?" she asks me.

"Forget-me-nots, I think." It's a bookmark, some pressed flowers—a spray of half a dozen small, deep-blue, five-petal blossoms. I hand her the flowers. "They were in the book."

"They're not from around here," she says.

"Of course they would be."

"Huh-uh." She shakes her head. "They're Alpines. Let me see."

I hand her the dried flowers and my loupe, because she doesn't have her own loupe, because she's dressed for a run and not for work.

She says after a moment, "*Eritrichium nanum*, I think. Arctic-Alpine forget-me-nots. You won't find them around here, not on the forest floor, not at this elevation. They grow on rocks high above tree line. Awfully pretty though."

"They wouldn't grow anywhere around here?"

"The closest place well above tree line is Rainbow Peak." Maddie nods off to the northeast, where a bald peak stands above the surrounding tree-covered ridges about four miles away. The peak glows warmly in the early morning sun.

"The next nearest peak above ten-thousand feet is probably fifteen miles to the northwest," she says, nodding in that direction.

Rainbow Peak is brightly colored, with bands of red, yellow, and gray rhyolites cutting the white porphyry country rock: part of the volcanic suite that brought in late-stage gold and silver to the District.

"Do you need samples from there for your mitigation studies?" I ask.

"Yes, I was going to do it later this month."

"I might go up there tomorrow. Make a list for me of what you need for samples."

"I'll go with you," she offers.

"No, I'd rather go alone if you don't mind."

"Harlan, it's a big hike and you shouldn't do it alone."

"Goddamn it, is Andy telling you to look after me?"

"Harlan, it's just common sense. I don't want to waste a day on a search and recovery mission."

That would ordinarily piss me off, but I look up and she's grinning, and cute, so I say, "I won't stray from the trail; my body'll be easy to find. Try to get to me before the crows work me over."

"Take lots of water," she says.

"Thanks."

"Stay sober tonight, it'll hurt less."

"I appreciate your concern."

THE RECLAMATION

A soft yellow evening light reflects from high clouds above the hollow, and it pours through the open door of the shack as I thumb through Jolene's book of poetry. I've always liked Shelley; I don't know what Maddie was going on about. In fact, the passage marked by the flowers is a favorite poem of mine. There is writing in the margin but, held up to the light of the doorway, the faint pencil marks can't be made out. On the inside leaf of the book, though, Farrell Hammond presented the volume to Jolene as a birthday gift:

"Dear Jolene," the note reads, in a tight cursive hand,

"May you find as much pleasure in these sonnets as I have found in our many bright conversations. Let these books build your raft, the pages be as canvas hoisted on a fair breeze. There is a river of knowledge flowing through all the world, Jo. Set your course upon it, let it carry you away."

-Farrell

The profound Mr. Hammond. I have a drink to his river of knowledge. "Set your course upon it... by all means."

Except, it's the River of No Return in these parts, I remind myself. I don't drink to that, but pour one to the sunset, and then another to Madison Davy's generous concern.

*

Morning broke clear and promised bright, although the sun was still well below East Ridge. I ate a cold breakfast and packed up my gear, then headed over Lookout Ridge. There was no reason to stop in Stibnite, and I had no trouble finding the Forest Service road leading northeast from the airfield.

The road comes to an end at the edge of an aspen stand, where a trail takes off beyond a locked Forest Service gate. Maddie will be able to see my truck parked here from anywhere on the north side of Lookout, and she won't have to panic over what might have befallen me. Unless, of course, the truck is still here at sundown. I take a few minutes to fold my topo maps, finish a coffee, and re-lace my boots. I belt on my rock hammer and Brunton compass, and still it's a good early start.

The pack weighs a lot as I head out because I carry most of my water for the day; the trail will stay almost entirely on ridge tops, so no water will be found until I get up into the snow banks. The pack will lighten if I remember to drink.

Jolene would not have taken the same trail but would have started in Cinnabar, joining the ridge trail higher up. Whether or not she had maps to guide her I can't know; maybe she just knew the country from her hiking. This trail, though, is lightly used, and the path rocky and overgrown in places. Blue jays chatter around the first bend, and a deer and her fawn scare up out of the brush. The trail leads northeastward into the country and plunges at first, then stays low for the first half hour. It carries me through sharp-smelling sage and thick-trunked cottonwoods in the dank, cool, canyon bottom.

Soon, though, the path climbs up out of the shadows and side-hills into the yellow pine forest. In early July at this latitude, the sun rises early and it quickly heats the white volcanic rocks; the air is drier and cleaner as the dark bottoms fall behind. An up-canyon breeze whooshes the pines and chills the sweat already soaking under my shoulder straps; it smells of sweet pine sap warming in the sun.

The vegetation thins as I climb, and vistas open up through the early morning. Within an hour the trail has gained the ridge top, and the walk is easier between thin-trunked lodgepoles, through sparse grasses, and over carpets of low-bush huckleberries.

The ridge steepens and throws up a small rocky knob from where I get my bearings on the map. Rainbow Peak stands before me, deceptively close and garishly colored. No clouds clutter the sky yet, and my legs feel strong. The trail bends to the north, and Jolene's trail converges with it in the low saddle before the next promontory. My journey has been longer, but hers would have been much steeper to here.

The trail rises steadily, and wildflowers scatter in profusion over the rocky slopes, but not the sky-blue forget-me-nots. They'll be higher yet. I top another rocky knob and drop back down into the trees, and then another, until the ridge beyond the next promontory remains rocky with only a few sparse White Pines to dot the landscape. Samples will have to be collected on the way back down, of rhyolite lavas and tuffs swirled in bands of red, orange, and white; of marble, and dark gray basalt.

The climb steepens on the shoulder of the peak, and a bent trunk of an ancient pine offers a seat for a short rest. The trunk is weathered nearly bare of bark and shows all of the deep grain of the wood, and yet a few sprays of needles grow from the branches twisting above. There is almost no other life around; lichen-crusted scree covers a slope that falls away into an expanse of clear blue sky. I've not remembered to drink my water coming up the lower trail, and now it is warm and tastes of plastic, but it's wet and welcome, and I gulp down nearly a liter.

She was here and saw these same things. Jolene felt the hot sun and the cool breeze on her face and heard the hollow whisper of wind blowing over bare rock.

The altitude pulls like weights around my ankles. Breathing becomes more difficult in the thin air, though it would not have been for her. Jolene was young and fit, and I have to push myself to keep up. Platy rocks, kicked up in haste, clatter and scrape under heavy boots.

The trail, barely a trace now, dives at last under drifts of snow. Sun-cupped and rilled, it still clings to the ridges here and there. The wet, granular slush cools my bare legs, and I kick through up to my knees.

Another pause to clean the snow from my boot tops and to enjoy the airy expanse, and a scattering of alpine forget-me-nots dot the ground all around, growing like azurite crystals from crevices in the outcrops and spreading between the boulders in bunches. At this high elevation there are no longer bird calls to keep a hiker company, but instead the silence of the eagle circling overhead and the warning call of the indignant pica. I sit on the edge of a glacial cirque, a great amphitheater half a mile wide and nearly as long from bottom to top, and wonder if her footfalls might be heard, were it not for the wind.

†

She turned and turned, taking in all the alpine wonder around her. There are no trappings to be had nor gold to be panned at this elevation, so the world above tree line was rare to Jolene. The air was thin but full of new smells: of rock flour and meltwater; of pungent shrubs and snow-wetted lichens; mosses and bunchgrass. The air chilled her flesh as it rushed down off the snowy peak, swirling and mixing with air warmed near the ground until she wasn't sure moment to moment whether she should put on or take off her jacket. Jolene climbed on through that giant's amphitheater, around hummocky ridges of gravel, over polished and striated stone surfaces, and across broad slopes rippling with the curious patterns of solifluction.

She reached the peak breathless as the sun swept to its zenith. Patches of snow and white volcanic rocks burned her eyes until the deep blue sky darkened almost to gun-metal gray. The air was thin to breathe and cold, and the sun warmed but one side of her. She turned to warm her other side and came face to face with a frightening expanse of rocky ridges and peaks, all tumbling down into the awful chasm of the Salmon River. She caught her breath and turned quickly away. But the blue forget-me-nots gathered again at her feet, and she stepped back from the shadowy wilderness and followed the flowers to the other side, to a cleft in the rocks out of the wind where she could nestle and enjoy the warm sun.

The hollow of Cinnabar opened below in the distance, and Jolene smiled at the smallness of it. The wind swirled her hair, and she tied a scarf to keep it out of her face, then pulled her jacket around and draped it over her shoulders. The sun moved as she watched, and the shadows of the hollow receded, and all the small town was laid bare to view. Her own house stood among the shiny tin roofs below, but she could not make it out for the distance. It was all so trifling: the town and the mill and all the mining roads and trenches scarring the hills, all of the clamor and consequence of the mines amounted, she thought, to mere scuffs upon the great expanse of hills and canyons and time.

From her pack she pulled the book Farrell had given her; she opened and read a few lines, smiled, and called over the wind to the pica and to the eagle, *"I met a traveler from an ancient land..."*

*

"...Look upon my works, ye mighty, and despair!" Was it chance that caused her to turn to this page? It would have been an appropriate choice, if she chose it on purpose. The town, the mine, the strife below us; they are all inconsequential and vain. Sixty-five years have proven that to me, but Jolene was twenty-five years old and never finished high school; had hardly been out of Idaho. Her choice of poem was fortuitous, a lucky parting of pages.

The young woman, the child really, laughed at Shelley's haughty tone, waving her arm with a *"sneer of cold command."* It was midsummer and she thought of huckleberry pies and cool mountain streams. She set down her book and imagined the warm, white beaches of California, and the palm trees along every street. She dreamed by then of going to college in California; Dotty Giem once told me so. She'd got UCLA in her head and talked of going there some day with Ray working a good job in the shipyards.

The town below us now is dead and rusted; it could have ended no other way. The clamor has subsided; all the dreaming and suffering have come to nothing, and as Shelley would have it, *"...the lone and level sands stretch far away."*

But the cleft is warm under the unfiltered sun and hardly a breeze stirs. There is no reason to get up just yet. The book falls open again to the pressed flowers, and the margin scribblings I couldn't read last night in the gloom of the shack show more visibly in the stark light of altitude. The faint penciled words don't look at all like

Farrell's tight cursive; the hand is girlish with measured heights and open loops. Holding the page close I barely make out:

> *"Time and tears in torrents pour*
> *o'er monuments of hope and pride,*
> *till graven stones cascade and roll,*
> *crushed and worn upon the tide.*
> *Oh, heartless do we dreamers stroll*
> *that distant morrow's sandy shore."*

There is more verse, but it doesn't stand out: the pencil is smudged, written too lightly. There is something like, *"ever tell,"* or *"angel fell,"* maybe. And... no, nothing more. The rest is lost, though I turn the page to the sunlight and search the smudges for clues. It is gone, and it is a shame. She didn't trust her hand yet to press firmly.

"*Heartless do we dreamers stroll...*" I don't know this woman yet. She set her pencil down, though, and plucked a forget-me-not to mark the passage, then brought her legs up under her and pulled the jacket tighter around her shoulders. How long might she have stayed in this cleft, curled against the wind, words held tightly to her breast? She peered down upon Hollow Town—where did I learn that name? —looked down on her life in wonder and cried. Or maybe she laughed. I don't know her yet at all.

I could stay on this mountaintop a while longer, too, until the sun drops below the rim, I think. It would be so easy to stay. But there is too much left to do. All of Maddie's samples have to be collected going down, and the day and I are already past our prime.

The last sample brings the pack to sixty pounds, and it's almost too much to wriggle into the straps and lean and rise. The trail going back is not all downhill and easy, either. I had not paid attention to a lot of dips and swales on the way up. It is a hump.

THE RECLAMATION

Maddie has parked next to my truck, and I wave back as she waves to me from the bed of her truck. She has been watching and waiting. She means well, and she helps me to drop the pack off my shoulders and onto the tailgate, and that's fine. The shedding of that heavy load relieves the back and returns a spring to my step. Almost like youth.

"I'd have made it you know, you didn't have to worry."

"I didn't worry," she answers. "I just thought you'd like a cold beer after work."

The blue plastic cooler sits in the back of her truck, and under the lid is a six-pack on ice. I could kiss her, were I really so young.

We sit on the tailgate quietly, for the most part. Maddie asks what I saw, and I tell her about the geology along the trail. The yellowing light glimmers in our eyes through the stand of aspens, and grasses and scrub oak glow on the hillside as insects buzz and dart in and out of the sun's low rays. My legs soften with the beer, and it's a warm feeling. Maddie smiles and asks what else, and I tell her about Jolene.

"She was your mother," Maddie says. "Jolene was your mother."

"Of course she was."

"Earl told me."

"She wrote poems."

"In Cinnabar?"

"I'd heard it said, but it never occurred to me." From my shirt pocket I hand Maddie a fresh sprig of arctic-alpine forget-me-nots. *Eritrichium nanum*, I think.

17

I got word Andy wanted me to call, so I drove to the top of the ridge where satellite reception is good. We talked into the afternoon mostly about the mysterious underground workings that have be-deviled Bernie's and Honorario's drilling. Those stopes fall along a trend that runs oblique to the normal directions of the district. The stopes shouldn't be there at all—that's the thing. They're not shown on any of the maps, and yet someone seems to have carried out extensive mining along the trend.

I noted some time ago the samples we've drilled out along the bothersome oblique trend contain a different suite of minerals than elsewhere in the mine. It appears to be an overprinting of a completely different mineralizing event. But there is no description of it in any of the old mine reports. Now the assay results are beginning to come in, and they are equally odd—and a little troubling. The veins along the oblique trend carry less mercury, but more gold than other veins. A lot more gold.

Andy doesn't see where a lot more gold is troubling in the least, and I can't put it into words, either. But the oblique veins project right toward the muck bay where Matt Cairn and I saw the long, caved drift behind the spoil pile. Andy and I decided to have Cairn open up the drift as far as we need to, to see where it heads. Andy says this could change everything. He might be right.

Maddie was pulling up to Honorario's rig when I drove by, and I stopped to say goodnight to her. She said goodnight back. She greeted the night shift as I hung back at my truck, then told me she'd stay to write out a few notes for the head driller. The sky was still glowing, though the sun was long behind the trees on the western ridge. Maddie joked with the crew, and her laughter and theirs rose above the rumble of the machinery.

The rig's lights came on as I got home, and I watched them while I cooked dinner at the fire pit. It's a shame to waste a warm fire, so I sat and let the shimmering coals dwindle to a few red embers before stepping in and settling down with the faded pineapples and palm trees of my tropical retreat.

†

Harly rode over the hill with Jolene, and they met Farrell at the airfield at noon. It was close to a perfect September day, if there could be such a thing for Jolene. The sun was warm in a sapphire sky, but the air had a cool edge to it, and a few of the tall trees along Meadow Creek already showed gold trimmings in their crowns. Jolene brought Spam sandwiches and a macaroni salad, and they spread a blanket on the grassy apron of the field next to Farrell's plane. Farrell had brought a book of prints by Frida Kahlo, Diego Rivera, and other Mexican artists, and they talked unhurriedly of poems and paintings.

"You've been gone a lot this summer," Farrell said to Jolene.

"The weather's been good. I've sort of... I've found some nice trails."

"Maybe we should all go hiking sometime."

Jolene looked up from the book and gazed over the airfield to the hills beyond, where her trails lay hidden, each with its sights and scents and its own version of all alone. "Maybe someday," she said softly. She wore a red-checked shirt with its tails knotted in front, and she sat propped against her backpack in white shorts, her tanned legs pointing outward.

"Well that's a tepid invitation."

"She doesn't want to share all that gold she's been panning." Harly winked at Jolene, and she dropped her head and laughed.

"What were you doing all that time in Mexico?" Harly asked Farrell. Harly had dressed up for the picnic, in tweed trousers, which Jolene had never seen him wear before, and a jacket that nearly matched. His shoes were polished.

"Dodging the draft and staying out of trouble. I'd just graduated and was busy figuring out what to do."

Harly eyed Farrell and grinned. "The privileged American?"

Farrell dropped his head and sighed but then returned the smile. "No doubt, no doubt," he said. "I was good at it, too, and getting better."

Jolene craned around. "You were a professor, Farrell."

Harly laughed. "Oh, good Lord, Jo. He taught a few classes at the local college. English language and American civics." Again Farrell dropped his head. "Correct again, Har. Nothing to merit the vaunted title, 'Professor'."

"I'm sure your students were impressed," Jolene said.

"They were appropriately deferential." Farrell took off his jacket in the warm sun and folded it like a pillow on the blanket beside him. "There were some good students; keen, more interested in learning than in the tweed trappings of the learned."

Harly slipped out of his tweed jacket and tossed it aside.

Farrell said, "I wish I'd had more time with them." He breathed deeply. "But some idiot U-boat captain had to torpedo the—what was it? —the damned Potrero del Llano, may she rust in the deep."

"Well, Guadalajara's loss is our gain." Jolene handed the book over her head, and Farrell sat back up and took it from her. "Is this impressionism or post impressionism?" she asked.

Farrell glanced at the page. "What do you think, Har?" he asked.

Harly didn't take the book but glanced at the page held open in Farrell's hands. "Beats the shit out of me," he said.

"Post impressionism, for sure," Farrell said. "Look how geometric it becomes," he traced a finger above the page. "The walls and the trees build almost to a cubism. Is that how you see it?" He looked over but Harly was watching over his shoulder, back toward town.

Farrell handed the book back to Jolene. She looked for the cubism but didn't see it. Setting the book aside, she pushed the pack away, and lay down on the blanket with her arms for a pillow. There were no clouds to watch, so she closed her eyes. With her arms folded under her head, the knotted shirt climbed up and exposed an awful lot of her midriff, but both men were looking away, back toward town.

"I told you they weren't going to put up with it," Farrell said to Harly. A commotion was rising in town about a quarter mile away. A crowd jostled outside the Bradley Mining Company office; maybe forty men. "Things might explode if management keeps squeezing the workers like this. It could be a hot Labor Day."

"It's a sham," Harly said. He spoke into the ground, his jaw askew.

"What do you mean?" Farrell asked, "Because for all our protests the army gets its minerals and the people still die poor?"

"And your old man gets rich."

"Harly!" Jolene said.

Farrell said, "It's not about money. It's about respect for human…"

"Only the moneyed are respected."

Farrell started to say something but changed his mind. "The men would follow you if you stand up," he said. "You could still make a difference in all of this."

Harly's eyes shifted back to the crowd. "I'll make a difference, sure as hell."

Jolene said, "Not everyone is dying poor, anyway. "She rolled over on her elbow and hip and faced the two of them. "Some of the wives in Cinnabar seem to be getting by just fine. I said as much to Barney Applegate and he laughed and said they were probably digging out some of that gold."

Harly turned to Jolene, his lips parted; Farrell didn't turn from the trouble in town. "What are you talking about?" Harly asked quietly. "What wives?"

"Oh, nothing. Barney and I were just wondering at all the money that gets spent by some of the engineers' wives, is all. He said there was plenty of gold in those veins before the government took over, and said someone must be getting at it."

"We don't produce anything but mercury from the mine." Harly said. "Those are the kinds of rumors that can cause all sorts of trouble."

Farrell turned now, too. "It's a funny thought, but not possible," he said. "Not secretly, anyway. Maybe you could get the gold ore out of the mine, if the miners aren't discerning of geology. But you could never extract the gold from the ore without everyone in the mill knowing about it."

"Which wives are spending so much?" Harly asked.

"Let's talk about something else," she suggested. She rolled back and again threw her arms under her head. "Have you seen some of Harly's paintings and carvings?"

"Yeah," Farrell said. He stood with his back to the others and his hands on his hips. "They're good. You're an artist; you're a sculptor; you never belonged in the war…" He turned as he spoke, noticed Jolene's supine exposure, and quickly turned away. He tried to speak in another direction but couldn't gather his thoughts.

Harly hid a sneer. "What about you, fair Lorelai, are you an artist or a warrior?" He shook his head and pulled her by the hand back to a sitting position.

"Well, you'd better not ask Ray which I am," she said with a roll of her eyes. She turned and tugged her shirt down below her ribs. "I still can't see the cubism, so maybe I'd better stick to fighting."

The talk grew strained; Harly sulked a lot anymore, Jolene thought, and Farrell seemed more tongue-tied than usual today. She wasn't up to keeping things pleasant this time, and by midafternoon the sun found some clouds, so she packed up the picnic and shook out and folded the blanket. She asked Farrell and Harly to put their jackets back on and stand next to the plane for a picture before they went their own ways.

Harly said he'd walk into town from the airfield. He had things to think about, and he was sure he could catch a ride back to Cinnabar later in the evening, so Jolene shouldn't wait. Farrell had agreed to

THE RECLAMATION

meet with some workers, then he would head over to Cinnabar as well, if Harly needed a ride. No, Harly told him, he wouldn't be ready for a ride that soon. He had some meetings of his own to keep.

Jolene stopped to shop at the Meadow Creek Grocery because, she explained, they had better vegetables than ever made it to Cinnabar. She stopped at the Dry Goods to look at dress patterns, too, and no one stole glances or turned pointedly from her. She was still on the road in late afternoon, sitting in the clearing on Lookout Pass when Farrell drove by, saw her, and backed up.

"Are you okay?" he asked.

"I stopped for the view and it won't start."

"Do you think we should open the hood and look?"

"Why?"

"I don't know," He shrugged. "That's what people do. Haven't you seen people do that?"

Jolene found the lever to release the hood, and Farrell braced it up and looked in at the engine while Jolene tried the starter a couple of times. Nothing worked. "It's a shame Harly didn't get a ride with you," she said. "He and Ray have fixed this old thing a dozen times."

"Crying shame," Farrell said. He closed the hood and helped her to load her groceries into his car.

He drove with the top down, and as they started down the hill it seemed a completely different road to Jolene. She let the cool autumn wind blow through her hair and the warm mid-afternoon sun flicker through the trees onto her face. "I'm sorry you and Harly are fighting," she said.

"We're always fighting anymore."

"It's not anything to do with me, I hope?" She rolled her head on the back of the seat and laughed.

"No! No, nothing like that. Harly isn't happy with where he's at."

"Cinnabar?"

"Anywhere." Farrell glanced at the road and the trees and the sky—anywhere but at her as he drove. The conversation came around again to California and college.

She shook her head slowly. "I'm a married woman, Farrell."

"I'm well aware."

She turned and rested her chin on her arm as the valley spun through gaps in the trees.

He said, "It doesn't matter, you know."

"How in hell would that work? Who would keep the house?"

"Lots of married women do it nowadays. I knew married women at Yale."

"Really, you did? Well, still…"

"I'm just saying, it isn't unheard of. It's between you and Ray, of course, but don't stop thinking about it because you think it's impossible."

Jolene rolled her gaze to Farrell and then back up into the passing treetops. "How many of your Yale friends didn't finish high school, Farrell? I'm a miner's wife. That's what I am."

"You're more, a lot more. I think you know it too, in your heart."

They both let it hang for a few more turns of the road.

Jolene said, "Thank you Farrell, if I forget to say it."

"For the ride? It's nothing."

"For the daydream." She crinkled her eyes and smiled but turned back to the scenery.

The road entered the dry clay of the mineralized zone, and dark brown dust rose from the tires and chased them into town. "Take a left, here," she said. She sat up with a sigh. "And then a right at the fire barrel. Ours is the un-painted shiplap, two-story shotgun. The one with the dishtowel in the window."

Ray walked up from his shift at the mine as Farrell helped Jolene unload the groceries. "Where's the Studebaker?" he asked.

"It's at the darned pass, Honey. I stopped to look at the colors and then it wouldn't start again. I was there almost an hour before Farrell came along." Ray turned to carry his lunch pail and jacket into the kitchen; Jolene tugged at her shirt, although it was fine, and followed him in.

THE RECLAMATION

Farrell called in through the doorway, "I'm going to grab some samples at the mill, then head back to Stibnite. I can give you a ride up to the Studebaker."

"I don't need a ride."

"As you say. But I'm driving back to Stibnite in about twenty minutes. I'll be happy to give you a lift if you want to take some tools up."

"What was the problem with it, then?" Ray stepped back onto the porch. He'd showered at the mine, and his dark hair was still wet and combed back. His shirt was unbuttoned at the collar; it fit snugly over solid shoulders but hung loose around his narrow waist. In his boots Ray stood eye to eye with Farrell, although he had forty pounds on him.

"I'm the last person to ask," Farrell said. "But it seemed like the battery turns it over, but the engine won't fire. Like it's out of gas, but the needle didn't say so."

"It's the Goddamned fuel pump. I need a new one, but you can't find parts these days for love or money. I'll get some tools together, then."

"I wonder if you'd mind stopping with me at the mill, in that case. I could use some help loading a few samples there. I'll wait as you get your tools."

In the equipment barn at the mill, yellow late afternoon light filtered down from high, sooty windows into an expansive concrete-floored shop. Metal hammering on metal, grinding machines, and the thrumming and banging of fan wheels echoed off the steel walls. Ray entered behind Farrell and immediately felt the stares of the workers inside. The samples were located in a back room across the floor and around several rows of work benches heaped with bolts, wheels, and oily engine parts. Eyes turned with them as they zig-zagged between the benches. Mechanics, tools in hand, barely stepped aside for them.

"The mill is being hit hard by the falloff in mercury production," Farrell explained quietly. "It's pretty tense right now between these guys and us at the assay lab."

"Is production down?" Ray asked. "We haven't had a drop in tonnage. In fact, it's been increasing." He wasn't comfortable in the shop, and he rubbed his elbow as he glanced about at the men who watched him pass.

"Tonnage is up, and assay results are staying flat. But mercury is down, and these guys say nothing has changed in their circuit. They can't explain the falloff in production. They think the assay lab is screwing with them."

"The assay lab run by the owner's son."

Farrell kept walking, but said after a moment, "I'm sure that's not lost on them. Anyway, they're pretty unhappy."

"Over what?"

"They're losing out on bonus money. The mill is Union, you know, and the production workers negotiated a low base pay and a profit-share on the mercury they recover. It was pretty slim for them last month."

"I didn't know that," Ray said. He and Farrell collected the bags of crusher fines, and together carried them out in one load the way they'd come in. Ray kept his eyes forward and didn't meet the stares of the millworkers.

They loaded the sample bags in the trunk, and Ray got back into the convertible and took off his hat, holding it in his hands.

"There was more trouble at the mine office today," Farrell said. "A lot of the Cinnabar men are unhappy about the new hours." Farrell turned out of the mill yard and headed up Ridge Road.

"There's nothing I can do about that," Ray said.

"What side are you going to take? Harly was wondering."

Ray looked hard at Farrell and shook his head. "Harly doesn't need to wonder what I'm gonna do. He just better worry about whatever the hell he's doing."

"The longer hours are to make up for the lower metal production."

"I don't run the mill circuit, I drive drift, and my Goddamned tonnage is up." Ray jammed his hat on his head, pulled the brim down, and rested his elbow on the top of the door as they swung around a curve and the scarred and pocked valley opened below him.

"I'm not happy about the hours either," he said. "But I do what I'm told, and I expect my crew to do the same."

He took a pack of cigarettes from his jacket pocket. Leaning forward behind the dashboard he lit one, then offered one to Farrell, who declined. "What are you trying to do, anyway?" he asked Farrell, "working with the labor organizers. That's not so helpful to us, day to day, when we're trying to keep production up."

"I'm all for production. I'm just helping the men out with meetings and legal questions."

"You a socialist?" The setting sun flickered through the trees.

"I have no other aims than what your father worked for in the past."

"My old man tells me you can't lift yourself up by stepping on someone else. And that sounds pretty good from a pulpit. But at our level, day to day, that's just how it works."

"My point is, it shouldn't be."

"Yeah, well, that's the situation," Ray said. "You ever done a cake walk at a social? No? Well, when the phonograph stops everyone has to find a chair. Except there aren't enough chairs on purpose, so you'd better scramble or you'll be the one without. Now, maybe it ain't fair that someone takes a chair away each time, but that's the game, and we don't get to pick the game." He drew from his smoke and exhaled into the wind. "When it's just about cakes it's no big deal, but when it's men taking care of their families, then that's where you'd better be damned good and hard at scrambling."

"Who makes the rules of that game?"

Ray jerked his head around. "We don't have the luxury all the time of sitting around and postulating on themes!"

Farrell glanced over with raised brows.

"When you're up to your ass in muck and mud every day sometimes the romance of working-class values ain't so obvious."

"I understand," Farrell said.

"No, you sure as hell don't." Ray took in the whole valley again as they swung around another switchback. "And when you're stuck living in the Goddamned sticks, the rustic charm of the setting is often lost on you, too."

"Now, that much I've noticed for myself," Farrell said, nodding.

Ray glanced over and half grinned. "Okay, maybe that then," he said.

They reached the top of Lookout Ridge and drove into the clearing as the sun dropped to the hills beyond. Farrell slowed and pulled alongside the Studebaker. Someone had thrown a rock and smashed out the back window.

"What in hell happened here?" Farrell asked. "For Christ sake!"

"Like I said, that's just how it works day to day." Ray jumped over the door and grabbed the tool box from the back seat. "Thanks," he said, the cigarette bobbing between his lips.

"I can wait," Farrell said, "to make sure it starts up."

"No, don't trouble yourself further."

"It's no trouble."

"Look, I appreciate the ride." Ray turned and smiled at Farrell; a generous smile. "But under the circumstances me and you ain't gonna be good friends. Doesn't mean we've got to be enemies, I suppose, but you know what I mean."

"Yeah, I know what you mean."

"Did you have a lot of friends back in Yale?" Ray asked. "None of my business, of course."

"Yes, before the war."

"Men and women both?"

"Yeah, both." Farrell hesitated a moment and said, "You know, Jolene and I, we just like books, that's all. We talk about books."

Ray set the tools on the fender of the Studebaker and took another drag from his cigarette before turning back to Farrell. He dropped the butt to the ground and exhaled as he stepped lightly on it with his toe. He smiled again and said, "Hell I know that, bud. If I thought any different, you'd hardly be around to discuss it." His smile was not at all unfriendly.

Farrell held his hand up to the yellow light burning through the pines. "Just thought I'd say it once," he said. For the life of him, he wished he could find another reason to dislike the guy. "So, you're okay here, then?"

"I'm good. Thanks for the ride."

18

The project is going pretty well, and for it being late July we're about where we should be in terms of drilling. I got Cairn focused on the re-opening of the Oblique drift, and it's proving to be as much trouble as we'd feared. At least there've been no more misadventures with equipment. Maddie and I—well I, and I'm sure Cairn too—have kept an eye out for troublemakers. Maddie's been collecting rock and water samples from the drillholes as they advance. It's time consuming, and it keeps her around the rigs a lot anymore. Bernie doesn't cuss around her, at least not in English, and Honorario's crew absolutely embarrass themselves; they'd walk barefoot over broken glass for her. It's fine, if somewhat silly, and I've let her take on some of the responsibilities of overseeing the rig moves and setups, the checking of daily footage, and the downhole surveys.

It's a long hike up to the forks of Sugar Creek. The Paleozoics there are twisted and folded back on themselves and cut by an unusual sequence of dikes. Weird stuff. I got back late, and Maddie was at my place waiting for me. She'd been crying, I think, although she tried to hide it. I hoped everything was okay. "How's Stan the Ranger?"

"Dan? He's great." She shrugs and rises from the porch railing. "God, Harlan! You know, you'd like him." Her smile looks tired, even in the low evening sunlight. More tired than before. "Well, maybe you wouldn't," she says.

"I like people."

THE RECLAMATION

The volume of work is overwhelming her, and of course Andy has been pushing us to wrap things up and write a report. She's falling behind; I know for a fact a lot of waters and rock types haven't been tested yet. Maddie doesn't want to say so, but in the end admits, "I'm so screwing this whole thing up."

"Of course you are. You were hired to screw it up."

She gawks at me speechless, near tears. I explain, "This is a huge job that got dumped on you, Maddie. You had no idea when you took it on, but we did. Andy and I knew it would crush any one person. You've actually done a lot better..."

"Why?"

"So you'd cave in and write an easy environmental assessment."

She looks for a second like she would throw something at me if her hands weren't empty. "So, what? That's it? I'm supposed to give up?"

"No, it would screw up the project a lot worse if you were to cave. Andy doesn't get that, but I'm not going to let you fail. Let's sit down for a minute. We can fix this."

I step up on the porch and open the door. "Let's start by writing down the tasks you have to get done, then sort out which ones are critical-path and which ones run parallel."

She looks at me like I just dropped down from Mars. She looks at me a lot like that. But she follows me in and sits down and stares ahead with her arms folded across her chest.

"I do, you know. Like people."

She rolls her eyes and twists her lips into kind of a smirk, but sits and sticks her hands under her legs.

"What are these?" she asks.

Oh, just some photos and letters and things I'm going through."

"Really, of your family? Who's this, is this Jolene? She's beautiful, my God!"

"Yeah, that's Jolene."

"She's just a kid, though, isn't she?" Maddie picks a few more pictures from the pile and examines them. She asks, "Did she really pan for gold in the nude?"

"Where in the hell...?"

"Earl said so. He said he'd only heard it second hand and wouldn't swear to it..."

"For God's sake! But let's talk about you and your project." I find a bag of Cheetos in my kitchen box, and Maddie reaches for a handful. We list about a dozen major tasks she has to complete in two months. It's more complicated than even I suspected.

"Okay," I say, "which ones are you doing right now?"

"All of them," she says, munching.

"No, you can't do it all at once; it'll kill you. Let's go through one at a time and see which have to be started now and which we can back off on a bit."

She smiles and throws a Cheeto at me.

Maddie didn't have to work her way through school; her father, Reese Davy, owns half of Connecticut. Okay, yeah, I Googled it. Why in hell Maddie chose to grub around in the dirt and mud for a chicken-shit mining company is beyond me. It's beyond her mother too, I learn over a beer and the rest of the Cheetos. Her mother wants her to give it up and come home. Apparently, the place in the Hamptons echoes since the old man walked out.

"Why did your Dad leave?" I ask.

"Oh, who knows, Harlan. Why do people leave?"

"Lots of reasons, it turns out." I pop another beer.

She looks at me curiously but doesn't ask the question on her lips. "I don't know." She drops her eyes. "Some catastrophe or another came along, and the world fell to pieces for them. I don't remember Dad saying good-bye."

She stands. I stand, too. "Good night, Maddie. Do you think you could stop by Bernie's number-one on your way?"

"Sure."

From the porch I watch her lights climb the switch-backs till they're out of sight. Maddie thinks some catastrophe came along and shook her world. I could have told her, that's not how life works. That is *catastrophism,* and it is too simplistic. James Hutton gave us instead the principle of *uniformitarianism*. Simply put, the same processes working today have, over time, produced all the vagaries of our world. It is elegant, but not so easy: *The present is the key to the past.* I didn't tell Maddie that before she left, but I will next time.

In my trunk of memories, in my tilted shack on this warm night of crickets and mosquitos, there are large gaps, long periods of time between packets of photos; even longer between keepsakes and trinkets. And that means just what you'd think: the photos were taken of the good times; the mementos are of the special times. The times *not* photographed are the every-days that fade one into another; not standing out; not meriting remembrance. For that reason, it is the commonplace times that are so hard to grasp and to gauge. Unlike the boisterous parties, the picnics, and weddings, the in-between days of uniformity hide behind veils of time. But those are the very days that define us.

The traverse will be a long one tomorrow. But this is the time of year to be doing your long hikes; the weather is warm and clear, and the daylight lasts all day long and then some. You don't want to be out here when the weather turns bad, rushing to end things, struggling up the trails in a blowing rain, hoping for a blanket of snow finally to justify your disinclination. Autumn is still a ways off, but the chill is coming.

†

Jolene stepped into the street, picking a route where the puddles were small enough to cross. The mud sucked at her boots, and she struggled to be patient. The rain and sleet of October had taken it seemed like forever to have their way and blow the trees bare. She had stared out the kitchen window and her heart had ached to think the clean, deep snows of winter were still months away. But the rain had stopped overnight, and she'd forced herself to get up and wash and do her hair and put on a decent dress. She'd stepped out into a glint of morning sun only to be caught in another damned drizzle.

She had carried a letter to the post office in Stibnite almost a month earlier, and that was the last time she'd talked with Farrell. She'd written to UCLA's Dean of Admissions to ask a few questions about policies and tests, and things. Rain and road repairs had restricted traffic over Lookout Ridge since then, even if Ray hadn't insisted she stay tight because of the labor troubles. Harly hadn't come around either—he was too busy to sit and chat with a bored housewife. And now she'd received a reply to her letter, and she had to think how to deal with that, too.

But not today; today she just needed a cake. It was Myrna's birthday—she'd almost let it slip by—and Jolene needed to make a nice cake. She jumped the brown runoff rilling the road, but the move was too sudden, and it splashed mud onto her stockings and hem. She twisted and raised her foot out of the mud, and nearly lost her balance, stumbling, horrified, onto an island of hard sand. With a few more leaps she made it to the narrow boardwalk, but without the hopeful smile she'd worn leaving the house.

"Why can't someone in this town dig a Goddamned ditch?" she said aloud. "Or find a can of paint?" The walls of the buildings along the entire street were bare wood or tarpaper over bare wood. "Would a coat of paint suffocate the town of Cinnabar?"

The grocery door opened as she walked up to it, and Ellen hurried out, nearly bumping into Jolene. "Good morning," Jolene managed.

"Maybe to some folks it is!" Ellen didn't even look back but stomped away leaving Jolene watching from the doorway. Jolene took off her coat as she entered, shook it off outside, and hung it on the coatrack by the fire.

"You weren't at the funeral this morning," Hattie explained to her. "Wasn't Millie a saint, though." Hattie was waiting for Mister Baughman to wrap her groceries.

Baughman drew in an unhappy breath, when he saw Jolene, and went back to knotting his strings. Two other ladies were in the small store, but they said nothing to Jolene.

"I just need a few groceries; the weather's been so awful, hasn't it? What about Millie?" Jolene asked.

THE RECLAMATION

"Well, it was her funeral this morning and all."

"Millie Collier?"

"Of course Millie Collier," Hattie said. "You knew she fell ill some time ago."

"No. I... I've not been out and around town recently."

Hattie buttoned her coat as she talked and drew up her collar. "But nobody expected you to be there, given the circumstances."

"I don't understand, Hattie, what circumstances?"

"Well, I mean Millie practically worked herself to death after Pete got fired."

Baughman stood behind the counter watching, arms folded, looking over his glasses. "Do you want us to stand close, so you can hear better?" Jolene asked him. To Hattie and loud enough for Baughman and the rest of the store to hear she said, "Ray didn't fire Pete Collier; the mine fired him. Ray didn't have any choice in the matter."

"Fired him for unionizing, though of course he wasn't. All I know is what I hear, but they say Ray didn't like that Pete complained about the extra hours and the conditions in the mine."

Jolene stood with eyes and fists closed tightly. She drew short, measured breaths. "Well, I'm sorry about Millie," she managed.

"You know she was so ill all these two weeks; it was pneumonia of course, and she never had a strong frame." Hattie took her packages from Baughman and stepped toward the door. "Millie was a saint of a woman, Jolene."

"She was, yes. A true saint."

Tears welled up in Jolene's eyes. Hattie noticed. "It's been such a long while since I've seen you out in the town. Have you been feeling well?"

"We're all fine, thank you for asking." She found a kleenex in her pocket and wiped her eyes and nose. "I've been hoping for a break in the weather. It looks like I may have over-played my hand."

"It has surely been a difficult autumn," Hattie agreed. "It seems the leaves had barely started turning before they were stripped from the trees." She hesitated. "But when God takes from us he always brings something in return."

Jolene said nothing. Hattie tried, "I haven't seen you and Ray at church recently. It doesn't hurt a thing to sit in fellowship and learn the bible teachings. The Lord knows there's hardly a grace said in this sinful town."

"Ray says grace at home, and you know Axel wouldn't let us go un-shepherded." Jolene wiped her nose again and stuffed the kleenex back in her pocket.

"Axel is a God-fearing man," Hattie conceded. "But if that were enough, I wonder what we would need with churches at all?"

"Well, Hattie, where else would we train saints?"

"Amen. So, I'll see you all on Sunday?"

"Look for us at the front," Jolene said. She did her best to smile and nod as Hattie filled the doorway. The other ladies decided to shop another time and walked out behind her.

When they had gone, Jolene took a deep breath and said, "Jim, I need a dozen eggs, five pounds of sugar, five pounds of butter, sack of flour..."

"I can only let you have three eggs. There's a war on. And I've no butter at all this week and maybe this month."

"Yes, I've heard something about a war," Jolene said. She stood staring at the floor, her arms straight at her side. She bobbed her head once and asked, "Can I make a cake with shortening?"

"I believe you can."

"Then give me a big can of shortening, some vanilla if you have it, molasses, and anything else you can spare."

Jim Baughman wrapped her groceries as she put her coat back on. With an inkling of pleasure, he said, "You go on and get home now, Jolene."

"I'm sorry; what was that?"

"Jolene, there's going to be some doin's in the town today, or so I've heard. None of my business, but it might be better if you weren't walking around with a lot of angry people about."

THE RECLAMATION

Jolene handed Baughman her stamps and cash, took up her packages, and stepped outside. She noticed some people a good way off and heading in the other direction, toward the mill. With packages in hand she managed to button her coat and wrap a knit scarf over her head. "Colder than the hubs of hell," she said to no one. She took a step toward home, hesitated, then turned instead to face the commotion. Two blocks up the street streams of men gathered into a body. They appeared to be led by a tall bear of a man. Jolene stared for the longest time but couldn't be sure it was Harly in front.

Halfway down the block she was nearly run into by four men coming out of an alley. A tall, wiry man appeared to be leading the others. He stepped her way and started to say, "It's not safe here…" He stopped, though, and set his hands on his hips.

Jolene held her packages by the strings and said nothing, but studied the man, her lips slightly parted. He wore a tweed coat belted at the waist, corduroy trousers, and polished, though now muddy, high-top shoes. She wondered if one was expected to dress for an uprising, but then understood that he must have dressed for Millie's funeral, and not changed. His hands were rough, and his shaved face was pasty from underground work. He and the others likely worked for Ray. "Why is it not safe?" she asked.

"That's all Pete Collier asked, too, and he lost his job over it." A solid fireplug of a man thrust his hands in his pockets and nodded stiffly.

"It was your old man who fired him," the wiry man said, "so what do you mean by asking such a thing?"

"Collier? Ray didn't fire him or anybody; the mine hires and fires. Ray works in the mine just like you do. He has no more choice than you."

The fireplug said, "Pete sat home and watched his wife work herself to death."

"It isn't true. About Ray, I mean. I'm sorry about Millie, she was… a saint." Jolene tried to make some room between herself and the two men crowding from behind. "Harly Pruitt comes to your meetings. He's there in front, isn't he?" She craned to see down the street to where a phalanx of workers marched around the bend toward the mine portal. "Ask Harly, he'll tell you what happened."

A third man in a dirty denim coat turned and spit into the street. "Harly delivers a lot of shinola but not much else. Pruitts stick together is what I figure." He raised his cap and pushed back his graying hair. "Fuckin' Ray fired Pete for less than his own brother gets away with."

The circle closed a bit tighter. Jolene cocked her head, trying to see into their eyes, but most of the men wouldn't meet hers. "It isn't true; I can see you know it. But it doesn't matter anymore, does it?"

"What ain't technical true is true enough when people start dying," the man in the dirty coat said. He shrugged and swung his head toward the mill, signaling the others to go, but they weren't ready yet to leave.

Jolene stood a moment, trembling in the cold drizzle. "You're angry. I know what that's like," she said. "You feel naked and outraged, full of hate. I can see…"

The men laughed at her. "Sounds like you've been studying under Professor Hammond," the man behind her said. "Day and night, I hear," said another.

Jolene wheeled and looked from one to the other. "I don't like how that sounds." She tried to step through the men. Tears started in her eyes and she drew her arms and packages close.

"We supposed to feel sorry for you?" the fireplug asked. "Ain't we all done for you? Who do you think was out front looking for your damned kid last year? It was Pete Collier every day."

Jolene stepped forward and slapped the man. He grabbed her coat collar and swung her around, sending her packages flying. But instead of slapping her back, he pinned her arm in the crook of his, and pulled the coat sleeve back, exposing the red and ragged scars on her wrist for the others to see. "This is what I'm talking about, fellas, right here! They're all so proud and pretty, aren't they? Well this here's just under the surface."

Jolene yanked her arm back and twisted free, stumbling and falling backward into the mud of the street. She laid in the mud uncertain what had happened until the cold and wet began to seep through her clothing. But still she laid a moment staring, open mouthed. Directly above her the sky roiled wet and black, not softened by distance or tree lines; there was nothing at all between her and the storm. She struggled onto her elbows, drew her feet up, and waited as the four men slowly circled, their boots sucking loudly in the mud.

The man in the denim jacket stuck his hand out to her. "Well, come on," he said. Jolene shook her head and looked around for her purchases—the brown paper parcels Baughman had tied neatly with string. They too lay in the mud, and out of her reach, and she cried out because it was ruined: Myrna's birthday was ruined! She felt suddenly sick with shame for even thinking of making a Goddamned birthday cake. It was a stupid idea, and she sucked in her breath for the shame, then just as quickly felt a stab of anger at being made to feel like that.

The lower edges of the clouds were tattered, with fingers stretching down almost to the ground as if you could reach up and rip them down. Jolene's shoulders began to convulse, and she laughed out loud at the absurdity of lying in the mud of the street and feeling ashamed not of that, nor even at having her private pain put on display, but for wanting a Goddamned cake she didn't even have the butter to make. She laughed, and then cussed herself aloud for laughing, but kept laughing. "It doesn't matter," she said, and laughed again.

"We supposed to feel sorry for you?" The stocky man asked again. The clattering of rocks on tin siding echoed from down the street.

The wiry man swung his head toward the commotion at the mill and took a red bandana from his pocket. Tying the bandana around his neck, he looked down at Jolene and spit in the mud. "Crazy as a fucking loon!" he said.

Jolene sank into the cold mud and the tattered sky. The four men turned and walked toward the protest. She stayed where she'd fallen until the laughter turned to sobbing and her body trembled from the cold. She rose, then, and leaving the packages where they lay in the mud, headed home, wading through slurry down the middle of the street, making no effort to shy from the eyes that watched from curtained windows. Her muddied dress clung to her legs as she walked, and the drizzle grew to a steady rain that chilled her to the bone.

19

The waitress looked me over when she brought my hotcakes and eggs, as though she'd never seen me before. Earl came by and filled my coffee, then made the rounds with the pot. Maddie is sitting with her Forest Service guy, what's his name, Don. I sat down a couple tables away.

It's okay, I guess. We're all grownups. I do call the junior staff kids, but they're really grownups. I don't know about breakfast together, though. At the least, she should be concerned about his career, because he's the one who'll be questioned as to his objectivity when our applications are reviewed. It's his skin, not Maddie's or mine, although it doesn't look so professional for Maddie either. I wonder if Andy knows they're seeing each other. And that puts me in a bad position, too, because I should let him know.

The ranger guy stands up to go, and he's about medium tall but not very solid. A little pumping of iron wouldn't be wasted on him. But his face is pleasant enough; it's shaved at least. He shakes her hand as he leaves, and that's a good touch, anyway. It lends a certain deniability to their having showered together.

"In from the wilderness?" Maddie asks, and I almost drop my damned fork. She is standing right there smirking down at me when I look up from my eggs.

"What? I like hotcakes and eggs."

"I need to talk to you about Tracey," she says, pulling out a chair and sitting.

"What about her?"

While I'm looking at Maddie, Earl comes over and he sits down, too.

Maddie says, "You've had her stuck in the core shack for almost two months. She'd like to see the sun, hear some birds, maybe learn something about the project before her internship ends."

"Tracey? Small girl, short brown hair? She's the one who wears earphones when I'm explaining the geology to her."

"She's real sorry she did that, Harlan. She was really looking forward to learning something this summer."

"You can learn a lot in a core shack if you apply yourself." I take another mouthful of breakfast, but Maddie is still waiting, so I swallow and explain, "Every time I tried to say something to her I had to wait till she pulled a plug out of her ear. I got tired of having to annoy her so much. I figured in the core shack she could play her music till pebbles bounce off the hills."

Maddie glances Earl's way, and Earl says, "Tracey's a good kid, Harlan, she's real sweet. Hell, she's still young. Still learning."

Maddie nods at what Earl says.

"So, what's this about?" I ask.

"I'd like her to work with me on the stream sampling. I could really use the help, and we have some new blood, just came in, to help in the core shack."

"Fine."

"Fine?"

"Fine. Why even ask me?"

She thinks I don't notice when she shakes her head Earl's way as she gets up to go, her eyes no doubt fixed on heaven. The junior geologists at the next table all turn and look busy as my glance sweeps over, and they pay their bills and get out quickly, too.

"Well, Christ!" I say to Earl.

"Oh hell, Harlan, who knows about kids these days."

The new assays were not in when I checked at the office, but I ended up wasting most of the day there anyway. I had just enough time to check out the new guys at the core shack and make the rounds of the drilling before it was time to head back to Cinnabar and start dinner.

While at the office dealing with the mail I also got some 'met' data from Maddie. Maddie has compiled the meteorological records for this part of Idaho going back to 1932. She uses them to calculate a water-balance, and to predict the impacts the mine would have on stream flows and springs. Her data also help me to understand just what in hell Jolene and the others went through back then, the kind of weather they had to put up with through the years.

I guess the past can also be a key to the past.

†

The rains of October 1943 gave over to a bare, dry freeze. The house was cold, and Jolene was sitting in bed in her nightgown when she heard Ray's boots climbing the unlit stairs. She slipped the book under the bed as he stepped into the room.

"What's that?" he asked. He stood over her, put his hand on her, and stroked her shoulder.

Jolene turned away and replied, "It's a book. I was reading a little is all."

"You're always reading, so why did you stick it under the bed?" His eyes were watery, and his words a little slurred. He'd been at the Cattail since end of shift.

She didn't answer, so he reached under the bed. The box he pulled out contained half a dozen books. "They're books," he said.

"Yes. That's what I said."

Ray read the titles aloud. "Algebra and Geometry, Basic Chemistry, History of Western Civilization, English Literature… What the hell are these?" He held a couple books out and waited for an answer.

"They're what you think they are, baby," she said. They're books. It was going to be a surprise."

He looked down, puzzled, and then cocked his head at an angle. "Yeah. A surprise of what sort?"

"I'm just studying. I'm studying to take a test to get a high school equivalence diploma."

"Why would you spend all your time doing that? Am I going to get dinner tonight?"

"I made macaroni. I put it away, but I'll heat it up for you. Because I never got my high school diploma. We got married and I hadn't finished my last year." Jolene rose from bed and took her robe from the hook.

"You're still on about college, aren't you?" He stepped around to face her, holding a couple of the books now against his forehead. "Goddamn it, Jo, you've got to be realistic."

"You're always telling me what's realistic. Why don't I ever get to say?"

She put on the robe and reached for the books, but he held them away from her.

"Because it's me bustin' my ass just to keep a roof over our heads and food on the table—not that it's been making it to the table so damned often."

"There's more to life."

"Yeah, the best things are free. But the necessary things cost money, and it's me who has to work for it." He threw the books on the bed.

Jolene said, "I'm not asking you to work any harder. It's the same for me to have a high school diploma than not to. You got your diploma; why can't I?"

"We know what's really going on, don't we?" he said. The room was cool, but the liquor made him sweat, and he bit at his words. It angered him that his tongue was thick with drink and his speech slurred. "The real point is you aren't ever gonna be happy being a low-class miner's wife."

"I'm not a low-class miner's wife, Ray. You're a supervisor, and you make sure everyone knows you are."

"That's a problem, now?"

"You make a good living for us, and the whole town knows not to mess with you."

THE RECLAMATION

Ray leaned with his hands against the wall and rubbed his temples against his upper arms. "You're worried what the town thinks, all of a sudden? You're always off with Goddamned Fairy Hammond. Do you worry how that looks? You get ideas in your head that you're better than the whole town."

"Better? I can't even walk…"

"And I put my ass on the line every day, and I have to go down the hole with these people and stay a step ahead while you're frisking around. You're with Hammond all day," he insisted, "and then you hide his Goddamned books under our Goddamned bed."

"Oh, for God's sake, Ray. They're books, not rubbers!"

He flipped his arm out and up and clipped Jolene's jaw with the back of his hand. It was a swift motion with only the weight of his arm behind it, but it lifted her from her feet and she stumbled back through the bedroom door. She landed at the top of the stairs, her head and torso sliding downward, legs flailing. She grabbed for the banister and stopped herself. She'd almost fallen; another few inches and she'd have rolled to the bottom of the stairs.

She tried to right herself, but her left arm was twisted under her and she could only hold on with her right and stare through the banisters to the dark wood floor below. She closed her eyes and felt Ray's boot land on the tread beside her head. Letting go of the banister, she raised her hand and felt herself begin to fall. Ray caught her hand in his, and in one motion pulled her back, lifted her, and rolled her into his arms.

"I'm sorry, Jo. I'm so sorry, baby."

"You never used to hit me."

"I'm so sorry." He cradled her in his arms like a doll and sat with her on the top step. She pulled her arms in tight and buried her face in her hands. Ray held her at the top of the steps in a triangle of dim light from their bedroom door, rocking slowly like they were dancing. The house and home calmed down, and the neighborhood quieted but for a dog in the distance and the ball mill turning and grinding away. They stayed in the bedroom's glow until a half moon rose in the small stairway window.

"Jo?"

"I'm right here," she whispered over the scraping of the mill.

"When this war is over I'll take you to California the way we set out. I promise, babe, I'll take care of you."

They'd met at the fair in Boise. Ray was tall and handsome with a man's pay in his pocket, and Jolene had let him teach her to dance. They'd struck for California on a cool November morning with mist lying in the valleys and clouds hanging red in the sky.

Jolene stared at her half of the moon until her eyes burned and she had to turn her face from it. Ray's Chevy had broken down in Yuba City just three days out, and the preacher and a new carburetor took most of their cash. Jobs were scarce in the Valley with the harvest just in, but there was good work at Grand Coulee, they heard, and it didn't matter it was in the other direction, because they were together.

She rose, pulled her robe around her, and stepped past him. "Where are you going?" he asked.

"I'll warm some macaroni for you."

"You don't need to do that, babe. Come on to bed."

"You've still got to eat, Ray."

20

Our field office is a storefront on Stibnite's Main Street. It's something of a functional mess, with personal field gear piled in corners, rock and core samples lying everywhere, and maps and drill-hole cross-sections taped to walls. I stopped trying to keep a field office tidy thirty years ago. Computers and printers, copiers and small kitchen appliances clutter a lot of the table tops and are connected by tangled cables and wires into too-few wall outlets. There didn't used to be so many wires.

 I've noticed earplug cords lying around, and even some small speakers on the tables, but I don't remember hearing music in the office. Maddie grins when I mention it, and shrugs. Several of the young hands grab what they need and head out into the field as I look around. The few who remain seem pretty busy.

 Mike Lovitt appears to be letting his hair and beard grow out for the summer. I wonder if it's related to having—or maybe by now not having—a girlfriend. Mike is putting together a 3-D computer model of the drilling intercepts, and he rotates the image for me this way and that, and cuts slices through it to show how all of the folded limestone beds, contact zones, and cross-cutting faults fit together. He's done a good job compiling it all so far, and it seems like a useful tool, I tell him, for visualizing the veins and contacts and whatnot. The truth is, I prefer the old paper maps, but I don't say so to Mike. I don't want to break his heart any worse than it might already be.

 One of the young interns brings me the full reports from the assay laboratory, and I thank her and sit down with my flat maps and plot up the numbers. The assays include significantly more gold than we expected. The increase is remarkable, really, and exceeds even our more optimistic projections. As before, most of the gold shows up in the intercepts along the Oblique trend—a lot of high-grade material.

The odd thing is, all of the gold recorded in the old government reports is commensurate with the low grades in the mercury veins. There is nothing reported—not an ounce of gold—to account for what had to have been mined from the Oblique drift.

I call Maddie and Mike over and show them my analysis. He says he can plot it up in his 3-D computer model, and I tell him that's exactly what I need him to do, and the sooner the better.

"But I see what you mean," Maddie says about my gold calculations. "It doesn't add up. Somebody was making more gold than they were reporting. That's great news for Castle Mining Company, though, right?"

"Hmm? Yeah, this is... it's good."

"Don't sound so jubilant."

It's looking like a pretty heavy afternoon storm, and I should get my headlight fixed because the road back down the ridge when it's stormy is not easy to follow with just the one light.

And Maddie's right, I should be happier about the assay results. The thing of it is this: The War Production Board kept the mines of Stibnite and Cinnabar operating year-round to produce antimony, tungsten, and mercury. Munitions and armament factories around the country depended on those metals. The government's men and money kept the roads open to the district and maintained the power lines strung through the canyons. Government trucks kept food, supplies, coal, and oil rolling in, all to keep the men in the mines swinging their picks day and night. The Bureau of Mines understood small quantities of gold would be produced as by-product; metallurgically, some gold was unavoidable. But gold mines across the country had been shut down to focus on the production of war materiel. The mining of gold for the sake of gold distracted from the war effort and was outlawed.

THE RECLAMATION

†

Ray found Harly at the bar waiting, as they'd arranged. Ray had come from dinner with Jolene, but Harly hadn't stopped before coming to the Cattail, so he'd already had a couple drafts. Ray sat on a stool and the bartender brought him a beer. The place was half full, but almost entirely with young men. It was a week night, and there were no dates and no single women. There was no music and little conversation, just the clinking of glasses, the scraping of heavy chairs on the plank floor, and the thunk of beer mugs on tables. Harly and Ray were given room at the bar to speak privately.

"Your men aren't keeping up with the advances," Ray said to Harly through the back-bar mirror. "The face at thirteen south has sat idle for two shifts because the shoring work isn't done. Two full shifts."

"Had no timbers," Harly said. "No timbers 'cause no trucks, no trucks 'cause the mill had to haul in a new grinding circuit. We had no trucks most of last week."

"You're responsible for the timbering. You're supposed to have your tools and materials. No excuses."

"I'm supposed to have my trucks, too, no excuses. But I didn't."

"I'm serious, Harly."

"I can get serious, too, Ray. If you think I'm fucking up, then replace me. But don't talk down at me like some kind of Goddamned company man."

"And you can get off my ass about that, too. You and Dad both. I'm doing a job, making a living, and I'm tired of getting crapped on because I do it right. And Dad doesn't seem to mind the Company so much he won't live in a company house or pick up a company pension check."

"He earned it," Harly said.

"And I earn my check. You'd be earning yours, too, if we could get in to advance on thirteen-south." Ray drank from his beer, lit a smoke, and turned from the mirror to face Harly directly. "I'll get your damned trucks back. Tomorrow morning."

The lights were kept down low and the sunset burned its way in through the door left open for the tobacco smoke. The room darkened and lightened as large men came in or out through the rich, golden light. Boots thumped on the boards and men's voices laughed aloud to coarse humor.

Ray snuffed out his smoke. "Harly, how does Jolene seem to you?" he asked.

"She seems happy. Doesn't she seem okay to you?"

"I don't know anymore. How do you like that?" He looked at his reflection in the back bar. "She's spending a lot of time with Junior Hammond. People are talking."

"Who's talking?" Harly set his beer down and scowled. "I'm with her and Farrell most of the time. When I'm not they just sit at the café and talk about books, and that's all there is to it. There's none of that other shit going on."

"Nothing's going on now, but maybe he's got designs on her?"

"It's nothing like that." Harly nodded to the bartender for another and took a handful of peanuts from the basket on the bar.

Ray said, "He's putting all sorts of ideas in her head."

Harly laughed. "Jolene is more than capable of her own ideas. If you're talking about the college thing, it's harmless. It gives her something to dream about when the days get short and the weather goes to hell on her. Let her keep dreaming and she'll be better off. Really. Trust me."

Someone put a nickel in the jukebox and loud, tinny music broke the spell of the place. A couple dozen men shifted uncomfortably. Ray turned away from Harly, pushed his fingers through his hair, and studied through the mirror the crowd behind him. It was a cowboy tune on the jukebox, probably Gene Autry, and it annoyed the men who wanted to talk and smoke and drink. Ray called for another couple of beers.

"I want to take Jolene away when this is done; just get the hell out of here," Ray said. "There won't be a lot of jobs right after the war, so it'll take money." He waited for an answer, but Harly sat and drank from his beer.

"Harly?" Ray started again. "You said you knew a way to make some money. Some real money, and there wouldn't be no laws broken. Is that still out there? It's legal, right?"

"I can't say legal or not; I'm not a lawyer. But nobody gets hurt by it." Harly never liked the song: *South of the Border*.

"If it ain't stealing and it ain't hurting nobody," Ray asked. "What's the money for?"

"It's for doing what you do, and nothing else." Harly laid his arm on the bar and turned to Ray. "You're a miner. All you have to do for a share is be a miner and don't try to be anything more than what you are. You don't try to be an engineer and tell them what heading you're on, and you don't try to be a geologist and tell them what minerals you see or what vein you're in. You keep your head down where it's supposed to be, and you don't ask questions, and you make sure everyone on your crew does the same."

"It isn't caught up with that socialist bullshit?"

Harly laughed. "Same outcome, I hope; different means." He glanced up and caught Ray's eye in the mirror. "Nobody gets hurt."

"This something your friend Farrell thought up?"

"No. And we're not such good friends. It's just something a couple of the engineers brought to me."

"Fucking engineers." Ray exhaled and dropped his head. Harly stared ahead with his lips pursed and worked the shells off some peanuts.

The song ended. Ray said under his breath, "Okay, fuck. What is it?"

The two of them talked quietly for a while longer as the light in the room began to dim and the men in the crowd got louder with liquor. Ray rose and leaned his hands on the bar.

Harly said, "I'll see you at thirteen-south tomorrow, mid-shift, after I get my crew on the trucks. I'll have a friend with me."

Ray nodded and stretched. He slapped Harly on the shoulder, finished his bottom swallow of beer, and walked over and said hello to a couple of men at a nearby table. He walked out through the last of the sun's rays and returned to Jolene under roiling clouds.

Harly sat alone at the bar after Ray left. He grunted or nodded to the men who said hello or clapped him on the back but didn't turn and didn't open himself to conversation. He was left to sit alone, staring into the mirror of the back bar.

The crowd didn't stay long. It was a week night and most of the men had early shifts in the morning. The Cattail by dark had quieted to just glasses clinking and the occasional scrape of a chair. A big man came in the door, dressed in slacks and a pressed shirt. He sat next to Harly and ordered a beer.

"How did it go?" the man asked.

"He'll do it," Harly replied into the back mirror. "There's no funny business in him."

The man talked a little more, finished his beer, and left. Harly switched from beer to whiskey and stared into the mirror until the bartender helped him out the door at midnight.

Ray waited for Harly in the main adit near Forty-eight hundred west, stepping aside for ore cars as they passed. It had been a couple days since they'd talked at the Cattail. Harly showed up and asked why in hell he waited here, under the worst ground in the mine.

"We want to drift on this trend," Ray told Harly. He looked around as he spoke.

Harly swept his lamp beam over the heavily-timbered ribs, along the straining solid planks and the beams holding up the crumbling back. He laughed. "You want to advance a drift in this shit?"

"Yeah, the geologists say it's a horsetail extension off the Midas Vein. We want to drift into it from right here and see where it goes."

"This ain't the Midas Vein, and it ain't no fucking horsetail. It's a cross-cutting shear, and it's pure shit-rock."

THE RECLAMATION

"You're a geologist, now, Harly? Goddamn, give me some of them books to read." Ray tossed his cigarette into the side ditch. "It's your racket," he said quietly.

Harly stared over Ray's shoulder. Underground, a miner will not look directly at you when he talks to you but will look away, so his lamp beam doesn't blind you. Words are rarely spoken directly, then, but downward or to the side. If a miner looks you in the eye when he speaks, he does it out of the corner of his eye. The habit carries over to the surface, and because of it miners are thought by others to speak deceitfully. Ray caught Harly's eye and pointed back with his finger. His voice wavered a little. "This is what the guy told me. We're gonna drift into this horsetail. We need you to shore it. Make a plan."

"Whatever," Harly said, "but drifting into it from here is suicide. We should move a hundred feet farther in and cross cut to it from the side."

"No, we don't want to cross cut."

"Why the hell not? It's the only way to start a safe heading. If we come in from where we're standing, we'll cut the fractures at too low of an angle. We'll lose what vertical support we have, and rock'll just explode out of the back. We'll lose the main adit, guaranteed."

"Aren't you a Goddamned genius? Make it work."

"I'll build you a Boulder Dam if you want, Ray, but it'll take a month—at least a month, if there's enough timber in the hills to do it. "We need to approach in some solid rock, then enter the bad rock at a cleaner angle."

Ray said, "Fuck it then. Drop to the outside a hundred feet and start a shallow cut there. We'll drift along the Midas trend and swing into the horsetail from that direction. It won't look like a cross cut. You can timber that, right?"

"Yeah, I can, but that's a lot of extra mining. Wouldn't it be a lot easier to just…"

"Harly, are you a geologist, or are you an engineer now?"

Harly looked away and spit. "I'm a miner."

"Then do your fuckin' mining."

Roger Howell

    Harly watched his brother walk away toward the portal, watched until the cap lamp disappeared around a distant bend of the tunnel. He stayed a while to size up the job.

21

Maddie has been out with Tracey taking stream samples for a couple of days, but today Tracey wasn't feeling well. I didn't want her to work all alone; it's pretty big country. We've been filling suites of bottles above every major confluence. We worked off of a good Forest Service road along the main stem of Monumental Creek, which saved a lot of time, but in the larger tributaries we've had to hike up some long valleys to sample at the main forks.

Maddie leads the way back out to the pickup, and we enter a cool, deep dell as the sun drops low. It is a narrow rock-walled ravine with a damp, leaf-strewn bottom. Tall, thick aspens grow sky high around me, and the trees and rock walls darken the way down by the stream. Except it's not dark. The low sun shines in the tops of the yellow aspens, which reach just above the rim of the ravine. The dell where I stand glows with the warm gold of the aspen crowns. I sit to rest and to enjoy the unusual light and try to remember if I've ever seen anything like it.

Maddie brings me up. She's had to walk back to find me and is rightly impatient. "Stay a while," I suggest and nod to a smooth rock a few feet away. "When have you ever seen light like this?"

She looks around and seems to notice for the first time what she's been walking through. She smiles and turns a slow circle. We don't say anything for a few minutes. When she speaks she asks me the oddest thing: "Who is Carly?"

"Carly is my daughter. Why would you ask that?"

"You called me Carly the other day." She looks me over curiously. "You have a daughter?"

"Why is that so hard to believe? She's a few years older than you. She has dark hair, too; a real pretty girl. Woman now, of course."

"How long has it been since you've seen her?"

"Eight years, nine months. It was Christmas at her mother's house."

"What came between you?"

"Well, I did. I mean, you know me pretty well now, right?"

Maddie is quiet again, and that's okay because the light is so beautiful here in the dell. There isn't a breath of wind to shake the leaves.

"I used to take her hiking, when she was younger," I say. "We had great times when she was a kid."

"My dad took me hiking in the Adirondacks. I miss those times, though I always thought it was a pain in the ass at the time."

"Yeah, time has a way of doing that. Time smooths over a lot of rough spots until we just remember the parts that made us smile." I take out my water bottle and drink the last couple of swallows, and Maddie does the same.

"And her mother?" she asks.

"Susan. She's great, really. She lives in Tucson now, a few miles from Carly. We're divorced, of course."

"I'm sorry, it's hard to picture you ever married."

"Twice," I admit before I can stop myself. It always brings the inevitable questions.

"Twice? Was Susan the first or the second?"

"Both." I sigh; Maddie gives me exactly the stare I expect.

"We got a divorce but then thought better of it and got married again. Things fell apart for good a few years after that."

"I'm sorry," Maddie says again. We watch the ravine mellow to deep amber while a warm, up-canyon breeze mixes with a cool down draft and rustles the leaves above us.

"So, let me get the score right," she says, now with a tight-lipped grin. "With just one woman you've failed at two marriages and a divorce?" Her eyes close and she looks like she has to sneeze, as hard as she's pinching her face between her hands.

"Well, I guess a cynical person could put it like that," I say. "Are you laughing? This isn't grist for humor."

"I'm not laughing," she says, laughing.

"These are people's lives we're talking about."

"Really, I'm not laughing. Give me a second." She chokes back a laugh.

"Real people with real feelings." I reach my hand to her. "Help me up!"

But she has tears in her eyes. "You're right," she forces out, pressing her fist to her lips. She asks, "And so far, the second divorce…?"

"Appears to be a success, thank you! Help me off this rock, you Dartmouth shitheel."

We got back from our hike just in time. The rain has started up again, and it hammers now on the tin roof and blows in through the open chimney hole. But the plastic around the windows still holds. I don't really have a plan if the plastic tears away. For now, the room stays reasonably dry.

†

The snow was plowed down the middle of the street, leaving a canyon between walls piled so high fences were no longer visible. A few cars were buried on the sides of the road and had been for a month. The bulldozer had to weave between them to keep the main streets open. A trench led Jolene from her covered porch through the snow and down into the dark, pre-dawn street. The bulldozer was working on the next block, and bright reflections and black shadows shifted as it moved. The frigid air hung heavy with diesel exhaust.

There had been so much snow by mid-December that even trampled by foot traffic the trails down the side streets were packed four or five feet above the ground. Her backpack shifted and almost threw her down as she climbed back up from the main street into the side street at the intersection. The snow had been sliding from tin roofs for four weeks and piling up the sides of her neighbors' houses, so now only faint glows emanated from buried windows, and Jolene had to pick her way carefully by starlight.

The packing and rutting of the snow lessened near the edge of town, and there Jolene set her snowshoes down and stepped up onto them and strapped her boots in. She walked out of town in the early darkness as she had so many times, climbing the ridge this time without the glow of a sunrise. There was no sunburst to greet her at the crest, either; the sky lightened just enough to show the trees in silhouette. Jolene didn't pause on the ridge, but pushed on through the deep powder, found the game trail, and watched hard for and turned onto her blazed trap line.

She saw the ghostly white mist rising from the seep before the cabin appeared out of the gloom. The drifts were deep around the cabin, but the wind had blown a well in the snow on the front side, and it took her only half an hour to dig out the door.

A yellow light was soon glowing in the open door of the stove and flickering around the dark cabin, and for an hour or more Jolene stared into the fire, letting darkness close in her vision and her chest ache until she thought her heart would stop. She'd yelled at Ray until the neighbors' lights had come on. She'd made him cry, she remembered, and Jolene cried now to think of it.

He'd lied to her and broken his word, and she didn't know the man anymore—the man she slept with and for whom she cooked and cleaned. She didn't recognize the man who'd swept her out of Boise and who'd held her hand in the tall grass above Coulee City with the summer wind nearly tearing their shadows away. Nor the man—the boy really—who'd stolen apples for her when she craved them, driving through the orchards of Wenatchee when her dreams were his, too, and all her hopes for the future were alive and kicking.

They'd fought all evening. Jolene had found the gold in a sock in the closet. Almost a dozen metallic yellow buttons spilled out onto the bed, each about as big around as a quarter and flat on the bottom

THE RECLAMATION

but rounded up like a gleaming caramel drop. The buttons burned in the lamplight, and Ray had rushed over and scooped them up.

"Stay out of my Goddamned stuff!" He'd grabbed her by the arm and spun her to face him, but let her go just as suddenly.

"What's it about, Ray?" she'd asked, her voice shaking.

"It's for you, baby. It's to take you wherever you want to go. We can get a new start in California, and you can go to college if you want to. This is our chance!"

Their chance! Jolene stuffed another piece of wood in the firebox and watched until her face burned, and she had to shield it in her hands. Grand Coulee had fallen away in the mirror and they had their chance again on the coast, but in stormy La Push, crossing the Cascades in midwinter with two-year-old Myrna on her lap. And even in that mossy gray port the three of them found a warm fire, and so much love she could have burst. The war came, and he promised he would stay and take care of her and their child, if she would follow him and be satisfied and make a home. And then when it all crashed down, and she felt like she'd died and gone to hell he promised again he would make things right if she would just trust him—endure the pain and trust him.

The yellow flames fluttered and popped each time Jolene shoved wood into the stove. The stovepipe smoked as it warmed, and the roof timbers creaked. She had promised him, and she stayed in this dreary dark hole because they both had promised. Now to throw it all away, to break every promise for pieces of gold. She didn't come here for gold! *Did Myrna die for Goddamned gold?*

"It's horrible!" she'd yelled. "Nobody gives you hundreds of dollars for nothing. What do you do for it?"

"You don't know what you're talking about."

"I know what gold is about!" she'd shouted back. "I've panned it from the streams. Honestly!"

"Have you? You think I don't know you go up on Alec's claim? That's company land, Jolene. If I stole and cheated for this, then you stole and cheated too!"

She'd rushed at him then, and he'd pushed her back—just raised his arm to fend her off, and she'd fallen against the dresser and hit her head. There had been blood; just a little, but Ray was sick about it.

"Is this why you dragged us to this hell hole?" she'd shouted. "Is this what Myrna died for? Did you let our baby die so you could fill your pockets with gold?"

Ray had cried right in front of her. "Am I supposed to feel sorry for you?" she'd yelled at him. Ray, in the end, had slept on the davenport, and he woke to find Jolene getting her trappings together.

The coals shimmered red, and her head pounded where the dresser had broken the skin. It was all such a waste. She drank from her water and tried to eat but the food was tasteless to her. When her socks felt hot and dry she waxed her boots again and put them back on, then set the stove to burn slowly all day. She climbed her way back out into the deep snow and the frozen fog, and started up the line.

Two pine martens hung in her snares, twisting by their necks on gleaming wires, stiff and cold, their eyes frozen open and lips drawn back from small white teeth. Their paws hung, praying, in final submission.

The sun never showed itself as she worked up the line, but lurked behind broken, shifting clouds. It was all an awful waste. As she made her way back down the line Jolene sprang all of the traps, knocking away the bait.

The cabin was still warm when she re-entered. She hung the pair of martens on a nail, loaded up the firebox again, and set a big kettle of snow to melt. While the water warmed she ate what food she had left and drank a good deal of slushy water. She sat by the stove and tried to read a new magazine in the dim light of the small window, but it bored her, and she took instead a book from her pack. It was a volume of poetry, and she leafed through the pages: Whitman. She hadn't read poetry in weeks, but now she relaxed a little in the freedom of the verse and smiled at the images it brought to mind and at the carnal passion behind the images.

The water in the kettle steamed in the shaft of light, and Jolene put down her book and set the carcasses onto an oilcloth on the table. They were barely thawed; ready to skin. There was nothing more to it than cutting up a steak or killing and plucking a chicken, of course, and Jolene had helped to skin plenty of deer, but this was a more delicate task than any of those—more terribly personal. She separated the pelts from the flesh, making long, shallow cuts where the skin joined the muscle, lifting the skin away with each stroke, taking care not to let the knife cut up into the hide. The skinning laid bare a cold, pink musculature; strong, lithe bands tied by ligaments to the bones and the intricate joints.

She did not sing as she might have another day, but spoke in meter as she worked, softly, the unfettered words of Whitman. She set down her knife from time to time and read again from the book, marking the pages with her blooded fingers.

She had to work quickly now, because there was no light but the light of the fire and the winter day through the window, and both were dying away. When she'd finished, she cleaned her knife and rolled the bloody pelts up in a canvas bag, then washed her hands, dumped out the water, and threw out the carcasses for the foxes and badgers.

Jolene left the cabin as the pale, shrouded disc of the sun neared the far hills, and re-traced her steps to the game trail and up over the ridge. The snow had thawed slightly during the day and was quickly re-freezing, and her snowshoes crunched through the surface layer.

Cinnabar Valley was awash in the last purple of frozen dusk by the time she made her way to the edge of town. Wood smoke rose in straight white columns into the hazy glow, and yellow lights shined already from upper windows. She took off her snowshoes and walked down the narrow side street. A few people turned and watched her go by, but she nodded to no one and no one greeted her. The new blanket of snow where she had left her tracks that morning was rutted and trampled, and on the rooftops and over the buried gardens a light dusting of mill ash covered what had been fresh and white.

Ray met her at the door and helped her with her pack and her coat. He'd showered, and his hair was still wet and steaming in the bare light of the frosted mud room. He wore a clean wool shirt and denim jeans, and Jolene smiled a little as he shuffled around in unlaced snow boots. She let him hold her as she kicked off her boots. Their faces nearly touched, and she saw in his relief that she had found her way back to him. There was an uneasiness in his smile she hadn't paid attention to but now understood. It had already been such a cold, dark winter and his smile, once sure and proud, made her heart ache.

She squeezed his arm and whispered into his shoulder, *"These dark and twisting sullen ways, long wintry woods my heart can abide."*

She walked past him through the kitchen and started upstairs to compose a letter. She sighed as she climbed and spoke only to herself, *"But roads without distance, days unlit, words never sung send me ravening to windows bright."*

22

A breeze kicks up, and the smoke from Honorario's drillrig clears away, and Cinnabar opens directly below in her dark green hollow. The tin roof panels shine in the afternoon sun and glint as the wind lifts them. The banging and shrieking of the old place rises faintly to where I wait, and I wonder if there isn't some place midway, some mathematical halfway point between the rumbling machinery and the twisting, rusted tin where the air is calm and the hillsides are neither forested nor laid bare; where men work rich veins with sledge and shovel, dodge machinery and warm at smoking forges; where women call from doorways for their husbands to take care and watch for children who run wild and reckless. But the furnaces dim and the trucks slow and stop, and brush and bramble take root. The men pack up their families—their women and children still living—and carry them to new Cinnabars in other sad canyons. They drive away full of new hope or old resignation saying hurried goodbyes to a few friends, and eventually find new friends if they are lucky in that way. Some find new lovers. All make new dreams and endure new disappointments because that is how life is lived.

A plume of smoke carries on a change of wind, and the diesel engine races. Honorario's voice lifts above it all, shouting directions to his men.

Jolene moved along the boardwalk slowly, so the passing air wouldn't sting her face. Her breath froze in front of her and blinded her in a momentary sliver of sunlight. The frost on the walk had been scuffed by only a few boots, although it was already mid-morning. She closed her eyes and tried to remember when the trees had flickered yellow, when warm reds had tinged the tops of the grasses and she'd laughed and talked of poems and paintings. But it was no good; the soft glow of autumn was so far gone now she had barely a feeling for it. A deep freeze had taken hold after the heavy snows of December and had tightened its grip in the first weeks of 1944. Frozen fog hung low over the rooftops, just out of reach, shrouding the tops of buildings at the upper end of the street. In the other direction, just under the gray ceiling, three planes were parked in a narrow arc of sunlight.

Harly and Farrell were already seated at their table, and they rose to help her with her coat. She had to look down to see what it was she was wearing underneath. It was a wool sweater and house dress, disheveled but clean enough, worn over heavy winter boots. She accepted a cup of coffee with cream, managed a smile, and pushed back a mop of hair. The warm coffee made her shiver even in the heat of the wood stove, and she turned and watched out the window as the sky lost its scrap of light and the street darkened again.

Her eyes drooped, and she sipped from her cup as Farrell described the literary influences of their book, *Moby Dick*. She'd hated the book; Farrell's explanations all sounded wooden to her, and she couldn't engage at all. As she turned away, an elk darted out from between two tall drifts of sooted snow fifty yards up the street. A young cow elk, she pranced into the frozen ruts of Main Street with her head back, nostrils flaring, and the whites of her eyes showing. Jolene wondered for a moment how the elk might have got so misdirected and separated from her herd, and then thought maybe it was running from a hunter. She wondered if a hunter would shoot

THE RECLAMATION

her just like that, in the middle of town, and leave her guts glistening in the gutter. But the big graceful animal dodged once up and then down the street, then loped back to where it had appeared. Harly's voice caught her attention, and she turned as he gave Farrell what she thought was a perfunctory answer: 'The whale, of course, represents man's eternal struggle with nature...'

'Well, that's bullshit, isn't it?' she heard herself say. She turned away from the men to peer again down the street, but it was empty.

"What was that?" Farrell asked.

"Bullshit," she said quietly, without looking.

Harly looked across at Farrell, a hopeful smile fading from his lips.

Farrell looked with raised brows and pursed lips. "What do you mean?" he asked.

"Your whole premise of the redoubtable hero battling against odds, legs braced, trusty harpoon in hand: it's a lot of ridiculous bullshit."

The tables nearest them went silent for a moment. "I kind of miss your simpering giggle," Farrell said, smiling, trying to lighten the mood.

"Yes, you would. You've never really wanted to hear what I have to say, as long as I sit here prettily and cling to your words."

"That's unfair, Jo. I do want to hear your thoughts."

She met his eyes but turned away. "They would frighten you. You've no idea." The swelling was long gone and the bruise on her forehead had faded to a pale green shadow, hardly noticeable under a little makeup. "Why are we here?" she asked. "Why do we even come anymore?"

Farrell and Harly both looked down, but in opposite directions. They waited as a man and woman moved past their table toward the door. The woman screwed up her lips and panned as she edged by. The diner droned with uninterested conversation; chairs scraped the floor, and boots clumped in and out with the patrons. Farrell looked over Harly's way, exhaled, and said to Jolene, "It's true, I've always thought you pretty, but never just pretty. Not since that first day in the library. I don't think Harly ever has, either. You're an intelligent woman." He said it almost angrily. "So please respect us enough to tell us why it was so damned important to kill the white whale."

Jolene started to smile as Farrell had started to speak, and she looked away now, the smile sitting sadly across her face. She opened her mouth, but then paused, near tears, hoping that the knot in her throat would go down. She bided her time with a sip of coffee and wondered if she was supposed to apologize, but didn't care and wouldn't have anyway. She closed her eyes, breathing deeply and, but for clattering dishes and other people's conversations and shouted orders to the cook, the room quieted.

"They were all cowards," she said matter-of-factly. "Ahab, the bullying preacher; Starbuck, the spineless officer, the company man. Ishmael pretended to be a common man, but he was a detached, self-righteous intellectual. The whale was their common nightmare: the preacher's doubt, the academic's ignorance; every man's impotence. It isn't about Man's struggle with Nature; it's about every man's struggle with his own unimportance. That's what the Goddamned book is about."

Farrell sat upright and leaned forward, eyebrows arched.

Harly stopped with his coffee cup halfway to his lips, the brim catching the glint of another momentary sunbeam. "Is that what you think, really?" he almost whispered.

"I don't know if it's what Melville meant," Jolene said, looking away again. "But nothing frightens a man more than the idea he can't best something, can't stick his Goddamned harpoon into something."

She opened her lips to apologize for her words and tone, and then didn't, but turned again to the window and waited. A small patch of sunlight wedged open and drifted across the airfield, and the tail rudders of the planes glowed brightly. The gap closed as quickly as it had opened.

Harly sat back and watched from one to the other, a tentative smile returning to his face. "What about Queequeg?" he asked.

Farrell raised his hand peremptorily, and Jolene heard Harly answer him sharply. The room seemed to darken, and she dropped her head. *It isn't 'nature that can't be conquered,'* she thought. *It's a goal, an ideal that teases and evades...* From the corner of her eye Farrell threw up his hands, and Harly rose and stomped to the door. *They're all the same—all of them: desperate, scared. They fear the whale because it won't be taken—not can't be, won't be!*

Farrell remained at the table, and he waited until Jolene breathed deeply and looked up. "Have you heard back from UCLA?" he asked her.

"UCLA is just more bullshit!" The whole room went quiet, but Jolene ignored the stares and turned again to the window. "Another letter came from UCLA," she murmured to the reflections in the glass. "Ray brought it back from the Post Office. At first, he got angry again. It makes him feel, I don't know, insignificant. But then I explained it really is just a lark; I'm happy being who I am."

Farrell shook his head and turned his gaze out on the dark, fog-shrouded street. Jolene met his eyes in the reflections of the glass, and they both turned away.

"Jo... What did the letter say?" Farrell asked, not turning from the darkened street.

"You know what it said, just what you said: there's no reason I can't go to school there."

Farrell turned then, "There, you see, it's within your grasp."

"My grasp. God!" She shook her head. "We're not like you; our dreams have edges."

"Not like me?" Farrell's voice was pained. He squared himself at the table and pushed his teacup aside. "What is that supposed to mean?"

Jolene breathed in and again didn't apologize. "There're lots of jobs in the L.A. shipyards now, and in the mines and factories everywhere," she explained quietly. "But what do you think is going to happen when the war is over? Millions of men are coming home and they're going to wear their uniforms to the job interviews and get first crack at the jobs. There won't be anything for us in California; hell, we'll be lucky to hold down a job in Cinnabar."

"I know it's been rough," Farrell said. "Listen to me: it isn't a lark." He tried to catch her eyes, but she avoided him. "At least I thought it wasn't. Is it really so easy for you to give up on a dream?"

"Don't instruct me, Ishmael! Don't talk down to me the way you do to Harly!" She stood. "Not about dreams." She folded her arms and paced in the small space between table and window. "Teach me all you can about irony; you're great at irony. But not dreams. I can tell you about dreams."

She sat back down, leaned forward, and looked tiredly at Farrell. "I'm sorry," she said at last.

Farrell waited, watching her face change. She wrapped her arms across her front, leaned back in her chair, and closed her eyes. When she spoke, it was almost in a sigh:

> *"Green the days of youth beguiled, of sunny, callow, carnal schemes.*
> *In reckless, tangled twisting wild glimmerous naked bathing streams*
> *is born a dream, a summer's child.*

Farrell sat back, his mouth curved into a curious smile. He threw his arm over the chair back and leaned away. Jolene bent forward and rocked slightly as she found the meter. But the summer dream of her first stanza grew weary:

> *...dulled with rouge and sated need. Where Autumn's withered fields are plied*
> *in drunken hope and wasted seed."*

Farrell's smile hung loosely, his eyes narrowed. Jolene rested her elbow on the table and rolled her forehead on the ball of her hand, her eyes closed, letting the words tumble. She barely whispered now,

> *...gray the color of dreamlessness, of darkly knowing eyes withdrawn*

THE RECLAMATION

from hollow town and barren crest."

She started the next line, *"The dream, the child in wintry dawn..."* but stopped and shook her head. Farrell leaned away in his chair and pushed his hair back with his fingers. Other customers were looking their way, curious now, listening in. When he looked back to Jolene, she was silent, her head resting in her hand, tears streaming down her cheeks.

"Are you all right?" he blurted.

"I'm fine," she said. "Christ, just give me a handkerchief, would you."

After a moment he asked, "Good God, Jo, when did you start writing poetry?"

"It's bullshit," she answered, looking into the glass again, "just a lot of bullshit."

*

I found the lines on a scrap of paper jammed between pages of a book. It was titled *Colors of a Dream*, but the title had been scratched out. There is no signature, but I know it's Jolene's hand. It is the girlish cursive I saw up on Rainbow Peak, but more forceful—resentful perhaps—with long, stabbing loops.

23

We're pushing the end of August, and the cool morning breezes warn of a change of seasons. Already the sun rises later and sets earlier than I need it to. Earl brought my hotcakes and eggs and filled my cup, and I asked him to sit and talk if he had a minute.

Outside the morning shadows contract, and a light frost sublimates as the sun hits it. "I thought Harly was dead by then," I say.

"Naw, hell no. Harly didn't die for a whole 'nother year. He died early in nineteen forty-five."

"Oh yeah?"

"February nineteen forty-five. The twentieth."

"Well, that was just eight months before I was born. So Harly and Farrell and Jolene stayed friends all that time?"

Earl takes his time answering sometimes, like he's describing an old movie, "No," he says, "the boys had a falling out, a pretty mean one."

"What caused them to fall out?"

"Oh, hell, Harlan, maybe they just grew apart. It was tough times; it was tough times on everyone, in the mines, and in the streets. Who can be blamed for what happens in times like that?" Earl doesn't look at me as he answers and shifts around in his chair. "You don't go messing in other peoples' lives. It never leads to anything but heartache."

"What does that mean?"

THE RECLAMATION

"It doesn't mean nothing. Leave me alone." He jumps up and stomps back to the kitchen.

I was out of coffee this morning, so I came in for breakfast again. Two times at the TNT in two weeks, and I seem to have everyone in a kerfuffle. A short, stocky kid with a ruddy complexion eats ham and eggs two tables away, listening to music through his earphones. He must be the new blood Maddie was talking about. Someone whispered something to him, and he half-glanced in my direction and took out his earplugs. Hell, that wasn't the point of the Tracey thing. I like music.

It's time to get to work, but it's raining like hell out there. Rain in the high country usually comes in the afternoon, so when it rains like this in the morning you're in for a lousy day. The junior geologists, though, have the energy that comes of youth. They stand and shovel their last few bites in as I glance around, pack things up, and head out into the weather. Good for them.

Earl came back with coffee and a couple doughnuts. "Harly didn't show up for many of the book discussions as the winter wore on," Earl says. "Then in late winter the road between the towns was closed as much as it was open."

"Harly didn't get into town at all?" I ask.

"Oh, sure, I'd see him; we'd get together, but usually not with Farrell." Earl looks away as he pours, then carries the pot back to the counter, his eyes fixed on the windows.

When he returns he says, "No, Harly lost patience, anymore, for Farrell Hammond's elucidations. Jolene coaxed him to come and she would kind of smooth the discussions when he did, but Farrell lost interest in the friendship as fast as he'd found it. Now I'm just saying what it seemed like to me, and I'm sure I have my particular perspective. Someone else might have seen it different."

Earl stares off over the room as he talks and rubs his hand over his head. I look over as well, and the three of them sit in the window, sipping tea and talking quietly.

"There were laughs of course," Earl says, "some good times still. But more often than not they would get into it about something, and that would really hurt Jolene. I'm sorry she got caught in the middle."

"What did they argue about?"

"Oh, I don't know. Harly and Farrell were as different as two men could be. There were tough times in the mines, too, remember; '44 was a tough year on everybody."

"So, there was nothing specific they fought about?"

"Well," Earl says with a nod and half a grin, "Harly did steal Farrell's plane."

He gets up and pours us both fresh coffees, then sits and leans on his elbows. He takes his time explaining. "Snow built up in the mountain passes steady from mid-December almost to March. God, it was a hell of a winter. The Army used plows to keep the roads open through Christmas and for a few weeks into January but avalanches finally closed them tight. Planes came in and out whenever the sky opened up, and they brought mail and medicine and some groceries, but not enough, and they left with concentrates from the mills. But there were long stretches when the snow and fog would sock in Stibnite's airfield, and nothing or no one came or went. Supplies couldn't get in, and the towns got by on elk and powdered eggs sometimes, and damned little of that. Folks got hungry and tempers wore thin.

"Of course, that also meant the antimony and tungsten and mercury couldn't get out on a regular basis. By March they said a whole bomb factory in Nebraska shut down waiting on mercury fulminate. The Army was desperate for mercury.

"One morning the sun came up in a sky as blue as a robin's egg, and everyone said hell, there's Farrell's plane at the airfield, let's fly a few flasks of mercury out to Spokane. Farrell said sure, he'd do it, and they brought a truckload of flasks over the hill. But when Farrell checked the weather he said he couldn't do it today; the radio service was saying another storm was blowing in from Canada. It would be clear day after tomorrow, he told everyone, and he would fly then."

THE RECLAMATION

Earl leans back and crosses his leg over his knee and nods. "But damn us!" he says. "We all knew Farrell was anti-war by then, and some wondered if maybe he wasn't glad the bomb factory was shut down. The sky looked fine to us, and the plane was fueled, and the runway plowed and groomed. But still Farrell stayed in town and said no, he would wait for the storm to come and go.

"Well, Harly didn't wait. He tossed a few things in a bag and climbed into a car, and he and some guys drove down to the airfield. Harly told them, 'Hell, boys, load up ten flasks, and somebody hot-wire the starter for me.'"

"Just like that?"

"You got to understand, Harly was in deep—there were troubles. It's easy to re-think it, looking back. But Harly needed to get out of Dodge." Earl stops to clean his glasses, and stares past me through the window. "Maybe he was just kidding at first, but maybe not... Anyway, ten flasks of mercury is darned near eight hundred pounds. Harly jumped into the pilot's seat, and somebody knew how to hot-wire the engine, and it kicked over and that was that."

Earl lets a grin take firm hold, then leans forward and looks out the window again and nods down toward the airfield. "Farrell sat right here at this table, him and Jolene having coffee, when he looked up and saw his plane taxiing down the runway. Hell, he jumped in his car and went tobogganing down there just cussing and bitching." Earl laughs. "But Harly made his turn and was wheels-up before Farrell got to the field, and he flew that plane off down the valley. I watched the whole thing from the boardwalk there. Farrell came back white as a ghost crying, 'It's just a window, it's just a narrow window!' But Harly had climbed and circled, and right then flew over the town waggling his wings, and there were men in the street laughing and cheering.

"Eight hundred pounds of cargo was too much weight, of course, and he had a couple bags of mail to boot, and Farrell said later Harly would have crashed on takeoff if the air pressure hadn't been as high as it was. But the high barometer meant another arctic system blowing in—and that weather closed in on us in less than an hour.

It hit us hard, and the cheering stopped. Everyone knew right away Harly was in trouble, and they were on the radio telling folks everywhere to keep an eye out.

"Harly told me he saw the storm the minute he climbed up out of the valley," Earl says. "It was like a white wall, still well north of the Salmon Canyon, but extending east and west as far as he could see, and a high rounded ceiling to it. He skirted it as much as he could, but it finally swallowed him up, and it nearly froze him. He was flying totally blind at times, he said. The storm blew him so far off course he came down near Walla Walla instead of Spokane and landed on a highway in a blizzard. He was damned glad to find that highway."

"Walla Walla? That would have taken him right over the Seven Devils."

"That's exactly what Farrell figured later. He would have had to pass right between the high peaks."

"Jesus!"

"Anyway, the local law found him and thawed him out, and once the storm passed they refueled him and plowed the highway for him to take off for Spokane and Fairchild Air Depot."

Earl topped off our coffees again, then sat back down with his story, "Well, Christ, you can imagine. He was treated like a hero; wined and dined by the officers at Fairchild. He met the Mayor of Spokane and slept in the Davenport Hotel. Harly tried to join the Army right then and there, and they almost took him. Just in time they got a call from the mine saying they needed him back, he was a strategic exemption. Still they damn near took him. The C.O. of Fairchild—a Goddamned General—said they couldn't take him, but he pinned a set of silver wings on Harly's chest. A Goddamned general!"

"So, how'd all that sit with Farrell?"

"Not worth a damn. Harly teased Farrell about the wings, and about how Farrell's name hadn't been on the exemption list so Harly had gone ahead and volunteered him for next summer. Farrell was angry for the ribbing, and for what he called the 'vulgar ignorance of the whole stunt'—those were his exact words. But Harly got to be a big man around town. In Spokane he'd bought himself a leather bomber's jacket; he pinned the wings on the front. And he brought back ten copies of the *Spokesman Review* with his picture on page two. I've still got a copy back at the house. And, well, Farrell's stock fell pretty hard, the arrogant bastard."

"But Farrell was right, that was just stupid."

Earl looks down and barely nods. "Stupid, maybe. It was desperate for sure."

"How do you mean?"

"He needed out, like I said. It nearly killed him when they sent him back."

Earl gets up and stretches. "Either way, though, it was just like Harly to try something like that. Just like him." Earl buses our cups and saucers, and he's grinning again. "Harly was bigger than life for a while. A man's man is the way to put it. He was something, boy!"

24

I have a couple pictures of late winter, 1944, and a few more of the spring. The winter pictures show impossible snow drifts, and roads carved between towering walls of white.

No winter lasts forever, though, and the towns of Cinnabar and Stibnite woke from their internments cold and muddy, but with no permanent damage. April conjured a little sunshine and some willow shoots, and May brought aspen and cottonwood buds. As the snows disappeared, lilac bushes leafed out, and a scattering of crocuses and daffodils burst into the sunlight. The streams and the fields and the streets flooded, and the floods receded. Then everything flooded again, and ponds burst, and roads rutted and rilled, and a few houses washed off the hillsides. But June rallied some longer days, and the ground finally grew solid under a dogged sun.

†

Jolene sat on the boardwalk with her legs and feet in the street, leaning against a light pole. The pole was dirty with dry, spattered mud and her dress was clean, or had started that way, but she seemed not to mind. The sun shined brightly, and she raised her hand to shield her eyes. She laughed at a thought that occurred to her just as a man and woman walked by. They paused their conversation and tried not to glance down as they passed. Jolene leaned her head against the light pole and laughed again as one car and then another drove up the street.

THE RECLAMATION

Paul Osterkamp was the civil police in Stibnite. He stood in the barbershop window keeping an eye on the street and listening to the mayor, who got his hair cut on Wednesdays. Osterkamp knew Jolene—or knew of her. Everyone knew of beautiful Jolene Pruitt, and he shook his head because it was such a shame things were not right with her. Folks in Cinnabar were concerned over the woman's behavior. She cussed loudly in public, threw rants in the shops, and yelled at people on the street. She wasn't drunk, they said; drunkenness was common enough and easily forgiven. This woman wasn't well in the head. Osterkamp leaned heavily against the window frame as the mayor went on about road repairs. He sighed. He didn't know how to deal with things like this. But there she was on his sidewalk today, talking... to no one.

Harly Pruitt, the union troublemaker, was coming down the sidewalk. Pruitt stopped to talk with Jolene, and that was some relief to Osterkamp. They were close, Harly and his sister-in-law; everyone knew that. Well, that was something he didn't need to worry about; the two deserved each other, he supposed. And he would let the hothead get the knot head off the street. Osterkamp smiled at his own wit.

"Jolene what in heaven's name are you laughing about?" Harly asked.

"Harly! Look there in the street," she said. "No, wait 'til this car goes by. There, what do you see?"

"I'm sorry, Jo, I don't get you."

"It's dust, the cars are kicking up clouds of dust!"

"I'm sorry, I don't get you," Harly said again, still smiling.

"Oh, don't be obtuse." She looked up at him with a hand pressed to the sun. "It's dust. I haven't seen a cloud of dust in nine months. Nine months, Har, think about that! Nine months of rain and mud and snow and ice and drizzle and fungus between my wrinkled toes."

Jolene laughed again and Harly laughed as well. He stood on the boardwalk above her and took her outstretched hand. "Have you heard anything yet?" he asked.

Oh, God no, it's way too early." Harly looked good, she thought. She'd seen him at Sunday dinner and he'd looked happy then, too. Ray had asked him at dinner if he was seeing someone and he'd turned beet red, and Jolene had nudged Ray to drop it. Jolene was glad it was so hot today and Harly couldn't wear the bomber jacket. He'd hardly taken it off in months, and the silver wings would start a fight if Farrell should change his mind and join them.

Harly helped her to her feet, and she gave him a big, long hug. "You've been gone too long, you old grizzly bear. Don't do that to us."

"So, dust?" Harly asked.

"Dust. Glorious, terrific dust. Nebulous swirling billows of wonderful dust." She laughed again.

"Jolene, you're not going nuts on us, are you?"

"The first dust of nineteen forty-four, I'm going to immortalize it," she insisted. "I'm going to write a great sonnet about dust. No, an Ode to a Dust Mote."

Harly nodded, hands on hips, and told her, "I doubt it's been done. Be the first."

Jolene narrowed her eyes, smiled, and said, "I'm serious. You have to help me." She stopped to let two men in dungarees hurry by to the hardware store, then lifted her head high and began,

> *"Oh brave, you mote there drifting free*
> *above poor, timid, earth-bound me."*

Harly scrunched his lips and laughed at her. She said, "Okay, don't be a smartass, help me out."

He cleared his throat and glancing at her, raised his eyebrows and said with a flourish:

> *"What hast thy wing-ed form to thank,*
> *what...uh...*

He hesitated for a beat, but finished with:

THE RECLAMATION

"What freed thee from the low and dank?"

Jolene laughed at Harly's idea, punched him, then hooked her elbow with his, and they started toward the TNT. She lifted her head skyward as they strolled and continued to rhyme:

"Taw's summer's sun did desiccate
the mucky grimy winter's pate."

"Few sonnets, to my knowledge," Harly said, "have made so engaging use of 'mucky' and 'grimy'."

"You don't hear it every day," she agreed.

"Farrell would tell you it's not really a sonnet."

"It's an Horatian Ode, for Lord's sake," she cried. "Less bullshit and more verse, please."

Harly's lips ran silently back through the lines, and he added:

"...And loosed thee that thou might take flight,"

"in multitudinous clouds, unite!" she cried.

Jolene stopped and there were tears in her eyes. She held her brother-in-law's arm tightly and said, "I love you guys, you know. Don't ever leave me. Promise."

"More verse," Harly said after a beat, but smiling warmly, "enough of the sappy stuff."

Jolene took a moment to dry her eyes, then butted Harly's shoulder hard with her head, and said with a smirk,

"Be thee true the earth's own spoor,
must thou just in dust endure?
Dost the dust not lusty dream
of gusty destinies subleme?"

"Sublime?"

"Whatever."

Harly bent himself double laughing. He laughed so loud Paul Osterkamp stepped back to the barbershop window and shook his head at the two fools on the walk.

At the door to the TNT Jolene let go of Harly's arm and, clasping hers around her middle, gazed out across the sun-brightened valley for a moment, holding her breath and framing with her mouth an expectant smile, as though a song sat waiting to be sung. The windsock at the airfield hung empty, and the air was so still she heard birds chattering in the line of trees all the way across the meadow.

"Finish it, Jo," Harly urged.

"No, gosh no. Does it have to end?" She turned slowly and looked up the walkway. All was sunny and still in that direction, too: not a soul walking nor car moving nor flag waving. She breathed in and out and heard her friend's voice again and laughed aloud. Finally, to his comic pleading she replied, "Oh, for Christ's sake." Then with a sigh, and softly, she said, "Okay, how about,

> *Fly on brave mote without repress,*
> *but in thy rising nebulous,*
> *take care thou dost not blot the sun,*
> *by which thy freedom new was won."*

"Come on you lonely mote." Harly said, putting his hands on her shoulders. "That's worth the price of a cup."

Earl saw them come in, gave a shout, and jumped up to clean off their favorite table. He brought a beer for Harly and apologized to Jolene because he had no coffee this week, just pure chicory. She asked for a tea.

"Night shift again?" Jolene asked Harly.

He nodded. "Did you get over the ridge much through the spring, Jo; did you still get together with Farrell?"

"Just a couple of times, unfortunately. The road opened for a short time in March, but Ray couldn't get the Studebaker to start. Well, you know, you helped him work on it."

"Gas line was froze."

"Then of course there was the test in April…"

"Have you heard anything yet?" Earl broke in.

"Still too early," Harly answered for her. He winked.

"…and Ray drove me over once again—when was it, Earl? — second week of May. He had work at the mine office, and he and Farrell and I had lunch in town."

Harly asked "How is Farrell doing, anyway?"

Earl slapped the towel over his shoulder and walked back to the counter.

"It was a long winter; it was hard on everyone." Jolene looked back from the window and shook her head. "What in God's name, Harly? What were you thinking?"

"Is college boy still angry over the mercury express?" Harly grinned.

"I'm still angry—you could have died, Har."

"Not Harly!" Earl called from behind the counter, "It'll take more than a storm to kill him." He scrubbed the grill and shot a sideways grin, but Harly was focused on Jolene.

"Maybe I just wanted to see the end of the world." Harly said to Jolene. "I mean, what in God's name is in your head, hiking the hills in mid-winter?"

"I have to get up into some sunshine, you know that—and don't try to make it the same as flying off into a stupid blizzard."

A caravan of army trucks, five or six deuce-and-a-halfs, rumbled up Main Street—probably hauling barrels of caustic for the tungsten mill. Harly waited until they were past, and the street was choked with dust. He said quietly, "I had to get away, Jo. I still have to get away. There are some people…they got me over a barrel."

"What are you talking about, what have they got on you?"

He sipped from his beer and glared for a moment through the window at the sunshine and the settling dust. He turned back with a grin. "I only regret I didn't offer you a ride."

Jolene took his hand and tried to smile. "I wish it were as simple as a plane ride."

"You're not caught up in chains. Not like I am. You can get out. Hell, Ray would give you money for a vacation away. He would."

She got up, walked to the door, and leaned her head against the frame, pressing her forehead against the solid coolness of it. "There are different kinds of chains," she said.

"Don't I know."

Jolene came back to the table and sat. "Maybe you should step back some from the labor movement, Har. Get your feet back on the ground."

"I'm afraid this isn't a leadership position you retire from." A couple black sedans followed a minute behind the dust of the heavy trucks and pulled up to the Bradley Mining Company office. "Government plates," Harly said, "Bureau of Mines. This isn't good."

Jolene looked hard at him. "I don't know you anymore. You're in trouble and I don't know how to help."

Harly shook his head. "Who knows who anymore."

"Whom." She blew her nose and leaned forward with her chin on her hand.

"Whom." He nodded and finished his beer. "You can leave here whenever you like. Really, Jo, you could, and I hope you do. But imagine if you couldn't go. And imagine you couldn't stay either. And then a way opens up. Well, I may die, but I'll be damned if I die in this shithole." There was a long pause. Without looking up he said, "You know what I mean, don't you, guys?"

Earl was listening with his arms crossed. He called, "Do you want some more tea? Another beer?"

"Sure, thanks bud." Harly pushed Jolene's cup forward. Earl came by with fresh hot water and a tea bag and asked if Jolene was feeling all right. "She's okay, aren't you Jo," Harly answered. He looked up and caught Earl's eye and gave a grin and a wink.

Jolene watched Earl until he was back cleaning the grill. "I know what you're saying about feeling trapped, not knowing which way to turn," she answered, now more softly. She took his hand again and brought it to her cheek. "But we shouldn't mistake chains and bonds, should we? They're not always the same."

THE RECLAMATION

They hadn't read a book in common for months; not one, and they kidded each other about that. Otherwise they had little more they were ready to share. Harly had read Jolene's short story and wanted to see more, but she apologized and explained she'd run out of paper and had been too blue to shop for more.

"Jo, I'll get you all the stationery you want if you'll write," Harly said.

"Farrell told me the same. He said he'd steal reams of it from the mine office."

"And what about your trapping?" Harly asked. "Did you make out on your line this winter; do you have a fur coat yet?"

"Oh, hell, I got a few pelts in January, but I just shut the line down after that. I'll start it up again next year. I guess I thought the poor things were having a hard-enough winter of it, and they didn't need me adding to their misfortune."

"So you didn't get out into the sunshine after all?"

Jolene ran her fingers through her hair and smiled crookedly. "Actually," she said, "in fact, I uh... I got up to the cabin a few times anyway." She took a sip from her tea as Harly and Earl both cocked their heads back. "Well, it's a great place to read and think, and no, I didn't exactly tell Ray the trap line was shut down, because it was just…"

"Well, you little liar."

"… it was just easier that way. And shut up!" she said, laughing at last.

*

The Ode to Dust was written down on a scrap of paper—the yellowed back of a menu folded twice and kept long in a drawer. Earl gave it to me. "Me and Harly wrote it down later," he said when he handed me the paper. "They had a lot of fun. I think the lines are accurate; Harly thought they were pretty close." I stuffed the paper in my pocket as Maddie and I were leaving his house that first time.

25

The geological contact zone at the old West End Mine manifests as banded assemblages of ferromagnesian and calc-silicate… well, bright green and amber crystals that sparkle in the late-morning sun. Maddie's been gone for a week, and it's been kind of quiet around here without her. Quiet isn't good on an exploration project with a looming deadline.

A week ago, she was at Bernie's rig number-one, and you could see right away there was a problem. She wasn't paying attention to the core sampling, and her eyes were red when I walked up. Her dad was sick, she'd learned from her mother; he was in the hospital in San Francisco. "You can get there best from Boise," I told her. "Boise's not even three hours away. What's he got?"

"It's his heart; he's had trouble with it for a while. But he's okay, they have it stabilized."

"Have Lovitt go online for a ticket. You can be in Boise by eight."

"Harlan, I'm too busy to go right now. The project is still way behind."

"No, it's not; not critically. You have a good team working for you, and I can loan you Mike for a while. You're not the only one who can get things done, you know. You have to trust other people can take care of things, too."

She laughed at me when I said that, but then got serious again. "It's not going to work out. Thanks, really, but I can't go see my father right now."

"Right now is when you've got," I said. "The project's fine. Get Tracey to direct the spring and stream sampling, and Mike can get your core samples; he's been lost in his Goddamned computer long enough. You can be in San Francisco tonight."

"Harlan, really, it's not that simple. I haven't seen him in years."

"Maddie, it's important."

She stood glaring at me with her hands on her hips.

"I'll watch things," I told her. "I'll be extra nice!"

She chuckled at that, went right to her truck, and headed down to Stibnite. She made it to Boise that evening and caught the ten-o'clock to San Francisco.

The crystals formed by metasomatic replacement, but that's not important right now. I noted a big cloud of dust rising down valley, and Tracey came bounding up the two-track road in the roustabouts' Chevy, honking her horn and waving her arm out the window. I boot-skied down the mine dump and hurried over.

Maddie was back in town, Tracey explained, and there was word we all had to get down to Stibnite as quickly as we could.

"What is it?" I asked.

"I don't know, I got a call on the radio. They said to find you because your radio isn't on."

Shit, I didn't know I had a radio. I ran to my truck and raced Tracey back down to the Yellow Pine road and on into Stibnite.

Maddie is easy to spot. She's with most of the rest of the crew out in front of the hotel, gathered around the tailgate of her pickup. She looks fine as I step out of my truck, and she smiles mischievously and hands me a big plastic bowl.

"What is it?" I ask, "What's the emergency?"

"Five gallons of ice cream," she says, "strawberry, butter pecan; rocky road of course—I thought the rocky road would be appropriate." She cocks her head and looks at me with a bright smile, but oddly. I can't place the look; it's like I don't scare her a bit. "I thought ice cream would be fun," she says, turning and filling more bowls, "but Earl just got a grocery delivery, and his freezer is full to the brim, and the ice chests won't keep it. It's turning to soup."

"Maddie…!"

She laughs again, bumps me with her shoulder, and says, "Everyone's got to pitch in. Take one for the team here, you old bastard."

She actually says that to me. I stand, eyes down and take a breath. She puts her hand on my shoulder and, with raised brows says, "Harlan, it's important." It's almost Labor Day, she reminds me, and some of the young hands will be leaving us, going back to college. "It's important," she says again, this time with a wink.

So I have a big soft scoop of each flavor. Earl stops by, and he and I take our bowls and sit down on the boardwalk in the tempering afternoon sun and watch the kids go on like it's Christmas. Several of the Forest Service crew come by; their summer internships are ending, too, I suppose. The young people all gather around Maddie, and she sits on the sidewall of her pickup bed and serves them up, laughing and answering all of their shouted questions. Her dad is going to be okay, although it was serious, and she barely made her flight out of Boise. The roads out of camp were wash-boarded so bad it made her teeth rattle, and there was a flock of sheep blocking the road through Johnson Creek. But she made it, and the midnight streets of San Francisco shimmered in a summer rain, and the taxi drove her right through a parade, or carnival, or some bacchanalian thing or another.

It's all exciting at that age. The ice cream is smooth and cool, though, like I haven't tasted in years, and Earl and I sit quietly and watch the kids go on.

Maddie brought back a dozen fresh-cut rib steaks, too, and about five pounds of shrimp. I guess she takes Labor Day seriously. She got the steaks at a place in Boise but brought the shrimp all the way from San Francisco. Two big coolers full of food, and it obviously won't keep, so I tell Maddie to give me the receipts for the food, so I can expense it properly.

THE RECLAMATION

We take it down to a big fire pit at the airfield, down by the old hangar: down to where the old folks once danced, and Jolene set her table, and where Ray and Harly stared up into an unfamiliar sun. Maddie wonders if I could help cook, given I've been grilling on coals all summer. But this isn't where I belong—not really—and I can't afford to stick around with all there is to do, so I apologize and say no.

Mike Lovitt says no problem, he'll do the cooking, and that's fine. But then Mike says he's going to Google how to do it, and I say, "Jesus Christ, Mike, forget it, I'll cook. But stay and watch and learn something." Maddie laughs, punches Mike, and walks over to the fire pit where Don—Dan, her ranger guy—is unloading some cord wood.

It's a big bonfire, and it draws people like moths. The morning waitress at the TNT brought a bowl of potato salad, and a couple of other salads show up and sit on a shed door someone propped up for a table. The laundress/mail clerk helped Earl tap a keg of beer. Our whole crew is here, including a couple of new faces I haven't seen before, and that bothers me because no one is supervising the rigs over across the ridge. The day-shift drillers are here though, and they let me know everything is drilling okay. The night shift drillers get screwed, of course, but that always happens.

As I'm poking and smoothing the coal bed, getting ready to cook, Maddie brings by a few of our juniors who will be leaving soon. She helps me to remember their names and to say some nice, encouraging things to them. They've done pretty well this summer, really, and I tell them so, and they lie professionally and tell me it was a pleasure.

"Everyone is ready to eat," Maddie yells over to me, and that's good because the coals are ready, too. They're burned down to a shimmering red carpet, and I get a dozen steaks hissing at once on the grate. The smoke swirls around in a gentle, down-canyon breeze in the last faint light of the sunset, and the sizzle and aroma of the cooking meat turn people's heads around. I throw salt and pepper by the handful.

Someone lights a couple of lanterns, and that's good because the moon will be late and spare tonight, and someone else starts up some music, but then it ends almost as quickly, and a few people laugh.

Maddie brings me a beer and a kiss on the cheek from out of nowhere. We confer a little, and now she calls our people to bring plates over quick or they'll be eating shoe leather. She doesn't have to tell anyone twice, and I serve up the first round of steaks in a heavy smoke of pine wood, beef fat, and a little dust kicked up by the crowd. One of the kids brings me another beer, and Cairn's guys step over with their steaks and ribs and I tell them hell, I have the coals just right and I don't mind a bit, so I'll cook them up if medium rare is okay. A few of the drilling crew say, yeah, they're down for that, too, so I keep cooking. I don't do chicken though; the people who brought chicken are on their own.

Mike sticks around and watches like I told him to. But he's young, and there's a pretty, dark-haired girl in government green he's been looking at like I'm blind or something. I tell him to get the hell out of here, he's just in the way, and I don't see him for the rest of the evening.

The last of the steaks are claimed from the grill. I take one I've set aside, and some potato salad, and wander off to a tailgate to eat and rest my back. Earl joins me with a couple more beers. We sit quietly and watch the young people laugh about God knows what and talk and yell about God knows what. Music starts up again, and this time they leave it on, and everyone seems like they're having a pretty good time. Several people try dancing in the gravel runway, but they make a mess of it. They'll try again later under a crescent moon, with a few more drinks in them.

Maddie stands effortlessly in the center of it all, talking and listening, glowing in the firelight, reaching to touch people; laughing. Dan stays by her side, beaming—as well he should. She sees me and Earl sitting apart and comes over and takes our hands and pulls us, though we complain, back over to the circle by the fire, which someone has kicked up into tall, yellow flames. We stand and talk a bit, but it doesn't take long until Earl and I ease back out to

THE RECLAMATION

the periphery. Matt Cairn joins us, too. I like young people, but they're gregarious and loud when they drink. That's as it ought to be, but it can be an awful lot to take, too, especially when someone turns up the music. I have a smoke with Cairn and watch the long shadows of the dancers jump and glide around the meadow.

I don't bother Maddie to say goodnight. I let her be and get back to Cinnabar while I'm still of a mind.

*

As cold and stormy as was the winter of '44, the summer of that year came hot and dry. Springs and small streams dried up, and fires burned over the horizons. With no men to fight the fires they burned for weeks and more, choking the skies over the mining towns. Jolene's yellow-gray dust kept rising, then settled with mill ash and now with forest-fire ash in fine laminations over everything that didn't move. The hot weather was matched by tempers of both labor and management as they all strained under the demands of war production.

For the family photo, Jolene put down her book and stood directly behind Ray, who sat on a log in his fourth-of-July suspenders between Axel and Ethel. Jolene's hands are not on Ray's shoulders, nor are her eyes focused on the camera. Harly set the shutter timer and jumped back beside Jolene but ended up slightly blurred.

†

They set up a table under stout cottonwoods at the edge of a green meadow. Other families did the same, with plenty of room to spread out across the meadow. Men—just the managers and shopkeepers this year—stood around the bed of the company timber wagon, Harly's wagon, where a large metal chest held ice, soft drinks, and beer.

Jolene walked through the tall meadow grasses still blue that Dotty wasn't there with them today. But she made a point all day of not saying anything about it. Dotty had gone back to Boise as soon as the roads opened in the spring. The day had been warm and full of sunshine, and the bus picked her up in front of the recreation hall on Main Street. Jolene and Ray came to see her off. Jolene cried all morning but couldn't find the words to apologize for not visiting her friend for months. She couldn't explain staying away as she had; she didn't understand it herself, really. Dotty tried to apologize, too, and they both had cried. Ray made himself useful and helped the driver load Dotty's things up onto the bus, and he gave Dot a big hug good-bye.

"Take care of my girl," Dotty had whispered to Ray. "She needs your help, Ray."

"She'll get better in no time," he told her. "We'll fix things up; we'll be fine."

Farrell came by to see Dot off, too, and he and Dotty talked awhile. Jolene was grateful to him for his kindness. Harly hadn't shown at all, and you could see Dotty was hurt. Ray was angry at his self-centered brother and let him know it through a good part of the spring. But Jolene hadn't expected him to show. She understood Harly better than anyone, almost, and she quickly forgave him.

Now Jolene walked all around the Fourth-of-July picnic, keeping to the edges. The dirt road bordered one side of the five-acre clearing, with a split-rail fence running alongside. Opposite the road, Meadow Creek flowed along the west side of the meadow, which was appropriate, she thought. The south and north ends were bordered by cool, leaf-strewn woods of aspen and spruce. They were neatly boxed in. Jolene gazed in as she walked the perimeter, at the families inside. All alike, she thought. Maybe two dozen tables were set up with engineers and their engineer wives; supervisors and foremen and their fore-wives, she supposed, of which she must be one; a couple merchants and their shop-keeper spouses. She watched them all as she walked, and few met her eyes or held her gaze if they did.

Farrell was not at this picnic. He'd made a point of sharing Fourth of July festivities with the miners and millworkers in Stibnite.

"It galls the old man, you can tell," Ray said quietly. "Farrell carrying on like a socialist. But I doubt he ever turned down a dollar handed to him."

"It galls our old man you've gone Company the whole way."

Ray glared at his brother. "You know better than that." He dropped his head to light a smoke, and said between puffs, "But I'm still getting my tonnage in. I'm still doing my job. Or I would be if you'd do more of yours and less protesting."

"I do what I have to," Harly replied. "And Farrell has more to worry about than his old man." He looked around at the other tables in the meadow. "He's getting on the bad side of some tough customers."

"Yeah, well. Shouldn't you be there with him today?" Ray asked, quietly again. "Won't being here raise questions of loyalty or something?"

"I'm just reconnoitering the opposition." Harly squinted up into the sun and emptied his beer. "Ray, it's killing me," he whispered. "I can't hardly look anyone in the eyes."

"Get out, then."

"There is no out." He punched open another beer and up-ended it.

"Join the Army. Get the hell out of here."

"I tried in Spokane—I begged them. I'm still exempted."

"Even with the labor violations against you?"

"Apparently we have friends in high places."

"There was a time you had friends in low places," Ray's father rasped from behind them, "Deep places." Harly and Ray glanced at each other and made room for Axel to step up. "There was a time you would have ate your picnic with the miners and millworkers. The both of you," he said.

"Harly's still with the workers, Dad. He's just here because he likes Jolene's fried chicken."

"And you? You don't think the workers matter anymore?"

"It isn't me who doesn't think they matter." Ray started loud but eased his tone. "When a man doesn't worry about bringing the right tools to the working face, it's him who doesn't think his time matters." He waited for an answer, but Axel stood sideways to him with his arms crossed. Ray dropped his cigarette to the ground. "When he doesn't bother to fill his skip before sending it up, it's him who doesn't think his labor matters. Who am I to argue?"

Oscar Hammond had been speaking with the men around the beer wagon, and now started toward the Pruitt's table, hands on hips. Axel didn't look up in time, but Harly saw him coming and side-stepped into the brush.

He found Jolene reading, leaning against a smooth white cottonwood log at the edge of a grassy clearing. "Did you notice the day?" he asked. "Do you see things around you when you get lost in a book like you do?" He sat in the grass and leaned with her against the log. "You get lost a lot anymore," he said.

"It keeps me from getting lost."

"I know; I do it as much as I can, too."

"I don't think lost in a bottle is really the same thing." She reached over and touched his shoulder. "You're going to kill me, Har. I'm so scared for you half the time."

Harly took her hand, and they both closed their eyes and stayed quiet for a while. "I'll be okay. And so will you, Jo. You have everything, you know. I'm jealous."

"I've nothing at all. Is that the same as everything?"

"And vice-versa, sometimes."

"Why won't you see Farrell anymore?"

"Farrell and I have nothing in common." He found a smooth stone under him and gave it a toss.

"You've got me."

"I don't wish Farrell ill, but there's only so much talking down to I can take. Besides, when you and he get going, you hardly know I'm there."

"That isn't true, Har."

"What's this, Anna Karenina?" He pried the book from her hand. "A beautiful Russian duchess in Moscow society. Parties, balls, operas. That's not a bad escape."

"You left out Anna grows unhappy at home and screws the prince."

"Yeah. And gets run over by a Goddamned train."

Jolene dropped her head and laughed. "Oh well, now I don't have to finish the thing."

"Oh, damn me! Sorry about that." He handed back the book and they sat quietly awhile.

"Jo, have you heard about your GED test?" The sudden recollection caused him to smile ear to ear. "Did you pass?"

Jolene closed her eyes; the air was warm and dusty, and sweet-sour with cottonwoods and tall grass. It had been such a lot of trouble back in April, and so many people had helped her set up an official test. Farrell had asked the chief engineer of the mine to serve as proctor, and the Army supply officer, a Major Duncan, had agreed to preside. In the end, Ray had even driven her in to town. She had taken up the meeting room at City Hall for half the morning; God, she'd been nervous. They'd sealed the test with official signatures and witness signatures and sent it off to UCLA with embarrassing ceremony. So many people had helped, and now she hadn't bothered to tell anyone about the letter.

Harly said, "A lot of people don't pass the first try, I hear. You can re-take it; take it again as many times…"

"I passed it, Har. I got a high score."

"Well, hot damn! When did you hear?"

"Two weeks ago. UCLA wrote and congratulated me. They invited me to apply next spring."

"Jo, that's super, just super!" He jumped up and pulled her up, too, and spun her high above him in a single motion. "Well, hell, we have to celebrate!" He set her back on her feet.

"No, no celebration. Please don't tell anyone, especially not Farrell, not yet." She sat back down and hugged her knees.

"Why the hell not? This is wonderful."

"Is it wonderful? I guess maybe it is." She leaned her head back against the log and stared through the tops of the pines. "Harly, I'm going."

"You're damned right you are."

"I don't know how yet, or when, but I can feel it sometimes. I can feel the road bouncing under me and the wind in my face." She laughed and punched his shoulder. Her face turned serious again. "Don't tell Ray yet, either. Let me work some things out."

"Happy families are all alike. Unhappy families are all unhappy in their own ways."

"That was Tolstoy, wasn't it?" She grinned and thumbed the pages of the book.

"Yeah. The problem is there are no happy families. Tolstoy was just another fool."

"Yeah." She closed the book and turned back to him. "Anyway, you should hardly be the one lecturing about happiness."

"Things'll quiet down at the union hall."

"That's not the unhappiness I mean. Harly I know, I think... what's come between you and Farrell."

He didn't say anything but looked off across the clearing. She leaned her head sideways against the log and looked long into the sun at her brother-in-law. Harly was a big, handsome, troubled bear of a man, and she loved him and wished she could reach him, probably like he wished he could reach her. "Maybe no happy families," she whispered, "but there are happy people now and then."

26

Rain came late the night of the bonfire, and it's kept up for several days, and about half of our junior interns have now gone. We'll push the season as hard as we can, but realistically we have this month and as much of October as we can get, and that's it then. The snows of November will sweep in and shut us down.

Cairn found me at the drillrig at dawn as a wet gray sky was trying to lighten. He saw I was having a coffee, so he poured himself one from his thermos before walking over. I didn't like to see him walking over because I knew what it was about. He stood watching Bernie wrestle the hydraulic head back into place as the helper slipped in some bolts. "They gettin' any footage?" he finally asked.

They weren't, and I wasn't happy to be up early in a cold drizzle with no progress being made. "I have a drilling foreman to worry about that," I said. "Are you getting any Goddamned footage in the Oblique?"

Cairn dropped his cigarette in his coffee and sloshed both onto the ground and said, "C'mon. I need you to come to the portal. I need you to sign off on something."

I shifted to get up, but then exhaled and rocked back for a moment longer. They had mucked and shored the Oblique drift all the last two weeks and had gotten now to over three hundred feet beyond the entrance. It had been slow progress because the miners had expected to find body parts in the muck the whole way; they had found shattered timbers, old electrical wires, piping, and rubble. Last night they had probed ahead and were pretty sure an open chamber might lie just beyond three hundred fifty feet.

I emptied my coffee and screwed the cup back onto the thermos and stood. I didn't want to see a body, for Christ's sake, especially not this one. But Cairn nodded and said sure as hell there were remains in there, and they had to hold up work until something was done. The operation was shut down and his crew were on standby in Stibnite.

The oxygen-generating self rescue hasn't gotten any lighter on the belt, but I buckle on the gear and we brass in. No one else is around, they're all on standby, so I don't know who is going to check the brass or when, but we hang our tags on the pegs. The portal is shut up with heavy wooden shed doors, and big iron crossbars to hold them in place. Cairn takes a key from behind a desk drawer and unlocks the chain across a smaller man-way door.

We make the long hike to the Oblique drift in silence through warm, wet, sulfurous darkness. This is not the same place as when the guys were working. The lights and the air have been turned off. Men's shouted voices don't greet the ear and my chest doesn't reverberate with the rumble of machinery. And of course, it's where we're going and what we're going to see. But even still, a shut-down mine is lonely and quiet as a tomb. We walk steadily, quietly.

The lamp battery and the heavy rescue pull on my belt, and it cuts into my waist, and the weight causes me to shuffle crookedly. Cairn notices but says nothing. Without the ventilation the air becomes hotter as we make our way back into the hole. Our boots scrape, and the narrow beams of our cap lamps sweep side to side. Groundwater flows around our feet as thick and red as blood.

At the entry to the Oblique drift we stop for a rest and a drink of water from our packs. The low-slung mucking machine is parked in the main adit just outside of the Oblique, and Cairn hops up and sits on the engine compartment. I join him and adjust the battery and rescue unit on my belt. It's a relief to be free of the weight for a minute. Cairn talks to me, and I nod, our beams crossing. The oblique drift has been shored, but barely, he says. The ground is too heavy, the clays squeezing in, and timbers won't be sufficient for long.

"Listen," he tells me, and we hold our breaths. I can hear the faint groaning as the new timbers deep in the drift deform to the stress of the squeezing clays. Steel framing will be needed, he says, before large-scale sampling can be done. There isn't the slightest breeze inside. The Oblique is a dead heading—unconnected with any other workings. The air is stagnant there and could collect gases bubbling out of the seeping groundwater. Cairn reminds me to turn on my organic-vapor meter and to keep it in front of me.

That's all that needs to be said, I guess, so we jump down, and Cairn leads the way into the drift. It is narrower than the main adit, eight feet wide or so, and the back is a lot lower over our heads; I have to duck under some of the lower timbers and old ore chutes. The drift is more brightly lit by our lamps because of the closeness, and because the walls, where exposed between timbers, are almost entirely of a white clay. Against the whiteness our cap lamps don't cut narrow holes in the darkness but brightly light the space, and our eyes have to adjust. Clay slimes and iron solutions rill down the ribs and drip from the timbers, and we slog through the orange-white slurry halfway to our knees.

The odor of sulfate is strong, and diesel smoke still hangs in the air from the work done last night; the air is lean of oxygen and doesn't satisfy the lungs. The new timbers groan and pop around us. Most of the shattered timbers have been hauled out and replaced, but those that remain from the original square-set shoring are completely coated by iron sulfate crusts and slimes.

At about three hundred-fifty feet in from the entry the new timbering stops, and the old original timbers are still in place, though not in such good shape. We are nearing the face, the end of the drift, and that's where we find him.

He was not caught in the collapse of the drift but lies on the wedge of rocks below the face, at the very end of the tunnel where the roof didn't fall. A few timbers have come down and a few others are near to falling; the back above us strains even now as if ready, finally, to give way, and I have to hunch over to fit into the space. Cairn remains outside the chamber. I don't blame him.

The dead man lies on his side on the apron of broken rock, which keeps him partly up out of the deep sludge that pools in the chamber. His head and shoulder and part of his torso remain above the muck. The chamber remained intact through the years, but was dammed by the collapse of the drift, so it had, of course, partly filled with groundwater. He has lain submerged in the acid mineral water for sixty years until the re-opening drained the chamber. The mine waters have eaten away the fibers of his clothing but have tanned and stained bright red the flesh until all that remains is a leather-encased skeleton half entombed in muck and dusted with sediment and iron oxides depositing slowly from the solutions.

A bomber jacket, or red-stained remains of it, hangs from a peg to one side. Harly's flying wings are still pinned to it where the heart would be. The tip of a miner's hard hat juts above the muck a few feet away. He lies on his side, an arm crooked over his head, mouth agape, crying out it seems, as if agonized by the light of our lamps, unable to bear the intrusion. Cairn and I stare for a few moments at the body. There is nothing to talk about.

There is not much to be done, either. "That's that," I say finally. "Let's go."

Cairn agrees readily. He starts away from the chamber. "Are you coming?" he calls back.

"I'll be a minute."

He nods, and with a word to be careful of the old supports, starts out. I sit for a while on a timber lying near the red, mineralized body, and wait for Cairn's sloshing to fade away. It seems right to sit for just a while.

He seems fragile somehow. Not the bear of a man Harly was described to be. Is that how we all are in the end? I don't know why, but I brush the muck from around him; I clean away the muck a little, and right there is the handle of a hunting knife protruding from his chest. The handle and broad steel blade are just visible in the slurry of sediment.

This isn't right. It makes no sense at all. The steel of the blade is partly replaced with bright red cinnabar—like a coating of fine rubies encrusting the metal, and that makes chemical sense. The handle is, or was, hand-carved bone or antler; it was Harly's own knife, I'll bet anything. I splash muck and slurry back over the blade to hide it, to get it out of my sight, and I stand, bumping the timber above me, causing it to groan. This isn't as it should be. Jesus loving Christ, it's all wrong!

So now what? I have to leave, but how do I do that? Do I back out and bump a pillar and bring the whole place down, or maybe stumble over a fallen timber or, Christ, a second body? Or do I turn my back on the corpse and rush out head first, with the awful blackness closing in behind me, chasing me? I'm too old to panic like this, but how do you control a cave-in once it starts? I kick through the muck too fast and it splashes up, filling my boots. My heart pounds in my ears, and I turn back with my light to fend off the pursuing darkness. I trip and fall to my knees in the muck, flail, rise and splash forward until I escape breathless into the main adit.

Cairn is waiting on the mucker, smoking a cigarette, and he glances away to let me think he didn't notice my panic. I wait a moment and catch my breath. The tobacco smoke is familiar and comforting as I walk forward, and he offers me one. I wipe my hands on a burlap rag and they're still shaking, but I take the smoke and he lights it for me.

"So what do we do now?" he asks, when I've drawn a few puffs.

"I guess we'll have to call the sheriff. Isn't that what you do when you find a body in a mine?"

"First time for me," he says. "We'll have to go on stand-by till then. It fucks with our schedule."

"It fucks with everything," I tell him.

*

It fucks with everything, and the wind never stops blowing through this rusted rat-shit town. The wind sets the tin panels tearing against their nails, bending and slapping against the timbers until thoughts won't gather in my head. I've day-dreamed away a whole summer; confused myself and patronized myself like a weak old man. The geological map, my summer's work, covers the sawhorse table. The contact lines sweep and bend, break apart and re-join, and the history of these mountains spills from it. It's almost complete and I could finish it now with my eyes closed. Drillhole cross-sections hang by tacks along the wall, and they chronicle the mineralization and the mining. The geological reconstruction was easy—child's stuff.

A gust howls in the treetops; a front is moving through. There's been no rain yet, but it's coming. Hopefully Bernie and Honorario will have the sense to shut down the rigs for the storm. I'll stay put; they know what to do. Maddie knows, too, and I suppose the geology team, those still here, will find safe harbors for the night.

The cave-in was no accident, that's simple enough. All it would have taken was a well swung sledge by someone who knew where to swing it; someone motivated to risk his Goddamned life, too, because once the timbers start going in ground like that they'd go fast—unstoppable as a freight train. By Ray's own words he and Farrell were the only ones with Harly, and Farrell left in a panic. So, Ray had to have brought down the timbers to cover up the killing. If he didn't kill Harly, then he made up a hell of a story to cover for Farrell Hammond, and that isn't likely. I wonder if Farrell knew. He left town about then, so maybe so.

But I can't put a knife in Ray's hand! Harly had to be deeply involved in the gold scam, but Ray would not have killed his brother for gold, nor even for fear of prison. There's mean and there's murderer, and though a hard bastard—or whatever, I don't know anymore—my father wasn't a murderer. God, I hope he wasn't.

THE RECLAMATION

The storm is gaining on the night; the trees on the hills bend and wave, whistling frantically in the half light. The photos from that last fourth of July picnic still spread across the packing crate. Some of the pictures have Harly in them, and I rustle through the mess for my magnifying glass. There is nothing to show he will be killed in half a year. He stands tall and broad shouldered, handsome, and smiling. Ray is with him, and they tip beers and stand arm over shoulder and laugh half-drunkenly, as brothers should. Jolene is there in the photos, too, of course; she's the center of a lot of them, and no wonder, as beautiful and graceful as she is.

Ray could have killed for Jolene. Jolene was the only thing in Ray's life he would have killed for. A big, hollow, empty wind rocks the shack and shakes the lantern on its hook, and the wind can take this place and the whole damned town, for all I care.

†

The violence returned late in the summer of '44, as Earl tells it. A miners' picnic turned into a rally with too much beer and ended with broken windows up and down Stibnite's Main Street. The TNT was not spared. The hooliganism brought in the National Guard, and that brought a wildcat walk-out at the Bradley Mine. The Bradley was by then the country's largest source of tungsten, and the shutdown brought the United States Army rolling in the next day. Idle miners were rounded up and drafted into the Army on the spot, and as a result, tungsten production hit a new peak by late August. A few of the Guardsmen stayed on into September to break up public gatherings and to keep an eye on the offices and homes of the mine owners.

As the summer burned its way into autumn, Ray began to fear the labor violence building beneath him, and he took what steps he could to keep his family safe. Jolene refused to stop going into Stibnite, though she agreed to drive the road only in the daylight hours. Harly drove her sometimes, although his own work schedule was full.

When he did go, he would not come in to talk, but would disappear on his own and not be seen until she was ready to return.

Ray pleaded and then demanded Jolene not hike alone in the woods. In the end, she just said, "Fine!"

It was early by the calendar, but the dryness of that summer had already caused higher stands of aspen to yellow, and the underbrush was rusting leaf by leaf. Jolene sat on a soft carpet of low-bush huckleberries, hugging her knees, savoring the lassitude, enjoying the chatter of birds and the warmth of the dappled light on her shoulders and back. The valley below lolled in a blue haze, and she smiled as she thought of a couplet to describe the land's helpless descent into Autumn. She pulled her blouse on over one arm then the other and fumbled with the top button, glancing upward as she did at the treetops barely sweeping in a light breeze.

His hands reached under the blouse, massaging her back and curling up around her shoulders, and she leaned back into it, rolling her head against his fingers. His kiss on her neck was cool and wet and she laughed and shook him off, but he moved his hands down and across her stomach, and pulled her back to him, onto the green carpet, sliding his hand down to unbutton her shorts. She laughed again and sat up, shushing him. "No, for God's sake no," she whispered. "I'm not going to walk through the middle of town with huckleberry stains on my blouse."

Gently, persistently, he eased the blouse down over her shoulders and off one arm and then the other, and she gave up and turned and kissed him long and softly and slid out of her shorts and lay down for him and took him in her arms again. Her hair tangled in the low-bush undergrowth and twigs scratched her back as she moved with him. Sunlight sparkled in her eyes through the trees waving above, and the scent of kinnikinic and warm pine sap, decaying leaves, and the smell of his body intoxicated her.

"Ssh, ssh! Someone will hear," he said in a whispered laugh.

"Well, you should have thought of that, shouldn't you?" she answered breathlessly.

THE RECLAMATION

Her blouse was stained, but not badly, and it sat soaking now in a basin with Clorox. She'd cleaned herself and sponged the stains from her back and shoulders. Her back was scratched, but there was nothing to do about that. She put on a Sunday dress with a full back and collar, too hot for the season but what the hell. She breathed deeply, opened the door, and hurried down the stairs to get dinner on the table before the family arrived.

A leaf fell into the sink when she ran her fingers through her hair. She ran back up to her room, slammed the door, and pulled the brush roughly through her tangled locks. A few more twigs and leaves fell out. "Oh, God," she whispered, and leaned her head against the doorframe. She could walk through this damned town a dozen times and not get a nod, but today everyone had wanted to stop and chat her up. And her hair... "Goddamn! Won't they all just have something to talk about now."

*

I woke in my camp chair and could barely move, but remembered Maddie and I were going to go out to the new road cuts to map and sample some good exposures of alteration and veining there. We were supposed to do it yesterday, but her boyfriend wanted to go berry picking, and I guess the Goddamned social life comes first.

Her boots thumped on the steps, and I sat up, combing my fingers through my hair and blinking the creases out of my face. I checked to see I was fully dressed, which was a little shameful on one level, but was fortunate on another. The bottle sat on the table, nearly empty, and I set it underneath as Maddie knocked and walked in the door.

"Well, good morning, Sunshine," I tried to say, but my voice broke and I had to cough and clear my throat.

"Rough night?" she asked.

"I'm fine. You don't have to worry about me."

"So you've said. I worry about the project."

"I worry about the project, too. Do you ever stay home at night? It's not safe. You think they'll care for you, but they don't, and they won't, and you're worth more than all of them put together."

"Who? What are you talking about, Harlan? What do you have against Dan and the others?"

My head was a mess. "They're fine people. You're fine, too; that's all I'm saying." I sat up straight as I could and smoothed my shirt. I needed a shave, and I know I must have smelled of whiskey. I pushed the bottle farther under the table with my foot.

"You might try to be a little sociable once in a while," she said. "It wouldn't kill you to get out and get to know some people, get to know your own staff."

"You might try coming home sometimes. It wouldn't kill you to keep your knees together once in a while," I answered. I felt sick.

"Are you joking?"

"I'm sorry, I didn't mean that."

"You can't say that shit."

"I'm sorry, I didn't mean to."

"My personal life is none of your... Fuck you, you broken-down, drunk son of a bitch!"

She threw open the door, the light raked through the room, and I raised an arm against the pain. I jumped up as she left but only made it to the door. I watched her stomp to her truck in tears.

27

I don't know what Jolene was doing in 1944. I don't know what I'm doing today. I don't know how to talk to Maddie now that I've screwed things up between us; I don't know what to say. I know I messed up, and I know a broken-down drunk son of a bitch has no right to judge whom a young woman in the fullness of life should lay in the huckleberries with.

A couple of the photos in the stack are out of sequence, I think. There is a picnic on the bank of a stream. I know the place, it is a few miles up the valley from Stibnite, by the headwaters of Meadow Creek. They probably drove up to see the sockeye spawning. Bright red fish used to swarm by the hundreds. Before the dams on the Snake River depleted their numbers, I watched salmon, some more than a yard long, writhe and dart under the waves so thick in places you could walk across crimson backs from bank to bank. I'll bet it was an early salmon run, toward the end of August.

†

Jolene rode with Farrell in his car with the top down, and they met Harly who had gone ahead in the company truck. The day looked sunny and warm, but there would have been a cool edge to the breeze. They stopped at a grassy clearing where the gravel road crosses the headwaters of Meadow Creek.

Harly, Jolene, and Farrell watched for a while from the bank in the shade of a tall birch, talking pleasantly as they hadn't in months.

They shared fried chicken and potato salad. Jolene's chicken, the guys agreed, was getting pretty good, and she laughed and said it was nice to be good at something. It had taken a week of begging to get the two men to agree to a picnic.

After lunch Harly took a pitchfork from the back of the company truck and speared half a dozen fish from the stream. He kneeled on the bank and cleaned them, putting the dressed fish in a garbage can of water to haul back to town.

"Is that legal?" Farrell asked.

"Oh, please don't ask, Farrell," Jolene called over. "It isn't elk, and I'm just dying for a big salmon steak tonight."

"I'm not sure if it's legal or isn't," Harly said in mock earnest, weighing the knife in his hand. "If it's breaking the law, though, tell me who's hurt by it."

Farrell turned away, shaking his head. Harly laughed and pushed his hunting knife up the belly of a large fish. "Come on, college boy; surely it wouldn't be your first poached salmon."

Farrell ignored the cut. Harly laughed again and put his head down and focused on his work. The air had calmed, the sun burned down hot without the breeze, and Jolene wanted to talk, but didn't want the guys to stop talking with each other so she didn't say anything more for a while. She left them and walked out onto the low bridge.

Harly looked up from time to time and smiled her way. Farrell hardly took his eyes off her except when she or Harly glanced toward him. She was wearing shorts and a white shirt with the tails tied around her middle. The long summer had tanned her hiker's legs to a golden radiance. She must have found wild irises growing in the grassy field; delicate purple and yellow blossoms. Harly decided fair Lorelai needed a crown, so during lunch he and she twined them into a circlet for her hair.

Harly finished cleaning the fish and washed his hands. He and Farrell hoisted the full garbage pail sloshing up onto the flatbed and tied it down, then came over and joined Jolene on the bridge. They stood for a while and watched the spawning mass below them. The

THE RECLAMATION

Forest Service bridge was made with thick, squared, creosoted timbers that soaked up the sun till it was blazing hot.

"Last winter was just awful," Jolene said. "It was hell. You guys remember. It was so hard on... I was hard on all of you." She laughed but sniffed and pushed her hair back. "Goddamn it, you know, winter's just around the corner. Ray thinks I should go down and stay with Dotty, instead of wintering here again."

Jolene spoke matter-of-factly, but her eyes searched the hills. "Dotty is settled in with a job and said she'd love to have me, and they're always looking for help at the sugar-beet factory." She turned and pushed herself up backwards to sit on the timber rail of the bridge. She tried to marshal a smile but ended searching the hills.

"See?" Harly asked with a big grin. "You said you were going, and you're going."

"I'm not ready, yet, Har. Not to take that road out of town, to drive out of the canyon—alone. Not yet."

He and Farrell leaned their elbows on the timber rail, facing the stream below with Jolene between them. They debated: maybe she should go or maybe it would be better to stay, and whose business was it anyway. Farrell thought some new vistas would do her good.

"That's really not for you to say." Harly's tone was short, and he didn't hide a scowl. "You're not the Goddamned expert on everything."

"I can't express an opinion?" Farrell said.

"You don't know anything about us. Your whole egalitarian principle is just a theory to you."

"What have I ever done to..."

"Oh, stop it, you guys," Jolene cried.

Harly looked away and tossed pebbles at the fish below, and the fish rose and struck at the ripples. Farrell put his hand on the rail and it brushed Jolene's. She looked away, over his head, her eyes misting. Harly said, "It's good of Dotty to offer, anyhow. How's she getting on back in Boise?"

"Oh, good, Harly. Real good, and I'll write her you asked," Jolene said, wiping her eyes now. "She misses you of course. Misses all of us."

Farrell jumped up to sit on the rail but saw right away Harly was getting ready to leave so he jumped down again. He glanced over sideways at Harly, and as Harly said his goodbyes, Farrell nodded curtly and managed a smile of sorts.

Jolene felt even worse now because the day had been a failure after all, and the two of them were still hardly talking. She glanced at Farrell as Harly ambled to his truck, but she couldn't judge his thoughts. Harly turned the truck around in the meadow, and drove away town-ward, slowly at first, so he wouldn't raise dust on the two of them.

"Harly liked Dotty," Jolene said after Harly had gone around the bend, "but it just wasn't going to work out. I mean the two of them."

"I know," Farrell said. "Harly will never really love anyone."

A pang shot through her. "Farrell, Har didn't mean the things he said…"

"Yes, he did."

"I need you both."

Farrell looked up to answer, to say something to her, but her face was shadowed with the sun behind her and he couldn't see her eyes and didn't trust he would say the right thing. "I guess we'd better get going, too," he managed. "We wouldn't want people to think we were out here alone and get the wrong idea."

"God, no," she laughed. "Imagine my reputation." She tossed the iris crown into the water, and they both watched until it sank under the glimmering waves. He lifted his arms to her, and she let him help her jump down from the rail. They walked to his car with their arms at their sides and enjoyed the sun and the wind as they drove back toward town.

Her hair blew in her face. She held it back with her arm and turned to him. "Why did you give me that German folk tale to read?"

"*Germelshausen?* It's a classic. You didn't like it?"

THE RECLAMATION

"How much of a classic? It seems pretty obscure to me. What made you choose it?"

"I don't know what you mean."

"Okay."

The road wound with Meadow Creek around rocky knobs and through flat parks of sage and balsamroot where Harly's dust still hung in the air. They drove slowly and watched through bends of the road as the cuts and scars of the mining district drew nearer and sharper on the hills.

"Did you like the story?" he asked, "*Germelshausen?*"

"A cursed town doomed to disappear for a hundred years; an impossible choice—of course I didn't like it. I wasn't supposed to, was I?"

"I don't know what you mean."

They rounded the last bend, and Farrell had to raise his arm to the harsh light. Jolene closed her eyes. "Okay," she said, "never mind."

*

I woke to the sweet, acrid smell of burning paint and plastic. I wondered, as my head cleared, if I'd left embers to billow in my garbage barrel. But the barrel and the fire pit were both cold. The smoke was drifting down the hill from the New Main portal, where yellow light flickered in an otherwise murky pre-dawn.

By the time I dressed and drove to the portal, flames engulfed Cairn's office trailer, the showers, and the tool shack. I dropped my tailgate and watched from a safe distance. Mike joined me after a quarter hour or so. Mike is covering night shift for the week. We sat together and watched the place burn down.

The sky lightened, as it will do, and the surface facilities were pretty much smoking ashes when Cairn and the sheriff drove up. Today was the day the sheriff was to go in and examine the body. They got out of their trucks, kicked through the ashes for a minute, then came over to where Mike and I were still sitting. Cairn looked at me funny. "The gate was locked," he said. "The night-shift drillers were drilling, right?"

"Yeah, they were making good footage all night," Mike replied.

"Who all knew a body'd been found, and who knew the portal was going to be shut down last night?" the sheriff asked.

I shrugged.

Mike said, "Everyone."

Cairn couldn't take the sheriff underground to look at the dead man, because we no longer had safety facilities on the surface. So, after poking around the ashes for clues, the sheriff drove back to Cascade.

Maddie showed up as the sheriff was leaving. She kicked through the ashes too; she'll have to write up a toxicity report for whatever chemicals burned with the tools. She didn't even look at me, and I couldn't think of anything to say to her.

*

It was going to take "about a week," we learned. The Valley County Board has to approve the sheriff and coroner coming back out to recover the body in the drift, and someone in Cascade decided they should check on the county's insurance coverage for the task. It wasn't something that came up every day, as it would in Shoshone County. Andy blew his stack because Cairn had to send his crew out on break or pay them a fortune in standby.

The sheriff thought it wouldn't be "too much more than a week" when we spoke again this morning. He wanted to line up a mine-rescue team to come along. "It's a little late for a Goddamned rescue," I assured him. But he said that was how these things are done.

Andy was back on site this morning and in one of those moods where you don't mess around with him. "Why are we even fucking with that caving drift?" he wanted to know. "We've spent more money there than on the rest of the damned mine."

"It's the locus of gold overprint," I explained. That probably kept him from firing me right then and there. He told me and Maddie point blank we have to finish our study before the snow flies. "The analyses have to be done and reports have to be written before Christmas. That's a drop-dead date," he emphasized, "so field work stops with the snows—no plowing!"

Maddie hasn't said 'boo' to me in three days but neither of us let on to Andy there was a problem. I thought that was pretty professional of her, anyway. We haven't been out yet to map and sample the new roadcuts. Andy suggested that, given the season, we might want to get our asses on that.

The given season is high-country autumn, and it's been an awfully nice one, with warm, dry days under lapis skies. The cottonwoods are close to full color in the valley bottom, and our new roadcuts lie below a broad stand of yellow aspens that borders the hollow on the west.

"What is it about the smell of a new-cut road?" Maddie wonders aloud as she walks ahead of me. "Opening up new beginnings, new possibilities?"

"They cut open the hillside and expose the A and B soil horizons," I answer, pointing to the bank above us. "It's the organic acids you're smelling. They'll dry out in a month or so, lose their volatile-aromatics, and it won't smell like new anymore."

She doesn't look back. "You're a regular poet," she says.

"The road pushed through a lot of pine saplings, too, and you can smell them dying in the sun. And, of course, the dozer rips up and crushes a lot of different bushes and forbs: kinnikinic, snowberry, sage, balsamroot. That's like crushing a handful of herbs and holding it to your nose."

"Yeah, thanks, Harlan."

Maddie writes her notes sitting on the ground at the base of the cut with her legs folded under her to make a table for her field book. Her back is turned to the warm autumn sun, so she writes in her own shadow and her face is darkened. But she pushes her hair back with her hand and slides a ball cap on to keep the hair out of her face. She gazes out over the valley for the words to describe what she sees in the rocks and soil, and when she does find the words, I can see it in her face, by the glint of blue sky in her eyes.

†

Jolene sat on a gray, weathered tree stump on the deforested hill above town. The stump was fully four feet across, and she sat comfortably with her legs crossed, bracing a book in her lap. Tying her hair back with a scarf, she began to write. The last of the autumn sun burned softly on her back as she searched the valley below for the words to render the sad, hapless town, the empty hollow, the forsaken lives. The sky to the north darkened with an early-season storm, but she thought she had plenty of time.

She ran her finger across the rippled tree rings and counted but stopped at a hundred and frowned. The town lay below her, but not so far below she couldn't make out the houses and streets. They were all there: the dreary pine-clad homes from where Hattie and Ellen watched out; Axel and Ethel's place with its neat garden, and her own house with its tangle of a yard, all gone to seed. She picked out the homes of a dozen others she knew: the Baughman's, Tammy's house newly painted, and what had been Greta's house before she and Fred moved to a nicer place in Stibnite.

The hillside between Jolene's perch and the town was covered in brush and bramble which had taken over after the pine trees were logged, and the brush was afire with the colors of the season. The brush all but hid the hillside cuts and trenches the mining companies had made over the years. In the distance she watched winches pull up and down in towering headframes, spewing ore through chutes into waiting trucks. The rocks rolled down the chutes, the rock dust rose, and she counted two, three, four seconds to hear the clatter and rumble of the loadings. The mill stood far below on her right, its stacks billowing black smoke as ever, the grinding clatter of its ball mills riding the breeze, faint but incessant.

Just a couple of cars and a truck were moving on the uneven roads of Cinnabar, but that was enough to raise billows of dust into the warm, still air. The town, coated with the dust, looked tired and lost. *Germelshausen,* she thought, *one hundred years of exile, and all who live here doomed to solitude. All who don't escape.* She sat up and hugged her knees. "Am I going to have to do it all alone?" she asked aloud.

*

"Am I going to have to do all this myself?" Maddie calls over.

She's right; I'm not doing my share. I stand quickly, but I'm a little stiff as I hurry over to help her with the sample transmittals.

"You hurt your back?" she asks accusingly.

"I didn't hurt my back."

"Then why are you hunched over and hobbling?"

"Because I got old, Goddamn it!"

She shakes her head. "I want to die young."

"I'm rooting for you," I say, before I can stop myself. Thank God she laughs.

"You never lose an argument, do you Harlan?"

"I don't want to win an argument with you. I want things to go back to the way they were before I fucked everything up."

"When was that?"

"You know, before I said what I said, the other day, in the morning."

She closes her pencil in her book and turns my way, squinting against the sun. "How do you think things get messed up, Harlan? All at once? Things never fall apart all at once. Isn't that what you said, *uniformitarianism*? They go to hell piece by piece, one missed smile, one selfish moment, one insult at a time."

"I'm sorry for all of them."

"Oddly, I believe you. It doesn't make it better, but I believe you're sorry."

28

"Gold? I never knew anything about gold. But yes, that would have been trouble. People would have gone to jail—hell, if they lived long enough. More likely it would have got some heads busted."

Earl's tavern on main street is called the Prospector Bar and Grill. The grill is no more—those operations have been consolidated with the TNT. But the bar still pours hard liquor from bottles lined up on glass shelves. The shelves hang on a Plexiglas wall that glows with the colors of a tropical sunset. A couple of my junior geologists sit at the bar tonight, and I get the feeling several more would be here if I hadn't showed up.

I sip my beer and consider Earl's answer. I say, "Someone had to be taking gold out of the mine."

"Sure looks like it," Maddie agrees.

Earl waves it away, a scowl beginning to darken his face. "A miner digs where he's told; he loads his ore car and sends it out and loads the next one. So sure, I guess it could happen. But it makes no sense once you're on the surface, does it? Because how could they work the ore? How would they mill it? You don't recover gold the same way you recover mercury."

"I guess they could run it through with the other ore and let the gold accumulate down in the circuit."

"Then how would they clean out the circuits and recover the gold without the whole mill knowing?" Earl raises his brows and shrugs, satisfied with his argument.

Maddie's eyes turn from me to Earl as I ask him about the mill circuit. She asks, "When did the mill ever shut down?"

"Christmas."

"That's it?"

"That's it," Earl grumbles.

I say, "That's the schedule, but that's never it, is it?"

Some of the smugness leaves his face, replaced by another satisfaction I can't quite place. "And I guess whenever there was a strike," he admits.

"A strike? You don't say."

†

Farrell was to give Jolene a ride into Stibnite after he looked in at the mill. He had to collect a few bags of ore samples in order to re-run the assays. Jolene would meet him out front, but she wanted first to stop at the grocery for some sugar cubes, since Earl had been out of them at the café last week.

Jim Baughman stood with a sour look on his face. "Just the sugar, then?" he asked. He'd told the story for a year, how he'd tried to warn Jolene of the labor action, but her own moping and willfulness had got her into trouble. *And well, you seen what happened. Can't say I was surprised.*

His dislike of her no longer bothered Jolene, nor did she bother to pretend friendly feelings toward him. "Just the sugar," she said.

"There'll be trouble in town today. Not a good day to be out sightseeing. Remember what…"

"Oh, God. Now what?" she said.

Baughman scowled and said one's view of the strikes probably depended on how high on the hog one was dining. "But the ordinary mill workers are damned tired of crooked assays getting reported, and losing out on a fair share of profits."

"The mill is striking?" she asked. Baughman nodded and continued with his explanation.

Farrell, she knew, would be walking into a trap. Jolene left the sugar on the counter and ran for the door, with Jim Baughman shouting, "Don't you be getting into foolishness. Jolene!"

Two blocks away the street had filled with scores of men in work clothes and boots. They stood with arms crossed, wordlessly stamping their feet against the cold, or arguing in small groups. A few heaved rocks at the mill, but from a good distance so that only a few stones banged against the corrugated steel walls.

Jolene pulled a scarf over her head and crossed the street to avoid men still straggling up from behind. Muddy ruts had frozen in the road overnight, making the crossing uneven and difficult, and she stumbled where the road became slick—where the unreliable mid-morning sun had thawed patches of the mud. On the boardwalk she edged close behind the mass of men, turning her collar up and wrapping the scarf around her face. She couldn't see a way past and into the mill to warn Farrell.

But Harly's voice suddenly boomed over the crowd. She was certain it was him, and his words rising in an affected oration called the men to action. She couldn't make out all he said, but the tone of anger and indignation was unmistakable. At Harly's crescendo the crowd turned as one and surged up the road toward the mine portal. Jolene watched them trot off and was relieved and grateful Harly had found a way to protect Farrell. She thought for an instant of Ray's safety, at the mine, but then decided Harly would not let him be endangered.

The low morning clouds had lifted to halfway up the ridge, and they parted now, letting through scattered shafts of light. Jolene followed one shaft of sun down the middle of the suddenly quiet street but lost the warmth and light under the shadows of the tall mill building. She hesitated, not knowing how to approach it. No smoke rose from the brick chimneys although smoke and noise seemed always to come from the mill. She'd never been so close before, except in a car, and the rust-red metal walls towered high above her so that she had to strain to see the long row of windows at the top. They were sooted and showed no evidence of light from inside. Soot and ash coated every surface and made the thawing mud in front of the mill black and sticky. She stepped carefully through the sludge, trying to keep from staining black her already muddied dress.

She didn't try the broad front doors, which she presumed would be barred against the protesters, but crept around the side of the building, running then along the rusted metal wall, ducking under windows as she came to them, listening but hearing no sounds or voices.

She found a low, open window and peered through, and all was empty and silent inside. The place seemed deserted. She found the next door unlocked and entered into a vast hall, dark but for streaks of gray light from third-story windows. As far as she could see in the filtered light, machinery of a scale she'd never imagined filled the hall. Jolene crept between iron struts and massive timbers that crisscrossed like great traps and snares. A wet, greasy walkway led her between ball mills—iron drums fifteen feet in diameter, turned on their sides and rotated around massive axles. She ducked under long, inclined roasters, and recoiled from the heat of furnaces two stories high, banked, and glowing red. Belt lines and conveyors sat idle with their loads of crushed ore, and water spilled in torrents from washers and screen classifiers.

Jolene dodged the waterfalls and edged along a network of concrete chutes and flumes. The walkway led her up iron stairs and along a catwalk to wooden steps that took her to just below the high windows. Soot and clay and grease caked half an inch thick on the heavy beams and planks in her timbered loft.

Faint voices rose up from below, and she had to duck behind a heavy timber. After a minute the voices grew nearer, or maybe, she realized, she could hear them better because the water had stopped splashing. She peered around the beam, and far below Fred Hogue and four other engineers she recognized entered, carrying heavy tools and lanterns. Two of the men had guns belted to their hips.

The men went to work quickly, prying up wood planks covering the concrete-lined waterways. With heavy chains they pulled out iron grids from the bottoms of the chutes, and with shovels cleaned sand residues from the ditches. Jolene crept to the edge of the loft and barely breathed as she watched the goings-on below. Hogue and his men shoveled the black sands into canvas bags, tied up the bags, and stacked them into wheelbarrows.

They're cleaning up a sluice—recovering gold! she realized; she had to duck back and lean against the beam to quiet her breathing. Jolene didn't understand the workings of the mill—didn't know a flotation tank from a jaw crusher. But she'd panned streams and could recognize a natural gold trap, and she'd cleaned out the riffles of old-man Alec's sluice box enough to understand what the men were up to. The engineers worked quietly and efficiently; they'd done it many times before, she could see.

Sunlight broke through clouds outside and glowed suddenly through the sooted windows. Hogue looked up, and Jolene again ducked behind the beam. There was a loud metallic bang on the side of the building, and then another, as if rocks being thrown. When she dared to look down again the engineers had stacked their tools and were returning the last screens to the concrete waterways. They lay back the wood planks, and without a word carted off the canvas bags of concentrate.

Jolene knelt in the shadows of the loft until more rocks on the metal skin, shouts, and the sound of breaking glass told her the mob was returning. She retreated slowly at first, back over the catwalk and down the wooden steps, not sure of her way, confused by the enormity of the machinery and the suffocating heat still radiating from the roasters and twisted retorts. She heard voices again—just a few men, she thought, but in a panic now, she hurried down the greasy walkway, trying to remember the path she'd taken from the door.

A sudden splashing of water startled her, and she turned toward the source. But as she did, an arm grabbed her around from behind while a hand covered her mouth. Jolene twisted and struggled in the man's arms but was lifted from her feet and dragged into the

THE RECLAMATION

shadows of a concrete vault. A strong chemical odor filled the room. She tore against the hand on her face and tried to call out.

"Ssh, ssh! Someone will hear." Farrell whispered. He pulled his hand away slowly.

She barely calmed. "Well you should have thought of that, shouldn't you?" She turned and threw her arms around him. "Thank God, you're okay!"

He held his finger to his lips as the sound of heavy boots approached then receded. The door was not fully closed, and voices could be heard deep in the mill, muffled by the timbers and the splashing water. "They'll re-fire the furnaces right away." He whispered. "But they won't run a shift tonight. It won't be ready again until morning."

"What is this place?"

"A chemistry lab. We're okay here for a while. We'll just have to wait them out."

"I saw Hogue and some of his engineers, did you see them? What were they doing?" She tiptoed to the door, still ajar, and peeked out. "It looked like they were cleaning out a sluice box," she whispered, "like they were recovering gold."

Farrell stepped over and eased the door closed. His face was ashen in the dim light of the single, high window. "That's exactly what I thought, too. But where in hell could the gold have come from?"

"Barney Applegate says the Cinnabar ore always carried some gold."

"Never in those concentrations."

Jolene started to speak but then drew in a quick breath and turned away. "Maybe it could have come from somewhere else," she said. "Maybe it has nothing to do with Cinnabar." Her eyes wouldn't meet his.

"No. It would have to come from the mine, wouldn't it? No other ore is brought in for processing. But how?" He sat on the edge of a work bench. "Some of the miners would have to be in on it… Jesus, what has Harly got himself into?"

"What do you mean? What has Harly got to do with it? No, it's not him, it... it was the engineers."

Men's angry voices argued just outside, interrupted by bursts of shouting in the streets and the sounds of whistles and massed pursuit. Farrell and Jolene both stopped, barely breathing. But a diesel engine started inside the mill, slowly at first, coughing and chugging. It caught its rhythm and raced, deep and throaty, and the rumble of it vibrated in the floor and walls. In the covering drone Farrell spoke softly, "Harly led the strike, Jo. He turned the mob—led them up the hill, away from the mill."

"Yes. He did it to save you." She stepped in front of him to speak, but still couldn't hold his eyes. "I know about this. Ray has been... Never mind, Harly can't be involved."

Farrell held his finger to his lips again, and whispered, "What about Ray?"

They both started at the banging of a heavy door. Farrell said, "Harly didn't do it for me—he didn't know I would be here today. I think he did it to clear the way for Hogue."

She turned away, hugging her arms to her, then turned back, glaring at Farrell until she had to look away again. Farrell noticed; he said, "I love him too, you know."

She didn't answer, and Farrell pushed himself up to sit fully on the lab bench, his shoulders hunched. "What the hell?" he asked under his breath. "God almighty, this is why the samples make no sense!" He looked up at Jolene, "This is trouble. I need to get away for a while; I need to sort this out."

She was still angry and hurt by what she'd seen—and by what she knew it meant. "If you need to get away, then go," she said. "You know the way."

He jumped down from the bench. "No, I won't... I don't want to tangle you up in all this."

"But I'm already tangled up, aren't I?" The wind outside rustled the corrugated skin of the building and corn snow pattered against the glass in the dim afternoon light. It was Harly, and she knew it. He was doing it for no one but Harly. She wanted to shout but didn't dare. She breathed in and out and it was like someone else's lungs filling. "Winter's come," she said, and even her voice sounded distant in her ears. "It's too soon. It's too damned soon."

"Ssh."

For a long time she stood in his arms trying to stop shaking, but she might as well have been alone in the blizzard again, in the wind and snow, huddled against the darkness. Another gust riffled through the tin panels and a ball mill began suddenly to turn over, its load of rock banging frantically against the steel walls of the drum. She pulled her arms to her and rested her head on his chest. "How do we escape?" she whispered.

29

Maddie and Tracey have most of the stream and spring samples collected now, and my geological mapping is done as it will get. The junior-geo staff is even catching up on the logging and splitting of the core, and screen shots from Mike's much-loved computer model are showing up on websites and in news releases.

Andy called somebody who knows somebody who knows how to light a local fire, I guess. The sheriff and the mine recovery unit will be here day after tomorrow. We need to get Cairn's crew back to work or they'll be caught by the winter snows. Not that snow falls underground, of course, but imagine all that equipment wintered-in at Cinnabar, sitting idle, costing stand-by charges for five or six months.

Maddie and I have been driving around in her pickup with the heater on, checking up on the drilling and sampling. We could have found other things to keep us busier today, but I remind her one should slow down once in a while and take stock of things. She pours me another coffee from the thermos and hands it over with a roll of her eyes. I don't know why people feel that's a form of communication.

The last sun of September barely glows through wrinkles and seams in low gray clouds that sweep just over our heads. More distant clouds drag white veils of snowfall across the hills. The aspens and the underbrush have begun to lose their colorful leaves, and on the ridgetops they are already bare. The air is cool today; the season has turned, and snow has begun to fall at Bernie's rig high on the ridge. We've talked a little about Jolene and the others; I had to say something because it all seems so incongruous suddenly. Maddie listens and asks a question now and then, but I leave off after a bit, so I don't bore her.

Bernie is breaking down his number two drillrig for demobilization. The drilling program is winding down, and we'll just need Bernie's number one along with Honorario's rig from here on out. Bernie goes on with his hammering and wrenching and clanking of pipes, and Maddie and I leave him to it and walk down to the edge of the drill pad.

From the high berm I can point out where the proposed open-pit mine would lie. She asked to see the impacts. At full build-out, the mine would be nearly a mile long, rim to rim, and half a mile across. The excavation would encompass all of the ridge to the east of us, well beyond the New Main portal, and extend a ways west of where we stand. The south rim would reach down the ridge a little way toward Stibnite, but the town of Stibnite would be preserved. The north rim of the pit, though, would plunge down the ridge and take in everything right up to the edge of the old town of Cinnabar.

"Cinnabar won't be mined out then?" she asks.

"No, it won't be taken in the pit. But it will be covered by a leach pile about two hundred feet deep."

"Oh," she says. "What about Cinnabar Creek?"

"Most of the upper drainage will be filled with leach pads." I point up along the shallow, heavily-forested valley beyond the town. "What streamflow there is will have to be diverted."

The pads will be lined with thick poly-ethylene membrane, acre on acre, and stacked with run-of-mine ore. Sprinklers will apply cyanide solutions to trickle down through the ore, leaching out the gold. As we talk, the country beneath our feet changes. The aspen groves tumble down, and the red, rusty undergrowth disappears under bulldozer blades. The hill is laid bare then stripped away, bench by Archimedean bench, as a pit spirals deeper into the earth. Smoking, pivoting shovels lay back the highwalls of the pit and push into and scrape away the pine forests all around. Outside the expanding pit, stacks of broken rock grow, building up by terraces like vast ziggurats, covering the headwaters and the town.

Maddie closes her eyes and for a moment stands still and quiet. "Where will the big overburden dumps go?" she asks.

"The waste rock will fill most of Alec's Canyon."

There was little else to be said. Maddie and I finished our thermoses and finished our rounds of the drilling, then she dropped me at my place just before dusk. We nodded our goodbyes. I stood awhile on the porch to make sure she made it back up through the slick red clays. A narrow beam of sunlight managed to pry through the clouds as I stood, so I walked with it a ways between snow-dusted piles of rubbish and wild rose.

All the streams I can see from these ruins, and all Jolene could see, flow down into the River of No Return. The waters tumble into chasms, roaring and hissing, tearing and grabbing at roots and boulders. They carry soil and twigs, bones, and bits of mountain down with them. Loneliness and regret rise too, from this damned soil, and spill down the canyons beyond where the eye can see. It has probably always been so in this place.

†

Fast moving clouds filled and darkened the gorge, and it seemed to Jolene the very cradle of storms. The days grew cold and dark and there was nothing she could do about it. But snow began to fall in earnest in mid-November, bringing some relief, and by the end of the month the snow lay deep enough over the hills to float snowshoes and skis.

Ray worried for his wife and urged her to get out of the dark, echoing house and away from the mean-spirited town. "Go rest your eyes on something better," he said. "Get out of this awful canyon."

And Jolene did get out when the storms would let her, but not by Ray's urging. By late December Ray believed that the freshness and the occasional sunshine were doing her some good. She brooded less and began to show interest in things again. And if that meant she stood up and fought a little more with him and Ethel, well, that was a good thing all in all.

She got her trap line going again and spent long days in the hills—sunny or dark—and seemed pleased when she brought home a pelt or two.

"I should go."

"Yes."

He rubbed his hands over his head and asked, "You'll be okay getting back to town?"

Jolene reached from the edge of the cot to set her tea on the iron stove, shook her head, and scoffed. "If anyone is going to need rescuing it's you. Did you park where the road crosses the canyon? The right canyon this time? Do you know which way to turn when you get back to the road?"

"Really Jo, I'm not lost."

"Not perfectly lost. Thanks for bringing the tea, by the way." She threw the quilt off and stood naked on the cold plank floor in the light of the open stove. "Aren't you going to say thanks for the screw?"

"For God's sake, Jolene."

"What's the matter, Pygmalion, are you shocked? Don't like your Galatea so much?"

"I like her very much."

"You like to fuck her very much."

"I like her all the time, even when she pretends to turn back into stone."

She raised her chin high, clasped her arms across her breasts, and turned slowly on her toes, goose bumps rising in the light of the fire. "How would you fix her, sculptor? How would you make her better next time?"

"I wouldn't change a thing."

"You are perfectly lost."

"Come with me to Los Angeles, Jo. The sun shines every day there. It's never cold and never gray. We can live with palm trees and flowers every day of the year. Think about it. You can go to college; hell, you can get a PhD. I have money and we can live well there."

"Ray has money too, and he's a better lover."

She wet a sponge from one of the steaming pots and cleaned, then dried herself. She pulled on her underwear and her wool pants, aware that he stood watching. She turned and reached for her brassiere and sweater. "I've hurt your feelings. I should be more considerate."

He helped her snap the brassiere as she held her hair out of the way. He asked, "Is he better afterwards, too? Does he see the colors in your moods and hear the pain in your verse? Does he even know who Galatea is?"

He tried to hold her, but she pulled away. "Leave me now, Pygmalion. Go home." She squeezed her eyes shut and felt tears on her cheeks.

"Have you shared a single poem with Ray?"

"Get the hell away from me," she said, now angrily.

"You haven't. He's never heard a word of it because you know he'd be stumped."

"Get out. Get the hell out of here. If Ray found you here he'd kill you. He'd kill us both, and I wouldn't stop him. I'd dare him to do it!"

She wiped her eyes and nose and finished dressing. He waited, leaning against the door. She took two half-thawed martens off the hook and dropped them onto the oilcloth, moved a steaming pot of water nearer to the table, and cleaned and tested the hone of her knife.

"You should go," she said more kindly. "I'll be alright."

"I know you will. I wanted to watch you skin them this time."

"No, you won't like it; it's monstrous."

She wiped her eyes on her arms and started a long incision down the chin, neck, and belly of the first animal. "Please go. I didn't mean the things I said."

"I know you didn't."

"I'm sorry."

"Don't ever be. You're crying."

"It's none of your business. Leave me, I want to cry a little."

"I love you." He waited, but she turned away. He stepped out the door, and Jolene slumped heavily against the table. "Don't," she whispered. She waited until he'd put on his snowshoes and the crunch of his steps faded down the canyon. She stropped the knife and tested the edge, drawing a bead of blood on her arm, then went back to her skinning.

30

Earl cleans his glasses, holds them to the light, and cleans them again. "Beats me; you've got your assays. I don't know what good it does you, though, to dredge all that up now. Even if it was true."

"I thought it might explain some things," I say.

He says, "And I don't know what… explaining things doesn't change things."

"True enough. Still…"

The woman behind the bar brings us two more beers, and another coke for Maddie. Maddie has night shift tonight.

"I guess things came to a head one day in late January," Earl says after studying the beer mug for a minute. "Maybe February, but the dark of the winter anyway. The engineering office got pretty tense; I didn't like being there. Talk went around of inspectors from the Bureau maybe coming out, and everybody wanted to avoid that. Tempers wore thin."

The song blaring from the jukebox, Johnny Cash walking the line, comes to an end. Thank God, because the noise and the tropical lights were giving me a headache. But when the room quiets down Earl stops talking as well, and there's a moment of silence as we drink from our beers. Earl stares up at the ceiling and continues quietly only when the jukebox starts up again.

"Everyone figured it was Farrell Hammond stirring things up. He said he was going to have a talk with the shift supervisor—Ray Pruitt—and that was the last I would have seen him, I'm pretty sure.

He left town; ran out just before things went to hell. So everyone said."

Maddie asks, "Could Farrell have been skimming off the top, is that what you mean? Do you think he was part of a scam, he and his old man?"

"I don't know about that. I doubt Farrell was liked well enough by anyone to form a conspiracy of that kind." Earl shakes his head. "Toward the end, I didn't really see much of him. He came in with Jolene a few times that winter. Harly had lots of friends, and by then the sense to be done with Farrell. I'd see Harly when he came to the café now and then, and sometimes he came in with Jo—your mother." Earl wipes the condensation rings from the table with a napkin. "I'm sorry she got caught in the middle. She was one classy lady, your mother. She was always good to me and Harly."

Maddie nods. I shrug, and Earl says, "They had plenty of reason to fall out. Neither one of 'em needed gold to come between them."

"You mean Jolene?" I ask.

"I don't know what you're talking about."

"Harly was seeing Jolene, wasn't he? Did Farrell find out? Was it a case of jealousy?"

"You're off base. There was nothing between Harly and your mother but friendship."

"She was seeing someone—the evidence is pretty clear. And Harly must have been seeing someone—that's why Dotty left town." I sip my beer, and Maddie and Earl both look down and shake their heads slowly. I say, "That'd be pretty low: to take advantage of Jolene when she was still mourning the loss of her child."

"I told you before, your mother was nobody's victim. If anyone was messing with Jolene... well, it wasn't Harly Pruitt."

"I know you admired Harly, but it doesn't fit. Harly died in the mine..."

"And you should leave him in peace!"

"Except he was murdered."

Maddie nearly chokes on her Coke, but what should have been shock on Earl's face doesn't get beyond contempt. I say, "He was murdered, and Jolene's husband was the only witness, and Ray lied to everyone about the cave-in."

"Farrell Hammond was there too, in the telling, and he skipped town, didn't he?" Earl's anger rises.

"It doesn't fit; Farrell was probably gay," I answer. "That seems to have been the consensus."

Maddie chokes on her Coke again and tells me to drop it.

"You're a pretty good geologist, I'm told." Earl rises from the table. "Stick to rocks, Harlan. You haven't figured out a Goddamned thing." He walks from us shaking his head. "Loretta," he calls to the barmaid, "Their drinks are on the house."

I'd like to finish my beer, but Maddie is ready to head out. I get up, too, and walk her to the hotel where we're both parked. But for the neon Budweiser sign in the window behind us and a streetlight a block ahead, the night has gotten pitch black and chilly. The wooden walk is old and spongy, and I stumble here and there on the twisted boards. "What was Earl so damned stressed about?" I wonder.

"Earl has more invested in your family story than you give him credit for." Maddie seems to know where all the broken boards are, so I follow behind her.

"What does that mean?" I ask.

"I'm not sure. But watch what you say, Harlan. Earl's gay."

"That's ridiculous."

"You're ridiculous."

†

"I didn't even go up the line today," Jolene said. "I didn't bait the snares last time. I don't want to trap them anymore." The fire had burned down to glowing embers; she lay on her side on the narrow cot, with his arm around her, holding her tightly. Jolene took his hand, scraped and bleeding, and held it to her lips.

"I just throw the bait out by the cabin and let the martens feast on it," she said.

"Good, don't do it anymore. There's enough trapping going on as it is. I feel my own head in a noose." Farrell rolled away, threw the quilt off himself and climbed over her to the cold floor. He still didn't know how Jolene could do it, could stand bare as she did in this frozen cabin. He stepped hurriedly into his long johns and rummaged around for his jersey.

"Are you getting up?" she asked. "It's still early."

His breath billowed in the mid-afternoon light streaming through the window. He kneeled in front of the fire box, stoked the coals with the poker, and threw in a couple pieces of wood. Turning on his knees, he smiled wanly, leaned over, and kissed her. She put her hand behind his head and smiled for him. His lip was cut, and his face bruised, but still handsome, and she kissed him once more, gently. He winced as she brought her hand down across his chest; a large blue bruise colored the ribs on his left side.

Fred Hogue had asked Farrell to stop by the engineering office a couple days before. Hogue had shown great concern over a report of possible fraud. What did Farrell know about it? Farrell tried to act surprised; he stammered a denial, sure his nervousness was apparent. Someone, Hogue told him, had called in the Bureau of Mines for an official inspection. Would his assay results stand up to review? As Farrell walked home from the office that evening he was jumped and beaten and had only gotten away because Chief Osterkamp had stumbled onto the scene and had drawn and fired his gun.

"We don't have to go yet; there's lots of time," Jolene said. "Come back to bed."

"No, we're running out of time. I'm afraid we really have to talk about this." He found his jersey under the bed and struggled into it, then rose and pushed a pot of water onto the hot part of the stove.

Farrell's voice shook as he spoke, and Jolene wasn't sure if it was from the cold. Her guarded smile disappeared, and she threw off the quilt and stood and warmed herself by the fire. He stepped behind her and wrapped her bare body in his arms, and she turned and put her arms around his neck and kissed him hard.

With so little room in the cabin they helped each other to dress. She snapped his suspenders over his shoulders; he helped her to step into her wool pants, and she put on her undershirt and heavy knit sweater. The day outside was clear and bitterly cold, and a shiver took hold as the chill finally found her. She dipped two ceramic cups into one of the pots of steaming water and trembled as she made tea.

The tea steeped and neither spoke. Farrell folded a set of flight maps and set them on the small table. He handed her a cup, then wiped the steam from the window panes with his hand and peered out on the snowy glade. Tall, thick aspen trunks and dark, intergrown fir trees walled-in their sanctuary. Mist rose from ice-rimmed pools at the spring and glowed in sunlight shining through bare branches.

Jolene sat back on the cot. Farrell stepped away from the light, sat on the floor at her feet, and laid his head in her lap. "You have to go," she said. "If you stay, they'll send you to prison or they'll kill you."

"*We* have to go."

"If you get started somewhere, I could meet you. I could get by till then."

He climbed onto the cot with her. "Jo, one dark day will turn into another, and the passes will close, and you'll get by," he explained. "And when the passes finally reopen the sun will come out too, and spring will turn into a glorious summer, and the fall will be not so bad—until the rains comes again. And when another winter sets in you will just die away."

"I know. I know how it works."

"You'll die here."

Jolene leaned her head on his chest, and he winced again from the pain. Sunlight filtered through the bare trees and knifed through the small room. She said, "Fair, why did you show me that story last fall, the one about *Germelshausen*? It's an unimportant German folk tale. What did you mean for me to gain from it?" She leaned away from him and looked into his eyes. "You knew you would ask me to go away with you, even back then."

She slipped out of the quilt, kneeled, and stoked the fire, then sat on the floor and added another piece of firewood. Farrell asked, "What did you gain from the story? What did you read in it? Did you see a town entombed in sin and ignorance, where time is meaningless because future is as useless as past?"

"You're being mean on purpose. You could also read of two people who loved each other, but one's faith wasn't strong enough and their love was lost forever." She drew her knees up and hugged her arms around them, warming her hands in front of the flames. "I could read it that way if I tried."

Farrell spoke softly, "And what would their lives have been if they'd stayed together in that cursed town?" He tried to stroke her hair but couldn't reach her for the pain. "A hundred years of sameness, of nothingness. We've made the right decision, Jo. We'll escape together."

She wouldn't look at him. "And shall I just forget everything I am, everything... I leave behind?"

"I won't dismiss your feelings. But it wouldn't be long before it all hardened you and filled you with hate. You'd hate Ray for the person you'd become." He rose from the cot, kneeled, and took her gently by the shoulders. "You'd hate me, too, by then..."

"I already do." She fought for a smile.

"But mostly you'd hate yourself for who you don't become."

Jolene sat on the cold floor, leaning against him, gazing into the firebox with her arms wrapped around her middle. For a long time her face burned in the red light of the coals. She whispered, *"Desire like a river flows...never twice the same."*

"What was that?"

She closed her eyes tightly. "When would you... when would we leave?"

31

Could it have been Farrell all along? I woke in my chair at midnight, still with no answers but finally with the right questions. The lights were off at the portal of the New Main, and the big doors locked and barred. But moonlight flooded the waste rock dump as I drove up. I pulled in with just the running lights of my truck and parked behind the new office trailer. I didn't want to draw a lot of attention if the drillers on night shift happened to look down this way. The maw of the adit stood dark against the silver-washed hillside. In another thirty minutes, I guessed, the moon would drop behind the ridge and the doorway would be lost, but that would mean nothing underground.

The new changing shack was cold, they haven't replaced the heaters yet. I decked out in the dark, donning boots and slicker, a lamp pack, and the oxygen-generating rescue. If things go badly in the Oblique, the self-rescue will do me no good. But I belted on the damned heavy thing, and I brassed in. Old habits, I guess. Cairn's key hung behind the desk drawer; I took it and unlocked the chain over the man-way door.

Entering an underground at night is always dispiriting, a far different experience than entering out of the daylight. The mind carries no sunniness down with it, the retinas no reserve of photons. A dreadful, lonely resignation enfolds you as you descend from shadow to perfect darkness. The Main adit feels colder and emptier to me than when I walked in with Matt Cairn. Boots scrape loudly on the floor, and the lamp beam sweeps back and forth in rhythm with my steps, as a cross might be brandished when walking through a graveyard. When yours is the only cap lamp in the darkness, all your world exists in that cone of light projecting from your head. It moves you forward but gives no relief at all to any peripheral unease you may feel. Your arms swing disembodied in darkness; your feet, too, unless you point your head directly at them. You walk with your own breath sounding different in your ears. Even your thoughts seem foreign now, and they echo in your head from far away, reaching back to images of light and life.

The Oblique opens unexpectedly in front of me. I have walked too quickly, didn't pace myself, and it takes a while to catch my breath and to screw up enough courage to re-enter the drift. I'm not afraid of him, of course; he is dead for a practical certainty. Still, dread weighs on my limbs. Fear of your own fear can exceed the terror of any demon, and it is a struggle to rise and put one boot in front of the other, to wade in through the white sludge under the creaking, groaning timbers. Ducking and weaving under the beams, I reach and touch the solid things, leaving hand prints behind to mark my passing.

He lies as I left him, the poor half-interred man, on his side with his arm draped over his head, agonized again by the light and the intrusion. I rest on the broken timber and lean back against the rib. It seems to me his arm bones are not unusually strong; the shoulders seem less massive than they should be on one who shaped and hefted timbers for a living. The finger bones are delicate, could not have swung a sledge all day. My own hand compares large next to his. The lamp beam catches a glint, and there is a tarnished ring hanging loosely on the mummified finger. A fraternity ring, its Greek letters glisten in the beam of my lamp. "Well, Christ," I say aloud, and my words resound in the emptiness. "Christ Almighty," I whisper, "how did this happen?"

The red sludge I moved last time oozed back and filled around his torso, but the knife is still there when I brush the sludge back again. It didn't disappear into my imaginings. Ruby-red cinnabar crystals still encrust the steel rivets and steel hilt; the handle, the antler, is exquisitely carved as only an artist could have done.

I reach up and turn off my cap lamp and let the darkness rush in and bury me: pure darkness, not just dark as a moonless night. Night is a faintness of light, a shadow between your eyes and the sun. The darkness of an empty mine—or of a tomb—is no shadow but an opposite of light, as perfectly different as death is from life or evil from good. The darkness wraps around and constricts my breathing, and the silence rushes over me as well. No drips of water, no rustle of winds or shifts of sand can be heard. The darkness and silence are endless.

†

Farrell hated and feared the underground. Still, he waited at security for someone to show up and sign and brass him in. But the mine was working an irregular shift that night, and when no one came by, he headed in alone.

He would have needed a good reason to enter the mine. Had Ray or somebody given him a message, arranged a meeting? What else but to get an explanation of the sample results and the mapping discrepancies? *Change of plans - meet me at this drift, at this time.*

Faint hammering clanked through the wallrock from somewhere in the mine, but no rumbling machinery nor shouting foremen broke the stillness at Forty-eight hundred west. The new jumbo drill was down, so the main face was idle and most of the night shift in this area were standing down, too. Men were working on the surface, cleaning and repairing until the mechanics could get the machinery up and running.

Farrell found the entry to the Oblique and followed it as it headed along the Midas trend. A hundred feet beyond the pretense though, the drift swung off on a separate trend, not following the map at all. Farrell easily saw the divergence, and he followed on toward the working face, though he was not experienced enough to recognize the poor ground conditions he was entering. In the drift the air was

THE RECLAMATION

hot and humid without the ventilation, and it smelled sharply of wet clays and sulfates. Bright red mercury and arsenic oxides dripped out of the overhead stopes and pooled on the floor. The heat and dampness increased as he walked deeper into the drift, and Farrell took off his full-length Ulster topcoat. Heavy Donegal tweed, it was a ridiculous thing in the mine, but he hadn't intended to enter the mine. As he approached the working face, some of the square-set timbers, just a few days old, had already begun to strain and heave. Farrell paid them no mind.

The furtive glimmers of another cap lamp darted in the passage ahead, and he stepped forward, ducking under beams. Harly, not Ray, sat waiting. Harly wore a hard hat but otherwise was not dressed for work either. His airman's jacket hung on a nail on one of the wood pillars. He sat on a timber near the end of the drift.

"Harly." Farrell stepped into the light. "Where's Ray?" he asked. "Is Ray coming?"

"Ray is probably waiting where you arranged to meet him," Harly said. His laugh was nervous. "I didn't think you'd want him to be part of this discussion."

"You're in on it, aren't you? I knew when I saw you lead the strike away from the mill." Farrell stepped around and stumbled on the rock-strewn floor. "Still, I hoped you weren't." He looked down at his old friend for a long moment. "Was any of it genuine, Har? Did you care at all about the workers, about justice?"

"Oh, justice! Good God yes, I've been working overtime for that re-distribution of wealth. You ought to be proud of me, professor."

Farrell looked for a place to lean or sit but saw nothing he could be sure of. He dropped his coat on the apron of rocks below the working face and wiped his head and neck with his handkerchief. "What the hell are you doing, Harly?" he asked. "When did gold become your priority?"

"When I noticed I didn't have any." Harly lifted his cap and wiped his arm over his head. He pursed his lips and returned Farrell's stare, but then looked away and exhaled. "I need a way out. It's nothing personal, college boy, but I need a way out."

"Way out? I don't understand…"

"That doesn't surprise me, rich boy—golden boy. When the war's over you'll go wherever you want in the world and do whatever you want. Well, I'm not staying behind in the muck and mud. I've got my own way out, now, and I'm gettin' while the gettin's good."

Farrell shook his head. "You've been angry for a long time, and I don't know why."

"It's not enough you're screwing my brother's wife?"

This time Farrell turned away. "When did you learn?"

"You're not as clever as you think."

"Jolene and I… it was never meant to happen. I just wanted to help."

"Well, now you can."

"How can I help, Har?"

"By going to jail." Harly stood up and stepped toward Farrell. "Inspectors are on their way. Someone's got to take the blame."

"I didn't call them."

"They're going to find this drift and figure it out in no time, and all the fake assays you've reported, too. You're taking the blame for the missing gold." Straining toward Farrell, barely able to hold back tears, he said, "You and your old man. Someone has to."

"Why did you bring me here, then?" Farrell asked, now a deeper concern sharpening his voice.

"See, you don't know a fucking thing. You're going to admit to it all, or Ray's gonna find out about you and Jolene. He'll kill you both."

Farrell stared down at Harly's feet, his legs going weak as an understanding slowly came over him. He shook his head. "Who called the inspectors, Goddamn it?"

But Farrell wasn't used to being underground, and as he yelled he swung his head and looked directly at Harly, blinding him with his cap lamp. Harly threw up his hand to fend the light, and Farrell thought it was a blow meant for him—he ducked and swung at Harly with a fist. Harly knocked him away with a hard backhand that sent Farrell flailing into a timber; a shower of broken rocks fell from above, nearly knocking Harly to his knees. Farrell rushed for the exit, but Harly, still reeling from the rock fall, blocked his way. They struggled and in an instant Harly's knife was in his hand, and Farrell crumbled to the floor.

*

The drumming of my heart tells me I don't belong here. It won't calm but gets louder. It breaks the silence and breaks my thoughts and echoes through the chamber. My breaths come heavily through my mouth, and the sound helps to focus my mind. The air is thin, and my head spins. How long have I sat?

The stiffness in my knees and back almost drop me again as I rise to go, and I sway into a timber and knock my cap off. The beam above my head groans and pops. In the dark I fumble for the cord that ties lamp and cap to my hip. As I do, flickers of light, gleaming sylphs, reflect against the face of the chamber even before the slushing and splashing reach me. Goddamn it!

But the wading is too tentative to be Cairn, too cautious. I pull my cap to me and switch the lamp back on. She calls to me; Maddie calls out my name and steps uncertainly into the chamber.

"Maddie, my God! You shouldn't have come; it isn't safe here."

"I was at Bernie's rig and saw your lights. I was worried. Harlan, what the hell are you doing here at this hour?"

"I lost my keys," I try to joke. "Just trying to retrace my steps." I step over and take hold of her and try to turn her away, but she tenses all at once and stops breathing for a moment. She doesn't scream, as I worried she might, but she stares, still as death. We both shudder.

"Harlan!" she says.

"You go on, it isn't safe here. Wait for me at the entrance of the drift. I'll be right out."

"Come with me."

"I'll be right out."

"Come out with me, Harlan."

"I'm almost through here. You go on out. Step carefully. I'll be right behind you."

Maddie's splashing recedes down the drift, and when she is well out I sit and turn off my lamp again. But the darkness this time is too heavy, and I have to turn the lamp back on. I just close my eyes.

†

Ray entered the mine already upset because Farrell hadn't made their meeting. The useless old security man told him he thought Farrell had gone in, and that Harly might be inside, too, though neither had brassed in. Ray knew where they would be.

He heard Harly's sobbing before he got to the face. Harly's cap lamp was broken, Farrell's was pressed against Harly's shoulder, and the chamber was nearly dark. Ray stepped in and found his brother holding Farrell. Ray didn't see the knife at first. "What's happened; is he hurt?" Ray asked.

"Oh, God I didn't mean to do it," Harly cried. "He came at me, Ray."

"What the hell did you do?" Ray grabbed his brother's shoulder, and Farrell rolled away with the knife hasp protruding from his chest. No breath came from Farrell, no pulse.

"Oh Jesus," Ray whispered. He pulled the body back and laid it down on the rocks.

"I had to; he called the Goddamned inspector on us," Harly lied.

Scared now, and confused, Ray asked. "What happened, for Christ sake?"

"He had it coming, the arrogant bastard. I had to do it." Harly pushed himself up to stand in the small space. "I did you a favor, dammit," he yelled at Ray. "He's been with your wife."

"Shut up, Goddamn you! I have to think." Ray paced for a minute, near tears, nearly blinded by fear and confusion. He stopped and listened, then held his breath and put his fingertips to the walls to feel the distant hammer ringing through the rocks.

THE RECLAMATION

"Look," he said, "everyone's gonna know you were in here, and everyone'll know Hammond was here, too."

Harly nodded, still crying. "I didn't mean to do it, honest to God," he sobbed.

"We have to close this drift, bring the roof down so no one ever sees what happened." Ray took his brother by the shoulder and shook him hard. "Listen to me!" he cried. "No one is gonna believe you would run from a cave-in, Harly. And no one will doubt Farrell did. Only one of you can leave, understand? You've got to die here tonight. Do you understand?"

Harly raised his head and tried to talk, but his blubbering made no sense. Ray shook his younger brother again. "Do you understand? Take his coat, leave yours. Take his papers and his keys. Listen to me, Harly," he said, now crying himself. "You always wanted to be Farrell Hammond, didn't you? You wanted to join the Air Corps? Well, take his stuff right now and run. Put your collar up when you leave here, shine your light in men's faces as you run. You gotta get to his plane and fly out of here, and don't you ever look back."

Harly, trembling now, and sobbing, had to be helped to put on Farrell's big overcoat and his hard hat and lamp. He looked back once but couldn't hold his brother's eyes; he tried to speak but choked. He turned and ran from the drift.

Ray sat alone, now, with Farrell's ghost. He turned from the dead man and lit a smoke. His fingers trembled as he drew on the cigarette. He finished the smoke and lit another; he wanted to let Harly get a good ways out before bringing the whole company running. His eyes couldn't look at the body. He finished the second smoke, tossed the butt down, and picked up the twenty-pound double jack. Only one way out remained for him, but it was going to be tricky.

Several sets out from the face the ground was straining and the ten-by-ten timber above him was already groaning. Ray took a couple of breaths, stepped to the exterior side, and swung the sledge at one of the six-by-six diagonal braces. On the second swing the brace exploded out, the ten-by-ten beam above started popping and screeching, and splinters shot from it. The ribs started spalling, and the back bowed down.

Ray ran out a few more steps and swung the sledge hard at another brace and it, too, broke loose. He knocked out the brace on the other side and started to run then, following Harly out. He swung hard at the braces at every other set as he passed them, about every ten feet. Behind him, the groaning and screeching of timbers grew to a tempest. A crack of thunder shot by him, and a *WHUMP*, and a blast of wind and water nearly knocked him from his feet as the first square set finally collapsed. He kept running and swinging the sledge. The other timbers now were all popping and shrieking as wood fibers tore apart. Ray knocked out one more brace, then dropped the sledge hammer and ran as fast as he could for the entry. He miss-timed the collapse, he realized; the whole thing was coming down too fast. He still had twenty feet to cover to get to the main adit, and the firecracker sound was non-stop, the screeching deafened him. And then silence—and a blast hit him in the back like a cannon shot and lifted him, arms and legs still running, throwing him from the drift to roll against the far rib of the main adit. He bounced off the rock wall and raised his arm to cover his head as rocks pummeled him, and broken timbers stabbed at him, and white clay and red ooze splattered over him.

The barrage stopped, and he stood, but fell again. The concussion had bloodied his ears and eyes, and the impact broke some ribs and a shoulder. He struggled again to his feet and stood in the sudden silence, and… Jesus Christ, the knife, he realized. He'd left the fucking knife!

His cap dangled behind him by the lamp chord, and he retrieved it with his good arm and stumbled toward the portal. The watchman and another miner met him as they ran in toward the disaster. Ray slumped against the rib as they approached, their lamp beams scanning him all over, searching him but seeing a ghost in white clay and blood and miner's gear.

"Ray! Christ Almighty, Ray!" the watchman yelled.

There was no going back. Ray raised his good arm and pointed toward the Oblique. "Harly," he croaked.

"Are you okay, Ray?" the miner shouted.

Ray nodded and pointed to the Oblique again, and the men hurried in that direction.

Two more miners rushed in, and Ray asked them about Hammond. "He just ran out, the fucking coward," one told him.

"Let him go," Ray gasped. "He never had balls for the underground. Let him go!"

The men ran toward the cave-in, and Ray stumbled out toward the portal, leaving Farrell Hammond lying alone in Harly's tomb.

*

I kneel once more and put my hand over his, over Farrell's, and slowly, carefully slide the ring off the leathery bone. Reaching under my slicker, I stash the ring in my jeans pocket. Farrell is left to his peace, at last, I hope, and the sloshing out through the timbered drift is easier, quieter this time. I have no strength left for panic.

Maddie waits in the main adit. She sits on the mucker, sighs when I appear, and marshals a smile. I stand erect, finally, stretch my back, and wipe my hands on some burlap. Cairn keeps his smokes and a lighter in the jockey box of the machine; Marlboros, and I take one and light it. Maddie takes one, too, and I light it for her.

"You're full of bad habits," I say, returning her smile.

"Well, Christ..." She tries to laugh. "If you can't have a smoke at a funeral..." Then she gets serious and asks, "Who was that? Was that Harly?"

"No. My father, I think."

"Ray?"

"No." I shake my head.

She nods and doesn't pry. "So, what do we do now?" she asks after a few puffs. "The sheriff will be here today."

"Close the drift," I say, and I'm surprised at my own words. "We can get the samples we need by cross-drilling from the main adit.

The drift is too dangerous. I wasted Andy's money opening the damned thing."

Maddie agrees with the plan, but says, "The authorities might be interested in that knife."

I jump up on the mucker with her and loosen my utility belt. "What knife?" I blow a bright plume of smoke across both our lamp beams. "Maddie," I explain, "Farrell Hammond died more than sixty-five years ago. Every person he ever loved or hurt in his life is gone, every last soul. Every hope he had and every pain he ever suffered has dissolved away to nothing. I'm all that's left of any of this, and I didn't see a knife. Did you really see a knife?"

Maddie turns and stares away down the adit; straight down so her cap-lamp beam disappears into the emptiness of it. She doesn't answer for a long while, and I realize she might see the story, understand every part of it better even than I can. She breathes in heavily and flips her cigarette into the red waters flowing under our feet. She says, "Harlan, I didn't see a damned thing."

We sit for a little longer, I light another cigarette, and she asks, "So what do you want to do?"

"Pull the timbers." I jump down from the mucker. "I have to bring it down. Now if I can. I don't want some Goddamned sight-seer going in to gawk at a rotting corpse and getting his stupid ass killed. And I don't want the sheriff in there digging up that body or calling for some lurid inquest. It's no one's business. I'm going to pull the Goddamned timbers."

Keys are rarely taken from underground equipment unless the mine is shut down for some time. Sure enough, the key is in the mucker, and with a push of the ignition the diesel engine turns over and fills the adit with deep rumbling. The diesel exhaust is like black perfume, and the lights glare off the wet rocks for fifty feet in both directions.

With a little concentration, I get the machine swung around so the winch on its back-end points toward the Oblique entry. Leaving the engine in idle, then, I pull the big hook line from the winch and start back into the drift. It's heavy work once around the corner, snaking the three-quarter-inch cable over the rocks. I didn't raise the timbers up as Ray and Harly had, so I don't know the best way to bring them down. The cable is heavy, and it fights me, but I get it snaked around the bend and into the deeper part of the drift, then pull some slack, as much as I can. The cable goes up over a roof beam, then around a pillar, then up over another beam, and so on into the drift, working closer and closer to the chamber at the far end. The slack of the cable has to be pulled over each beam or around each pillar before the next one can be started. I loop the cable behind a couple of pillars, then twice around another roof beam and snap the hook around the cable to tie it off.

That's that, and I stop to rest and to catch my breath. But I was wrong: I'm not the only one left of all this. The open chamber lies fifty feet farther in but it is a long slog. I am exhausted, weary of the place, dreading the return.

My light intrudes upon him one more time and I try to speak, to apologize, to explain my actions, but my voice breaks and nothing sensible comes out. The leather jacket is too crumbly and falls apart in my hands. The wing medallion is intact, though the silver plate is partly replaced by cinnabar crystals; it comes off easily. That will do, and my offending light retreats from the chamber a final time.

Maddie agrees to wait at a cutout about fifty feet out toward the portal where she can watch in relative safety. From the operator's seat the controls for the hydraulic winch are easy enough to figure out, and I set the brake and give Maddie a thumbs-up. The engine revs, and with a light pull of a lever the winch turns and the slack comes out of the cable. The drum keeps turning, pulling the cable taut and crushing the rock where the cable bends around the corner into the drift. As resistance builds the winch whines and strains, and I gun the engine a little more and feel the mucker pull and lean toward the Oblique. A beam far down the drift breaks away, and the mucker rocks back at the release of tension and nearly throws me from my seat. The drum winds a couple of turns more and the cable tightens again. Another release of tension rocks me; the drum winds and tightens, and another release, and by now the shrill groaning of timbers rises over the sound of the diesel. Two more beams break away and that's all I can stand. The tunnel is rumbling like a freight train as I jump down and run toward the main exit. Maddie calls and gestures to me, but I don't hear her words. My legs strain but it seems I barely move, and I get just a few steps before the floor bounces up and throws my feet from under me. I come down hard on the rocky floor and feel another bounce lift me. White-red muck explodes out of the drift and blasts against the opposite rib with a roar of wind. Timbers crash against the wall, and muck splashes and flies my way, spraying me with clay and gravel and splinters.

The blast is over in a few seconds, but the ground bounces for a while longer, and my ears ring from the concussion. Maddie runs to me and when I can stand, helps me up and over to shut off the mucker. With a hack saw I try to cut the winch cable, but my shoulder is banged up, and she has to finish cutting it. The tension pulls the cut end back under the muck. Maddie finds a burlap rag and wipes my prints off the machine's controls. I shake my head but tell her she's a fine co-conspirator.

As we turn to leave I'm not walking too well, so she props me up under my good arm, and we begin the long mile to the portal. I let her help me. "I'm sorry for all the trouble," I tell her.

"I'm fine. What do you need to be sorry for?"

"God, I don't know. I'm sorry for all of it. I'm sorry for things I don't even understand yet."

We scuffle through the darkness together, and like no time before I yearn for a rising sun and the sounds of wind and living things.

32

We stepped out into the barest illumination of dawn, and even that dulled by a mist that blew in while we were underground. But even the murky half-light was a deliverance to our eyes. I put the chain back around the man-way door, and re-locked it, then found a long crow bar, and with Maddie's help, broke the chain. I returned the key to its hiding place. We hung up our brass and our lamps, and stowed our diggers behind the seats of our trucks. It looked plausibly, if anyone were to ask, like another anonymous act of vandalism.

With an hour left before sunup, I told Maddie to hit the sack and suggested if she were to sleep for most of the day she would have to answer fewer questions. Maddie drove back to Stibnite, and I headed to my place to clean up a little. There was more to be done before I could sleep.

The clouds were hanging just out of arms reach at my place when I climbed back into my truck, and my headlight beams bounced eerily off their swirling bottom surface. I entered the murk as I started up Ridge Road, and it grew heavier as I climbed. Toward the top of the ridge, though, the fog thinned, and the sun must have been rising, because the haze grew glaring, even painfully bright.

†

Harly ran from the mine in Farrell's big Ulster coat and felt the bounce of the ground under his feet before he found Farrell's car parked behind the tool shop. He jumped into the car and drove down under the ore chutes and up onto Ridge Road, the siren at the mine wailing behind him. He passed rescue units at the top of the pass coming the other direction. Scared and alone, he raced through the south-side curves, his bright headlight beams slicing through the black night, sweeping the trees and the snowy brush. The road was rutted and icy, and he spun out and slid on the turns, but made it down to Stibnite. Foot traffic was heavy in the town, so he dodged over to side streets and crept to the airfield, parking at the far end where Farrell's plane was tethered.

Hoarfrost thickened the rushes and tree branches at the edge of the runway and glistened in the beams of his headlights. Harly jumped out of the car, put the collar up on Farrell's big tweed coat, and tied the belt tightly around. His boots crunched in the dry snow as he checked over the plane: fuel, oil, battery, engine compression; it was ready to go. The airfield was abandoned and dark, the small hangar and office obscured by a freezing ground fog. Another car could have been parked in the shadows behind the hangar; someone could have waited unseen.

Harly found a bag in Farrell's car, packed for a trip. He threw it into the plane's cabin and climbed in. He started the engine and didn't wait for it to warm but gunned it hard and sputtered and backfired to the far, dark end of the runway. The plane's wing lights swept narrow beams across the snowpack as he turned and started his run. Someone could have dashed out then, waving with suitcase in hand and easily not been seen, had someone come to the airfield, if a person had been waiting.

†

"I'll try Fair," Jolene told him. "I'll try to come, I promise." She turned on her knees to face him. "But if you don't see me there, you have to promise you'll get in the plane and fly away, and never look back."

THE RECLAMATION

"Dress for icy cold," he said, and he raised her up from the floor of the shack and held her in his arms. "It'll be cold in the plane. Bitter cold." Fighting through tears he said, "I'll meet you at the airfield at nine o'clock, so we won't get caught on the roads with a shift change."

Jolene nodded, her face buried in his shoulder. He tried to smile but couldn't, tried to speak again of their life together, of his love for her. She nodded but didn't raise her eyes to his.

†

The plane bounced down the frozen surface and lifted eastward into the night sky. The engine warmed as it climbed, and its high-pitched drone echoed through the hills as Harly banked into a tight turn. It vibrated in the window panes as he flew back over the wintry town, humming a Doppler farewell through the tin roofs of the small, timber-framed homes.

*

I watched out for Cairn and the sheriff coming up the road, but the hour was still early, and I passed no traffic. A number of trucks, including Cairn's and a couple of government-looking vehicles, were parked in front of the TNT, so I avoided Main Street and found a back track to Earl's place, to the old mansion on the rise. I must have looked a sight from hell standing at his door in the morning mist.

Earl answers my knock in less than a minute. He's already dressed, as though expecting me. "I felt the bounce, just like sixty-five years ago," he says.

"Yeah, I closed the drift," I admit.

He leads the way down the hallway to the dining room. "I wondered if you would," he says without turning.

"I thought I'd better do it before you killed yourself trying."

Earl turns and looks hard at me. "You should never have gone in there poking around," he says, then walks from the room.

He returns with a pot of hot water, and a plate of biscuits. We sit at the grand mahogany table as the tea steeps, and watch gray fog billow against the window panes. A marble clock ticks on the mantle. "Did you find... Oh, God!" he says, and nearly chokes up. "Did you find all you need?"

I nod, and when he asks me what it was like, I tell him. He hears every detail of how it smelled with the red sulfurous slime oozing from the walls and how the clays glistened in the beam of my headlamp, and the darkness deeper than anything you can imagine on top of the earth when the lamp is turned off and you sit alone with a dead man. I tell him about the knife—the cinnabar-crusted hilt and the carved handle.

He knows who it belonged to; his eyes tell me so. He nods without speaking.

I polish the wing medallion against my shirt, and hand it to him. He clasps his hand gently around it, holds his closed hand to his head for a moment, then sets the wings on the table.

"He was bigger than life," Earl says. "The best friend I ever had." He closes his eyes and nods a couple times. "Harly knew about me— the way I am. 'Don't you ever feel bad about who you are,' he would tell me. 'Anyone gives you trouble, you come see me'."

Earl cries softly, and I could give him a minute, but I say, "There was more." He clasps his shoulders and looks away. I take the ring from my pocket and lay it next to the wings.

He looks at the ring for a long moment, expressionless, then shakes his head and barely whispers, "I feared so... and I guess I feared not. So, it was Harly who flew away." He breathes deep and says, "Your uncle was a good man. Whatever else you believe, Harly Pruitt was a good man. The best friend..."

"You didn't know who died that night, did you?"

"No. Never for sure, because.... Well hell, he couldn't just stop at the café for a chat, now could he?"

"No, I guess he couldn't. It was you, wasn't it? You betrayed Farrell and Jolene."

"Betrayed them, is that what you call it?" Earl shakes his head and turns away. "I'd have died and gone to hell for your mother. Why she took up with that fancy shirt I'll never understand. He took advantage. Your mother... she wasn't strong yet; she was still hurting, still searching."

"You said she was nobody's victim."

"Goddamn you, if you came here to twist my words! Farrell Hammond took advantage!"

"Harly never got over his jealousy of Farrell, did he? Was it just the wealth and class, or was he jealous over Jolene, too?"

Earl stands and looks like he would come right over the table at me if he were a few years younger. "Harly wasn't jealous of nobody. He didn't need to look up to that elitist, that arrogant..." He raps his knuckles on the table, but sits eventually, and pours himself a tea. Tears well again in his eyes before he can stir in the milk, and he speaks almost in a whisper, "It was me. I told Harly he had to save Jo. Harly let it go for a long time. He didn't give a damn what happened to him or Farrell by then, but he waited because of what it could do to Jolene. She was fragile—more than anyone knew, he told me.

"But Goddamn me all to hell, I put the idea in Harly's head that he might kill two birds with one stone." Earl's head jerks up. "Hell, you know I didn't mean it like that!" He's shaking and can hardly go on. "'Call the inspectors in,' I told him, 'that'll end it for you, and you can make Farrell pay for what he's done'."

I wait as Earl watches the fog blow against the window. He says, "Harly was scared; Hogue's scheme was killing him. He needed to get out. Did you get that it was the engineers?"

"It had to be. And in the end, it had to be all about gold, didn't it?"

Earl lifts his eyes, and the fight's gone out of him; he's just a tired old man. "No, you got that part wrong," he says softly. "It was never just fortune to Harly, nor to Ray—anymore than it was to Jolene out panning the streams."

It's not what I expected, but maybe I should have: Earl starts to sob, just softly. He says, "It was... a reclamation—do you know what I'm talking about? —a chance to get back something of what was taken."

He leans forward, touching his head to his fists on the table. I don't know what I'm supposed to do. I step around and pull out the chair next to him and sit. I put my good arm around his shoulder and hold him for a bit. "You shouldn't have opened it," he says. "I didn't mean for them all to die. You should have left it be."

It's no skin off my nose, so I sit with him a while longer. He's okay after a bit, although he keeps apologizing. He doesn't need to apologize; he doesn't need to worry about any of it. Life may be catastrophism after all, but we are the martyrs not the agents of the calamities. It is eddies and pools, falls, and bends until there's no way back. I make us another pot of tea, and we sit at the table, watch the morning sun burn through the fog, and talk about the old days.

33

There were some hard questions about the broken lock and the cave-in. My answers were all factual. The sheriff wondered if we shouldn't re-open the drift to recover the body. I told him it would be dangerous; Cairn was half beside himself, but he had to agree. I showed the sheriff the wing medallion and explained that it was given to my uncle by a general at Fairchild. I said it was my own flesh and blood lying under the rocks, and I'd prefer to let him rest in peace.

It was all factual. But the thing about sticking to the facts is this: for all that people go on about them, facts have a completely different meaning when seen from different perspectives. Working theories are better; that's how you approximate the truth in geology. Truth is the working theory at any given time that most fully calibrates to the evidence. So, a lie isn't really a lie in geology. It's just a working theory that discounts, for one reason or another, some of the facts.

I left the wings with Earl.

The fog returned in the afternoon, but it has nearly lifted again, and I can see the road clearly. Everything else, though, remains in shadow and I don't know anymore where to turn. Jolene might have gone to the airfield that night—or she might have stayed home in her kitchen instead and heard the changing whine of the plane's engine as it neared, flew over, and flew by.

But she might have gone to the airfield. Frightened, hopeful, in love; would she have seen Farrell in his coat or would she have recognized Harly? Did she return slowly down this road to Cinnabar, suitcase still beside her on the seat, broken hearted and shamed as she faced Ray at the kitchen door?

And what could she have said to her husband? What could Ray have said to his wife after what he had seen and done?

There is so little left in the trunk of photos and letters. So damned little to go by.

*

A light snow fell again during the day, and most of the aspen and cottonwoods have dropped their leaves. The higher peaks are still dusted with white, and the crisp air tells me the dusting is here for the long haul. Maddie saw me cooking dinner out front and she stopped in.

"Rough day yesterday. Have you caught up on your sleep yet?" she asks.

"Just about. This steak and a bottle of wine should do the trick. Join me?"

"Can't. Have a date. But I'll take a cup of that coffee." Maddie comments on the stark whiteness of the late autumn sun as it drops to just above the tree tops. "A harsh judgement of all our labors?" she wonders.

I explain that in fact the air near the ground is colder this time of year and therefore holds less moisture, so the light coming through is not as refracted by water molecules and, as a result, the sunlight really is whiter and more intense.

She wags her head around and glares at me through her eyebrows. "You're a poet, Harlan," she says.

I clear my throat and suggest, "Bright heaven's window, 'neath we toil in temp'ral drear..."

"Huh?" she laughs.

"Do me a favor, Maddie, spend some time with Earl if you get the chance; hear what he has to say. If you feel comfortable about it, maybe talk to him about what you saw underground."

"Even about the knife? I thought that was…"

"He knows. I think he could use a friend to talk to."

Maddie has a warm smile, I've always thought so. She left for Stibnite and her evening with Stan, or Dan, or whoever the hell. The sun went down as scheduled, the down-canyon wind picked up as physics require, and the tin shacks of Cinnabar started to hammer again, as they must. But not so bitterly tonight.

May 8, 1945

Dear Dot,

The sun is out and warming things, and in just a few hours the icicles have fallen away, and snow drifts have melted back from fences and walls, and the roads flow now like slushy rivers. If this keeps up I believe the daffodils will be up and the lilacs will be blooming before another week goes by. Myrna so loved the daffodils. You remember, don't you? But you've probably been thawed for a month there in Nampa.

Dotty, I haven't been able to write since the accident because there just aren't words to express what I feel, what I know we both feel. I have lost you all. All but Ray and thank God for him… and for the baby. If Ray didn't tell you in his letters, then surprise! It's due in late October.

We don't talk of California anymore, it makes Ray upset when we do. "I can't leave," he tells me, and he means he can't leave Harly behind in this cursed ground.

Dotty, I made a terrible mistake and I don't know that I'll ever climb back from it. The spring has been so wet and cold, and I haven't read a book, and I can't seem to lift a pencil to write anything…

Roger Howell

*

The drilling program is almost finished, on schedule, and only a quarter-million or so over budget. It was a good day today: a warm, dry wind blew in, and I believe we may get a little Indian summer now. Mike and his team can enjoy that weather as they wrap things up. I'm not needed here anymore.

Honorario told me he'd like to come back in the spring for the fill-in and geotechnical drilling if we need him. I said he'll be the first one I call, and I meant it. Bernie has been in a good mood, too, for a Maritimer, and we've been cussing at each other a lot less recently. That word he's been yelling all summer: *tabernac?* It means church. He's been yelling *'church!'* at me. Whatever, right?

Maddie drives up as I poke the coals around into a shimmering bed for cooking. It's good to see her; I hoped she would come by. She steps up onto the porch, sets down her map case, and finds a beer in my cooler. Sitting on the railing, she hooks her foot around a baluster for balance like a first-class cowgirl. Except for the running shoes.

"I thought you were going to quit drinking," she says.

"It's just beer."

"Just beer is still drinking."

"Hardly. How about a grilled chicken breast? Got to eat 'em, can't take them with me."

"Chicken?"

"Cholesterol."

"Why not?" she says. "I've officially had everything on Earl's menu ten times."

The chicken breasts sizzle as they hit the grill, and while I push them around in the smoke I tell Maddie a little more about Jolene and Farrell, at least those parts I think I know. The chicken is white when I cut into it; I don't know how to tell if a damned chicken breast is ready. "Is this ready?" I ask.

She leans over and pokes the chicken with her finger, "Oh yeah, it's ready. Why didn't Jolene leave—did she leave?" Maddie asks.

"When it all went to hell did she at least get out to the city to stay with Dotty?"

"To Boise? No, she didn't go, not like that."

"Was she afraid of Ray?"

"No, I think Ray was... gentle with Jolene for the most part, as gentle as he knew how to be."

"He wasn't gentle with you."

"Not always, but he did okay by me, considering." I poke the coals with a stick until they glow bright red. "Ray was chained to Cinnabar," I say.

"How do mean?" Maddie's eyes are closed, and her head tilts back to the murmuring pines and the shifting and tearing tin.

"While the mine stayed open, all the gold in his hands meant nothing. He was a prisoner of the secret down there in the caved drift. As long as some eager engineer might try to re-open the Oblique..."

She throws her paper plate onto the coals and watches it blacken and twist and catch fire. In the sudden glow she says, "Well, all that won't matter soon. The acid-leach tests came back. The tailings can be neutralized, as you probably already guessed, and the surface-water impacts can be mitigated for the most part. The Plan of Operations will be approved."

"Yup, a million and a half ounces of gold will buy a lot of mitigation."

"So you tell me. I guess that's it then. I'll write my report when I've wrapped up here. The mine will go in, and the acid and the arsenic will be swept under the marshlands."

She's really a pretty good environmental engineer; a lot tougher than I expected her to be, and not nearly as much a pain in the ass. "Madison," I ask her, "what do you know about pine martens?"

"*Martes humboldtensis?*" she glances back at me. "What's there to know? They're endangered. I don't think there are many left in the central Rockies."

"What does their scat look like?"

"Well, it's a little like a real small bobcat's," she says curiously. "They eat mice and voles and the like, so it's usually full of hair, like a twisted rope. Like a weasel's scat, in fact, though larger."

"That might be what it was then," I say as I open another beer.

"What *what* was? Where?"

"Up in Alec's Canyon. There's an old cabin and some diggings up there by a spring. It might have been weasel scat, except I've seen weasel scat and this, I thought, was from a larger animal."

"Weasels are a lot smaller," she says. "Martens are more like the size of a Fisher almost. Where exactly did you see this?"

Another armful of wood makes the fire crackle and throw up streams of sparks. In the light of the fire I show her on the topo map exactly where I'm describing.

"Harlan, pine martens are endangered. They're *listed!*"

"So you tell me."

"It could kill the mine. If it's true, it would change everything."

"Yeah, that's the damned thing about truth." I toss my beer can into the barrel.

The days are much shorter anymore, and this one has faded gracefully to a moonless night. The wind picks up a little, and Maddie and I stare into the coals for a while longer and listen to the town hammer and shriek. I don't mind it like I used to, it's just the wind sorting through the last of the rust and memories. The firelight glints on the lettering of the ring: sigma gamma epsilon in gold and black onyx. It fits well on my finger, and I think Farrell Hammond would not mind at all that I wear it. Maddie agrees he would have wanted me to have it.

She has to get on back to town to get ready for a hike tomorrow, and I have some packing to do, if I get around to it.

34

June 12, 1945

Dear Dot,

...If it's a girl, we'll name her Dorothy. You won't mind, will you? Ray says if it's a boy he wants to name him Harlan. I don't understand Ray at all, but he is treating me kindly; you don't have to worry about that. Ray tries to get me out walking when the weather's good, and I go with him, but it's been hard. I can't read, and I can't write. But I'll share a thought I just had, if you can stand it:

> A part of me caught up in your distant drifting dreaming
> lost sight of you wondering, lost sight of me misting your
> eyes.
> I smiled, lips waiting your pause; sparkling uncertain,
> enduring the autumn in our skies.
>
> Do you stand deep in blossoms, sweet fields waving red with
> new blossoms aching, reliving the frost and ember?
>
> Did you soaring, in your wake our promises breaking o'er
> granite walls crashing over empty hollow lives, through eyes
> now amist guess that part of you caught up in me?
> Did you turn, Love, and wonder; pause and wonder?

There, you see, Dotty, I'm back to writing awful poems. The church ladies found out I'm expecting, and they've been coming by with meals and such. They sit with me now and then during the day. God, can you imagine?

Ray has the mine manager's job, he finally got around to telling me. It's a good living, as you know, so I guess we'll be staying here a while longer.

I'm so sorry for all the trouble I've caused you all..."

†

Jolene sat on the front porch in the sun, its rays warming her back through a thin cotton shift. Ray had gone to work earlier, before sunup, and today Jolene had felt good and she'd cleaned his breakfast dishes and swept the floor. He had left her a fried egg and some bacon in the Frigidaire, and she'd felt suddenly ravenous and ate them cold. The cupboard was almost empty, and there was nothing else in the ice box to cook for supper. She remembered, though, that Ethel was going to bring over something today, a soup or a stew. She'd found a single tea bag on a high shelf in the cupboard, and it floated now, in a big mug of hot water.

She closed her eyes and smiled with her first sip of tea in the longest while. Shift change had come and gone some time ago, and it was too early yet for shoppers or visitors, so the town was quiet and nearly empty. A car drove by on the cross street, half a block away, and raised a puff of dust at the intersection. The dust rose and billowed and drifted on a light breeze, and Jolene made herself watch it until it was too thin to see. She raised the cup slowly to her lips and sipped.

From her porch she could see up the street as far as Ethel's house, and a couple houses down the cross street. And she could see Lookout Ridge, of course, above all of the rooftops. She sat on the porch all morning, getting up only a couple of times when the wind shifted, and she couldn't stand the banging and scraping of the ball mill.

Yellowjackets buzzed her as the sun got hotter around noontime. They had a nest somewhere, she imagined, because they'd been around the last several days. Yellowjackets live awhile, she supposed, not like house flies, so why didn't they learn there was nothing sweet to feed on here and they'd just get swatted at? It made no sense if these were the same yellowjackets, which she wasn't sure. Other than the yellowjackets and the loud, banging mill it was pleasant on the porch.

She thought she might walk to the grocery for more tea, but she couldn't remember where the money and stamps were kept now. Besides, her clothes didn't fit right anymore. Her belly was starting to swell, and when some of the ladies were passing by a week or so ago they had noticed. "Your cheeks are so flushed, Jolene," one had said, and another asked, "Are you okay, dear? Are you feeling at your prime?" They had seemed a little like goats to her, bleating and butting and straining for something, and it had made her laugh aloud. They hinted without asking until Jolene conceded, "Yes, actually; I'm expecting in late October or November." They'd come right up on the porch with her then, horns and hooves and all, and talked for half an hour until she excused herself back into the house.

Ladies came by more often now, especially from the church. They brought casseroles and soups and gave her to understand she was special, being not well as she was, even aside from the child. She laughed at that part and didn't care so much, really; she let them minister to her, and Ray seemed grateful for the regular meals.

Hattie came by in the afternoon as Jolene sat in the sun. "How long do you suppose yellowjackets live?" Jolene asked.

"Yellowjackets? Well, I don't know the number. But I'm sure it's not more or less than God intends."

"I guess that's the measure, then, isn't it?" Jolene said. "Yes, that must surely be the measure."

Hattie glanced at the teabag drying next to the cup, and Jolene noticed her glance and said, "I'm sorry Hattie. I wish I could offer you a cup, but I think that was my last bag."

"When were you last to the grocery?" Hattie asked.

"I'm not sure. I think in March. Or early April."

"For Lord's sake, child!" Hattie said, "Let's you and me walk on down there and get some tea and sugar. What else do you need?"

"I don't remember where the ration books are kept anymore," Jolene nearly cried, "or the money!"

"Jolene, you have a credit account with Jim Baughman."

Jolene sat for a moment and thought about it. "My clothes don't fit; do you think it will be okay? And I'll have to find some shoes."

Hattie and Jolene were back on the porch drinking their tea when Ellen came over. She'd seen them walking back from the grocery. Jolene asked Ellen to sit, and they all enjoyed the afternoon sun. Jolene served tea to Ellen, who wasn't used to the beverage, and another cup to Hattie, and opened the box of graham crackers that she'd just had to have at the store.

"Why is nothing in this town ever painted?" she asked Ellen and Hattie.

The two neighbors glanced all around as though they hadn't noticed the gray drabness of the place until then.

"Well, Jolene, they're all company houses. Who's going to paint a company house?" Ellen asked.

"Well, I don't know," Jolene answered. "The company. It's just ugly this way, don't you think? It wouldn't take but a cheap coat of paint to make the town decent."

Hattie glanced at Ellen and smiled politely. "Maybe we could do something," she suggested. "It wouldn't hurt anything to ask the company, I guess."

"Just a cheap coat of paint is all it would take. I swear, that's all, and this could be a decent town. The company could buy the paint," Jolene suggested, "and the men could paint their own houses."

Hattie nodded at the thought. "Why, the whole town could paint on a Sunday, as a communal service."

Ellen turned and shook her head with a shrug, but Hattie nudged her under the table. Jolene searched up and down the street as far as she could see. She promised to have Ray push the idea with Oscar Hammond.

†

"See, I knew you had a smile in you, Jolene," Hattie teased. "You just have to remember how to use it."

"Of course I can smile, when there's something to smile about," Jolene answered softly, glancing at the ladies around the table.

"Then what are you smiling at now?" Ellen wanted to know.

Jolene sat with Hattie and Ellen in the basement of the Baptist Church along with Berta Applegate and one other woman whose name Jolene couldn't get straight. She paused and smiled again, just a little. "I was thinking we should draw up this dress pattern and submit it to Vogue Magazine," she said. "It could be an instant hit, I think."

"For heaven's sake, we don't need a pattern for this," Ellen said, "just a few measurements on you. Lord knows we've all sewed enough maternity shifts."

"I think Jolene was telling a joke," Hattie said. "Did you want to go with the red gingham or the blue calico, honey?" she asked Jolene.

"I don't know, Hattie."

"The blue, dear," Hattie decided. "The gingham would look like a tablecloth on you." Hattie watched her face to see if Jolene would smile at that, too, and she beamed when the corners of Jolene's mouth tugged upward.

"Hardly much of a tablecloth," Berta complained. "She needs to eat more than she's eating."

The other women took turns agreeing. "You're too thin, dear. It ain't good for a baby to be carried around in a sack of bones," the woman with the difficult name said.

"Are you eating any of the casseroles," Ellen asked, "or is Ray eating it all?"

"No, Ray makes sure I eat," Jolene said quietly. "He takes good care of me."

"Well, all's I can say is the Lord makes some folks hard to figure," Ellen pushed her red hair off her face and glanced around at the others, who kept their eyes down or away.

"He does, that's for sure," Jolene agreed.

It was not a tablecloth, but something of a tent once they started sewing. Ellen would not consent to trim it down, insisting that a woman as tall as Jolene was would certainly add girth by her seventh month. Especially carrying a boy like Jolene was surely doing. And they didn't have to worry because she would eat more when her body was ready for it. Jolene nodded and said they should cut it Ellen's way. Hattie and Berta shrugged, but Ellen had carried eight children to term, so nobody argued.

On Sunday afternoon a social gathered at the church, and Jolene wore her new blue dress. She couldn't be dissuaded from bringing a plate of fried chicken, too. The day was beautiful for early September, not a cloud in the sky, and children played in the church yard. Ray and some other men smoked cigarettes by the gate as the women set up tables in the basement hall.

Jolene helped to lay out the buffet and talked with the ladies about today's sermon, about the sin of sloth and idleness. They were all sorry Jolene hadn't felt up to the picnic back on the Fourth. It had been so nice, and so peaceful this year. Jolene followed the talk as much as she could, but her mind was not there.

Ray had come out the previous night, and he'd sat with Jolene on the porch and they'd talked a bit through the best part of the setting sun. "How ya' doing tonight, babe?" he'd asked. The breeze blew from the east and carried the loud scraping, clattering sounds of the mill over the rooftops and down to their place on the porch.

"It's a semi-autogenous grind," Jolene had replied.

Ray leaned back and laughed aloud. "That's right, hon, that's exactly what the mill circuit is. Where in the world did you hear something like that?"

"We've lived with it since we moved here," she answered. "It's big steel drums that keep turning and never stop. Chunks of ore are thrown in all together, and they roll and tumble and bash into each other, crashing and breaking and wearing each other away. And that's the whole point: they wear each other down. And there's no way out; no way but to wear down so small there's nothing left to you at all and you fall out through the screens. But then there's nothing left but sand and dust."

Ray had stared a moment, then tried to say something, but he had to stop and turn away. He kissed her hand and told her they should start getting ready the baby's room. But Jolene had said no, she wasn't ready to clear away Myrna's life just yet. Ray had gone silent at that, and Jolene knew he was crying but couldn't help him. And then he said maybe Jolene could visit and stay awhile with Dorothy in Boise; it wouldn't take but a bus ticket. But Jolene said no to that, too. The road was too long and too bumpy, she lied.

Tears came to her now to think of Ray sitting sad and quiet under the golden clouds. One of the ladies noticed the tears and suggested Jolene sit a spell, and someone else fetched her some water.

35

August 15, 1945

   Dear Jolene,

   There was a story in the Boise paper, Shirley Knott showed it to me—Farrell Hammond was killed in action. He was shot down over the Pacific. I learned about it a couple weeks ago, but waited for a letter from you...

   What must it be like there in Cinnabar? I'm sure everyone is talking about it. Everyone liked Farrell...

   I just don't get it. They told us the war was almost over. Please write to me Jolene, I miss your letters.

                                      Love, Dottie.

I find no other letters after that one, nothing more in the trunk to go by. The autumn of 1945 does not stand out in the meteorological records as any worse or any better than autumns in other years. The days shortened and the air cooled, and leaves drifted down from the trees. Jolene sat on her porch and bore witness to the seasons working their way through the canyon. Her neighbors found their boots and jackets, and they remembered how to skirt mud holes and to leap puddles. They turned gradually inward, to their homes and families, and when out in the town they hunched low and hurried from door to door. Rains set in as they do in the high country, and by October towering thunderstorms gave way to nebulous white skies sweeping down from the north, leaving thin blankets of snow in the mornings. Jolene watched it come, and she listened and breathed and trembled until Ray brought the table and chairs in from the porch.

*

It took almost no time to pack up my things, the camp stove and the chair, the damned painful old cot, the trunk of memories. I loaded them into the back of my pickup and looked around one more time as the dawn broke. It's unlikely I'll return.

I didn't bother making coffee but will stop at the TNT for breakfast; there's no reason in the world I should not. I'll be in Boise tonight, and with good roads, in Tucson with Susan and Carly day after tomorrow.

The air was crisp and promised a dry, sunny day as I walked to my truck, and in the stillness and mid-light of early morning, birds seemed to call from every bare branch and every bush; the chorus was astounding. The birds must be passing through southward, I think; a seasonal thing. It's the sound of birds, then, and not the banging of tin I will take with me of my leaving.

From high on Lookout Ridge lilac bushes border empty yards and forgotten plots, and the remnants of tin and old timbers stand like monuments over distant lives. Harly died a working-man's hero. All of Idaho knows the story of his strength and courage, standing like Atlas to hold open the escape route. Farrell died a patriot over Leyte Gulch. He came late to the war but sacrificed all for his country, and the Hammonds took pride in his service.

And that is the working theory we'll put forward. I have no facts at hand to say any of it is untrue.

Jolene gave birth to a son on a bright day in earliest November as chinook winds blew over the valley. The child was strong, I'm told.

She nursed him for a week, then rose from her bed while her husband toiled in the darkness and walked alone into the Salmon River wilderness.

A small figure in a bright red jacket hikes from town and out of the valley north-westward: a woman by her stature and gait, but strong and sure on the trail as she pushes through scratchy brush and vaults over wind-felled trees. I stand a while longer as Maddie Davy hurries up the winding path. Glimpses of her flash through the forest branches.

She stops at the crest of the ridge and turns slowly, catching her breath, taking in the cool breeze and the bright morning sun. She moves on, and I watch until she is no longer visible, until she has dropped down the other side into Alec's Canyon. She'll find the markings of pine marten she seeks, lying all around the clearing and the seep. She'll find the cabin, repaired anew, swept clean, and the cot made up with new bedding. Books lie on the table if she has time for them, and a small stack of field notebooks with Jolene's story written in an old man's hand.

Below me, the town and the old roads are fading away. The rusted sheets of tin quake silently in a morning breeze; it is slowly disappearing into the pine and brush, healing in nature's time. My own drill roads crisscross the ridge and stand out harsh and raw, and I'm not proud of the work I've done here this year. But these cuts, too, will be re-contoured and re-vegetated. It won't take long. Maddie will see to the reclamation, and she'll do it right. And the wounds will close, and the trees will grow up, and silence will spread over the town and the hollow. And all will lie in solitude again, perhaps until a hundred years have passed.

As I look out, timeless dark forests rise from the town, and granite porphyries stack up ridge behind ridge in all directions matching the breadth of the sky. There are no edges to emptiness, no lines or limits or rows of ancient lilacs you can point to and say that is where it ends and where hope begins again. My mother pulled her coat around her as she walked, as the November sky darkened with winter's first storm. She followed the road north out of town until it became a trail, and the trail until it faded to a track. And when there was nothing more to follow she climbed rock over rock, as castaways do. In a cleft in the granite she closed her eyes and whispered verse and rhyme to the buffeting winds.

--- END ---

Made in the USA
Monee, IL
16 July 2020